HALL OF SECRETS

Books by Cate Campbell

Benedict Hall

Hall of Secrets

Published by Kensington Publishing Corporation

HALL OF SECRETS

CATE CAMPBELL

KENSINGTON BOOKS
www.kensingtonbooks.com

For Nancy Crosgrove, R.N., N.D.

and

Dean Crosgrove, P.A.C.

Thanks for everything!

CHAPTER 1

Everything under the soaring dome of the First Class Dining Saloon of *Berengaria* seemed to glitter. Beyond the draped windows, the North Atlantic night was dark as pitch, but within, crystal goblets, silver flatware, and Minton china gleamed. The candelabra sparkled, and the linen tablecloths and waiters' jackets were blindingly white. Even the instruments of the string quartet glistened, their varnished surfaces catching the light as the ship rocked. Allison Benedict could see the musicians scraping and sawing away beneath potted palms at the far end of the room, but she couldn't hear a note for the whistle of the wind past the funnels.

The ocean had no sympathy for the passengers of *Berengaria* this night. Candle flames swayed with the ship's rocking. The white-coated waiters, approaching with the first course, teetered dangerously on the parquet floors as the ship plunged and jolted. The middle-aged woman on Allison's left gasped and seized the edge of the table. Half the seats in the Dining Saloon, including those at the captain's table, were vacant, their intended occupants nursing *mal de mer* in their staterooms.

The seas were rough, there was no doubt. Before dressing for dinner, Allison had spent an hour watching the waves splash up the sides of the ship to wash over the lifeboats in their webs of rope and to soak the promenade decks. Whitecaps formed and then dissipated, spitting foam over the dark surface of the water. The deck creaked beneath her, and the curtains at the windows rippled and swayed.

Her mother, Adelaide, was in their suite even now, groaning and miserable. She had taken to her bed, and ordered her maid to bring a vinegar compress for her forehead. Allison's own maid was in her bunk in steerage, unable to open her eyes or set her foot on the tossing deck without being sick. Only tonight's invitation to sit at the captain's table had saved Allison from being trapped in the suite with her mother. Adelaide had spent the first days of the voyage angling for that invitation, and she couldn't bear to waste it.

The waiter safely reached the table, his tray of hors d'oeuvres intact. He bowed to the captain and began to serve the first course, tiny anchovies quivering in a bed of tomato aspic. The older woman waved hers away, and pressed her gloved fingers to her mouth. In defiance of this, Allison spooned hers up in two bites, aware that her neighbor shuddered, watching her.

Captain Rostron smiled. "Miss Benedict, you're a very good sailor."

"Thank you, sir," Allison murmured, glancing demurely up at him. He was quite old, forty at least, but he cut a dashing figure in his dress uniform, with gold epaulets on the shoulders and ribbons draped across his chest. "I like the storm. It's thrilling."

"I don't know how you can say that," her neighbor moaned. "The ship sounds like it's coming apart!"

"Not at all," the captain said smoothly. He waited while cups of clear consommé were placed before them, then added, "I assure you, Mrs. Benton-Smith, there's nothing to worry about." He winked at Allison, and she felt her cheeks warm. "Miss Benedict is quite right. It's exciting to watch a good ship brave a storm."

"Miss Benedict," Mrs. Benton-Smith said, turning an inquiring look on her. "You're traveling with your mother, I believe. Is she not coming to dinner?"

"No," Allison said. "She's not feeling well."

"Of course she's not. No one is."

"I am," Allison said. "I feel perfectly well!"

"A good sailor," Captain Rostron repeated. "We should give you a job, Miss Benedict. An officer of the Cunard line!"

Allison laughed, but Mrs. Benton-Smith scowled. She said stiffly, "Perhaps, Miss Benedict, you should be in your stateroom, tending to your poor mama."

Allison's laugh died. She said defensively, "Mother's maid is with her."

Mrs. Benton-Smith sniffed. "Well! I do find that curious. In *my* day, a young girl did not come to dinner unchaperoned."

"I'm out, though," Allison protested. "I made my debut this year, and I've just finished my Grand Tour."

"Even so. There are proprieties to be observed, especially for girls of our class."

"Come, come, Mrs. Benton-Smith," the captain interposed. "We're well into the twentieth century. We've fought the Great War. Young people are different now. The world is different from the one we grew up in."

"Different," Mrs. Benton-Smith said, pursing her lips, "does not mean better."

The ship lurched at that moment, and the gentleman across from Mrs. Benton-Smith spilled his bowl of consommé down the front of his starched white shirt. A flurry of waiters descended on the table to mop him up, to escort him to his stateroom to change, and to reset his place. During the fuss, Allison rested her chin on her hand and contemplated the view of the Dining Saloon from the captain's table.

In the past three months, she had seen so many Gothic cathedrals, baroque concert halls, and rococo palaces that her visual palate was exhausted, but she thought the churches and halls and palaces had been appropriate in their historical context. This ship—designed by a German before the war, so perhaps it was understandable—was overladen with flourishes and scrolls and gilt.

For her mother, the opulence of *Berengaria* was perfect. The glow of gold leaf, the shine of enameled flowers, the elegant moldings and carved archways, all supported Adelaide Benedict's sense of status. She felt the elegance of the ship was only her due, and she found it a comfort after the shortcomings of the European hotels, the inconveniences of the trains, the refusal of waiters and maids to speak English.

It all made Allison feel like a caged bird, restive and fluttery and trapped.

She had felt that way most of her debutante year. She had wearied early of the dull parties, the proper dresses, the careful hairstyles. She found her mother's obsessive perusal of society columns humiliating, and Adelaide had haunted every step, managed every move her daughter made, analyzed everyone she met. Allison lost her temper once, after a reception when Adelaide had pushed her in front of the newspaper photographers so often they began turning away when they saw her coming. That night, Allison snapped at her mother that *she* should have been the debutante. Adelaide retorted that she had not been so fortunate as to have a debutante year, and she seized upon the moment to hold forth at length about how grateful her daughter should be.

Occasionally, Allison had observed other girls and their mothers laughing together, embracing, whispering secrets. Such moments left her confused and uneasy. She had never whispered in her mother's ear. No one in her family embraced. She felt as if there were something she should understand, something these other families knew that hers didn't, but she could never quite grasp what it was.

She had nursed a hope that the Grand Tour might be different, but in that, too, she had been disappointed. Her mother crowded every day with lectures, guided walks, shopping excursions, teas and suppers with other mothers and daughters traveling the same route. They had been in Europe no more than a week before Allison understood that her Grand Tour was not hers in any sense. It was Adelaide's Grand Tour. Allison was only the justification.

Dinner in the First Class Dining Saloon proceeded. A dish of cucumbers in dill sauce appeared, then steamed sole, followed by roast beef. Allison could have eaten it all, as she had the anchovies, but even in her mother's absence, habit persisted. She cut everything into tiny pieces, tasting two or three morsels and making little piles of the rest on her plate. She drank two full glasses of champagne, though, something Adelaide would never have allowed, or would have ruined by adding water. Mrs. Benton-Smith tutted when the waiter refilled Allison's flute a third time. Allison was tempted to point out that Mrs. Benton-Smith herself was on her fourth glass, but she held her tongue, despite feeling wonderfully giddy from the champagne. She had no doubt the old fussbudget would find a way to report any incivility to her mother.

The chocolate soufflé made Allison's mouth water so intensely she had to dab her lips with her napkin. She couldn't resist taking a spoonful before mashing the rest into dark paste. Mrs. Benton-Smith, she noted, overcame her malaise enough to devour all of hers. Her long silver spoon rattled in the empty glass.

"Girls," Mrs. Benton-Smith lamented, casting an eye over Allison's figure. "I used to be slim myself! It's not easy getting older, Miss Benedict, I promise you. I hate being so fat, but what can you do?"

Allison was certain Mrs. Benton-Smith didn't expect an answer—or want one—so she didn't offer it. She was, of course, an expert on the topic, thanks to Adelaide.

Captain Rostron pushed back his chair, rose, and bowed farewell to the ladies. The other diners rose, too, in a flutter of furs and silks and opera scarves. Most of them staggered off to their staterooms to wait out the storm. A few made their way into the First Class Lounge, and Allison, draping her silk wrap around her shoulders, followed these hardy ones. On the stage of the lounge the orchestra was tuning. Allison settled into an upholstered chair, and a waiter appeared with a small silver coffeepot and a cup on a tray. She smiled her thanks, smoothed the embroidered gauze of her evening dress, and sat back to enjoy the music and her precious moments of solitude.

Her respite didn't last long. The steward, the man who cleaned their suite, kept their flowers fresh, and brought them tea or coffee when they wanted it, appeared beside her chair and bowed. "Pardon, Miss Benedict. Mrs. Benedict is asking for you."

Allison set down her coffee cup and gazed out at the listing dance floor. The orchestra had begun a Viennese waltz, and a foursome of dancers was trying to execute the steps despite *Berengaria*'s pitching. They laughed as they clutched one another to stop from falling.

The steward said, hesitantly, "Miss Benedict?"

Allison stood up, drawing the length of her silk wrap through her fingers, and cast the steward a pleading glance. "Could you tell her," she begged, "that you couldn't find me? Just this once?"

The steward's eyebrows rose, and his lips parted as if to make some protest. Allison murmured, "Please."

He suddenly grinned, and she saw that he couldn't have attained many more years than her own nineteen. His uniform and the solemn expression he affected made him appear much older. She wondered what he must think of the Benedicts, of her imperious and demanding mother, of her own mostly silent presence. She realized with a pang that she hadn't even learned his name.

If any of this bothered him, she couldn't tell. His grin faded as he glanced around the room, then pointedly gazed over her head as if she had become invisible. He cleared his throat, and turned his back to her.

Allison whispered, "Thank you!" and hurried away before he could change his mind.

Margot Benedict watched Blake rise and walk toward her, leaning on his lion-headed cane. His right leg still dragged, and neither she nor his cardiologist could predict how much that would improve. But he was walking. And smiling.

He settled into the Morris chair Dickson had ordered for him, but he sat erect, disdaining the chair's reclining position. Margot drew up a straight chair. She threw her coat over the back and sat down with her medical bag at her feet. "Blake, you're looking well. You seem to be feeling much better."

"I do feel better, Dr. Margot." *Ah do.* Since the stroke, Blake's accent had reverted to his decades-old Southern roots. Margot took care not to comment on it. She knew, the moment he realized it, he would make every effort to shed that resurrected drawl.

"Are you walking every day? With Sarah?"

"Of course," he said. With a hand that trembled only a little, he gave a mock salute. "Following doctor's orders."

"It's good to hear someone follows them," she said with an affectionate smile. She tried to look him over without being too obvious. She was gratified by how clear his eyes were, how much his color had improved. He had lost weight, but that was natural. His speech had been distressingly slow to return, but now he was forming his words—and his thoughts—with ease. Only the Southern vowels, the slight slurring of the consonants, gave evidence of the aphasia that had persisted for so many months.

It had taken a long time, but Blake was making his way back from the cerebral apoplexy that had made them all fear for his life. "I'll be back at work by Christmas," he said, but she saw the quiver of his eyelids. He was worried she would deny him.

"We mustn't rush things," she said. She lifted a forefinger and shook it in gentle warning. "I'm not going to let you work sixteen hours a day anymore! There may be some damage to your heart, and we don't want—"

With a touch of his old dignity, he interrupted her. "I appreciate that, Dr. Margot, but a man needs to work. And since Mr. Dickson has been so kind as to hold my job . . ." He raised his eyebrows and tapped his fingers on the armrest of the Morris chair.

She linked her hands loosely in her lap. "Your job will always be there, Blake, you know that. Father could never be satisfied with anyone else. We've had to borrow the Sorensens' butler several times, and that hasn't been entirely—shall we say—felicitous."

He said, "The Sorensens' butler is a dipsomaniac, I'm afraid. I expect Mr. Dickson figured that out."

Margot chuckled. "Yes. He dips into the brandy when he thinks no one's looking. In any case, everyone at Benedict Hall is waiting for you."

"That makes me a lucky man."

Margot's heart warmed with gratitude. It had been a terrible year for Benedict Hall, full of tragedy and sorrow. Blake's recovery seemed to signal a better year to come.

She stretched her legs out in front of her and began to relax. It had been a long day, and this was the brightest spot in it. "You might be surprised to learn we're adding to the household this winter," she said. "Do you remember my young cousin Allison? Mother's niece?"

"I believe I do. She and her mother—Mrs. Adelaide, I recall—visited once when Miss Allison was only two or three. I'm not quite clear on how she's related, though."

Margot laughed. "It's not easy! Cousin Allison is related to Mother and Father both. Adelaide is Mother's cousin on her mother's side, and she married Father's cousin Henry."

"So that makes her your third cousin, I believe—or is it fourth? Or," he said, lifting his thick white eyebrows, "both?"

"Oh, Lord, Blake, who knows? Mother's the only one who could keep those things straight, and right now, she doesn't really . . ." Her voice trailed off. It was painful to feel her mother's accusatory glances on her, or worse, to know her mother was doing her best not to see her at all. Sometimes it seemed as if Edith had found a way to look right *through* her, as if Margot had become transparent since Preston's death. It was a difficult situation, one she had solved, in part, by moving into Blake's apartment above the garage so she wouldn't have to meet her mother in the hallway. She hadn't told

Blake that, because she knew he would say it wasn't proper, but it was exhausting to have to confront her mother's pain every time they met.

Margot understood that her mother was protecting herself. Whether for good or ill, the family had a sort of unspoken agreement that allowed her to do it. Edith had concocted her own explanation for the death of her youngest son, and though it bore no resemblance to the truth, no one argued with her. No one troubled her with the exact account of what Preston had done or how he had brought about the disaster. Even Margot felt it would serve no purpose, and she was the one Edith blamed.

Hattie believed what Edith believed, of course, but Hattie's conviction didn't include making Margot responsible. She treated Margot with the same affection she always had. She fussed over her laundry, worried over the late hours she kept at the hospital, and insisted on carrying food out to the garage apartment when she missed dinner.

Margot gave a dismissive flick of her fingers. A year had passed, and there was no point in dwelling on things she couldn't fix. She said, "In any case, Allison is nineteen now. She's just completed her Grand Tour, and apparently something happened on the crossing. Uncle Henry is furious. Wants her out of San Francisco until the gossip dies down."

"I don't believe I've met Mr. Henry."

"No, you wouldn't have."

"He's a Benedict, though."

"Yes. From the 'poor' Benedicts, as Mother used to say!" She couldn't help chuckling. "I understand Uncle Henry didn't have a pin when Aunt Adelaide married him, but he's built up quite a successful import business. Father is impressed, although he thinks Uncle Henry should diversify. We're coming out of the recent depression, but Father sees trouble ahead."

"Mr. Henry should listen, then. No one excels at business more than Mr. Dickson."

"Very true. In any case, Uncle Henry wrote to Father, claiming that Allison has been diagnosed as a hysteric, which makes a con-

venient cover for whatever it is she's supposed to have done. As
nearly as I can tell, it's Aunt Adelaide who suffered a nervous attack, but they'll never say so."

Blake laughed, his old deep rumble. "Nervous attack. Is that
the medical term?"

Margot grinned. "I doubt Aunt Adelaide's trouble is medical."
She pushed her fingers through her hair, which she could never
remember not to do. It mussed her bob into a bird's nest. "Adelaide's a brittle sort of woman. The way she spoke to her daughter, when they were here last fall, set my nerves on edge, though
I don't know if anyone else noticed."

"It will be beneficial to Miss Allison, then, to spend some time
at Benedict Hall." He sounded so much like his old self that
Margot felt weak with relief. She had been terribly worried about
him. He was, of course, a servant, a colored man, the child of
slaves, but that didn't matter. He had always been like a third
parent, and she couldn't imagine life without him.

He said, "Mrs. Edith should be a good influence. She always
speaks kindly to everyone."

Margot said, "Blake, Mother's really not herself. You'll understand when you come home."

"I did see her, you know. She came to visit once, with Mr.
Dickson."

"She did?" Margot couldn't picture her prim, polished mother
visiting this nursing home in the Negro neighborhood. She
hoped Edith had not sniffed or kept a handkerchief pressed to
her nose. No doubt her father would have put his foot down if
she had. Dickson was sensitive in the matter of Blake. It was one
of many ways in which he had surprised Margot during this difficult year.

The smile faded from Blake's face. "Poor Mrs. Edith. It's been
terribly hard on her."

"Hattie doted on Preston nearly as much as Mother, but
Mother needed her, and that kept her going, I think. Mother,
though—" Margot brushed her hair back again. "She's terribly
thin, though Hattie does her best. Her hair has gone gray, and she

seems . . . I don't know, Blake. As if she's not quite *there*." Margot made a small, helpless gesture.

Blake said, "It hurts you."

"I can't make it right for her."

"That is correct, Dr. Margot. No one can make it right for Mrs. Edith. And none of it was your fault." Blake paused for a tactful moment while Margot blinked away the sudden sting in her eyes. "I'm surprised Mr. Dickson agreed to Miss Allison's visit, with Mrs. Edith still so delicate."

"It was my idea, actually. I hope I won't be sorry I suggested it. We have an abundance of space, and when Uncle Henry wrote to ask Father's advice, it seemed like a good idea. I hope I haven't made a mistake. I had this notion that having a young person in the house—a girl, you know, who would want to go to parties, buy clothes—I thought it might help Mother. Give her something to think about."

"It's worth a try," he answered, but she heard doubt in his voice, too.

"Well," she said, with some briskness now. "Things can't be any worse than they are. Uncle Henry and Aunt Adelaide wasted no time accepting our invitation. Hattie's made up the south bedroom at the back, the one beyond the servants' stair. The window opens onto the garden, you remember. It has a bath of its own, though it's small. Allison can use either the kitchen staircase or the main one."

"What's become of Mr. Preston's room?"

Margot gazed into Blake's kindly face. His hair had changed, too, like her mother's, but Blake's had gone completely white during his long illness. Sarah had cut it for him into a curly cap that contrasted dramatically with his dark skin. Margot said, "Mother closed the door of Preston's bedroom the day of the funeral. Everything in it is just the way it was before he died. The maids are allowed in to clean, but not to move anything. She pretends—or she believes—that he's coming back."

"Mrs. Edith still doesn't understand about Mr. Preston."

"I don't think it would make a difference if she did. Sometimes I think she clings to her pain as a way of keeping him alive."

"Do you and Mrs. Edith—"

"No," Margot said, her voice a little rougher than she intended. "No, we don't talk about it. I'm certain she wouldn't want to hear what I have to say."

"Such an old, old problem." His gaze shifted away from her to the window of his room. Steady rain streaked the glass beyond the printed cotton curtains, and in the brief silence Margot could hear its rhythm on the roof. "I thought perhaps she would understand now. That she would see . . ."

"She doesn't want to see," Margot said. "She never did, of course, but now more than ever. . . . She imagines he was the victim. She sees him as a hero. Believes he sacrificed himself."

"I wish I could have attended the funeral."

"You would have hated it, Blake. I did."

"I'm sorry about that. I believe such ceremonies are meant to be healing to those left behind."

"This one wasn't. It was just Gothic! The empty casket, the reception with all those society people murmuring platitudes—it was ridiculous."

"Not to Mrs. Edith, I suppose."

"She went through all the motions, and I thought at the time it was a good thing. She wore a black dress and a hat with a veil, black gloves, insisted on supervising all the food, the flowers, even instructed the priest what to say."

"Hattie told me that."

"Poor Hattie! It was awful for her. She cried for days, even while she was cooking. I was afraid she'd make herself ill, but Hattie's like you. Made of stern stuff."

That made Blake smile again. "Tell me about Major Parrish," he said. "Is he well? The new arm is working?"

A quiver of tension tightened Margot's belly, but she said with determined cheer, "The Carnes arm is the best there is, Blake. The elbow bends, the fingers flex. He uses it almost as much as he does his right arm these days. I'll bring him to visit, and you can see for yourself."

"I'd like that."

"It will have to wait, though. Bill Boeing sent him to March Field, down in California, to meet with some army pilots. Something about new developments with an airplane."

"Perhaps, when he comes back to Seattle, the two of you . . ."

Margot sighed, her tension subsiding into the more or less persistent melancholy she had felt since Frank left. "I don't know, Blake."

"Now, I was quite sure you and Major Parrish had an understanding."

"We did, Blake. We do, I mean." She shifted in her chair, trying to explain without saying too much. She said, "There are some things—it's just that, with Mother the way she is, we've felt we should wait until things are—settled, I suppose. As settled as they're going to be, in any case."

There were other issues holding them back, but she would keep those to herself. She didn't want to worry Blake with them, even though she really had no one else to talk to. What did it say about her, she wondered, that this old family retainer was her only confidant? Except for Frank, of course.

Blake, his eyes still on the rain-soaked darkness beyond his window, took a long, slow breath, and let his head drop back against his chair. Margot clicked her tongue. "Blake, I'm tiring you. You need to rest. I should get home to change for dinner, in any case. Mother hates me coming to dinner in my work clothes."

He turned his head without lifting it and gave her a weary smile. "I don't have all my strength back yet. But you tell Mr. Dickson I'll be back as soon as I can. As soon as my very fine doctor gives her permission."

She stood, and because they were alone, she bent to touch his hand. Hers was pale and narrow, and his was thick with age. She liked the way it looked, her young white hand on his aged black one. All her life, this strong dark hand had been her protection. She wished she could impart some of her own vigor to him now, through her touch.

"Don't you worry, Dr. Margot," he rumbled. "After all you and Mr. Dickson have done for me, I couldn't help but get better."

"Good, Blake," she said. "I'll hold you to that." Her throat tightened, and she turned away to pull on her coat and gloves and pick up the umbrella drying by the radiator. She coughed a little and fixed a smile on her face as she turned back to say good night. "I'll see you tomorrow," she said.

"No, no," he said. "You don't need to come all the way out here every day. Sarah takes fine care of me."

"I know she does. I'll come this weekend, then. Perhaps I can bring Hattie for a visit."

"That would be very nice, Dr. Margot." His eyelids drooped, and she saw that he truly was tired. He said in a softer tone, his vowels broader than ever, "Very nice. I will look forward to that treat."

Chapter 2

Raindrops skittered from the ribs of Margot's umbrella as she hurried through the squall toward her streetcar stop. Several people nodded to her, and two said, "Good evening, Doctor." She smiled and responded, cheered by their acceptance.

She had been uncomfortable in this neighborhood at first. The residents had been startled, even suspicious, at the sight of a tall white woman walking along East Madison. They whispered to one another as she passed, and some stared openly in ways that made her neck burn. There had been no respectful greetings in those early weeks.

One evening, just as darkness was closing in, a lanky young man in coveralls and a porkpie work hat had stepped right up to her and said, "Slummin', are ya?"

Margot had tried to walk on, but he stood in her way, leaning insultingly close, treating her to a sour gust of bootleg whisky and cheap tobacco. His eyes were red, and his dark face distorted with drunken resentment. He reached a grimy hand toward her medical bag. "Whatcha got there, missy?"

Margot instinctively pulled the bag away, out of his reach. Her hospital experience had rendered her reckless with her own safety, but in that bag—a gift from her father to replace the one lost in the fire—was a necessary supply of drugs. She carried morphine and laudanum, atropine and adrenaline chloride, none of which were safe in the wrong hands. There was no alcohol, but she knew that for some, any drug would do. She tried to sidestep the young man. He laughed and mimicked her steps, reaching around her toward the handle of her bag.

It could have been a bad moment. It would have validated everyone's worries about Margot's trips on the Madison streetcar. Blake, in particular, once he was able to speak, worried over her visits. Her father, Hattie, even Sarah Church had tried to dissuade her from coming so often, and so late in the day.

But that night, an elderly woman in a shapeless housedress and an assortment of shawls resolved the situation by bursting from a nearby house with an attention-arresting bang of her front door. She stood on the stoop, hands on her skinny hips, and called, "William Lee Jackson, you get on in this house right this very minute!"

The hapless William started as if someone had struck him. His shoulders slumped, and despite his adult height, he seemed to shrink to little-boy size. He dropped his head and backed away from Margot. As he turned and started up the cracked cement walk of the house, the old woman glared at him as if daring him to disobey. She was half his size, but that seemed to make no difference. Under her gaze, he slunk into the house without a word. The woman followed, but not without casting Margot a hard glance. She didn't scold her, but that glance told Margot she was in a place where she didn't belong.

That had been months ago. Now that Blake had been in the East Jefferson Convalescent Home for more than a year, her regular visits had made her a familiar sight. Sarah had been a great help, informing the families who lived around the Convalescent Home that one of its residents had a white doctor. A young lady doctor.

As the word spread, it became common for Margot to find

someone waiting on the steps of the Convalescent Home after one of her visits. Occasionally, one of the workingmen of the neighborhood had an injury or an ailment, and no time during the day to visit the office of one of the Negro physicians. Often it was a worried mother with a baby on her hip or a gaggle of toddlers clinging to her skirt. Margot followed these people to their homes, single-story houses built like little boxes, divided into three or four sparsely furnished rooms by the thinnest of partitions. In these modest places she treated earaches, burns, sprains, fevers. Once she attended a case of food poisoning that kept her at a bedside all night, administering saline and a mixture of bismuth carbonate and salicylate until she was certain her patient, who was the sole support of an alarmingly large family, was going to recover.

The families rarely had any money. They paid Margot with what they had, and without apology. She had carried away jars of homemade jelly, loaves of freshly baked bread, once a vast blackberry pie that Hattie very nearly refused to admit to her kitchen, but which proved so delicious Margot had to beg Sarah to go back to its baker for the recipe.

Margot was aware now, as she strode through the rain, of protective eyes on her. Curtains were drawn over lighted windows, but they twitched occasionally as the women inside watched her pass. Men smoking on their cramped porches nodded to her, and one or two stood up politely. William Lee Jackson, that unhappy young man who couldn't find work and who occasionally consoled himself with a jug of two-dollar whisky, materialized out of the dusk, touching his dilapidated hat brim and grinning at her. His teeth were very white in the darkness, and on this evening Margot detected no acrid smell of whisky.

"My Granny Jackson sent me," he said. "She says she won't give me no dinner if I don't see you to the streetcar."

Margot said gravely, "Please thank your grandmother for me. I hope your dinner is excellent."

They walked side by side the remaining two blocks. William didn't speak again, but he stood beside her as she waited in the darkness. The rain fell hard enough to splash from the sidewalk

and wet her ankles. Her umbrella dripped furiously, and she
began to shiver despite her woolen coat with its warm fox collar.
She was relieved when the streetcar came clicking up East Madison from the lake.

She thanked William again, and swung up into the car's
lighted interior. She dropped her nickel into the fare box and sat
down in the first available seat. The bench seat was hard, but the
car was blessedly warm, and she shivered a little with relief. She
shook the rain off her umbrella as she rode up the hill and out of
the Negro district. She had to change cars at Broadway, dashing
through the rain.

In the second streetcar, she propped her umbrella against her
knee and gazed out the window. The houses seemed to grow, bit
by bit, as the car clicked its way northward. Neat picket fences
appeared, occasionally flanked by garages. The gardens expanded and the rooflines rose. This alteration of the landscape
from one neighborhood to another was a phenomenon she hadn't
really noticed before this year, when she had begun taking the
streetcar everywhere.

She thought wistfully of the days when Blake, rain or shine,
light or dark, would wait for her outside her clinic or in front of
the hospital. She loved riding in the polished Essex with its
sparkling windows and cozy plush seats. Blake was inevitably attired in his driving coat, cap, and gloves. There had been something restful about the ritual, something comforting about being
welcomed into the automobile's warm interior, relinquishing her
responsibilities, relaxing into Blake's hands.

She chided herself for her nostalgia as she climbed down from
the Broadway streetcar and started up the steep slope of Aloha
Street. Those days were never going to return, but that didn't
matter. What was important was that Blake was healing. There
had been a very real possibility, after the heart attack and its sub-
sequent complications, that he might never wake again. She still
had questions about the event, about the accident his heart attack supposedly precipitated, but he refused to speak of it. He
said it made no difference now, that there was no point in

dwelling on it, and perhaps he was right. Her younger brother, Preston, her tormentor since an early age, was gone. She was safe from him, and though the family was bruised and nearly broken, it would recover. Except, perhaps, for Edith.

Margot's stockings were soaked by the time she reached home. She hurried to her apartment above the garage, stashing her umbrella at the bottom of the stairs before dashing up to get out of her wet things and change into a suitable frock for dinner. She caught sight of the blue celluloid clock on the bedside table, the one she and her brothers had given Blake for Christmas long ago. She was late again.

She shrugged out of the shirtwaist and skirt she had worn all day and into a wool crepe sheath with a dropped waist and shawl collar. As she pulled on a fresh pair of stockings and fastened them, she remembered that the last time she had worn this sheath had been a dinner date with Frank. A sudden rush of longing for him made her press one hand to her heart.

She blew out a breath and dropped her hand. There was no time to indulge her weakness. She had to gather herself to face the gantlet of dinner, her mother's wan face, her father's struggles to behave as if nothing were amiss. Her older brother's genial bewilderment didn't help. Her sister-in-law, at least, though her efforts were sometimes awkward, was doing her best to step into her mother-in-law's place and keep the house running smoothly. Without Blake, that wasn't easy.

All Margot could do was be present for dinner as often as she was able. She washed her hands, straightened her frock, and went down the stairs to take up her still-wet umbrella and cross the back lawn into Benedict Hall.

Allison tossed her hat onto the green frieze plush of the Pullman drawing room seat. "It's pouring out there," she said. "We'll be a sodden mess in five minutes!"

"I have your umbrella." Ruby spoke plaintively, a bit defensively, as if responsibility for the weather in Seattle fell squarely on her own habitually hunched shoulders. "And we won't be

walking that far. The Benedicts are supposed to send a car . . ."
She broke off in the face of Allison's irritated glance.

Allison knew she wasn't being fair, but she was in a ghastly
mood. She had been imprisoned in this compartment with Ruby
for the entire journey from San Francisco, and she was nearly
rigid with boredom.

It was that silliness on *Berengaria*, when she hadn't done a single thing wrong! Well, hardly anything, at least nothing that mattered. She protested over and over that nothing had happened,
really, nothing to be upset about, but her mother had raged on
and on about her ruined prospects, her compromised reputation,
carrying on until she made herself ill. Ruby and Jane, between
them, hadn't been able to calm her. She had shut herself up in
the stateroom for the better part of the crossing.

Allison had been humiliated. Adelaide emerged to sit at the
captain's table the next evening, but Allison had to stay in their
suite. She was allowed to walk on the deck only in the company
of the two maids, and forbidden to speak to anyone. Adelaide ordered her meals brought to their rooms, where the steward laid a
table nearly as elaborate as the ones in the Dining Saloon, and
Adelaide sat with her, glaring, ordering her to eat something.

Allison refused to touch anything but water and an occasional
cup of tea. Though Adelaide raged at her over this, as well, Allison would not relent. It was the only weapon she had, and it was
all the more powerful because it was one her mother had given
her. She hoped Adelaide grasped the irony of that.

The moment they reached home, after the interminable train
journey from New York, her mother closeted herself with Papa.
Allison and Ruby, unpacking upstairs, could hear Adelaide's
shrill complaints and Henry's loud, terse answers, their voices re-
verberating through the tall, narrow house. The next day a doctor
showed up, ordered by Henry, admitted by Ruby, and ushered
into the parlor where Allison and Adelaide waited in tense and
antagonistic silence.

Dr. Kinney seemed ancient to Allison. He had white hair
growing out of his ears, and his foul breath made Allison wrinkle

her nose when he leaned close to look in her eyes and her mouth. He pinched the flesh under her arm and pressed on her belly with blunt, icy fingers. He didn't speak to her at all. He directed all his questions to her parents, as if Allison were an infant, unable to answer for herself. Or a mental defective, not to be trusted.

Dr. Kinney listened gravely to Adelaide's account of Allison's depraved behavior aboard *Berengaria*. When Allison tried to interrupt, to tell her own version, he held up a hand to silence her. Papa joined in, growling at her to be quiet. Adelaide, with the air of a warrior winning a battle, tossed her head in triumph.

In the end, Dr. Kinney handed down his diagnosis in the manner of a great judge sharing his learned wisdom. Allison, he declared, was a hysteric. He used some sort of complicated name for her condition, repeating it several times, a little louder in each instance, as if that made it more convincing. Allison suspected he would charge Papa three times over for using Latin no one could understand.

Allison, deflated and defeated, burst into tears. She sobbed, over and over, that it was not she who had had hysterics but her mother. Her protests were worse than useless. For Dr. Kinney, her uncontrolled weeping was merely the confirmation of his diagnosis. He took a slip of paper from a pad, wrote something on it with a shaky blue-veined hand, and gave it to Papa. Henry read it, then made a great show of folding it and placing it into his breast pocket.

Later that day, Adelaide disappeared into her room with her maid in attendance while Papa called Allison into his study. He made Allison sit on a stool beside his heavy leather armchair while he took a long time fussing with his pipe, tamping the tobacco, striking a long match, puffing on the stem with his thick lips. When the pipe was drawing well, he pulled Dr. Kinney's paper out of his pocket and brandished it between two fingers.

"You know what this is, Allison?"

She glanced up at it, then dropped her gaze to her folded hands. "No, Papa."

"This," Henry pronounced, in a tone of gravitas, "is the name of a sanitorium. Bella Vista Rest Home in Sacramento. It's a place for females of fragile mental health. This is where Dr. Kinney has suggested I send you to deal with your hysteria."

Allison gripped her hands together so hard her fingers ached. "I'm not hysterical, Papa. You know I'm not."

"You're out of control, Allison."

"I am not!" She released her hands and wrapped her arms tightly around herself. "It's not true!"

"Your behavior on board ship—"

"Papa!" Allison jumped up, still hugging herself, and stared down at her father. "It was nothing! We were just having fun—do you even remember what it's like to have *fun?*"

"Your mother says—"

"Mother! Mother *hates* me!"

Henry glared at her, but she saw the flicker of his eyelids, the slight compression of his lips. He knows, she thought, and a wave of sadness swept over her. She hugged herself tighter, frightened by the realization. He knows. But he doesn't care.

That meant she was alone. She must have always been alone.

Her knees felt suddenly weak. She sank down again onto the childish stool and stared helplessly up at her father. He said, "You're not a child anymore, Allison."

"No," she said through a tight throat. "I'm not."

He pulled down the corners of his mouth and stroked his chin as if contemplating the gravest of thoughts. "You will learn one day," he said heavily, "how difficult it is to be a parent. It is a terrible responsibility."

"What do you want from me, Papa?"

"I want what all fathers of our class want."

"Our *class?*" she repeated. "I'm not sure we really fit into *our class.*"

She saw fresh anger spark in his eyes, and she knew she had made another mistake. It was one of the barbs Adelaide had been tossing for years, because she knew it was the one that hurt the most.

"Listen to me, my girl," Papa said stiffly. "I've come up in the world. I take pride in that, and you should be damned glad I've done it." He pushed himself out of his chair and shoved the slip of paper back into his pocket. "Your mother and I want the best for you."

"The best for me? You mean, marriage."

"Naturally. That's the proper course for a young woman of means."

"What if it's not the course I want to follow?"

He shook his head. "Your parents know what's best for you."

Allison jumped up once more, then had to seize the edge of Papa's desk to fight off the sudden dizziness that assailed her. She blinked hard, hoping he hadn't noticed. Breathlessly, urgently, she said, "Papa, listen to me. You want to be a modern man, I know you do. Women can do other things, have careers."

"I disapprove of that," he said ponderously. "You'll understand when you have your own home, your own children."

"I'm too young," she said.

"No younger than your mother was."

Allison gazed at his heavy features, his stubborn mouth, and wondered if there was anything at all she could say that would move him. "Do you think being married so young made Mother happy?" she asked, half under her breath. No one in their home could think Adelaide was happy.

"What else was she going to do?"

Miserably, in a barely audible voice, she said, "A hundred things, Papa. A thousand!"

"She knew her place. And we raised you to know yours."

"But, Papa, I want to study, to work. I'm *smart*," she said, her voice breaking on the word.

"What difference does that make? It's my job to see that you're settled. This—this incident—it threatens all your chances. What good family is going to accept you if this news gets out?"

"Papa, I told you. I didn't *do* anything."

"That's not what Adelaide says. She says all it takes is for one person to get word of your escapade, and—"

"Get word? Why should anyone *get word?*" Her voice rose, sounding thin and childish. "No one from San Francisco was on board, Papa. No one would know anything if Mother would just—would just—shut up about it!" Her father's face darkened at the insult, and Allison clapped both her hands over her mouth to stifle a sob.

It was a circular argument, in any case. Allison was, in fact, a smart girl, smart enough to know she had lost this battle. In the ongoing war with her mother, the advantage rested with Adelaide. She had maneuvered Allison into a position of weakness, and Allison, foolishly, had allowed her to do it.

"I have written to our family in Seattle," her father said gravely, doing his best to affect an air of the benevolent paterfamilias. "You were there in the fall of last year, I believe, so you've met them."

"Papa—"

"Don't interrupt. Your cousin Margot—the doctor, you remember—telephoned this morning. Your uncle Dickson has generously invited you to stay the winter with them."

"Papa!" Allison cried. "No! I want to go to college."

"No point in sending girls to college," he said. "Waste of time—and money."

"But you said, after my Grand Tour—you said we could talk about it!"

"You should have thought of that," he declaimed, with a pomposity that made her want to scream, "before you stripped naked to jump into a swimming pool with a young man you barely knew!"

"I wasn't *naked!*" she cried. "Ask Mother! Make her tell you the truth, Papa! I *was not naked!*"

"If Adelaide says you were, of course I accept your mother's version of events."

It was bitterly, extravagantly unfair. More protests sprang to Allison's lips, but she let them die unspoken. She almost wished she had done the thing she was accused of. It might have been her last chance at any excitement.

He pulled out the slip of paper again and waved it at her. "It's your choice, Allison. The sanitorium or Seattle."

Which was, of course, no choice at all.

On the platform of the San Francisco train station, Mother had dabbed at her eyes with a handkerchief, pretending sorrow at the parting. Papa had gripped Allison's arm with his short fingers and growled that she was not to set foot out of the drawing room he had reserved for her and Ruby. She was forbidden to go to the dining car. She was under no circumstances to step out to the lounge. The Pullman porter, under his explicit orders, would bring all their meals in.

"And for God's sake, Allison," were his final words, "eat something. You look like a starving sparrow!"

At this, Allison turned her head to meet her mother's gaze. Adelaide sniffed her imaginary tears, and Allison, with a toss of her head, claimed this one small victory for herself.

During the whole slow trip north, the porter did just what Papa had said. He showed up often, bringing tea, offering newspapers, carrying fresh towels or pitchers of water. Allison had no doubt Papa had paid him well to spy on her. She felt certain Ruby was making a little extra for the purpose, too. Between them, they had trapped her. She wondered if Cousin Margot was also on Papa's payroll and had accepted her at Benedict Hall as her prisoner.

Seattle, for pity's sake! Rain and dirt streets and fishermen. No doubt lumberjacks overran the town, swearing and spitting.

Allison sagged back on the sofa, arms folded, fingertips tapping. "Can a person die of boredom, Ruby?"

Ruby looked up from an apron she was stitching together with tiny, precise stabs of her needle. She was a wizard with a sewing needle and really good with a flatiron. She had an amazingly unsubtle mind, though, and she never laughed at any of Allison's jests. "No, Miss Allison," she said now, placidly. "I don't think so. But then I'm never bored."

"Oh, you have to be! Following me around all the time, or Mother? It must be excruciating."

"Not in the least. This is a very good position, and I'm happy to have it."

Under normal circumstances, Allison would have let that drop as a subject that would only intensify her ennui, but now—there was literally nothing to do but stare at the rain-washed view of trees and water and mountains, all blurred to an anonymous gray by the steady downpour. "You must have hoped for something more," she prodded the maid. "Some excitement! Didn't you ever want to be a film star, or a vaudeville dancer, or—I don't know, something interesting?"

Ruby gave a prim little tut before she bit her thread neatly in two. "Oh, no," she said. "I always knew I'd be in service. Mama trained me for it, starting when I was just young."

Allison tilted her head, eyeing Ruby's sallow face. "How young?"

A bit of color tinged Ruby's cheeks at the unaccustomed attention. "I was ten," she said. "Older than some, you know."

"Ten! How old do other girls start—what do you call it, training?"

"Oh," Ruby said with a little shrug, lifting the apron and scanning the hem for stitches out of place. "Some start when they're just four or five. They don't go to school at all. I," she said, with simple pride, "was in school until the fourth grade."

"Oh," was all Allison could say. "That doesn't seem fair at all."

"It was fair enough," Ruby said. She spoke in her usual monotone, as if the subject weren't of much interest. "Mama wanted me to know how to read, so I could follow recipes and read patterns."

"Where did you go to school, Ruby?"

"In the city. But the earthquake, you know. The school fell down."

"Oh!" Allison said again. "I was only four. I don't really remember."

Ruby seemed no more interested in this than she was in her own history. She shrugged. "After the school fell down, there didn't seem to be much point. We had to go to Oakland, because our house fell down, too. And burned," she added indifferently.

"So, Ruby," Allison pressed, her boredom eased by this bit of information, "was your mama a lady's maid, too?"

"Oh, no," Ruby said. She folded the apron neatly, smoothing the sash and tucking it under the bodice. "Mama's a laundress."

"Was anyone hurt in the 'quake? Your family?"

"My father disappeared, but we never knew if he got killed or just ran off."

"That's fascinating! Tell me about it."

But Ruby seemed to have exhausted her supply of entertainment. She got up to pack the apron into her valise, and though Allison tried to draw her out again, she had no success. After a few moments, she dropped her head on the seat back again and stared disconsolately at the rain-blurred view as the train chugged northward.

Every click and clatter of the wheels seemed to spell out her sentence. Winter in Seattle. Months of rain. The dreary company of conventional relatives, Aunt Edith, Uncle Dickson, Cousin Dick and his wife, Cousin Pres—oh, no. Preston was dead. There had been a fire in Cousin Margot's clinic. Somehow Cousin Preston got caught in it. Cousin Margot had lost everything, Papa said, and Uncle Dickson was helping her rebuild. Papa thought that was a waste of money, because how was a woman physician going to succeed in a private clinic in a poor neighborhood?

Allison's lips pinched at the thought of Cousin Margot. Papa wouldn't have thought of packing his daughter off to Seattle if Cousin Margot hadn't suggested it. Allison remembered her from her first debutante party, tall and remote in a beaded silk dress and headband. Her young man had been interesting, the one-armed officer in his dress uniform, with vivid blue eyes and a touch of silver in his black hair. And he'd gotten into an actual fistfight with Preston! That had been marvelous, just like a film.

She hadn't been allowed to watch it, of course. The moment it started, her mother had dragged her into the house and up the stairs, as if watching two men fight would soil her forever. She kept the curtains drawn and wouldn't let Allison come downstairs until Uncle Dickson came up to tell them the excitement was over. Allison had been forced to miss the end of the drama, and the rest of the event was just like all the other deb parties, boring, predictable, stifling in their sameness.

Her adventure on *Berengaria* had been the only real diversion since the fistfight. She remembered it with longing.

She had hurried out of the First Class Lounge and slipped down the staircase amidships. It was the first time since leaving Southampton she had been alone, and though she knew her mother would be angry, Allison felt alive, bubbling with champagne and reckless with freedom. She soon found herself standing in the doorway of the Second Class Lounge, where she gripped the doorjamb to keep from losing her balance as the ship rocked.

The molded ceiling here was low, trapping the haze of cigar smoke emanating from the smoking room next door. A jazz band was playing a sloppy but energetic version of "The Sheik of Araby." Men and women, some not much older than she was, were dancing, many more of them than in the First Class Lounge.

They wore all varieties of evening dress, from smoking jackets and loose ties for the men to georgette dresses for the ladies, some of which reached no lower than midcalf. Beads and feathers, all of which Adelaide deplored, flew as the dancers spun around the parquet floor. They made Allison's embroidered gauze dress, which trailed to the floor at the back and had been purchased just weeks ago in Paris, seem staid. The *vendeuse* had sworn it was going to be all the rage in the coming year, but now it seemed already out of date. Allison dropped her wrap and tugged at the neckline of the gown to make it dip a little lower. She couldn't do much about the length, but she strove for a sophisticated pose in the doorway, hips thrust forward in the S-silhouette the *Vogue* models used. She tried not to look lost as she glanced around for someplace to sit.

Before she found it, a man strutted up to her, grinning. "Gosh, a new face!" he said, in an accent she couldn't quite place. He held out his ungloved hand in invitation. "Where've you been all this time, fair lady?"

Before she could answer, the ship pitched wildly. Allison found herself gripping the strange man's hand for balance. The people on the dance floor cried out and seized one another. Even the band faltered for a moment.

As *Berengaria* righted herself, the man holding Allison's hand laughed down at her. He was young, she saw, redheaded, and liberally freckled. He exclaimed, "Aren't you scared?"

"No," she said. She tried to free her hand, but he refused to give it up.

"Then dance with me, strange maiden!" he demanded. "I swore I would dance with every beautiful girl on this ship, but I've missed you somehow!" Still holding her hand, the sweat on his palm visibly staining her white gloves, he bowed, more deeply this time. "Tommy Fellowes, at your service. Newly freed from Exeter College, Oxford University, and de*lighted* to make your acquaintance."

Tommy Fellowes's hands were bare, but he was otherwise properly attired in a tuxedo with a white vest and tie. He sported a wonderful set of dimples in his freckled cheeks, and Allison couldn't help laughing with him. She was quite sure Adelaide would have despised him, and though Tommy Fellowes couldn't know it, that was the highest recommendation he could receive.

Using her free hand, Allison unwound his fingers from hers and smoothed her sweat-stained glove. "Allison Benedict," she said, dropping a mock curtsy. Then, laughing, "Newly freed from the First Class Lounge."

"Golly!" her new acquaintance cried. He clapped his hand to his starched breast. "Too posh! I'll bet they're all wearing tails up there!"

"Of course they are. And gloves, too."

He was utterly unabashed by this. "Got too hot!" he declared. "But I promise, I wore them at dinner." He pulled a pair out of his pocket and waved them at her before jamming them back in and seizing her hand again. "Come on, old thing," he cried. "Let's cut a rug!"

A quartet of young dancers, still struggling for balance on the dance floor, called Tommy's name, beckoning to him. He tugged Allison toward them. The jazz band had found its beat again, and the music struck up more loudly than before. It was all irresistible.

Allison, her silk wrap trailing behind her, followed Tommy, and in moments was trying to dance the Black Bottom in her too-long skirt. *Berengaria* rolled from time to time, and she found herself holding on to whoever was nearest, sometimes Tommy, sometimes one of the other men, once even one of the girls, a plump, red-cheeked brunette wearing a short beaded dress. When one song ended, the band went straight on to another. Allison, caught up in the moment, stripped her own gloves off and tossed them on one of the upholstered chairs, along with her silk scarf. When the musicians finally took a break, the dancers collapsed into chairs, calling for drinks and grinning at one another. Allison was perspiring, out of breath, and happier than she had been in weeks. In months.

And, she thought now, disconsolately staring out at the drab landscape beyond the train's windows, if she had stopped then, returned to the suite and to her mother, she would probably be safely at home in San Francisco. She might even be choosing her clothes, packing up her tennis racket, and buying books for her frosh year at Mills. She most certainly wouldn't be on this train, imprisoned by a turncoat maid and a warden in the form of a Pullman porter, chugging her way toward the most boring winter ever.

Yes, it was her own fault. She should have left brash Tommy Fellowes and the rest of his gay group in Second Class and trudged back up the stairs to the stiff confines of First. Where she belonged. Where, as her papa reminded her endlessly, her future was. Where, her mother would say, she would associate with people of her own class.

She couldn't make them understand, Papa and Mother and all the other parents who meant to mold their children into younger versions of themselves, that the world was changing. The lines were blurring, not only between social classes but between men and women. Women could vote! Women could serve in Congress! She had been born in the *twentieth* century, a new world of opportunities! Why, look at Cousin Margot!

But that was a thought she didn't want to pursue. She was still nursing her resentment of Cousin Margot for suggesting this whole stupid scheme.

In some ways, she envied Ruby. There were many advantages Ruby didn't have, but Ruby, at least, could change jobs if she wanted to, live where she wanted to, choose her own life's path. She was limited only by her ability.

Of course, Allison thought, casting her maid a guilty glance, Ruby's abilities were unremarkable. She knew that.

But what was she supposed to do in Seattle? Was she supposed to play the role of companion, solace to her poor bereaved aunt Edith? Not that she didn't care! It must be awful to lose a son, such a handsome and charming one, especially after having him come home safe from the Great War. Still, she didn't want to be trapped in a sprawling big house with a woman who by all accounts barely set foot outside her bedroom. The winter stretched ahead of Allison, dull and dim and relentlessly wet.

Maybe she should have chosen the Bella Vista Rest Home!

She pulled the curtains shut with a snap that made Ruby jump. Allison threw her head back against the sofa, an action that made her head spin. She closed her eyes, waiting for the dizziness to fade. There was nothing to look at in any case. She was already tired of the monotonous view, rain and clouds and tossing gray water, and they hadn't even reached Seattle.

Ruby was wrong. A person could easily expire from boredom.

CHAPTER 3

In the Moreno Valley, where Frank Parrish stood ankle-deep in yellowing grass, late autumn sunshine slanted across the barracks and mess halls of March Field. A dry wind fluttered the brim of his Stetson as he squinted into the afternoon glare to watch the JN-4, dubbed the Jenny, joyously carve the empty sky with turns and rolls and dives. Its double wings flashed in the sunlight, and he had the odd, poetic thought that the airplane seemed to be laughing.

The Jenny banked, angled toward the runway for a touch-and-go, then sailed up and over Frank's head where he stood with Captain Carruthers. His ears thrummed with the sound of the engine, and the airplane was so close he could see the vibration of the struts between the double wings. The student in the front seat was grinning ear to ear. The instructor, in the back, waved to the men on the ground. Frank tipped his head up, one hand on his hat, but keeping a close eye on the undercarriage, the slight movement of the lower wing, the landing wheels spinning in the wind.

"What do they say about the stick?" Frank asked, after the noise of the plane's motor died away. "Advantage over the

wheel?" The Jenny had previously been controlled by a Deper-
dussin control wheel, but this version, sometimes called the
Canuck because of the Canadians who had redesigned it, used a
stick. Frank's right hand twitched with the urge to know for himself what it felt like, to understand the connection between the
control and the craft.

Carruthers said, "Depends who you ask. Some like it better.
Some think the Jenny was fine the way it was." He clapped
Frank's shoulder. "You can ask the pilot yourself." The two men
started across the field. The desiccated grass rustled under their
feet, and the sun burned Frank's shoulders through his jacket.

He had arrived just that afternoon, climbing off the train in
Riverside to be met by one of Carruthers's sergeants. The
sergeant had installed him in bachelor officers' quarters, then
brought him to the airfield to meet the captain.

Captain Carruthers was exactly the sort of clear-eyed, broad-
shouldered military man that a younger Frank Parrish had
dreamed of becoming when he enlisted in the King's army. He
had been impatient to be in the show, to ride off in glory to fight
the Hun. The British Army had snapped him up in a heartbeat,
eager to commission a young officer with both engineering skills
and a lifetime of horsemanship to recommend him. Frank
thought he would be like Carruthers, career military, straight-
backed, proud, with clarity of purpose and a taste for adventure.

He sometimes thought, now, that the greatest shock of his war
experience was not even the loss of his left arm, which was misery enough. The worse shock, in many ways, was the profound
shift in his perception of the world. He came home stunned by
the carnage, the cruelty, and the excesses of war. He might, he
supposed, have regained his commission once he was able to tolerate his prosthesis, but he could never have accepted it.

None of that dimmed his respect for Carruthers. The captain,
and the others who labored here at March Field, had been essential to the ultimate victory of the Allies. Frank knew Carruthers
by reputation, and the efficient operation he saw around him
proved that the captain had earned it. Frank had saluted him in

all sincerity, and shaken his hand, finding his grip as firm and friendly as he could have wished.

"The Boeing Company appreciates this access," Frank told the captain.

Carruthers grinned, his face creasing in weathered lines. He looked every inch a flyer, Frank thought, with a twinge of envy. He looked to be a man as much at ease in the air as on the ground. Carruthers said, "Your company makes fine airplanes, Major Parrish, and has done wonders refitting some of the old ones. The army is happy to oblige Bill Boeing whenever possible."

"I'd like to talk to all your pilots," Frank said.

"You mean, the ones I have left?"

"Right." Since the end of the war, operations at March Field were being gradually phased out. The same slowdown of operations that had cut Boeing's army contracts in half had sharply reduced the number of pilots being trained. The Jennys were disappearing, one by one, mostly snapped up by barnstormers.

"I don't know what's going to happen in the flying business, Major," Carruthers said. They reached the mess hall, and Frank, a little self-consciously, reached for the door with his left hand, his prosthetic one. He had found, in the year he'd had it, that he wanted to use it as much as possible, not just for the practice, but to prove he could. He felt the curious glances when people noticed it, but very few made any comment.

He didn't blame anyone for looking. It was called the officer's arm because it was the finest of its type, the best modern technology had to offer. Still, it hardly looked real. It looked like what it was, metal and leather and rubber, but Frank didn't care about its appearance. He loved the thing. He felt as if it—and Margot—had given him back his life.

Thinking of Margot confused him just now. His feelings for her hadn't changed, but it had been something of a relief when Boeing sent him here to study the JN-4. It gave him time to think about what had come between them. He was embarrassed, though, to realize how much he missed her. At the thought of

her, his solar plexus ached with longing to see her tall figure striding toward him, shining dark hair ruffling in the breeze, clear
dark eyes lighting as she saw him. Damn, Cowboy. You have to
set this right. But he couldn't think about it now. He had a job to
do, and he was grateful for the distraction.

He and Carruthers poured coffee for themselves and sat at one
of the long tables in the mess, their legs stretched out from the
bench seats, a sheaf of blueprints between them. Carruthers
tapped the papers. "There's a lot of good work here," he said.
"Side benefit of war, I guess."

"Yes."

"You had a very different war from mine, Major."

"Expect so." There wasn't much to say about it, Frank
thought. Not that he ever had much to say. Carruthers had been
part of the supreme American effort to match the Germans' airpower. Frank figured that was probably more meaningful, and a
hell of a lot more productive, than his own service with Allenby
in the Judean hills. He tried, now that he had a functional hand
and arm, not to think about the day he was wounded, but sometimes the memory caught him unawares, and he felt the horror
and disgust of it all over again.

Carruthers didn't press him. He seemed an affable enough fel-
low, career army, well past his youth. Frank had studied his
record before he came, and he knew Carruthers had put up
March Field, with its machine shop, hospital, supply depot, and
aero repair building, in just sixty days. It was an impressive accomplishment.

Carruthers said, "So, Major. Your boss believes airpower is
here to stay."

"He thinks it's going to transform the world." Carruthers lifted
his eyebrows, and Frank smiled. He was on sure ground on this
topic. When it came to airplanes, and the Boeing Airplane Company, Frank could be more forthcoming, even talkative. He
shared Bill Boeing's passion for the possibilities and the opportunities available to the masters of the air. "We're already carrying

mail, a commercial enterprise. Building seaplanes, touring airplanes, the MB-3A pursuit fighters—there's no limit. We're going to build lighter airplanes, carry a heavier payload."

"Douglas got ahead of you with the Cloudster."

Frank chuckled. "That got under Mr. Boeing's skin, I can promise you."

"But now the war's over. I wonder if there's enough demand to keep all of you in business—Boeing and Douglas and Curtiss, too."

"Mr. Boeing's looking ahead, Captain. He's got all his engineers working on the next step."

"So he sent you here. He doesn't mind that Curtiss built the Jenny?"

"Not at all. He figured a good close look will help us understand why the Jenny is so efficient and so stable. Is it the ailerons, you think?"

"Maybe. The Jenny's slow, which is why the barnstormers like it. It won't ever work as anything but a trainer."

"We've heard the Canuck has a lighter interior. We're interested in that."

"Happy to help however we can." Carruthers emptied his coffee cup. "I'll give you a tour of the place, so you can look around on your own."

"Thanks."

"Maybe, if you feel like it, you'd like to go up for a spin?"

Frank set down his coffee cup with a decisive click. "Oh, yes, Captain," he said fervently. "There's nothing I'd like better. If the United States Army would allow an ex–British Army man in one of their airplanes, I would very much like to go up."

CHAPTER 4

Allison had forgotten the magnificence of Benedict Hall. Four white-painted stories were surrounded by a wide porch. There was both a large and a small parlor, a long dining room, and so many bedrooms she hadn't been able to count them yet. Her parents' house in San Francisco was tall and narrow, but Benedict Hall was tall and broad, sprawling among gardens that must be beautiful in the spring and summer. There was an old coach house in back, now converted into a garage, where the Essex motorcar rested in shining black splendor.

Cousin Margot, oddly enough, lived above the garage in a small apartment. Allison didn't know why that should be, when there was an enormous bedroom with attached bath right at the front of the house, a room everyone referred to as Miss Margot's.

Allison pictured Cousin Margot scowling, sour with disappointment over not marrying her major. She probably went around most of the time in heavy shoes like Ruby's, dark stockings, even spectacles. She probably wore a stethoscope around her neck and had a thermometer sticking out of her pocket. Maybe what happened at Allison's party had ruined everything, and now she was a bitter old maid ready to take her misery out on Allison.

Allison felt like a stranger here, even though they all bore the same name. She knew about the family mostly from letters and conversations with her parents. Papa said Uncle Dickson's business had thrived in Seattle, even after the war and the general strike that had brought down so many others. He always said, with gruff admiration, "That Dickson can see five years into the future! Hell of an advantage." Dick, the oldest son, worked in the business with his father, and his wife, Ramona, was a conventional sort, fair and pretty, not much at conversation but wearing very good clothes.

The Benedicts' cook, Hattie, was a Negro. Adelaide, after their last visit, had declared on the train back to San Francisco that she didn't know what Edith was thinking, hiring a colored cook. Papa had made some remark about Hattie being with the family a long time, and Adelaide had retorted that with all their money, Dickson and Edith could do better. She said it was all well and good to have colored help in the laundry or to clean, but she wouldn't have it in her kitchen. Allison had stopped paying attention then, because her mother never went in the kitchen that she could see, so she didn't think her opinion mattered much.

Hattie had made what she called her "special cake" on the night Allison arrived. She served it herself, so Allison had to eat a few bites to be polite. It was marvelous, flavored with almond and topped with coconut, and Allison could still taste the sweetness in her mouth when she went to bed that night.

Uncle Dickson had driven the Essex himself to King Street Station to meet Allison and Ruby. His butler and chauffeur, as Allison had learned from Papa, had suffered cerebral apoplexy the year before, and Uncle Dickson refused to replace him, which meant there wasn't a single manservant in Benedict Hall.

In Mother's view, this was foolish, and created more hardship for Edith. In Papa's opinion, Dickson Benedict was just looking for an excuse to drive his own motorcar, something no one in his position should do. Whatever the reason, Uncle Dickson had been at the wheel of the Essex, which was quite a respectable automobile. With him, to help with the luggage, was one of the maids, a redheaded, freckle-faced girl named Leona, who bobbed a curtsy every time anyone spoke to her, and whose presence had Ruby stony-faced with resentment by the time the valises and the trunk were wrestled into the back of the Essex.

Benedict Hall and the other grand mansions of Seattle occupied Fourteenth Avenue, opposite a park with a glass-walled conservatory and a brick water tower soaring toward the leaden clouds. It all would have been beautiful if it hadn't been for the unrelenting rain, which depressed Allison and made Ruby sniffle.

While Ruby unpacked Allison's trunk and stowed her things in the drawers of a massive oak wardrobe, she complained steadily, in a resentful monotone, about having to share a floor with Leona and her twin, Loena. Ruby had her own bedroom, but they all shared a bath, and the twins trotted in and out of her room without asking, as if it didn't even have a door. "They chatter at me all the time, and I can't even tell them apart," Ruby droned, all the while folding chemises and shirtwaists and pairs of stockings. "They're as alike as two peas in the same pod. I swear if you put 'em side by side even their freckles would match. And they're just housemaids, besides. There's no lady's maid in the house, not a real one. Who am I going to talk to?"

"Maybe Seattle ladies don't have lady's maids," Allison said absently. It wasn't an issue she cared about in the least. If Ruby decided she didn't like living in Benedict Hall, Allison would happily put her on the train back to San Francisco. She could fold her own clothes, surely. She couldn't mend them, or iron them, but she would get by. She had managed perfectly well on *Berengaria*, when Ruby was lying in her bunk in Third Class, clutching her stomach and moaning.

Now, Allison was seated at the vanity mirror, coaxing the sides of her hair into spit curls to frame her cheeks, the way the film star Louise Brooks wore her hair. Of course, Louise Brooks's hair was dark and Allison's was so fair it was almost colorless, but she thought the style flattered her small face and pointed chin. The trick was to get the curls to stay. She dipped a fingertip into the tin of pomade, delicately stroked it on, then turned her head this way and that, assessing it.

"You could be a hairdresser," Ruby said, standing behind her. "Monsieur Antoine couldn't do any better."

"Oh, he could," Allison said, pursing her lips. "He invented the bob, after all. And the finger wave."

Ruby pushed a strand of her own dull brown hair back from her face and scowled over Allison's shoulder. "I'd like to bob my hair, too," she said. "But who knows what the barbers in Seattle are like?"

"Cousin Ramona must know one. She has a perfect finger wave. Do you want me to ask her?"

Ruby shrugged. "Oh, I don't know. I'll think about it." She turned to shake the wrinkles out of Allison's pink georgette crepe, and Allison let the matter rest. Ruby often longed for this or that new thing, but when push came to shove, she was a coward. She still wore her hair pinned up in rolls. She would probably go to her coffin that way.

Allison added a touch of rouge to her cheeks, so subtle she thought only Cousin Ramona would notice. All the debs this year had worn a bit of makeup. She sparingly touched her mouth with color from a Levy Tube, then pressed her lips with a handkerchief so she wouldn't stain the table napkins. She gave her head a shake to be certain the spit curls would hold. She decided the look was good. Not as vivid as Louise Brooks, of course, but every bit as chic as the women she had seen in Paris.

Unfortunately, there was no one to appreciate her achievement except this house full of relatives. She had been here two whole stultifying days! Since her arrival at Benedict Hall, she hadn't been out of the house once, and it was too wet outside to just take a walk.

Her bedroom was very nice, though, with lace curtains at the window and more lace dangling from the vanity chair. A plump pink comforter filled the bed, and a pretty china basin and ewer rested on the bedside stand, even though she had an entire bathroom to herself. She wondered who had arranged everything.

It couldn't have been Aunt Edith. Such an effort was obviously beyond her. She was eerily silent and alarmingly vague in her movements.

Cousin Ramona was sweet, looking after Aunt Edith, asking in a distracted way if Allison had everything she needed. Uncle Dickson was brusque, but kind enough. Dick seemed a nice sort, but he was always talking with Ramona or going off to work with Uncle Dickson. Allison hadn't seen Cousin Margot once. She wondered if that was done on purpose, if Cousin Margot was avoiding her.

Allison took a last look in the mirror before she rose from the dressing table and held out her arms for Ruby to slip her dress over her head. She heard the door open down the corridor and her aunt's light, uncertain step on the stair. She would have to sit next to her again, she supposed. At least Aunt Edith paid no attention to what she ate. Or didn't.

She tugged her dress down over her hips and slid her feet into a pair of low-heeled slippers. She would go downstairs, sit in her assigned place at the dining table, make polite conversation, and pretend to eat dinner. She would serve her sentence here in Seattle, because she had no choice in the matter.

But, she promised herself, she would never, ever forgive Cousin Margot for making her do it.

Margot stood on the bare oak floor of the space that would soon be her reception room. She turned in a slow circle, admiring the new windows and the built-in shelves Frank had recommended. The shelves were already planed, ready for a coat of varnish. Her father had insisted on giving her a reception desk from his office that he swore no one was using. It sat under a dustcover off to the side, ready to be placed once the floor was sanded and polished. The glaziers were done, and the outside, despite the rainy season, was fully painted in an inviting shade of cream. Her sign, the one Frank had repaired for her, lay just inside the door, ready to hang. Tomorrow the Chinese gardener, recommended by the family of one of her patients, would come to start plantings in the small space between the clinic and the street.

She could begin organizing her small office, too. The floor there was finished, and her supply of books waited in cartons near a new rolltop desk. It was hard to tear herself away from that project, but she had missed dinner the past two nights, caught up in a rush of flu cases at the hospital. It wasn't anything like the epidemic of 1918, but enough to keep everyone busy late into the evening. She had assisted at an aspiration for an influenza patient with a sudden pleural effusion and rather dramatic cyanosis. She hadn't done that before, and she learned a lot from the procedure.

Tonight, though, she must get home in time, especially because, as her father reminded her, she hadn't yet greeted Cousin Allison. Undoubtedly, Ramona and Allison would have far more in common than she and Allison would—clothes and makeup and society, all the things to which Margot was indifferent. Still, her cousin was a guest at Benedict Hall. She didn't want to seem ungracious.

Margot shrugged into her coat, settled her hat on her head, and pulled on her gloves. As she picked up her umbrella and started out of the clinic, she wondered again what it was that Allison had done on the crossing. Margot knew all too well the real trouble a nineteen-year-old girl could get into, the kind of trouble that made a family send her away as quickly as they could. She hoped with all her heart Allison wasn't pregnant. That was one problem that would most certainly be hers to solve.

Allison watched from her window as Cousin Margot's tall figure, sheltered by an umbrella and encased in a long brown overcoat with a drooping collar of some kind of fur, crossed the lawn behind the house and disappeared into the garage. Such an odd choice, to live over the garage, in an apartment all by herself. Allison hadn't been in the apartment, but she could imagine it. It had been the butler's rooms, after all. It couldn't offer much in the way of comfort or elegance. Cousin Ramona said the best thing about it was the telephone Uncle Dickson had installed there, so Margot's late-night calls from the hospital didn't disturb the family.

Of course, Cousin Margot had the advantage of solitude, and Allison could see the appeal of that. There was hardly any in Benedict Hall. The two maids, Loena and Leona, were forever dashing about upstairs and downstairs, cleaning, dusting, polishing. Hattie, the cook, pottered between the kitchen and the dining room, offering to make tea or a sandwich. Allison's bedroom could have been a refuge, but Ruby spent far too much time there on trumped-up tasks—a shirtwaist with a tear, a skirt needing pressing, a woolen coat in need of brushing.

Allison turned from the window to face her maid. "Ruby, can't you make friends with the twins? They seem all right to me."

"You don't know what it's like up there, Miss Allison," Ruby said sullenly. She smoothed the panels of the wool crepe frock Allison was going to wear for dinner and held it out to her.

Allison stepped into it, tucking her silk slip down inside, turning for Ruby to manage the fastenings. "How bad can it be, really?" she said. "We're stuck here all winter. You can't spend all these months in my room."

"They come in and out of my bedroom like it was their own," Ruby said. "Always wanting to talk about this and that, show me some bit of frippery one of the family gave them, ask me all about San Francisco."

"Well, tell them," Allison said. "It's not like they get to travel. As *you* have done, remember." She turned back to the mirror, twitched the wool crepe into place, and touched her hair one more time.

Ruby bent to the bottom of the wardrobe and produced the pumps with the low Cuban heels, and Allison made a face. "Not those," she said. "The Louis heels, the pointed ones."

Ruby frowned at her. "Mrs. Adelaide says—"

"Mother isn't here, Ruby. She's wrong, in any case. There's nothing trampy about the Louis heels."

It was obvious Ruby had more to say on the subject, but Allison's stormy expression evidently dissuaded her. She brought the Louis heels, set them down smartly on the vanity, and departed, pointedly shutting the door behind her. Allison made a face at the closed door, then sat down on the vanity stool to put on the shoes.

She caught sight of herself in the mirror as she was adjusting the straps. The furrow between her eyebrows was hardly becoming, she thought. Her lips were pursed, making her look like a spoiled child. Or a sour old lady.

"This has to stop, Allison Benedict," she said sternly to her reflection. It wasn't, after all, Ruby's fault that she was dull. Nor was it her fault she was stuck here in a houseful of strangers. Allison sighed and rested her chin on her fist. It was all just so—so *stultifying*.

She hadn't wanted a maid in the first place. It had been her mother's idea, and her father had concurred, mostly, Allison suspected, because he thought it looked grand for his debutante daughter to have a lady's maid hovering around her. The two of them, Henry and Adelaide, insisted on quoting Emily Post at every opportunity, and Emily Post decried the sharing of maids between a mother and her debutante daughter.

Even after only two days, it was clear to Allison that the Benedicts of Seattle had no need to consult Emily Post in order to do things properly. Despite Aunt Edith's fragile state and the lack of a butler, the style and management of Benedict Hall was as effortless and elegant as any house Allison had seen. Nothing was ostentatious, but every piece of furniture, every bit of drapery, every decoration had been chosen with exquisite taste. The Seattle Benedicts wore their wealth easily, in a way that seemed vastly more sophisticated to Allison than her own family's display.

She had visited enough homes of the wealthy in the past year to understand that her parents' home verged on the vulgar. Its rooms were crowded with velvet davenports and suites of club chairs. Etageres and occasional tables and Persian rugs filled every available space. Allison had protested, once, when some new piece of scrolled and carved furniture was delivered, and her mother had spat at her that she wasn't going to live in an empty barn.

She had been more successful in talking her mother out of putting Ruby in a uniform, probably because Papa didn't want to have to pay for it. Allison had managed to head off the lace cap, pinafore apron, and black button-up dress by assuring her mother such a getup was much too old-fashioned. She hadn't used the word *pretentious*, but it was in her arsenal if necessary.

Looking at the servants' attire at Benedict Hall, she knew she'd been right. The twin maids, Leona and Loena, wore simple print dresses with long utilitarian aprons over them. Like Ruby, they wore dark stockings and flat, serviceable shoes, or boots if they were going outside the house. Ruby clarified her higher position as a lady's maid by wearing a white shirtwaist and a dark skirt that fell demurely to her ankles. She had a trim white apron to wear when she was doing wash or sewing or carrying trays.

It had been a lucky thing that Ruby was able to sew new skirts for herself. She had gained at least ten pounds during Allison's debutante season from sitting around in the kitchens of grand houses waiting for the parties to be over, drinking tea and eating leftovers as she gossiped with the other ladies' maids.

Papa remarked that it looked as if Ruby had gained all the weight Allison had lost that year. He supposed the excitement of being a debutante—photographers everywhere, dressmakers parading through the house, engraved invitations arriving in the mail—had made Allison lose her appetite. At meals she could feel his speculative gaze, assessing her hair and skin and figure as if she were a bale of dyed silk and he was trying to decide what price he could demand.

If he knew what her mother had done, would he send Adelaide to Bella Vista Rest Home instead of her? It had crossed her mind to just spill it out to them, to Papa and that appalling Dr. Kinney, tell them the whole truth of the matter.

They might not have believed her in any case, but more than that, it was part of her private struggle with her mother. To turn it over to someone else would be, in some obscure way, to give up. To surrender. Allison would never, ever surrender, even if she died.

She turned now before the mirror, noting with satisfaction that her breasts and hips were so flat she could have been a boy. She would have preferred being a boy, actually. Boys grew into men, and men were free. Men could choose what they wanted to do. Men had all the fun, men like Tommy Fellowes, late of Exeter College, Oxford.

Allison bent to take a handkerchief from a drawer. When she stood up she had to pause, one hand braced against the wall, until the black dots faded from her vision. She supposed she had better be careful about that. It was getting to be a habit.

Margot went up the back porch, leaving her umbrella to dry beside the kitchen door. She sidled carefully through the kitchen, apologizing for getting in the way of Hattie and the two maids, who were bustling between the stove and the counters, their hands full of spoons and spatulas and serving bowls. Hattie just smiled, and said, "Get yourself on in there, Miss Margot, and set down. Your mama gonna be glad to see you."

Margot doubted that, but she passed on through the kitchen and out into the hall, reaching it just as her cousin was descending the carpeted steps of the main staircase.

Margot's first thought was that Allison looked more like a thirteen-year-old girl than a young woman of nineteen. She was fair, and very pretty, but the bodice of her dress barely swelled over her bosom. The dropped waist made her lean hips look even narrower, and the points of her clavicle, revealed by the square neckline of her frock, stood out like those of an undernourished child. For a moment, Margot gazed at her in confusion, wondering why no one had mentioned Allison was ill.

Allison looked back at her from shadowed eyes that seemed full of suspicion. They gazed at each other for a suspended moment, until the door to the small parlor opened, spilling the murmur of conversation into the silence. Ramona appeared in the doorway. "Oh, Margot, good!" she said. "You're here. We were just about to go in to dinner."

With an effort, Margot recalled why she had made an effort to be present tonight. She took a step forward, and held out her hand to the thin girl standing on the lowest stair. "Cousin Allison," she said. "It's nice to see you. I'm glad you could come to stay at Benedict Hall for a time."

Allison shifted her handkerchief to her left hand. She extended her right, and Margot took it cautiously. Her bones looked as fragile as a bird's, and her skin was cold to the touch. "Cousin Margot," Allison said. "Thank you for"—there was the briefest pause before she finished, with deliberate inflection—"*inviting* me."

Margot heard the inflection without knowing whether it was intentional or inadvertent. She saw, though, the narrowing of the girl's eyes, the flash of emotion in her blue gaze. She lifted an eyebrow. "And how are you?"

It was a commonplace courtesy, a ritual question. For Margot, however, the query was not so simple as it was for most people. It had layers of meaning, elements of real significance. It was why she had chosen her profession, and the sight of this emaciated girl engaged both her interest and her concern.

At the very least, there was no question of Allison Benedict being pregnant. With her body weight so low she was doubtless amenorrhoeic. Margot had observed the condition in malnourished daughters of Chinese laborers and occasionally the crib girls of the Tenderloin.

Allison turned her face away and stepped down the last stair to follow Ramona toward the dining room. Over her shoulder, she said, in a brittle tone Margot thought was meant to be gay, "Oh, swell, Cousin Margot, thanks. I'm just swell."

CHAPTER 5

Allison's seat was on Aunt Edith's left, at the foot of the table. At the head, Uncle Dickson settled into his chair with a slight grunt. Cousin Ramona and Cousin Dick sat together on Uncle Dickson's left, the other side of the table from Allison, their faces all but obscured by a tall silver candelabra. Cousin Margot was on Allison's left, and directly opposite her, at Aunt Edith's right hand, one chair remained empty, though the place was set with a charger and a full complement of flatware and crystal.

Allison knew what it was, because the twins had told Ruby, and Ruby, unusually animated by the tidbit of gossip, had whispered it to her before her first dinner at Benedict Hall. The empty chair had been Cousin Preston's, set at his usual place at the table, on his mother's right hand. When Uncle Dickson had asked the maids to remove it, Ruby reported, Aunt Edith had screamed and wept, and slapped at the maids' hands until everyone was in tears.

It was hard not to stare at that empty chair with its plum-colored brocade and scrolled frame, and watching the maids remove the charger and unused silverware after each course made

Allison's skin crawl. No one else seemed to pay any attention. She supposed they were used to it, but it made her feel as if she were sitting opposite a ghost.

She wished Cousin Margot would sit there, instead, so she could take a good look at her. She was younger than Allison remembered. She wore the simplest of dinner dresses, just dark green wool, with a V-neck collar and a pleated skirt that fell to the middle of her calves. She wore no jewelry at all, and she certainly didn't have a stethoscope around her neck! Allison wondered where she kept it. Cousin Margot was no model of chic, but her hair was neatly shingled in back, and hung in straight, shining curves under her chin. Clearly, she didn't need pomade to wrestle her hair into the style she wanted. Allison suspected she wouldn't have bothered if she did, and probably no one could nag her, a doctor, about how to wear her hair or what dress to put on.

The two redheaded maids began serving a soup course that tasted strongly of onions. Allison tasted it, to be polite, before she laid down her spoon and folded her hands in her lap. She felt Cousin Margot's eyes assessing her from the side. Those eyes seemed to look right through a person. They were dark, like her older brother's and her father's, but they had a sort of gleam to them, as if she had one of those new X-ray things built right into her head. Allison resisted a foolish impulse to put up her hand to block Margot's gaze.

Ramona said brightly, "Margot, Cousin Allison was telling us last night about seeing the Eiffel Tower in Paris."

"Did you like it?" Margot asked, forcing Allison to turn toward her. "Many do, I think."

"Well, it is the tallest structure in the world," Ramona said, before Allison could answer. "That makes it interesting."

"And it has Otis elevators," Uncle Dickson said. "Some French ones, too, but I'm told the American ones work much better."

"Trust you to know that, Father," Margot said.

Uncle Dickson chortled and waved his soupspoon. "American industry, daughter. It's the best. Still, the tower is an achievement."

"I suppose it is," Margot said. "But I found it rather stark, in that city full of graceful old architecture."

Adelaide had oohed and aahed over the Eiffel Tower. She had made Allison stand in line forever in the hot sun so the two of them could have their photograph taken in front of it. Allison thought at the time that was the reason she disliked it. Now, Cousin Margot had perfectly expressed her reaction. Allison had found the Eiffel Tower crude and somehow aggressive, with its dark lattices and clanking lifts and exaggerated point stabbing the sky. Of course she hadn't said so. Her mother would have snapped at her that she didn't know anything about architecture, which of course was true, or that she should respect the opinions of people who knew better. Allison often didn't respect the opinions of people who were supposed to know better, but she had learned not to say so.

She found herself stuck now, not wanting to offend Ramona, but intrigued, and a bit confused, to find that someone—anyone—shared her unspoken opinion. She blinked, wondering what she could say. Finally, awkwardly, she said, "I liked Notre Dame much better."

"Yes, so did I," Margot said, nodding at Allison as if her thoughts mattered. As if she really wanted to hear them. She said, "I love the feeling of age in an old cathedral like that. There's a weight to it. A sort of rooted feeling. It makes me feel connected to all the other people who have been there."

This was so like the way Allison had felt when she entered the shadowy, cool interior of Notre Dame that she fell silent, remembering. Her mother had been impatient, saying they had seen enough churches, but Allison could have wandered through the cathedral for hours, discovering bits of statuary, interesting niches, enjoying the way the stained glass windows colored the sunbeams that fell over the marble floors. Her mother had tugged her away when she was trying to examine the gallery stalls, which had marvelous carvings. Adelaide ordered the maids to gather their things so they could go to the hotel, and ordered Allison to move on in exactly the same tone of voice she used with Ruby and Jane. Allison had snatched her arm away from her mother, fighting an urge to simply flee.

She couldn't have done that, of course. She didn't speak very good French, and she wasn't allowed any money of her own. There was no place she could go. Simmering with resentment and frustration, she had followed Adelaide out into the courtyard like a dog on a leash. All of this flashed through her mind in a moment as she looked up into Cousin Margot's searching gaze. "I'd like to go back," she said, and though she was afraid it was an obscure, even a childish, thing to say, Margot nodded again.

"I would, too. Some day when I can have a nice long vacation."

Ramona, bravely trying to keep the conversation going, said, "Dick and I honeymooned in Paris. Such a romantic city." Her husband smiled at her, and she blushed becomingly. She was plumper than Allison remembered, her cheeks rounder, her bosom fuller. It didn't seem to concern anyone, though. No one appeared to be taking note of what she ate.

"I went to Paris after I finished my undergraduate work," Margot said. "Paris and London. I didn't have time for Italy, because I was due to start medical school." She glanced at Allison, a clear signal that it was her turn to contribute.

Allison wasn't used to being included this way. It was hard to keep thinking of polite things to say, and Cousin Margot was so attentive, she didn't want to make a mistake. "Italy was my favorite," she said lamely.

There was so much more she could have said. She could have described the fabulous Uffizi Gallery in Florence, which had captivated her. She could have mentioned going to an opera in Milan, where the music had been heavenly, but which Adelaide had ruined by saying it was too hot and the Italians were too rude. She had ridden in a gondola in Venice, while her mother ran on about what a terrible place it must be to live, with mold and damp and peeling paint everywhere. Adelaide kept a handkerchief to her nose to shut out the stink of the water. Allison and the gondolier, who fortunately didn't speak a word of English, had exchanged rueful glances, so that Allison had to hide a laugh behind her hand. It had been one of her favorite moments of the tour.

She could find no way to express all of that. She could hardly even organize her private thoughts about it. She had loved Italy for its music and its art and its laughing people. The food, however, had been a torment.

Uncle Dickson saved her by saying, "Well, well. Allison, your aunt Edith also loves to travel. Don't you, Edith?"

Allison turned to her aunt. Edith, who hadn't touched her cup of soup, raised her eyes to her husband. "What, dear?"

Uncle Dickson said, speaking with careful clarity, "We were talking about travel, Edith. You always enjoyed traveling."

"Oh, yes," Edith said, but she dropped her gaze immediately, not looking at Allison at all. "Oh, yes," she said again.

When the salad came, Allison ate most of it, feeling the pressure of Margot's questioning gaze. She ate a bit of sea bass, and one bite of fried potatoes. The potatoes also tasted strongly of onions. She mashed them with her fork into a little pile at the side of her plate.

The maids came in with dessert and a coffeepot. Leona, Allison could see, was ever so slightly thinner than her sister Loena. Leona had a freckle beside her left ear, too, that Loena lacked. Allison thought she would point that out to Ruby so she would stop complaining about not being able to tell them apart.

As Loena poured coffee, Cousin Dick said, "So, Margot, how's the clinic coming? Windows all in?"

"Yes," Margot said, pulling her coffee cup closer to her. "The windows are in, and the floors are almost done." She picked up her coffee and leaned back, cradling the small china cup in long, strong-looking fingers. "Cartons arrive every day," she said with satisfaction. "The autoclave is here, a full set of storage jars, and the mattresses for the exam tables. Two of the doctors at the hospital have sent me extra specula and syringes, and one of them had a drug cabinet he wasn't using—" She broke off and gave

Ramona a wry look. "Sorry, Ramona. You don't like hearing all these details."

"Well, no," Ramona said, with a light laugh. "But I know it's a big undertaking, replacing *everything*."

"It is, in fact. So many details! Hattie's going to make curtains for the windows, bless her. I could have hired someone, but she really wanted to do it. I worry that she's doing too much, handling Blake's job as well as her own."

Dickson said, "Let her do it, daughter, if she wants to. She's proud of you."

"I know. It's awfully kind."

Edith looked up abruptly, as if something Margot said had startled her. "Curtains," she said.

Uncle Dickson frowned, and Allison thought his lips trembled. "What, dear?" he said.

"Curtains," she said again, as if he should understand. "I forgot to tell Hattie."

Margot leaned forward and set her cup down. "Mother, what about the curtains?" Her voice usually had a decisive tone, an authoritative edge to it. Now, however, she spoke carefully to her mother, as her father had done earlier. Allison wondered if this was how she spoke to her patients.

Edith turned her head to her daughter, but a trifle too slowly, as if she were having trouble locating the speaker. "It's the curtains in Preston's room. They're dusty. They should be—" She fluttered one thin hand. The skin was so pale it almost seemed a person could see right through it to the bones beneath. Allison glanced down at her own hand, and noticed, with a twinge of unease, that her fingers were nearly as bony as Aunt Edith's.

Ramona said, "Mother Benedict, I'll have Leona do it. Don't trouble yourself."

Dick covered his wife's hand with his. Dickson nodded and cleared his throat. Margot, on Allison's left, folded her arms, and Allison had the distinct impression she was holding herself in.

Aunt Edith gazed around the table as if she were searching for someone. Her eyes went from place to place, the empty chair, her daughter-in-law's face, her son, her husband at the head. When they reached Margot, they focused suddenly. The pupils swelled, threatening to swallow the pale blue irises. Her pale lips parted, and as she drew breath, Allison felt Margot tense beside her.

"I told you," she said in an urgent whisper. "I told you not to do it. You shouldn't have done it, Margot." Allison's arms prickled with gooseflesh. She realized her mouth was open, and she pressed her lips quickly together.

"Edith," Uncle Dickson said. "Margot didn't do anything."

"She did!" Aunt Edith's voice rose. "She spent all Mother's money on that clinic, and then Preston . . . Preston . . ."

Dickson shoved back his chair, the wood creaking in protest, and stood up. He strode around the table to Edith, surprising Leona, who had just come in with a tray. The maid made a small, startled sound and took a step back, the dessert plates on her tray sliding and clicking against one another. Dickson sidestepped her, reached his wife, and bent to take her elbows and pull her gently up and out of her chair. "Edith," he said, with a crack in his gruff voice. "Edith, come with me. Let's go into the small parlor." She protested, something wordless, and he kept murmuring, "Come now, dear. Come with me." He put an arm around her slender back and guided her toward the door.

Allison watched all of this, embarrassed but fascinated. The misery emanating from Margot, at her elbow, was like a wave of cold from an open window in wintertime. Dick, from the opposite side of the table, said, "Don't worry, Margot. She doesn't know what she's saying."

Ramona pressed her palms together, as if in prayer, and said, "Dick, I don't see how we can go on like this. Your mother's really not well."

Cousin Margot shook her head at Leona, who was trying to serve her dessert. It was some sort of custard, with a curl of whipped cream on the top of it. It looked tantalizing, but Allison also refused it.

Leona settled for placing dessert in front of Dick and Ramona, then backed out of the dining room, the tray in her hands. Loena peeked over her shoulder, and the two maids whispered to each other, something Allison couldn't catch. Dick ate the custard in a few quick bites, as if it were medicine he was forcing down. Ramona poked at it with a listless spoon, and gave Allison a sad smile across the table. "I'm sorry, Cousin Allison," she said. "Mother Benedict hasn't recovered from Preston's . . . that is, from losing Preston."

Allison found her voice at last, though her throat was dry. "It's very sad," she said. "Poor Aunt Edith." In truth, she was stunned by such naked infirmity, the evidence of real illness. Her own mother's nervous attacks appeared even less convincing in the face of the scene she had just witnessed. "What was she . . . what did she mean?"

"Nothing. Nothing," Dick said roughly.

Cousin Margot made a bitter sound that might have been a laugh. "Cousin Allison is going to be in the house for some time, Dick. She might as well know."

The dining room door opened once more, and Hattie's round, perspiring face appeared. "Miss Margot, a letter came for you." She pulled it out of her apron pocket, a slender white envelope with blue script on it, and handed it over. "It's from California. I thought you'd want to have it right away."

"I do, Hattie. Thanks." Margot took the letter and held it without opening it.

Hattie, scrubbing her hands on the hem of her apron, scanned the table and clicked her tongue disapprovingly. "Now, I made that nice butterscotch custard, and hardly nobody ate any of it!"

Dick said stoutly, "It was delicious, Hattie."

Ramona said, "Mrs. Edith was upset. It spoiled our appetites. I'm sorry."

"Now, don't you never mind that, Mrs. Ramona." Hattie bustled around the table to pick up the two dessert plates. "Don't you never mind. You all just enjoy your coffee, and I'll go see if

Mrs. Edith and Mr. Dickson are doing all right. Maybe some tea for Mrs. Edith . . .." Her last words faded away as she hurried out of the dining room and the door swung closed behind her.

Margot said, "I hope Mother isn't still taking laudanum. There are serious problems with long-term use. I'll speak to Dr. Creedy."

"He was here yesterday," Ramona said.

"Good." Margot pushed her chair back and stood up. "I'll call him tomorrow. Now, will you excuse me, everyone? Cousin Allison?"

Ramona said, "But we're going to listen to a concert on the wireless, from New York. Don't you want to—"

Margot said, in a weary voice, "Thank you, Ramona. I think it's best all around if I just go to bed." She said good night to everyone and walked out of the dining room. Her shoulders were hunched now, and her steps were shorter and slower. She carried the letter, seemingly forgotten, in her hand.

When she had gone, Dick growled, "This is unfair. None of it was Margot's fault."

"But what can we do?" Ramona breathed. Allison watched the two of them, at a loss.

"Not a damned thing." Dick threw his napkin down, rose from the table, and held Ramona's chair as she stood up. "No, if Father won't take steps, there's not a damned thing we can do."

Allison wondered what he meant by take steps, but she was sure it wasn't proper to ask. Whatever was going on, it was obviously making Margot unhappy. As she followed the family out of the dining room and down the hall to the small parlor, she felt more confused than ever. This woman she had designated as her enemy had big problems of her own. It was hard not to feel sympathy for her.

Margot gathered up her umbrella, dry now, and trudged across the lawn to the garage. The rain had stopped, but the cloud layer remained, thick and forbidding. Only the light she had left on at the foot of the stairs beckoned to her through the darkness.

She didn't remember the letter from Frank until she reached

for the doorknob and found the envelope still in her hand. She tucked it into the pocket of her dress, opened the door, and dropped the umbrella into the pottery stand inside. She would wait, she thought. She would get ready for bed, make a cup of tea, and settle down at the old, scarred table to read it. She would indulge herself in imagining Frank sitting opposite her, hearing his voice in the written words. If she closed her eyes, she could see the streaks of silver gleaming in his dark hair, be enchanted anew at the vivid blue of his eyes.

She found a fresh nightdress folded on the foot of her bed, and a wave of affection for Hattie swept over her. Hattie didn't like her living over the garage any more than Blake would if he knew. Margot, for her part, had forbidden Hattie a dozen times to climb these narrow stairs to "do" for her, but she might as well have saved her breath. There was daily evidence of Hattie's presence—a fresh bar of soap, a change of sheets, soiled laundry disappearing and reappearing clean, pressed, and folded. A bad cook but a good woman, the Benedicts said of Hattie. The truth of it brought a smile to Margot's lips even now, lonely and disheartened though she felt.

She lingered over washing her face, turning back her bed, putting on her nightdress, brewing her tea. The letter, with her name in Frank's cramped handwriting, lay in the center of the table. While it was still unopened, she didn't have to face what it said. It wasn't her nature to leave it there all night, of course. She was accustomed to facing her challenges squarely. The trouble with this particular challenge was that there seemed to be no answer. No resolution. There was no response she could think of that could bridge the distance between herself and Frank.

She sat down at the table, her teacup at her elbow, and drew the envelope toward her. Just looking at his handwriting reminded her of the comforting strength of his good right arm and the saving efficiency of his left arm. That left arm, and that mechanical hand with its cleverly jointed fingers, were a testament to how far the two of them had come.

Margot touched the unopened envelope with her fingers. Ten days had passed since they had said good-bye, a painful and poignant farewell neither of them wanted to make. It had left a sore spot in her heart, one she knew she should stop probing, but which she couldn't help revisiting, over and over.

She had walked with Frank to King Street Station that misty November morning. She was due at the hospital, but she had just time to see him onto his train, then hurry back up the hill. The car would have made the whole thing much easier, but she was used to its absence now. She knew the streetcar schedule, knew which taxicabs were best and which should be avoided. On this day she had walked, meaning to savor the crispness of the end of autumn. She met Frank at his boardinghouse, and they strolled down Cherry together, turning toward the campanile that towered above the train yard. The giant clock warned them they had only a quarter of an hour. Frank, handsome in his Stetson and his camel's hair coat, carried his valise in his left hand and a bulging briefcase in his right. Margot carried her medical bag. The breeze from the Sound had a bite to it, but her coat was buttoned up the front, the fur collar pulled high under her chin. She glanced up from beneath the brim of her hat and saw that Frank's mouth was as set as her own must be.

She stopped when they reached the entrance to the station. Automobiles rattled up in a continuous stream, their passengers disembarking with cries of farewell, calls to the porters, a great fuss of trunks and suitcases and hatboxes. Frank paused with her, and the two of them stood facing each other just under the awning, a little island of tense silence amid the flood of activity.

"Frank." Margot spoke through a throat aching with the pain of approaching separation. "I wish we could talk about what's happened between us. I still don't quite understand."

He looked down at her, his blue eyes flinty with distress. "I think you do, Margot," he said. The pain in his voice matched her own. "You should. It's a matter of principle."

"It's no less a matter of principle for me."

A porter approached them, touching the brim of his flat cap. "Luggage, sir?"

Frank shook his head without taking his eyes from Margot's face. A woman in a long fur coat, just being helped out of a touring car, called to the porter, and he wheeled away toward her. Frank set his valise down and switched his briefcase to his left hand so he could put out his right to Margot. "Nothing more to say just now," he said, a little roughly.

"I suppose not," she whispered. She put out her own right hand. Their fingers met, intertwined, and held. She felt the warmth of his skin through her glove, the pressure of his fingers gripping hers, pressing them more tightly than was necessary, and she understood he loathed this public farewell as much as she did. She wanted to lean forward, to press against him, to kiss the lines around his mouth that had become so dear to her, to feel his firm lips on hers, but of course she couldn't. Not here. And, perhaps, not now. "Frank, I—" she stammered, with an uncharacteristic loss of composure.

"We'll think about it," he said tightly. "We'll both think about it."

The whistle of the train, a blast of steam-powered noise that made Margot's ears ache, reminded them of the time. Frank released her hand, his fingers sliding away, parting from hers with reluctance. She wanted to seize them back, but of course she couldn't do that, either.

He bent to pick up his valise again. "Watch the glazier," he said unexpectedly. "The seals."

She could only nod. At that moment she didn't give a damn about the clinic's new windows.

"I'll write," he said, and then, swiftly, he turned, the hem of his coat flaring, and strode away. She watched his back, following the tilt of his hat, the set of his shoulders, until he disappeared through the glass doors of the station. There she lost him in the crowd, too many other hats and coats and raised arms for her to follow his progress. Her hand felt cold where it had just moments before been warmed by his. Her eyes stung embarrassingly as she turned away from the station and started up toward Fifth Avenue and Seattle General Hospital.

Margot Benedict had not expected to fall in love. She was, and had been since she was only fourteen, consumed by her ambition to be a physician, and once she achieved that goal, by the drive to establish herself, to earn the respect of older doctors, to resist the prejudice and ritual exclusion women physicians faced, more intense now than in a hundred years of medical practice. Part of what was wrong between her and Frank was that drive, that need to fight for equality for herself and for other, less privileged women. Romance had never entered into her plan, and now, with her heart aching over Frank's absence, she almost—but not quite—wished her life had followed its expected path.

"Too late for such thoughts," she told herself. She was learning that the heart, once engaged, was impervious to logic. It was hard to recall what her life had been like before Frank Parrish came into it. He had protected her, sustained her, supported her when her old supporter was laid low. No, there could be no regrets, and no turning back. Whatever was to be between them, she couldn't, and she wouldn't, wish they had never met.

Now, alone in the small apartment that still felt as if it belonged to Blake, she turned Frank's letter over and slid her thumb beneath the flap.

There was only one sheet, closely written. She hadn't seen Frank's handwriting often. The tightness of the script, the rather cramped style of it, surprised her. Her own handwriting was large, almost careless, and she had to take care not to scrawl. Frank's looked, she supposed, like the handwriting of an engineer. It was orderly, controlled, every word calculated to fit on its line, every line planned to fit on the page. She wondered if he had written the letter on another sheet, then copied it onto this stationery, with the March Field letterhead at the top. It read:

My dearest Margot,

You will find my address at the top of this letter. You can add "Bachelor Officers' Quarters" to be certain it reaches me. I hope to hear from you by return post. I want to hear how the clinic is coming. Are the floors finished? The glazier should be done by now, and Hattie can get on with her curtain project.

I hope you won't be too disappointed to learn I am staying on here longer than I expected. There is much to learn, and Mr. Boeing has asked me to look into several details we hadn't previously thought of. The airplanes are marvelous, quite light and easily maneuverable. Study of them should be a great help in the development of new designs. Mr. Boeing is going to join me here in a couple of weeks to see for himself.

The weather in California is remarkable for November. The sun shines, and a dry wind blows up the valley. It's the perfect spot for flying, and I've been privileged to go up almost every day with one of the army pilots.

Dearest, I hardly know how to address the other matter. I suppose separations never come at a good time, but this one has to be one of the worst. Are you going ahead with your plans? I long to know the answer, and yet I dread to hear it.

What I am certain of is how much I miss you. Nothing has changed in my feelings for you. I send you my deepest affection,
Frank

Margot read the letter twice, while her tea, forgotten, cooled in its cup. She wanted to cry out to him, remind him of her warning that she wasn't like other women. She wanted to argue, persuade, point out how he was wrong, but they had already done all of that. He was beyond any doubt a man of honor and principle. His war experience had only deepened those attributes, and she loved and admired him for it.

What he couldn't see, and what their bitter argument had failed to persuade him of, was that her position came from the same beliefs. Honor. Principle.

It wasn't that she and Frank didn't agree on the underlying necessity for women to have access to birth control. *All* women, as she had stressed to him, not just wealthy ones. He had no objection in principle, or even in practice. It was her association with Sanger that so offended him. The public and controversial nature of that association embarrassed him, even angered him. When she first understood the depth of his feelings, she was shocked. When she tried to point out that poor women were being imprisoned by continuous pregnancy, he had said he understood.

"But," he said stiffly, "it's a personal matter. It should be managed privately."

"Frank!" she protested. "If it's always private, most women will never know their options. I see poor women and girls all the time who have never heard of condoms or sponges. All they know is Lysol, and that can be lethal—to say nothing of useless."

She saw his slight shudder of distaste at her bluntness, but he said only, "It's against the law."

They were lunching at the diner on Post Street, having spent the morning with the workmen putting up the walls of the clinic, measuring for the roof. It wasn't lost on Margot that Frank was avoiding her eyes, gazing down at his fish fry as if the remnants of it were fascinating. She had convinced herself that meant he had doubts about his own argument.

She plunged ahead with her explanation, eager for him to grasp what was so clear to her. "Of course, Frank," she said. "That's exactly the problem. We're working to change the law, Mrs. Sanger, and I, and others in the movement."

At that, his eyes snapped up to hers, and she saw the glint of real anger in them. "Movement!" he said. "Suffrage for women, that was a *movement*. This—this is just—indecent!"

They both knew the word wasn't adequate for his meaning. Margot gazed into his eyes for a long moment, searching for encouragement or, at the least, for understanding. She didn't find it. In its absence, she felt a wave of exhaustion that made her turn away from him, gather her things from the chair next to her, and rise to go.

He said, "Margot, please. Margaret Sanger was sentenced to *jail*. Her husband actually went, and served thirty days!"

There was pain in his voice, pain mixed with anger, and with frustration that matched her own. She paused, looking down at him. "You went to war, Frank. You did it because you believed it was necessary."

"It was."

"I don't disagree with you, though the price you paid—which we all paid—was staggering. This is a war, too. It's my war. There's a price to be paid for it, and I don't see a way to avoid that."

They were interrupted at that moment by the aproned proprietor, a familiar face to both of them after months of work on the clinic. He said, "You going off to the hospital, Doc Benedict? No time for coffee?" He rubbed his thick hands over his grease-spotted apron. "Got some nice cobbler in the back. Last of the blackberries, and some fresh cream from the Valley."

She picked up her gloves and pulled them on. "Thank you, Arnie. I wish I had time. I have patients to see."

"How 'bout you, Major? Coffee?"

Frank only shook his head, reached into his pocket for money to pay for lunch, then held Margot's elbow in the most impersonal manner possible as they stepped past the cast iron rooster doorstop at the diner's entrance.

When they stood in Post Street, Frank said, "I don't want you to do it, Margot. I don't want your name attached to it."

She had said, in a tone as icy as his own, "I have to do it, Frank. It's impossible for me to think of *not* doing it."

And it was. Even now, alone in the dim apartment above the garage, where every corner seemed invested with Blake's generous spirit, she couldn't think of not doing it. The faces of women and girls who had sought her help, who were desperately searching for some way to take control of their lives and build better futures for their children, paraded through her mind as they had paraded through the charity wards of the hospital and the tiny waiting room of her original clinic. Some had burned themselves with the Lysol douche that was marketed as hygiene but which everyone knew was meant as a spermicide. Others had borne too many babies at too young an age and were in danger of not surviving another pregnancy. One had a husband who said if she didn't get rid of the baby she was carrying he would kill them both. Many wept that they couldn't afford more children, that the ones they had already were going hungry. How could she *not* do everything possible to give these women some power?

She wasn't even advocating for legitimizing abortion, although she fought hard for her patients who needed therapeutic terminations. It was the Comstock laws. Sanger and her allies struggled against them, those blind, shortsighted laws that made any mention of contraception an obscenity and therefore illegal. Margot understood this conflict very well by the time she left medical school, and the experiences of her hospital work and her private practice had made her a soldier in an irrational war.

She refolded Frank's letter and put it back in the envelope. She would answer it, of course. She would tell him how much better Blake was feeling, describe the approaching winter weather, tell him that Cousin Allison had arrived. There was no point in describing her mother's ongoing frailty, because he had seen it for himself. She wouldn't mention her worry about Allison's painful thinness, nor the girl's rather odd behavior, because she didn't know what it all meant yet. She would ask him if he might be back for Christmas, surely a happier Christmas than the last one.

She would omit any mention of Margaret Sanger's impending visit. She hadn't met Mrs. Sanger yet, but through the mail they had made their plans to create a chapter of the American Birth Control League in Seattle. As a physician, it was legal for Margot to prescribe—and teach women how to use—contraception. But without garnering some public attention, women couldn't know it was available to them. Sanger always attracted attention. She would be useful.

Margot stood up, carried her cup to the sink, and poured out the cold tea. She rinsed the cup and saucer and placed them on the drainboard. She pulled aside the curtains above the sink and looked across the lawn at Benedict Hall, dim and drowsy in the thick darkness. Just so had Blake always finished his long days, one last glance to be certain all was well.

Margot saw a single faint light in the house, a candle perhaps, in the bedroom now occupied by Allison. She wondered what was keeping the girl up so late.

She let the curtain drop and turned toward the bedroom. She was assisting at a surgery in the morning, and she needed to rest. As she passed the table, she picked up Frank's letter one more time, tempted to reread the last passage, but she laid it down again. She didn't need to read it. She had it memorized.

> *What I am certain of is how much I miss you.*
> *Nothing has changed in my feelings for you. I send*
> *you my deepest affection.*

She clung to those final words, drew comfort and reassurance from them. Frank never said anything he didn't mean. She knew that. She had to trust they would work it all out, somehow.

She wished she had some idea how.

CHAPTER 6

Frank peered into the brilliant sunshine glinting on the buildings of the airfield below him. Nelson shouted through the speaking tube, "Pull her left a bit, Parrish. Bit more. Bit more—there you go! Now, level out. Adjust the trim, so you don't—right, right. Line her up careful now, and start your descent."

Frank's cheeks stung with the wind blowing through the open cockpit. It was a thrilling sensation, a reminder that he was not tied to the earth, but sailing the skies. The sense of power and freedom was like nothing he had ever experienced. Flying made him feel like a mythological hero, a conqueror of worlds.

The double wings vibrated to his left and right. The stick felt easy under his hand, and the rudder bar was surprisingly sensitive beneath his foot. It amazed him how much flying the Jenny was like riding a horse, the airplane reacting almost the way a horse would to hands and heels, flexing, turning, speeding up or slowing down. He couldn't help grinning, and the air whistled against his teeth, making him laugh aloud.

He heard Nelson's chuckle through the speaking tube. "Yeah, Major, it's fun, all right. Just don't get carried away."

"I won't," Frank said. "Ready to go in now?"

"Ready. Be sure you listen!"

The aspect of the Jenny that still impressed Frank deeply, after several flights, was the lift of the double wings. The airplane could fly so slowly it was as if it had stopped in the air, and it made landing seem deceptively simple. He had learned that it wasn't, though, both by studying the manual and by listening to Nelson. Nelson was reminding him now about the sound the bracing wires made under the pressure of speed and wind. The joke was that if the pilot slowed down too much, the wires would hum a descending melody, "Nearer, My God, to Thee," and he'd better adjust the throttle and the altitude before he found himself at the pearly gates!

Frank listened, satisfied at hearing a steady hiss. He lined up, adjusted the trim, and pulled back gently on the stick to modify his angle of attack. He let the Jenny drift toward the ground, knowing if anything changed—an obstruction appeared, a gust of crosswind jostled him—he could ascend again in a heartbeat. His wheels touched down in a respectable three-point landing, the plane barely shivering on contact with the packed earth of the runway. It felt so natural, so instinctive, that Frank heard himself murmur, "Whoa," as he taxied to a stop.

Later, in the mess hall, he tried to explain the comparison to horsemanship to Nelson. The lieutenant shook his head. "I can't grasp it," he confessed. "I'm from Brooklyn. The closest I ever got to a horse was when the iceman came once a week. At least, till I went to France."

Frank said, "I didn't know you were in France."

"Battle of Saint-Mihiel," Nelson said. "I saw the horses hauling the artillery back, but I was in the Army Air Service, thank God."

"Brutal on the ground."

"Yeah. A hell of a lot better to be in the air than in the trenches." Nelson jumped up to bring the coffeepot to the table and refilled both their cups. The remains of lunch were spread before them, meat sandwiches and bowls of oranges from a nearby orchard.

Frank took an orange and began, with self-conscious dexterity, to peel it, using both hands. He felt Nelson's eyes on this process and glanced up. "Works pretty well," he said.

"Works damned well, seems like," Nelson said. Frank nodded. "Where'd you lose it, Parrish?"

It was the first personal question anyone at March had asked him. There was friendship among the pilots and technicians at the base, a camaraderie based on common experience, but the men who had been in the war kept quiet about it. That felt right to Frank, mirroring his own reluctance to revisit the war and its aftermath. He appreciated Nelson waiting until they had spent some time together, on the ground and in the air, waiting for mutual respect to build, for understanding to grow between them at its own pace.

He lifted the artificial arm now and flexed the fingers. "Lost it near Jerusalem," he said. "Shell caught me. I was fortunate. Ten inches to the left, and that would have been all she wrote." It was a Montana expression, but Nelson seemed to understand.

"I know the feeling," he said. A shadow passed over his face, darkening his usual cheerful expression. He was a Nordic type, blond, burly, with a pencil mustache so pale it barely showed against his skin. "I had a close call or two myself."

Frank inclined his head, acknowledging this. "We're luckier than some," he said.

A silence fell between them for a moment. Frank could guess that Nelson, like himself, was haunted by the memories of those less fortunate, those who never came home, but he wouldn't mention it. None of them ever did.

"So," Nelson said after a time. "Army gave you the new arm?"

Frank said, simply, "Yes," but his heart thudded under the immense weight of everything that simple answer left unspoken. He would never be able to forget the misery of that first year, the agony of the neuroma that made him unable to tolerate a prosthesis, a time when he was only barely able to bear the touch of a shirtsleeve or the weight of his jacket.

Or the touch of a girl's hand. His girl, the same one who became his doctor, against his wishes, but to his great benefit. He had no way to put any of it into words, not to Margot, or even, he acknowledged, to himself. Margot had changed his life. She had salvaged it from the ruin it had become. She was unlike any woman he had ever met before, and that, he had learned, was not an easy thing for a man to deal with. He could barely think of her now without a rush of confusion that tied his tongue and made him want to bury his head in his hands.

He wasn't going to blurt any of this out to his flight instructor, of course. He reflected, with private embarrassment, that the person he really wanted to talk it over with was his mother. She was far away in Montana, no doubt already looking out her kitchen window onto the snow filling up the home pasture and sprinkling the roof of the horse barn. He could write to her, but she had never met Margot. On paper, he feared his description of Margot could not possibly do her justice, and might make her sound unapproachable, possibly unreasonable.

He couldn't help wondering, though, what Jenny Baker Parrish would make of Margot's views on the public dissemination of information about what the papers called "family planning." It was sex, pure and simple, something private made public. It was scandalous, which was why Margaret Sanger had almost gone to jail, and why there were laws to control that sort of thing. But would his mother agree with him? He wished he knew.

"Lost you there, Parrish?"

It was Nelson, half smiling, eyebrows raised. Frank said hastily, "Sorry. Got to thinking."

"Dangerous business, thinking," Nelson said with a chuckle.

"True," Frank said. He smiled back. It had been a fine morning, the sun burning through his leather helmet, the wind howling through the ailerons and the struts, and Nelson encouraging him from the rear seat. "You're right, Nelson. Better not to dwell on things we can't change."

"You were thinking about your arm, I guess," the lieutenant said. "Can't blame you for that. But you're halfway to being a pilot, just the same. Got to take pride in that."

"I do. Thanks." Frank drained his coffee mug and set it down. "This is an opportunity I never expected, and I appreciate it."

Nelson made a deprecating gesture, a sideways movement of one hand, a brief shake of his head. "Nah, the captain and your Mr. Boeing are both happy about it. Seems like you're enjoying it."

"Yes," Frank said, inadequately, wishing he had a stronger word. "Yes, most certainly enjoying it."

Flying was, in fact, the most liberating thing he had ever done. Every time his airplane rose above the scrubby grass and low-roofed buildings of March Field, his heart rose with it. Every time he soared away across the valley, with the mountains in the distance and the blue sky empty and inviting all around him, he felt as if the problems of earthbound life fell away, letting him fill himself to the brim with confidence and joy. When he was flying, he felt whole, and that was more intoxicating than the whisky he used to drink to soothe the pain of his missing arm.

He gave his head a shake and pushed back his chair. "Better go write up a report for Mr. Boeing," he said.

"See you at dinner," Nelson said.

Frank bent to pick up his leather helmet and goggles from the chair beside him. "Thanks again."

Nelson reached for the coffeepot to refill his cup. He touched his sandy forelock with two fingers. "It's a pleasure."

Frank left the mess hall and turned toward his quarters. All this, he knew very well, was possible only because of what Margot had done for him. Without her skill—and her courage, which would make any soldier proud—he would still be suffering through long days of pain, searching for whisky every night. That, too, had been in defiance of the law of the land. Was it right for him to object to Margot resisting the law when he had broken it so thoroughly and regularly himself?

He stalked across the grounds to the barracks, suddenly angry with himself, with her, with life in general. He wished he could go straight to the airfield, untie the Jenny from its moorings, and take off, all alone. Leave the whole sorry mess behind on the mundane earth.

* * *

Margot, since installing herself in Blake's apartment, had developed the habit of breakfasting in the kitchen with Hattie and the maids. Hattie protested that this was unseemly, but Margot reminded her that her odd hours made it difficult sometimes to sit with the family at breakfast, and that she and Blake had often shared a pot of coffee before anyone else was awake. On this morning, when she needed to be at the hospital early to scrub for the operating theater, she quietly let herself into the kitchen through the back porch door.

There was no one about, but Hattie, bless her, had left the percolator ready. Margot plugged it in, and brought down one of the big china mugs that were only allowed in the kitchen. She found cream and butter in the icebox, and took bread from the box on the counter. Hattie would scold if she didn't eat more than coffee and toast, but she was no good with eggs. They were always either scorched or runny, and the smell of the sizzling butter and soon-to-be-spoiled eggs would only bring Hattie hurrying from her bedroom, dressed or not. Hattie would cluck, push her away from the stove, and urge her to sit down and "let old Hattie do for you."

Hattie had been "doing for her" as long as she could remember. As Margot waited for the percolator to finish its bubbling, she wondered how old Hattie really was. She knew Blake's age, fifty-something, because he had been born right after the Civil War. As a child, she had pestered him for his history, and he had given it to her in bits and pieces, glimpses into a life begun in the shadow of slavery, developing into one lived in the light and warmth of a family he loved.

But Hattie, as she often said, "kept herself to herself," and believed that was the proper way for a servant to behave. When the young Margot had begged her for stories of her childhood, Hattie only gave that familiar cluck, shaking her head so her round cheeks jiggled. "Ain't much to tell," she would say. "Nothin' a girl like you needs to know. You just remember," she sometimes added, shaking a surprisingly long finger, "how lucky you are, a bitty girl with this big ol' house and a sweet mama and daddy to take care of you." Margot had always thought Hattie was hinting at a hard childhood, but could wring no details out of her.

She'd asked her mother about it once. Edith had been the one to hire Hattie, she knew. Her father had said once, in Margot's hearing, that Edith should have asked her to cook a meal before she gave her the job, and her mother had heaved a sigh and spoken the line they had all used for years. "Well, Dickson. I know Hattie's a bad cook, but she's a good woman."

When Margot pressed her mother to tell her something about Hattie, though, all Edith would say was that if Hattie wanted the children to know her story, she would tell them herself. Hattie took pride in the reputation of Benedict Hall, in its proper complement of a butler, two housemaids, gardeners and handymen, and her own position. Margot guessed Hattie feared her background would make her ineligible to be on the Benedict staff. It spoke to the honor of her family that despite Hattie's shortcomings as a cook, there was never the slightest consideration of letting her go.

Margot put two slices of bread in the brand-new pop-up toaster. Toast, at least, Margot could manage. She had learned to make it by holding a wire toasting rack over Blake's hot plate, turning and turning it while trying not to burn her fingers. The automatic toaster did all of that for her, and renewed her appreciation for modern conveniences.

The toast popped up neatly, perfectly browned on both sides. The percolator finished, and Margot filled her mug and sat down at the table to butter her toast. The sky was still dark outside, but the warmly lighted kitchen was peaceful, fragrant with the scents of newly brewed coffee and toasted bread. Margot sipped her coffee and pulled Frank's letter out of her pocket to read one more time. After surgery this morning, and her rounds in the children's ward, she would find a quiet corner and write back. She would be as careful with her wording as he had been. She could fill her letter with reports on the clinic's progress, the stocking of the storeroom and the examining room, all the bits and pieces Frank had launched for her. She would tell him again how grateful she was for his help, and she would finish just as he had, with a restrained expression of her affection. The real issue that lay between them was, just as he had said, too complicated to be re-solved in letters.

She wouldn't tell him the funding from the Sheppard-Towner Act had come through. The Women and Infants Clinic would soon be a reality, and would teach hygiene, home health care, and contraception to women and girls. There was no point in an-nouncing that, because she was going to do it no matter what Frank might feel or say. All she could do, though it went against her nature, was postpone their conflict until they were face-to-face, until they could decide how big an obstacle it was going to be.

She finished her breakfast and was stowing the butter and cream back in the icebox when Hattie came in, smoothing her printed cotton housedress over her broad figure. "Oh, Miss Mar-got! Good morning! Let me cook you some eggs."

"Thank you, Hattie, but I don't have time. I'm assisting in the operating theater this morning."

"Oh, my goodness, my goodness, Miss Margot." Hattie bent to take a fresh apron out of a drawer, pulled it over her head, and began tying the ribbons. "You're gonna have a long day! Let me send you with a sandwich, at least."

Margot refolded Frank's letter and slipped it into her pocket. "I had some toast," she said. "And I can have lunch in the hospi-tal canteen. No need to trouble yourself."

That won not one but two resounding clucks from Hattie. As she selected eggs from the pottery bowl on the counter, she said, "Canteen food! Cold meat loaf and overcooked vegetables!"

Margot had to hide a smile. There were evenings in Benedict Hall when the canteen's meat loaf sounded appealing. Hattie was right, though. It was often cold.

"I wish you'd tell me when you got to make an early start, Miss Margot," Hattie went on. "I got me a perfectly good alarm clock, same one as you children gave me years ago, and I can sure get up to see you have a proper breakfast." She was in motion even as she spoke, opening a drawer for the egg whisk, taking a mixing bowl from the cupboard, setting the heavy cast iron skillet on the stove. "You may be a doctor now, but old Hattie knows what it takes to get a body through the day."

"I know you do, Hattie. Thank you. I'll try to remember to tell you next time."

Loena and Leona came in, yawning. It had been uncomfortable at first, Margot having breakfast in the kitchen, but the maids had gotten accustomed to it. They had stopped curtsying every time they saw her, thank God. They merely nodded politely, murmured their good mornings, and moved around her to begin assembling flatware and china for the dining room table, including the thin porcelain coffee cups Margot swore held only three thimblefuls of coffee.

Before she left the kitchen, Margot stepped close to Hattie to speak in an undertone. "Hattie, have you noticed whether Cousin Allison's appetite is everything it should be?"

Hattie's eyes came up to hers, a swift flash of whites and a gleam of dark iris, then back to the eggs she was whisking. "You ask me, Miss Allison doesn't eat enough to keep a bird alive," Hattie said. "Looks it, too."

"I don't remember her being so thin when she was here for her party last year."

"I'm cookin' Mrs. Edith's favorites all the time, tryin' to get her to eat a bite now and then. Maybe Miss Allison doesn't like what I'm fixing."

"It's hard to tell, isn't it?" Margot settled her hat on her head and pulled on her gloves. "I should be home for dinner."

"You have you a fine day, Miss Margot," Hattie said. "You go and make that poor soul all well who has the operation, and then you have you a fine day."

"You, too, Hattie." Margot turned toward the front hall, then thought better of it, and walked back through the kitchen to use the door onto the back porch. Just as she put her hand on the knob, Hattie called after her, "And don't you go making that bed up there, either. You don't need to fuss over chores like that. Leave it for Loena."

Margot, bemused, said, "Yes, Hattie," and made her escape into the gray morning before Hattie could think of something else to chide her for.

She would write all about this conversation to Frank, she decided. He was always entertained by Hattie, and he understood why Margot and all the Benedicts were so fond of her. It would make something safe, and might fill a whole letter. She wouldn't be tempted to tell him Margaret Sanger was coming to Seattle. If he stayed in California for another two weeks, he would miss Mrs. Sanger's visit entirely, and they wouldn't have to argue about whether Margot should be seen with her.

CHAPTER 7

Allison heard the porch door open and close, and went to her window to watch Cousin Margot walk around the back of the house and out to the street. She worked awfully hard, Allison thought. She left early almost every morning, and seemed to work late as well. She must be important at the hospital.

Of course, Margot knew she was important. You could see it in the way she walked, that quick, decisive stride, the way she carried her head. The way she spoke to people, looking right at them and acting like she expected an answer every time she asked a question. She was the opposite of all the women Allison knew, women who simpered and spoke in soft voices, who minced when they walked and deferred to men—all men. Cousin Margot certainly didn't behave that way. What an ego she must have! She spoke to Cousin Dick and Uncle Dickson as if she were also a man, and no one seemed to find that strange.

A surprising stab of emotion shot through Allison's breast. Was that jealousy? It couldn't be. It was only her temper. It had to be temper. She was *furious* with Cousin Margot, after all. At least, she was trying to be.

She pulled the comforter from her bed and wrapped it around herself. It was so cold in Seattle, colder and damper even than it was in San Francisco. She shivered with goose bumps half the time, here in this rain-soaked city. Her very bones seemed to ache, as if the chill could reach right inside.

Ruby gave a timid knock on the door, opened it, and put her head in. "Miss Allison? Are you ready to dress?"

Allison turned away from the window. "Yes. I suppose I'd better."

Ruby came in, already neatly attired in her skirt and shirtwaist and apron. She went to the wardrobe and opened the doors. "What about the plaid frock? You haven't worn that yet."

Allison shrugged. "That's fine. It hardly matters."

"Mrs. Adelaide wanted me to pack that one especially," Ruby said with confidence. "She says it makes you look so slim."

"Yes, I know she does, Ruby." Allison couldn't keep the sourness out of her voice. Even Ruby, not sensitive to nuance as a rule, gave her a questioning look.

Allison had liked the plaid dress when her mother brought it home from Magnin's. It was short, falling barely past her knees, with a dropped waist and a deep lace neckline. There had been one just like it in the last *Harper's Bazaar*. With her mother watching, she had put it on, tugging it past her hips, then frowning into the mirror. "It's too small, Mother."

Adelaide stood behind her, also frowning. They looked very much alike, everyone said, both of them fair, with light blue eyes and fine features. Adelaide's frown was perpetual, and had plowed permanent furrows in her forehead. Her thin cheeks bore a delicate web of wrinkles, accentuated by the face powder she used. She put her hands on her bony hips, staring past Allison into the mirror. "You've gained weight," she pronounced. "And the Pettersons' ball is this Saturday."

"I haven't gained weight," Allison protested. "It's this frock."

"It's your usual size." Adelaide twitched the skirt, but that didn't help. It still pinched and pleated above Allison's thighs.

"That doesn't mean anything," Allison said fretfully. "It's the way it's cut. It won't fit!"

"It will if you lose a bit of weight."

"Lose weight?" Allison said, startled.

Adelaide pursed her lips, drawing the wrinkles deeper into her cheeks. "For heaven's sake, Allison! Look at yourself!"

Allison gazed at her reflection. Her hair was still long enough then to be caught back and pinned with a silver clasp. Her cheeks were faintly pink, her lips full, if a bit pale, and her eyes were wide and clear. She had always thought it was too bad her lashes were so light, and her chin perhaps a bit too pointed, but she had never been unhappy about the way she looked. She hadn't, in fact, thought about it all that much. She had thought much more about her tennis serve than about the size of her hips.

But at that moment, under her mother's critical eye, the awful truth struck her. She experienced a sinking sensation that made her legs feel weak and her stomach collapse in on itself. She saw for the first time, as if her eyes had only just opened, how she truly looked. Her breasts were too big and too pointed, bending the pattern of the plaid wool crepe. Reluctantly, she turned sideways, and realized that her hips had swelled to humiliating proportions. There was also a hideous bulge around her stomach. She pressed her hand there, fingers splayed. She felt no more than a modest curve, but she knew it was there, right where the lines of the plaid refused to hang straight. She ran both hands down her sides, over the bunched fabric, feeling the lumpiness of her thighs. Even her legs had distorted as if overnight.

What, she wondered in desperation, had happened to her body?

"You'd better try on the blue gown," Adelaide said with a warning tone. "The one for the Pettersons'. It's Blue and Silver Night, remember? You *have* to be able to wear it!" She hurried across the bedroom to the wardrobe, pulled open the heavy doors, and rummaged through the clothes until she found the dress. Allison struggled to pull the plaid frock over her head, her throat closing with panic.

Her mother slid the white cotton cover off the gown and held it out. It was a pretty blue silk, shot through with silver thread.

There were pumps to match, and an embroidered headband. Adelaide shook the dress, and the silver thread shimmered with light. "I hope to God this still fits, Allison. What have you been thinking? You *know* how important this party is! All the college men have been invited!"

With difficulty, Allison extricated herself from the plaid frock, and she stood with it draped over her hands, staring at her mother. Adelaide Benedict seemed a stranger at that moment, a sort of angry monster, eyes snapping, sunken cheeks coloring beneath their layer of rouge. The hand holding the blue gown trembled, and Allison noticed for the first time how prominent the bones of her mother's hand were, how fleshless her arms, how fragile her figure. She spoke without thinking. "Mother. You're *so* thin."

It had not been intended as a compliment. Compliments were few enough in their family, hard to win, nearly impossible to recognize on the rare occasions they were uttered. What Allison meant was that her mother looked like an assortment of bones held together only by her expensive day frock. That she looked dried up, shrunken somehow, like an apple left too long in the pantry.

Her mother misunderstood. "Of course I'm thin, Allison," she said. Her voice was dry, too, and edgy, as if it had been sharpened. "It's hardly an accident, you know. It's a question of discipline." She thrust the blue gown forward. "Put it on."

Allison laid the plaid frock across the back of the white-painted chair beside her bed. She took the blue one from her mother, but stood with it trailing from her hands in sparkling folds. "What do you mean, it's not an accident?"

Adelaide fixed her daughter with a faded blue stare. "I mean that I take control of my own life. My own mother gained ten pounds with every one of her six children, and I decided early on I wasn't going to do that. Put the dress on, Allison."

"I don't understand. You only had me."

Allison didn't know why she had never noticed how sharp her mother's chin was. Her thinness made her teeth too prominent, her lipsticked smile grotesque. Allison shivered with a feeling that was both shock and revulsion.

Adelaide didn't notice. She said, "I never wanted children, you know. Your father insisted, and so we had you, but that was all. What I wanted was to keep my figure, and I have. I weigh less now than the day I was married. If I wanted to wear my wedding dress again, I'd have to have it taken in." This last pronouncement was issued with fierce pride, much the way Allison thought a general would announce that he had won an important battle. That he had defeated his enemy and decided the war.

Perhaps it was a war, Allison thought helplessly. She turned back to the mirror, holding the blue gown before her. Adelaide stepped forward to undo the hooks and eyes in the bodice, to help her drape it over her head, slide it down over her chemise. Allison couldn't bear to watch as her mother fastened the hooks into the eyes, starting at the top, working her way down. There were twenty of them, tiny silvery fastenings, and as each one slipped into place, the gown grew tighter and tighter. Allison held her breath. She pulled her stomach in until it began to hurt. She felt the tug of the fabric, the pinch of her mother's fingers, and then the last fastening was done. Cautiously, Allison lifted her gaze to the mirror.

"Well, I guess you're in luck this time," her mother said. "You can still squeeze into it."

Allison looked from her reflection to Adelaide's, and her heart constricted. She could have sworn that what she read in her mother's face was not relief but disappointment.

Allison took her seat next to Aunt Edith. Cousin Margot was off already, as she knew, but Uncle Dickson, Cousin Dick, and Ramona were all there. All Allison could see of her uncle and cousin was the back page of a newspaper section. Ramona smiled as she sat down and said, "Good morning, Cousin Allison. I hope you slept well."

"Yes, thank you." One of the twin maids came in with the coffeepot and filled the small bone-china cup in front of Allison.

Allison glanced up at her. "Thanks, Leona." The maid murmured something and dipped a small curtsy before she made her
way around the table to refill the other cups.

Ramona said, "You're so good at telling them apart, Allison. I
still have trouble, and I've known them for three years."

"That's what Ruby says. I can just see that one is a little thinner than the other, and Leona has a freckle Loena doesn't."

Ramona held her coffee cup in her two slender hands. Allison
liked looking at her, with her neat finger-waved bob and pretty
wool frock. Her wedding ring, a fat ruby circled in pavé diamonds, glittered under the light from the chandelier. "You have
an eye for detail," she said to Allison. "Why not come shopping
with us this afternoon? You can help me choose a pair of shoes to
go with my new evening dress."

"I would love that," Allison said. She felt a little rush of good
cheer at the idea of an outing. She had no money for shopping, of
course, because Papa had seen to that. It was part of her punishment. Allison didn't know if Ramona and the others knew, but
still, it would be good just to be out. Benedict Hall, despite its elegance, was beginning to feel like a jail. A cold, damp jail.

The maids came in with platters of griddle cakes and rashers
of bacon, just as Ramona leaned forward to look down the table
at her mother-in-law, who hadn't spoken yet this morning. In
fact, she had barely spoken since Allison had arrived. "Mother
Benedict," Ramona said, in the tone one might use to speak to a
child. "Won't you come, too? We could have tea at Frederick's.
You always enjoy that."

Aunt Edith turned her face to Ramona, but the gesture was
slightly off, sluggish, as if the thought trailed behind the action.
"How kind," she said vaguely. "Thank you, Ramona. I don't
think I feel up to it today."

"You might feel better for a little air," Ramona said. "Why
don't we talk about it after you've eaten something?"

Loena was at Allison's elbow, offering her the tray of griddle
cakes. They were the loveliest golden brown, crisp around the
edges, and smelling of butter and eggs. Allison's stomach cramped

with a sudden hunger that made her mouth water. She looked down at the plaid dress, at its snug fit around her hips, and then back at the platter. She took one griddle cake, the smallest one on the tray, and set it in the center of her plate. Loena waited for her to take more, but she gave a small shake of her head.

Uncle Dickson and Cousin Dick took several each, with slices of fragrant bacon. Even Ramona took three griddle cakes, and when she glanced across the table at Allison's plate, she raised her delicately painted eyebrows. "This is one of Hattie's specialties," she said. "I'm sure you'll like them."

Leona came around with a small carafe of warm maple syrup, and everyone took some. Allison poured a few careful drops on the griddle cake. She had refused the bacon. She was relieved when everyone began to eat, the men laying their newspapers aside, Ramona using her knife and fork to cut her bacon into bite-sized pieces.

While everyone was occupied, Allison picked up her own flatware. She cut the griddle cake in half, and then in quarters. She cut each quarter in half, and swirled the tiny pieces in the little bit of glowing maple syrup. She spread the pieces out, then mounded them to one side of the plate, so it looked as if she had eaten most of the griddle cake. She put just one morsel in her mouth, biting back a groan at the rich taste of good eggs and flour and butter, with the tinge of maple sweetness. She chewed it, swallowed it, then laid down her fork. She picked up her coffee cup and looked across its rim at the others.

Ramona and Dick were talking about a piece of furniture they were thinking of buying. Uncle Dickson was chewing huge mouthfuls of griddle cake and bacon, and looking down at the newspaper beside his plate. Allison let her glance slide to her right, to Aunt Edith.

Aunt Edith was perfectly groomed, her hair brushed, her face clean, her shirtwaist ironed and tidy. She managed, just the same, to give the faint impression of disorder. There was something about the cloisonné clip that held her graying hair back from her face, about the odd match of her shirtwaist and skirt, the slightly over-powdered surface of her face, that made her look as if she didn't quite remember how to put everything together. As if it were Aunt Edith who needed a lady's maid, far more than Allison did.

Aunt Edith looked up, as if she felt Allison's gaze. Her eyes drifted to Allison's plate, then to her own. She showed no reaction, but Allison felt a slight shock, the way you do when you catch sight of yourself in a mirror and realize your buttons are undone or your hair is standing up in the back.

Aunt Edith's plate looked exactly like her own.

Margot liked working with Dr. Creighton, who was meticulous and skilled, and they had an interesting case that morning. The preceding afternoon, a young longshoreman had been sent to the hospital from the docks. He had injured himself while unloading a pallet of cartons from a freighter. He presented with abdominal pain and a visible swelling of the groin, and Margot diagnosed an inguinal hernia. Due to the risk of peritonitis or suppuration, she recommended surgery the next morning, the earliest she could schedule it. The man's wife had been called to the hospital, and the two of them made an effort to be cheerful in the face of this information. It was clear to Margot they were both terrified, despite her efforts to be reassuring. The wife carried a baby in her arms and had a toddler whimpering at her knees.

The longshoreman was heavily muscled, and they proceeded with care in the first incision. Dr. Creighton allowed Margot to manage the dissection of the Cooper's fascia, which required special precision with the scalpel, and he nodded approval as she delicately exposed the hernial sac and then identified it by touch. Fortunately, the patient exhibited a healthy gut, with no discoloration, and the repair was made without incident or complication. When the final sutures were placed, Margot stood back with a feeling that she had, in fact, performed the operation mostly on her own. She was smiling beneath her surgical mask, and when she saw Dr. Creighton's eyes twinkling at her, she knew he understood.

She went out to the waiting family as soon as she could. The longshoreman's wife was fresh-faced, even younger than he was, wearing an inexpensive hat and a cloth coat. She shot to her feet when she saw Margot, waking the infant in her arms and startling the toddler. When Margot gave her the good news, she burst into relieved tears, and her two little ones immediately began a chorus of wailing. A nurse bustled over to quiet the group, but Margot waved her off, letting the young wife clutch her hand and sob for a moment, then crouching down to comfort the older child, to assure him his father was going to be returned to them in just a few days. When the fuss settled down, the young woman turned her tearstained face up to Margot and said, "Thank you so much, Dr. Benedict. We're so grateful."

Margot watched the little family depart with a feeling of profound satisfaction. She hoped she never reached a point where she took such moments for granted. Her intention, her promise to herself, was to always remember that this was why she had chosen her profession. She started back up to the wards with a light and energetic step, pleased by a good morning's work, content that there was more to come.

She finished her rounds in the children's ward in the early afternoon. As she took off her white coat, she was trying to decide whether to eat lunch in the canteen or at Arnie's diner before beginning the task of unpacking boxes and organizing shelves and cabinets in her clinic. The diner won, in no small part because of Hattie's disdain for the food in the canteen. Margot was fitting her hat onto her head, taking her gloves out of her coat pocket, when someone knocked on the coatroom door. Margot opened it to find one of the nurses from reception.

"Dr. Benedict," the nurse said. "Your family telephoned. It seems your mother and sister-in-law were having tea at Frederick & Nelson, but someone is ill. Fainted, the caller said."

"My mother fainted?"

The nurse shook her head. "I'm sorry, they didn't say who it was. Just that you were needed."

Margot thrust her arms through the sleeves of her coat. "Thank you. I'm on my way. Do you think you could put a call through to my father, Dickson Benedict? His office is in the Smith Tower."

"Yes, of course."

"I appreciate it." Margot seized up her medical bag and hurried out. All thoughts of lunch fled before the fresh tide of worry about her mother. Edith's grief over the death of her youngest son had subsided, over the past months, into a persistent listlessness. Margot had spoken to Dr. Creedy, and received his assurance that he had withdrawn the laudanum from Edith after Preston's funeral. He shared her concerns, but neither of them knew how else to help her. In another time, Margot supposed, a physician would prescribe a change of scene, perhaps a sea voyage. The presence of Allison had made no appreciable difference, unfortunately. What Edith needed was something to distract her. Something, in point of fact, to live for.

Luckily, it was one of the best November days, clear and cold, as if the recent rains had washed the sky clean. Margot hastened the few blocks to Frederick & Nelson, dodging the lunchtime crowd. The Tea Room was on the fifth floor, she recalled. She had been there a year ago with Ramona. Anxiety made her impatient, and she pushed her way through the crush of shoppers to the elevator. Clever Ramona had somehow managed to get Edith out of the house, which was a significant achievement. She wished her sister-in-law's kind gesture hadn't ended like this. She would have to address the problem with her father. Edith wouldn't listen to her, of course, but if Dickson . . .

The elevator operator opened the doors, and Margot stepped out to see a group of people clustered around a chaise longue just outside the entrance to the Tea Room. The maître d'hotel was obvious, with his black suit and bow tie. Ramona, her back to Margot, was on her knees beside the chaise, careless of the skirt of her frock. At the foot, wide-eyed and white-faced, stood Edith, twisting a handkerchief between her fingers.

It was Allison lying on the chaise. Drops of perspiration shone like chips of ice against her pale face. A waitress in a frilled white apron was handing a folded napkin to Ramona, who pressed it to Allison's forehead as Margot approached.

"Oh, Ramona!" Margot murmured. "I didn't expect this to be Allison! I was certain it was Mother!"

Ramona looked up, her forehead wrinkled with concern. "Margot, thank God you're here. Allison just collapsed in my arms! She didn't say a word, just—just fainted dead away!"

Without being prompted, Ramona stood up, making way for Margot to reach her cousin. Margot eyed Allison's still face as she reached for her wrist. The girl showed hardly more color than the damp napkin resting on her forehead. Her fair hair fell away from her face, revealing the sharpness of her cheekbones, the hollowness of her jaw. Her pulse was fast and thready. Margot set her medical bag beside the chaise, unsnapped the top, and pulled out her stethoscope. She put the bell to Allison's chest and the earpieces into her ears, and bent her head to listen.

A moment later, Margot folded her stethoscope. As she stowed it back in her bag, she spoke to the maître d' over her shoulder. "Can you bring me a glass of juice, please, something sweet? Orange, or apple."

He nodded and scurried away. Allison's eyelids began to flutter. She moaned something and tried to sit up. Margot slipped an arm behind her shoulders to help her.

Edith said, "What could be wrong with her? Cousin Adelaide will never forgive us if—" Her voice trailed away on a little sob. Margot cast her a wary glance, afraid she might have two unconscious family members at once, but Ramona moved to her mother-in-law's side and put a protective arm around her.

Margot nodded her appreciation. "As you can no doubt see, Mother," she said, "Allison is very thin. Her blood pressure is quite low, which could account for her fainting. I don't know yet if there's a reason for her being underweight, but for now, a little nourishment should help."

The maître d'hotel reappeared with a glass, and Margot held it to Allison's white lips. The girl's eyes opened, moving from side to side as she took in the scene, and an involuntary sound escaped her. "Drink this, please, Allison," Margot said. She used the matter-of-fact tone she employed with most of her patients, and Allison, obedient to the authority in her voice, drank. In fact, once she tasted the orange juice, she drank it thirstily, draining the glass. Her cheeks pinked up almost immediately, Margot noticed with satisfaction. She took Allison's wrist again and felt the pulse begin to steady under her fingers.

Allison blinked and brought her free hand to her forehead. "Oh," she said softly, her voice that of a child. "Oh, oh."

"You'll feel better in a moment," Margot said. She released the girl's wrist and moved the damp napkin away to the arm of the chaise. When Allison tried to move her legs, to stand up, Margot said, "Wait a bit, Allison. Give yourself some time."

"What happened?" It was little more than a whisper, full of confusion and fear.

"You fainted, that's all."

"Did I—did I—" Allison turned her eyes up to Margot, the pupils expanded, the lashes damp with sudden tears. "Was I sick?"

Margot's own eyes narrowed, trying to think what this meant. She said carefully, "I don't think so. No one has said that, only that you fainted."

Allison's eyelids fell, and she drew a shaky breath. "Oh," she said again, but her voice was stronger now. "Oh."

Edith, from the foot of the chaise, said, "Is she all right, Margot? Can we go home?"

"Yes," Margot said. "I'll come with you."

"I shouldn't have come out," Edith fretted, as if it were all her fault. "I told Ramona I didn't want to come."

Ramona ignored this, saying calmly, "Shall I go call a taxi, Margot?"

Margot cast her a quick, appreciative glance. Ramona was

proving, through the hardships of the past year, to be more level-headed and pragmatic than she would ever have suspected. "Thank you, Ramona. That's an excellent idea. If you could take Mother down with you in the elevator, Allison and I will come along shortly."

The maître d' said, "Thank you for coming, Dr. Benedict."

"Not at all," Margot said. "Is there a bill to settle?"

"Not today," he said. "There's no charge for the juice. And no one's eaten a thing."

CHAPTER 8

He huddled in the cold shadows cast by the water tower in Volunteer Park and watched Benedict Hall. He had done this for days, so many he had lost count. The more days that passed, the more his resentment grew. He wasn't sure, at first, why he came here, what he was looking for, but his thoughts and his need were at last beginning to come together, setting his purpose and focusing his mind.

When he saw the taxicab pull up on Fourteenth Avenue, he briefly wondered why they weren't in the Essex. He concentrated, pulling his scarred eyebrows together until the memory came to him. It was hazy, muddled by months of pain, but he remembered.

The Essex was smashed. He had driven it into the tree himself, and then—yes, even after that, he had gone on driving it, wrecked though it was. He had driven it into the city, inexpertly operating the pedals and the wheel, running it up onto the curb in front of Seattle General. Shouldn't have happened, of course. He was never meant to drive the damn thing. That was Blake's job. He was meant to ride in the back, properly, while Blake the butler drove the motorcar.

Blake had betrayed him. Turned on him. It was Blake's fault, really, almost as much as it was hers, but he didn't know where Blake was, and she was still taking up space in the family digs. He felt the grimace on his face, and he knew it was an expression that made him look like something out of a nightmare.

His laugh was rough, as ugly as he had become. He was even more wrecked than the Essex, and it was she who had brought him to this. She had taken his life and twisted it into something so macabre he could barely comprehend it, even after all these months.

He had to release the grimace. It still hurt too much, sometimes maddeningly. Something about the nerves, he supposed, though he was only guessing. *She* would know, blast her to hell. He could almost believe she had deliberately set those oxygen bottles in his path, but even in his pain-racked brain, that was a stretch.

No, it was just her customary obstinacy and arrogance that had destroyed him. If she had only gotten out of his way—better yet, if she had never been born—he wouldn't have to hide himself like this, pull his hat brim down so low he could barely see, pull his muffler up so it hid his twisted mouth and ravaged cheeks.

Yes, she bore the blame, there was no doubt about that. He had had everything, family, position, a job that brought him respect and even a small measure of renown. It was all gone now. Vanished. She was probably happy about that.

He straightened suddenly, wincing at the twinge that ran down his back as he did so. Who was in that taxicab? Oh, for God's sake, Margot, mannish as always. She was wearing last year's coat, with that moth-eaten fox collar! Why couldn't she make an effort to dress better?

Not that he cared. His column was ended, dead and buried, just like he was. Margot couldn't embarrass him anymore.

As he watched, she turned back to the cab and held out her hand to someone. There was a girl, slender, fair-haired. She looked familiar, but he couldn't get a good look. Margot encircled the girl with one arm and led her through the front gate as Mother climbed out of the taxicab. Ramona got out the other side, paid the cabbie, then hurried to take Mother's arm.

Since when did Edith need Ramona's arm to walk up the few steps to the porch of Benedict Hall? She moved so slowly, as if she'd been ill. Her hair had turned the most repulsive shade, yellow and gray all mixed together. Surely she knew there were things you could do about that!

But perhaps he was being unfair. Mother had always put him first, at least to the best of her ability. She could have done more, done something about Margot, but then, Mother wasn't the sort to stand up to people. Still, despite how unhappy she must be now, there was no point in letting herself go. She couldn't be much above fifty.

Why the devil didn't Margot make herself useful and do something to help her?

He watched as the group of women made a slow progress up the walk and onto the porch. Hattie appeared, wearing her apron, holding the door and fussing as they passed. Hattie looked much the same. She, it seemed, had recovered from the tragedy awfully quickly. Maybe she hadn't cared as much about him as she'd pretended.

He faded back into deeper shadows and started to make his way around to the far side of the water tower. The rest of it didn't matter. Who that girl was, the one who looked as if she could barely support her own weight, didn't matter. Blake didn't matter, because he had gotten what was coming to him. Father and Dick and Ramona were all right, even if they were fools to allow themselves to be taken in by the magnificent Margot. Even Mother didn't matter, not really. Seeing her so frail was troubling, but, sadly, she was an innocent but unfortunate bystander. Such things happened, and they couldn't be helped.

No, all that mattered—and his only reason for being alive, now—was Margot. The rest of it could take care of itself.

* * *

Allison could still taste the orange juice in her mouth. Its tart sweetness had thrilled her tongue and tingled in her throat, making her want to beg for more.

Now, in her bedroom at Benedict Hall, undressed by Ruby and tucked under a quilt, she rolled on her side to escape Margot's searching gaze.

She heard the murmur of a few words and the swish and click of the door as it closed. A chair grated on the floor, then made a softer sound as its legs settled into the rug beside the bed.

"Allison," Margot said. Her voice was low and clear, in a tone that meant she expected an answer. "I need to know what's going on with you."

Allison closed her eyes, crushing her lids together as if that would keep out the sound of Margot's voice.

"Your blood pressure got very low. That's why you fainted, and that's why the juice made you feel better."

Allison said resentfully, "I don't feel better."

"All right, you don't feel better," Margot said. She sounded as pragmatic as if they were discussing fabric colors or motorcar models. "But you're conscious," she added. "I think you would agree that's an improvement."

Allison opened her eyes to glare at the primrose wallpaper so near her face. A familiar bubble of resentment rose in her throat and choked off her voice. Usually, it was her mother who provoked this feeling. Now it was Margot, sounding so reasonable and concerned and . . . it was all too confusing. She wished she would just go away and leave her alone.

"Can you tell me what's bothering you?" Margot asked.

Allison narrowed her eyes, and the primrose pattern blurred into a mix of pink and green and brown. It made her head spin.

"Allison, if you won't talk to me, and explain what's wrong, I'm going to have to telephone your parents."

Allison whispered, "Haven't you done enough already?"

"I beg your pardon?"

Tears of anxiety suddenly pricked Allison's eyes and ached in her throat. She could feel the argument building, the explosion that invariably followed if she didn't think before she spoke. Hastily, her words tumbling over one another, she said, "Never mind. Sorry. I'm sorry. I didn't mean—" But she had. She couldn't think how to explain it.

Margot waited for her to finish her answer, and when she didn't go on, she said, "Allison, I'm sure your family would want you to see your family physician."

Dr. Kinney! Hair in his ears and rotten breath and the threat of a sanitorium! Allison groaned, "No, no, please. I'll be all right now, I promise."

"You're not all right," Margot said. Her voice softened, gentled into the one she used with Aunt Edith in the dining room. "You have to understand that I can't just ignore what happened."

Allison gazed at the blurred primroses, willing them to stop their mad whirling.

"Allison, we're family. We're living under the same roof, and we need to speak openly with each other. Are you angry with me about something?"

Allison rolled onto her back to get away from the primroses, and she stared up at the molded ceiling in an agony of confusion. She had never had such a conversation. She didn't trust it. Adults didn't ask her to speak her mind. This was like walking on quicksand, when the wrong answer would sink her straight to the bottom of the quagmire. She bit the inside of her cheek to stop her tears from falling, and she struggled to think of what to say, how to end this.

A strong hand came to rest on her shoulder. "Please explain to me," Margot said. "If I'm to help you, I need to understand."

Allison wanted to protest that she didn't need help, but it was obvious Margot wouldn't accept that. She said finally, resignedly, "Coming here—to Seattle—it's my punishment."

"Punishment?"

"Yes. But I didn't do anything!"

"All right. Let's posit that you didn't do anything. But why should that make you angry with me?"

"Papa said this was your idea. Me coming to Seattle."

"Oh, but, Allison—no one said anything about punishment to me! Uncle Henry was upset, and I gather something went wrong on your trip. I suggested you spend a few weeks with us when Uncle Henry said your mother was having difficulty coping—"

"Coping?" Allison cried. She knew her voice was rising, going thin and shrill so she sounded like a wounded child. Papa hated that voice, but she couldn't help it. She rolled to her left to face Margot. "My mother can't cope with *anything!*"

Margot lifted her hands and pushed her fingers through her hair so it stood out in little ruffles over her ears. When she spoke again, her voice sounded different. Less confident. "Oh, Allison," she sighed. "I know a thing or two about mothers. You've seen how mine is. If it weren't for your cousin Ramona—" She dropped her hands to her lap. The gesture, with her shoulders hunched and her eyes downcast, made her look more like a girl and less like a doctor. She looked sad. Hurt.

Allison didn't know what to do. Had she been wrong? Everyone told her something different, and it was bewildering. She was tempted, for one mad instant, to tell Cousin Margot everything, about Dr. Kinney, the sanitorium, explain what really happened on *Berengaria*, even tell her about the spoon—

No. She could never tell her about the spoon.

Margot lifted her head, but slowly, as if it were too heavy to hold upright. She avoided Allison's eyes as she rose, and replaced the chair beside the wardrobe. Her doctor's voice returned. "I do see why Uncle Henry was concerned about you, Allison. I can even understand why Aunt Adelaide felt she didn't know how to manage." She came back to the bed, and now she stood looking down at Allison with a composed expression that was impossible to read. Allison gazed up at her with apprehension.

Margot said, "It's not normal for a girl to be so thin. Along with everything else, I'm concerned about anemia. Are you fatigued? Are you often dizzy? I haven't been present at all your meals here, but you don't seem to have a strong appetite."

Even hearing the word *appetite* made Allison's stomach cramp with hunger.

"And I would guess," Margot went on, "that you have amenorrhoea. No menstrual periods."

Allison shivered with sudden anxiety and shame. It was true. She hadn't been getting her monthlies for some time. She hadn't told her mother that, of course. She knew such things weren't nice to mention. Ruby hadn't noticed, and Dr. Kinney hadn't asked. She had never thought it was a problem. Maybe even Cousin Margot would want to send her to the sanitorium!

After a moment, Margot said briskly, "You understand, I can't let this go on. Not as a physician, nor as a family member."

Cautiously, Allison pushed herself to a sitting position and found that her head didn't spin even a little bit. It occurred to her that the juice she'd drunk had actually made her feel a good bit stronger. She linked her hands, hoping to look demure, and said, "I feel much better now, thank you."

She looked up and saw the skeptical set of Margot's brows. "Really," she said.

"Yes," Allison said, and attempted a smile. "Yes, I do. Thank you for coming to help me today."

"You're welcome." Margot reached for her wrist, and Allison allowed her to hold it for a few seconds while she measured her pulse. "I'd like to see you eat something now. Will you come down to the dining room and let Hattie fix you a sandwich?"

Allison nodded. She didn't think there was much else she could do.

"I'll speak to Hattie," Margot said. "And I'll wait for you," she added.

Allison, her eyes on her hands, felt the faint brush of Margot's long fingers over her hair. Startled, she glanced up, but her cousin had already turned away and was crossing the room to the door. She reached it in two strides, opened it, and went out, leaving Allison staring after her. Why had she done that? No one really touched Allison except Ruby, and that was only because it was her job. When was the last time her mother had caressed her hair that way? Or her father? So long ago she couldn't remember. If ever.

She got up and crossed to the mirror to comb her hair. It was mussed from the pillow, and the plaid dress was creased on one side. She tried to smooth the dress, peering at herself in the glass. Only this morning she had been sure she was getting fat again. She had heard, in her memory, her mother saying she wasn't trying hard enough. That it was a matter of discipline. That she should follow her example.

But Margot said she was too thin, that it wasn't normal. And her monthlies . . .

She stared forlornly at her reflection, trying to see herself through Margot's eyes. Maybe it was true. Her wrists looked like sticks, and her collarbones stuck out like chicken wings. Yet, despite those things, the plaid frock was too tight, and even in her absence, Adelaide's critical eyes seemed to peer over Allison's shoulder, pointing out her flaws.

She swallowed fresh tears and turned away from the mirror, feeling as lost as a child in a dark wood. How could she know whose judgment to trust? She didn't know which Allison was real. Was it the fat one? Was it the thin one?

She couldn't tell, and that meant she couldn't trust herself, either.

"I've got two people starving to death under my nose," Margot said. Blake was stretched out in his Morris chair, his chin on one hand, listening with his usual patience as she paced his room, restless and out of sorts. "Mother looks like she'd blow away in a stiff breeze. And Cousin Allison! I know girls think it's smart to be thin, with styles so boyish these days, but she's nothing but bones. Hattie does her best—" At Blake's sudden wry expression, she chuckled. "Well, she does, Blake. It's hard to go wrong with a sandwich, isn't it? It was just a sandwich, fresh bread and butter and cheese. The child hardly touched it."

He smiled up at her. "Now, Dr. Margot, you stop that striding around here and sit down for a moment. You're looking a bit poorly yourself, you know."

"Nonsense." She pulled the straight chair close to him and

perched on it, grinning at Blake. "You always say that, but I'm just the same as always. I was never a Gibson Girl anyway."

"No," he said. "You're just you. Just as you should be."

"There's a book I need to get my hands on, something about girls who don't eat. I've forgotten the title, but I read an extract somewhere. There might be other cases like Allison."

"You'll find the answer," Blake said with confidence. "You always do."

Margot exhaled a long, slow sigh. "You place such faith in me! I'm not so sure. There's something odd about her. She's nineteen, an adult, really, but in many ways she's like a child, as if . . ."

"Perhaps her parents have kept her that way on purpose."

"Yes. Perhaps." She pushed her fingers through her hair. "So much is happening just now, all at once—the clinic is built, but there are a hundred details to be settled. Work at the hospital is going well, but it takes a lot of time, and then at home, with Mother . . . Well. It never seems to stop."

"I think," Blake said with deliberation, "that you are in need of some help. It's time I came back to Benedict Hall."

Margot tipped her head to one side, eyeing him. "Let me ask Dr. Henderson for his opinion."

"Dr. Henderson was here two days ago. He said I'm doing fine, and that he didn't need to make this long drive down here anymore."

"He did not!"

Blake chuckled, a deep, easy sound. "Yes, indeed he did, Dr. Margot. I've been most fortunate to have not one but two of the best physicians in Seattle, and it seems that one of them has now washed his hands of me!"

"Surely he didn't advise your going back to work so soon."

"I've been a layabout for more than a year," he said, with a spark in his eye that assured her the old Blake was still there. And that he had made up his mind. "I am most grateful to feel that I'm needed. I'm sure Hattie will be glad."

"I know she will," Margot said. "But, Blake—you will have limitations. You'll need your cane."

"I can work with my cane."

She shook her finger with mock sternness. "I'm going to set strict rules on your hours, I warn you!"

"You do that, Dr. Margot. You just do that. But tell them I'm coming home. Hattie can put fresh sheets on my bed."

"I'm sure she'll be delighted," Margot said. She looked away from him, wondering how to confess that she had been sleeping in his bed all this time.

"And you," he said with a straight face, "can go back to your own bedroom, where you belong."

Margot was startled into a laugh. "Hattie told you! She promised she wouldn't."

"Of course Hattie told me." He winked at her. "I have to keep my hand in, don't I? How else can I see that everything's done properly?"

"I was sure you wouldn't like me being in your apartment, but—"

"It wasn't what I would have chosen for you," Blake said, more somberly now. "But I know it's been hard."

"It hasn't been hard staying in your apartment, Blake. Actually, it's been a comfort."

"Now, how could that be? Your own bedroom must be much more comfortable than my little rooms over the garage."

Margot struggled to put her elusive feelings into words. "The thing is, Blake—I have always felt safe there. And happy. There were books, and cocoa, and—" She spread her hands and smiled.

"Such small things," he said.

"I suppose. But it was a place where I felt protected."

Blake's eyelids lowered in acknowledgment of this truth. He gazed down at his dark-veined hands, turning them this way and that. "It was difficult at times," he said. "I'm not sure I did all I could."

"Of course you did," Margot said. "You did everything possible. Preston was going to be lost no matter what, Blake. There are some people who are like that, I think. Born that way."

"Preston's been gone more than a year, though. Surely you could have moved back into the house. Let Hattie and the twins take proper care of you."

"It was about Mother. She holds me responsible."

"Well, that's not right, of course."

"I know that, and you do. Father does, bless him. She doesn't."

"I guess Mrs. Edith can't get over losing Mr. Preston."

"She hasn't accepted that he's gone. She keeps his place set at the table, and his room . . ." Margot leaned back in her chair to stare out the window at the dark street beyond. "She'll never believe it was his own fault," she mused. "Never. She has to have someone to blame, it seems, and I'm it."

"She doesn't really blame you, Dr. Margot."

"I think she does, Blake. You know, I'm afraid—" She broke off, shifting in her chair, bringing her gaze back to his dark, understanding one. "I don't think Mother's quite sane. I wish I had some idea what might bring her back to us."

CHAPTER 9

Allison had just taken her seat at the breakfast table when Hattie came in bearing a platter of ham steak and fried eggs. The family was all present except for Margot, who had set off early for the hospital. Uncle Dickson looked up, smiling at Hattie, even setting down his paper to speak to her.

"You're looking cheerful, Hattie!" he said, sounding unusually cheerful himself. "I suppose Margot told you the news."

"Oh, yes, Mr. Dickson, oh, yes. Praise the Lord! This is a fine day indeed." Hattie carried the platter to his end of the table and set it at his right hand. "I'm serving you all this morning so the twins can move Miss Margot's things back to her own bedroom and get that apartment shipshape."

Dick chuckled at this. "I'm sure you've kept it shipshape all along, Hattie."

Dickson served himself, and Hattie lifted the tray to carry it to Aunt Edith. "Well, we been trying, Mr. Dick, but you know how Miss Margot is. She don't like a fuss."

Ramona said, "It will be such a relief to have everyone back where they belong."

Allison said, "Cousin Ramona, what is it? What's the good news?"

Ramona smiled at Allison as she served herself from Hattie's platter. She took two eggs and a thick slice of ham. Allison watched her. No one raised their eyebrows when Cousin Ramona took toast for her plate, or potatoes, or enjoyed her dessert. She just—just ate. It was curious.

As Hattie moved on, Ramona said, "Blake is coming home today. Our butler. He's been gone more than a year."

Allison wanted to ask where he'd been, but she wasn't sure that was a polite question. Maybe he'd been in jail or something, and no one wanted to talk about it.

"We have to remember," Uncle Dickson said, "that Margot says he's not to work too hard. He may not be strong yet."

Oh. He'd been ill. Allison wondered what had been wrong with him.

"What about the Essex?" Dick said. "Are you going to keep driving, Father, or is Blake allowed to do that?"

"I made a point of asking Henderson about that," Dickson said. "He thinks if Blake feels up to it, he can drive."

"Won't that be nice!" Ramona said. "To have the motorcar to take us places again. I've missed that." She turned to her left and said, "Won't that be nice, Mother Benedict?"

Hattie had just brought the tray to Aunt Edith and was holding it out to her with a hopeful look. Aunt Edith took an egg and the smallest piece of ham, and murmured vaguely, "The motorcar? Oh, no, thank you. I don't want to ride in the motorcar."

There was a long, embarrassed silence around the table, broken only by Hattie coming to Allison and offering her the tray. Allison took an egg and slid it onto her plate. Hattie said under her breath, "Just a bit of ham, Miss Allison. You can manage that." Allison's cheeks warmed, but she took a piece of ham, putting it on her plate next to the egg. Hattie said, "There you go, miss. That's good ham. You gonna like that."

Allison had been careful to make a good show of eating something at every meal, especially when Cousin Margot was there.

She suspected Margot of colluding with Hattie to keep track of what she consumed. Every day she looked in her mirror, watching for signs of bigger thighs and a swelling stomach. Ruby had caught her at that just yesterday, caught her pinching the skin around her ribs. Ruby said, "Miss Allison, what are you worrying about? You're bony as a bird!" Allison had just shaken her head. She made a point of not telling Ruby any of her private thoughts, because she was sure they went straight to Papa.

Papa thought he knew all the secrets. He was wrong, though. He didn't know about the spoon.

Allison's mother had refused to send the plaid dress back to Magnin's. Though the gown for that weekend's ball still fit, Adelaide announced that Allison should take the incident of the plaid frock as a warning. She bade Allison take off the blue-and-silver dress and restore its cotton covering, then said, "Wait here. I'm going to bring you something."

Allison was seated at her dressing table, pulling on long black stockings, when her mother returned. Allison glanced up, searching her mother's hands for whatever it was she meant to bring her. Adelaide shook her head as she shut the bedroom door and turned the lock on the inside. She crossed the room again, moved the ewer from the bedside stand, and lifted the basin to carry it to the dressing table. From her pocket she drew a small silver spoon and laid it beside the basin. Allison watched, mystified.

Adelaide said, in a hushed, almost reverent tone, "This is a secret, Allison. A woman's secret. You're old enough to know some things."

Beginning to feel uneasy, Allison said, "What things, Mother?"

Adelaide's painted lips curled down at the corners, pulling long, shallow creases in her cheeks. "It's not easy being a woman in this world. I'm sorry to say that, but it's true. Our lot in life is to take care of men, to do what they want, to have their babies and raise them. The men never think about what we might feel, about how they hurt us, about how hard it is to keep them happy."

"Why are we expected to keep—"

Adelaide put up her hand. "Men," she said, "are slaves to their desires. They can't help it, and we have to live with it."

"I don't know what you're talking about." Allison fidgeted uneasily with the lacy covering of the dressing table. "What does any of this have to do with that spoon?"

Adelaide's lips pressed so tight they nearly disappeared as she drew a noisy breath through her nostrils. "Listen to me," she said. "You listen to me, Allison. I know you think you're smart, but I can tell you, it's one of God's little jokes to give women brains. They don't serve us very well, not the way the world is." She smoothed her dress over her flat stomach. "The only thing we have to work with, the only weapon we have, is our looks. Our—" Her voice lowered as if she were speaking a dirty word. "Our *bodies*."

"Mother." Allison gazed up at her mother, and a chill crept through her middle. She lowered her voice, too, although she wasn't quite sure why. "Mother—our bodies?"

"I'm afraid so," Adelaide said, with a tiny shudder. "But we don't have to talk about *that*. You'll find out when you're married. That's soon enough. That's when you'll understand how important it is to a man."

"How important what is?"

Her mother glanced away. "I don't like discussing this, Allison."

"I don't even know what you—"

Her mother sighed. "This is difficult for me, but if I don't tell you, I feel I'm failing in my responsibility." She turned a bleak gaze toward the window, where a San Francisco fog curled in wisps past the glass. "I saw it with my own parents, and I vowed I would never let it happen to me."

"What? Gaining weight?"

Adelaide blinked and looked back at Allison, startled and frowning. "Of course! Isn't that what we've been talking about?"

"Mother! I don't know *what* we're talking about."

"I'm talking about holding on to your husband. About not letting yourself go so that he looks elsewhere for his—" Her cheeks colored, and she averted her gaze to the window once again. "For his needs." She cleared her throat and said, "I'm sorry to be indelicate with you, Allison, but this is the truth of a woman's life." She coughed again. "My mother—your grandmother—got very stout, and my father was famous for his mistresses."

"*Grandfather?*" Allison couldn't help a burst of laughter. "He's so *old!* And he's awfully stout himself, isn't he?"

"He wasn't always old," Adelaide said. "Nor so stout. Everyone knew what he was doing, and he threw it in Mother's face every chance he got. He drove her into an early grave, and I swore I would never let Henry do the same to me." She reached for the spoon and held it out on her palm. "I'm going to show you how to do this, Allison. It won't be pleasant, but I'll only have to show you once. You'll thank me one day."

To say that it had been unpleasant was an understatement, Allison thought. In all her life she had never seen her mother undressed. She had never observed her in the bathroom or even in the bath. They were a private family, and such things were considered improper and distasteful for people of their class. Yet that day, her mother had pulled another spoon out of her pocket—her own, personal spoon, the silver nearly destroyed from years of use—and put it down her throat. She had vomited into the basin, a nasty thin stream that made Allison's own stomach spasm and her gorge rise in her throat. Afterward, Adelaide wiped her mouth daintily, cleaned the spoon, and took the basin to the bathroom to empty it. Throughout all of this Allison gazed at her in horror, eyes wide and throat convulsing with nausea.

"I'm sorry you had to see that," Adelaide said when she returned from the bathroom. "I felt it was necessary." She had rinsed the basin and wiped it dry, and she tossed the towel and her handkerchief into the laundry hamper beside the wardrobe. "Believe me, it's nothing compared with the mess of giving birth."

Allison was speechless. Even now, more than a year later, the memory made her skin crawl. When she tried the whole thing for herself, she was no less repelled. It was effective, that she couldn't deny, but it was a hideous practice. She loathed it.

Ultimately, to her mother's satisfaction, Allison fit into the plaid frock. The early victory went to Adelaide.

What Adelaide didn't understand, however, was that it was only the first skirmish. A prolonged conflict was to follow, and Allison would fight for her own side with all her strength.

She decided early on that not eating was much simpler than using the silver spoon. Why put food in her stomach only to bring it up again? Meals in her parents' overdecorated dining room were more about formality than food in any case. She found an added benefit, a private and unexpected satisfaction, in watching her father scowl over her uneaten meals, then turn an accusing look to her mother.

Adelaide didn't understand at first. She didn't have, Allison thought, the real subtlety of mind to wage this kind of war. She didn't comprehend any new tactic.

Allison fit into the plaid frock, but before long, all her other gowns had to be altered, taken in at the hips and bust, tightened at the waistline. Her father, who rarely noticed much about Allison except for the occasional tennis trophy, growled one evening that she looked more like a boy than a girl. He said, pointing a thick finger at her untouched serving of fried fish and buttered rice, "Eat something, for Christ's sake, Allison."

Allison said in a mild voice, "I'm just not hungry, Papa," even as she shot her mother a triumphant glance.

Adelaide had frowned, the thin skin of her face crumpling like dry paper. She looked down at Allison's plate, and then, her eyes full of suspicion, up at her husband. His attention was already directed elsewhere, but Adelaide must have understood, at that precise moment, just what was happening. The battle was joined, and this time, the advantage was all Allison's.

That had been a full year earlier. Allison had never intended to stop eating entirely, but somehow, once she got started, it was a difficult custom to break. Her empty stomach, the flatness of her bosom, even the persistent hunger she felt, had all become habitual. It was comforting in the way that any routine, however difficult, can be comforting. Even now, away from her adversary's eye, she sat at the breakfast table of Benedict Hall, cutting a piece of ham steak into the smallest possible pieces, moving them this way and that, managing to mix the ham and the egg so it looked as if she had eaten most of it. She was fiercely hungry, but she tried to quench her appetite with coffee. She let the ham sit in the broken egg until it cooled and congealed, and no longer held any appeal. When Hattie returned to clear the plates, she said, "Now, Miss Allison, I'll just let you work on that for a bit." Everyone else had finished, and Hattie carried the stack of used plates out of the dining room, backing through the swinging door and bustling away with her long apron flying around her like white wings.

No one else seemed to notice that Allison hadn't eaten anything. Uncle Dickson and Cousin Dick rose from the table and headed out to collect hats and coats and briefcases to go to their office. Aunt Edith stood up, and Cousin Ramona hurried to her side to help her out of the dining room. In the doorway, Ramona cast a glance over her shoulder. "Oh, Allison, I'm sorry to leave you on your own. I need to check that the twins have Margot's room ready, and I want to arrange to have her telephone moved."

Allison said, "Can I help with anything?"

Ramona was already halfway through the door with her hand under her mother-in-law's arm. "That's sweet, dear. If I think of something, I'll send Ruby for you."

Then she was gone, leaving Allison alone at the dining table, staring at the plate of cold ham and crusted egg. The place set at Aunt Edith's right hand was still there, as it was at every meal, clean plate and unused flatware, a crystal glass, a neatly folded napkin. Her own dirty plate looked even more revolting by comparison.

She heard the quick patter of feet on the main staircase, a

sound she had learned was the twins, working side by side. She heard the bang of the big front door as Uncle Dickson and Dick left the house, and a moment later the purr of the Essex pulling out of the garage and down the driveway to the street. A snatch of song wafted from the kitchen, where Hattie was doing the dishes. Allison rose, pushing her chair back, then shifting it into place beneath the table. She would have liked to scrape her plate clean, but that would mean carrying it into the kitchen, and she didn't know if . . .

She didn't realize the singing had stopped. As she debated with herself over the plate, the door to the dining room opened and Hattie looked in. She didn't notice Allison standing uncertainly behind her chair. Her gaze went to the clean place setting, and a sudden, distressing look of grief dragged at her face, making her eyes droop and her round cheeks sag. Allison, seeing, caught a little breath of dismay. Hattie started, turning in surprise. Her eyes had gone red, with generous tears forming in the corners.

Allison stammered, "Oh, I'm sorry, Hattie, I—I just—"

Hattie snatched up the hem of her apron and pressed it to her face. In a muffled voice she said, "Never you mind, Miss Allison. Never you mind."

Allison backed away from the table, her hands twisting in the material of her dress and her heels catching on the edge of the rug. She had never seen a servant weep that she could remember, and this one was so strange to her, with her dark skin and her broad accent. She couldn't think what to do, or what she could say. Behind the apron, Hattie sobbed twice, and Allison's heart ached, as if Hattie's grief were communicable, like a cold or influenza. She wanted to escape the room, but that seemed awfully insensitive, even if Hattie was a servant, and a colored one at that.

After an uncomfortable few seconds, she found herself saying, "Hattie, should I—do you want me to call someone?"

The cook choked back another hard sob and wiped her eyes

with her apron. When she let it fall again, Allison could see how her chin trembled with the effort to stop her tears. She was still searching for words when Hattie said, in a voice gone too high, "No, Miss Allison. I'm awful sorry—sometimes I get to thinking about Mr. Preston—" She bit down on her lower lip, shaking her head helplessly as tears slid freely down her face, sparkling against her mahogany cheeks.

Allison stood frozen, her back to the window, the weeping cook between her and the door. She fought an impulse to run to Hattie and take her hands. Her mother had taught her never, never to be familiar with servants. "They won't respect you," Adelaide had said, many times. "It's important to keep your distance." That was easy with Ruby. If Ruby even *had* personal feelings, Allison was unaware of them. But this woman, so much older, so alien to Allison, looked as if her heart would break, and Allison felt as if her own heart would fall to pieces in sympathy.

At last Hattie took a long, shivery breath. She pulled her slumping shoulders back as if that were all she needed to do to restore herself to calm, and she smoothed her tear-damp apron with both hands. "Oh, my lands, I'm so sorry, Miss Allison. What you must think of me."

Allison took a step to the side, hoping Hattie would move away from the door and let her pass. "It's perfectly all right," she heard herself say. Her voice sounded so cool in her own ears, so much like her mother's voice, that she could have wept herself. She said, awkwardly, "I was just leaving, to go—to go upstairs."

Hattie sniffed noisily. "You go on, Miss Allison. Never mind me, I'm just feelin' teary today."

Allison took another sidestep, but she couldn't help saying, "I thought you were happy, because your—because the—Blake—is coming back."

"Oh, yes, I am, I am," Hattie said, starting to sound more like herself. "I'm so happy about that, it's almost like—" She stopped, looking at the ruins of the breakfast Allison had barely touched. "Oh," she said. She started around the table and picked up the plate in both hands, gazing sadly down at it as if it were the cause of her tears. "I guess you just don't like what I cook, do you?"

A rush of guilt swept over Allison, joining the throng of her other jumbled emotions. She said desperately, "Oh, no, it's not that at all."

"I wasn't s'posed to cook fancy food," Hattie said heavily. "I'm just a plain cook, but I needed this job, and Mrs. Edith—"

"No, Hattie, please. Of course I like what you cook. I just . . . I don't . . ." She couldn't think how to finish the sentence.

Hattie looked at her, eyebrows raised. She held up the untouched plate as if they were in a courtroom and it was evidence of some crime. "Now, Miss Allison," she said in a voice so kind Allison's heart twisted. "What would your mama say about this?"

Allison had taken another step toward the door, but she stopped, folding her arms around herself and looking full into the servant's eyes. She blurted, "Hattie, my mama would be ever so pleased to see that plate. You can trust me on that."

Hattie's mouth opened in surprise. Allison knew she could never explain, nor could she take the words back. She whirled, and blundered out of the dining room. She bumped the door with her shoulder, and caught her foot on the doorjamb, but a moment later she was flying up the staircase, dashing down the hall to her bedroom. She shut herself inside and stood for long moments breathing hard.

She hardly knew what had just happened, what she had witnessed, what she had said. She had almost confessed everything to a Negro *cook!*

She didn't understand anything.

Allison spent the morning huddled in the window seat of her bedroom and staring disconsolately into the gloom of the November day. A shifting layer of gray clouds spat rain from time to time. She was accustomed to the fogs of San Francisco, but here the days were so short, the daylight so dim, that she felt as if she were living under a blanket. After the strangeness of the morn-

ing, she felt like a saucepan on the boil, the lid rattling and
bouncing under the pressure. Every so often she jumped up to
pace the room, to pick up a book and lay it down again, to riffle
through the dresses in the wardrobe. She thrust her hands
through her hair and then had to paste the curls down again. She
was ravenously hungry, but she didn't want to eat. Her tennis
racket stood in one corner, but she had no one to play with, and
even if she had, this persistent rain would make it impossible.

She heard the purr of the Essex's motor as it pulled into the
drive and around the house to the garage, and flew to the window. Uncle Dickson pulled the motorcar inside, and through the
open door she watched Cousin Margot help a colored man out of
the back passenger seat and around to the door that led to the
garage apartment. Allison leaned close to the rain-streaked glass
to get a better look at this Blake they were all so happy to see
again.

He was tall, with short silvery curls and white eyebrows, and
he leaned on a cane as he walked. Cousin Margot was right beside him, her hands slightly out as if to catch him if he stumbled.
He seemed to notice this, turning his head to smile and say
something to her. Margot laughed, and so did Blake, but still she
stayed close to him, opening the door, standing back to follow
him as he disappeared inside. Uncle Dickson stood at the foot of
the narrow stairs, his face turned up to watch their progress. After
a moment, they all crossed the lawn together toward the back
porch. Allison drew back behind the curtains, not wanting them
to think she was spying.

She wondered if it would be rude to go down and observe the
reunion with Hattie and the twin maids. She was debating this,
still haunting the window, when she saw a taxicab come around
the corner and halt just short of the driveway of Benedict Hall.

The driver hopped out and opened the back door of his automobile. The passenger climbed out and started digging in his
pocket. Allison gasped, and bounced out of the window seat. She
flew across the bedroom, opened the door, and dashed down the
main staircase. There were voices in the kitchen, the twins and

Hattie welcoming Blake home. Allison hurried to the front door to reach it before the visitor rang the bell.

She pulled the door open. He stood on the porch, his hat in his hand and a huge grin spreading across his freckled face.

He said brightly, as if they had only parted the day before, "Hello, old thing!"

Allison cried, "Gosh! Tommy Fellowes!"

CHAPTER 10

Frank arranged access to the telephone after nine in the evening, in hopes Margot would be at home. He placed the call with the operator, then waited beside the desk in Carruthers's office for her to put it through. He gazed out onto the empty airfield, made nearly as bright as day by an enormous white moon shining from the clear sky, and wondered if she could see the moon at home. When the phone rang, he picked it up eagerly, balancing the earpiece in his right hand and the receiver in his artificial one. "Margot? Are you there?"

"Frank," she said, with a warmth that even the great distance between them and the coldness of the telephone wires couldn't diminish. "It's so good to hear your voice. How are you?"

"I'm well," he said. "Very. And you? Tell me what's happening in Seattle."

He closed his eyes as she talked, shutting out the spareness of the military office, with its plain desk and stacked wooden cabinets. He pictured her with her dark hair brushed behind her ear so she could press the earpiece to it, her long legs curled under her. Perhaps, he thought, she was already in her dressing gown, getting ready for bed. The old camellia would cast thin shadows in her room, unless the clouds were too heavy for the moon to break through. Everything around her would be orderly, the way she liked it. There would be a book beside her bed, perhaps a glass of water. Her medical bag would rest beside the door, so she could seize it up if she had to make a house call or go to the hospital.

He could see Benedict Hall, too, as she described Blake's return, walking with his cane, with only a slight weakness of one leg. Blake, she said, wanted to resume the task of driving the Essex, and everyone in the house but Edith was enthusiastic about that. Edith, it seemed, was much as she had been.

"And how's the young cousin?" he asked. "Has she settled in?"

He heard her hesitate, that familiar little pause that meant she was considering her answer before giving it. "She's not a very happy girl, I'm afraid. She seems very young for her age, for a girl who's made the Grand Tour and done the debutante year. She seems—*unformed*, I think would be the best word. More importantly, she's too thin. Much thinner than when we met her last year, and although she behaves properly when I see her—at dinner and so forth—she gives me the sense that it's a deception. She seems both fragile and explosive, if that makes sense. As if she's barely holding herself together."

"Odd," Frank said, more to show her he was listening than because she needed a response.

"Well, yes, but if you knew my aunt and uncle you might understand," Margot said drily. "They treat Allison like a dog to be disciplined."

"You hoped she might draw out your mother."

"No joy there, I'm afraid."

"Is everything finished at the clinic?"

The change in her voice, as she described the completed work, was a thrill to hear. As she told him about the reception room, the two examination rooms with their brand-new beds and sparkling glass-fronted cabinets, the beautiful new desk her father had sent for her office, he felt a glow of pride. He had worked hard on those plans, had supervised everything in the construction, from the laying of the foundation to the Neponset asphalt shingles on the roof. Those would be more fire resistant than the wood shingles of the previous building. He had planned the entrance, discussed the landscaping with the Chinese gardener, chosen the exterior paint, and arranged the glazing of the windows. It was, he thought privately, *their* clinic, though it would be presumptuous to say so.

"I love it, Frank," she said. "I can never thank you enough for all your work."

"Don't," he said. "I'm just glad you're pleased."

"I'm afraid this call is getting expensive," she said. "But I want to hear how your work is going. Are you almost done?"

He understood the unspoken question. *Are you coming home?* But he couldn't do that, not yet. He wanted to surprise her, to surprise everyone, but he wasn't yet ready. "Not quite, I'm afraid. Mr. Boeing has several questions he wants answered, and I—I'm working on them."

"But you like what you're doing," she said.

He thought of the elation he had felt just that morning, as his airplane soared above the valley, shedding the weight of Earth and setting him as free as the birds that dipped and dived below him. He thought of the deftness he was acquiring with his artificial arm, of the mastery that was coming to him, bit by bit. It filled him with a satisfaction he hadn't ever expected to feel again. With all of this filling his mind and heart, he said, inadequately, "Oh, yes. Yes, I like the work very much."

Margot, thoughtful and frowning, replaced the earpiece on the telephone base. There was something Frank wasn't telling her. She knew it, with the same instinct that sometimes told her a patient was holding back, out of fear or caution or—what? Why would Frank keep secrets from her?

She got up from her bed and went to wash her face and brush her teeth, telling herself sternly not to turn into a jealous female, imagining slights or suspecting betrayal. He had called, after all. He had spoken with her at length, and it must have cost him a frightful amount of money.

And, of course, she reflected wryly, as she returned to her bed and slipped under the blankets, she was keeping secrets of her own. She would tell him, do her best to explain everything the moment he came home. She could see no reason to reignite their argument now, while they were so far apart.

She hadn't told her father, either, because he would object at least as strongly as Frank. Her conviction would have to sustain her against their opposition.

She had invited Margaret Sanger to Seattle, and the two men most important to her were going to be angry about it.

The press called Sheppard-Towner the Better Babies Act. That bit of humor offended Margot to her very bones. There was nothing funny about this issue. These were matters of life and death. Infant mortality among the poor was shockingly high, and women of that class still died in childbirth all too often, leaving motherless children behind. Education was the only answer. How could the Italian women, the Chinese women, the colored women, know any more than their own mothers had if no one would teach them? How could they improve the lives of their families if they couldn't control the size of them?

She reached for the book beside her bed, but then laid it down again, unopened. It had been a long day, and her list of duties for tomorrow was just as long. The first thing she had to do was to find someone to staff the Women and Infants Clinic.

She put out the lamp and rolled over, pulling the comforter up to her ears. Perhaps one of Matron's nursing students. Or perhaps an older nurse, someone with hospital experience, who was ready for a change. . . .

Or Sarah Church.

Margot's eyes flew open, and she gazed up at the dark ceiling, suddenly wide awake, energized by the flash of inspiration.

Sarah had left her hospital post in order to care for Blake. She had done so faithfully all this long, slow year of his recovery, and she was now without work. Margot wondered if Blake knew where Sarah lived, where she might reach her.

She sat up, put on her lamp again, and reached for her dressing gown. The oak case clock beside her bed told her it had just gone ten. Blake never slept before eleven. He should still be awake. She pulled on her dressing gown and thrust her feet into her slippers. She opened and closed her door quietly, in case anyone else was sleeping, and walked to the back staircase. She passed Allison's bedroom on her way. No light shone under the door.

Margot went down to the kitchen, where the appliances sparkled faintly with reflected light. The marine layer had blown away sometime during the evening, taking the rain with it. Now the full moon shone its cold winter light on the gardens of Benedict Hall. She let herself out the back door, and paused on the porch to look across the lawn at the garage.

The windows there were all dark. The curtains were open, but she saw no movement. She leaned against a pillar, thinking how rare it was for her to be awake when Blake wasn't. Of course he must be tired! It had been a big day for him. Benedict Hall was, she thought fondly, every bit as much his home as her own. Perhaps more, because he would no doubt live out his years here, whereas she—

She put her back to the pillar and tipped up her face to the moonlight. She hadn't asked Frank about the weather, because that would be such a waste of expensive telephone minutes, but she wondered. He was in the Moreno Valley, where the weather tended to be warm and clear, which was why they put the airfield there. Surely he could see this same moon. She wondered for a moment if he might look up at it, and think of her.

It was, of course, a silly, sentimental notion. She should know better, after her years of medical practice. She had been witness a thousand times to the bleakly unromantic effects of relationships, but that didn't seem to quench her own longings. Despite all that world-weariness, she was still capable of yearning to see Frank's tall, lean figure climbing the hill to Fourteenth Avenue, coming in through the gate of Benedict Hall. Wishing to feel his muscular arm around her waist, his cool lips against her cheek.

She took a long breath of icy air, trying to soothe the ache of loneliness beneath her breastbone. Yes, Frank could probably see this moon very well. He was probably considering what effect it might have on navigation!

The thought made her smile, and her heart lifted a bit. She pushed herself away from the pillar, and took a last look at the dramatic disc of the moon, blazing white above her head, before she turned to go inside.

She had just put her hand on the latch when a flicker of movement caught her eye. She glanced around the garden, but whatever it might have been was no longer there. She stood very still, listening. Was that a step on the wet grass? Perhaps a night creature rustling through the dry rose canes? She took one more look, but found nothing. She told herself it was the cold breeze and the ghostly light of the moon that made her neck prickle.

She pulled the door open and went back into the warmth of the house.

Margot rose early, showered, and dressed. With her shoes in her hand, she slipped down the back stairs to the kitchen and was rewarded by finding Blake alone there. The electric percolator was already bubbling, and Blake, when he caught sight of her, went straight to the cupboard for a second mug. He was leaning on his cane, she noticed, but he was deft with it, negotiating his way around the table to the icebox without difficulty.

"Good morning, Dr. Margot," he said. "I hope you have time to sit and drink your coffee. This is like old times."

"It's so good to see you here in the kitchen again," she said. She took a chair beside the table and slipped her feet into her shoes. "I do have time, as it happens. I'm not due at the hospital for an hour."

"You'll let me cook you a bit of breakfast, then." He poured coffee and pushed the jug of cream toward her.

"What I'd like best," she said, "is for you to pour your own coffee and sit with me. We can worry about breakfast later."

He filled his cup and crossed to the table. She noticed he lowered himself into his chair with care, but without any evidence of pain. He propped his cane, the old familiar lion-headed pine stick, against the table.

"I hope that won't hinder you," Margot said, nodding to the cane. "We could certainly get you a better one. A nicer one."

"Oh, now, Dr. Margot," he said. "No need for that. I have a fondness for that old cane."

"It's stained," she said. "It wasn't stained before."

His gaze met hers without a hint of dissembling. "It's old wood," he said. "It has history."

"Not much of an explanation, Blake."

He picked up his cup and smiled over the rim. "I've already told you, young lady. Best you don't press me on that."

She chuckled. "I won't, then. If that's what you want."

They drank their coffee in companionable silence for a few minutes. Margot didn't want to rush. The quiet would soon be broken by Hattie bustling in to begin breakfast preparations and the twins pattering around the kitchen readying the trays for the dining room. But for a precious space of time, she and Blake could sit alone in the shining kitchen, smelling the fragrance of freshly brewed coffee, comfortable and comforted.

Margot rose to refill their cups, waving Blake back to his chair when he started to get up. "Humor me," she said when he protested. She set their cups down and passed him the cream. "I want to ask you about Sarah Church."

He poured a bit of rich yellow cream in his cup, and tipped it to see it swirl into the blackness. "That is a fine girl, Dr. Margot. I feel bad that she gave up her post to care for me, and now she's without a job." He glanced up. "Perhaps you could speak to the hospital about engaging her again?"

"Of course I could, Blake," Margot said. "Especially if that's what she wants. But I have this other idea."

His white eyebrows drew together, and he looked troubled.

"Now, Dr. Margot," he said carefully, "you know Sarah can't come work in your clinic. Not that she couldn't do the job, and do it well, but you can't take on a colored nurse. You'll have no patients at all."

Margot sighed, tapping her cup with her fingertips. "Isn't that sad?" she said. "But I know it's true. Neither right nor fair, but true."

His face smoothed. "Well, then. What is it you have in mind for my little Sarah?"

She leaned forward, elbows on the tabletop, fingers steepled. "There's going to be a special clinic for women and infants, Blake. A law was passed, and it provided some money. This will be a wonderful clinic, available to anyone, whether they can pay or not. To teach prenatal care, home health and hygiene, and—" She paused. It suddenly occurred to her that she didn't know Blake's feelings about contraception. He tended to the traditional in his views, except when it came to her profession. He believed in people knowing their place and respecting it. He believed in the sanctity of the family—at least the Benedict family—and loyalty to it by family members and servants alike. He was not religious, as far as she knew, but he lived as if he were.

She exhaled, and parted her fingers in an uncertain gesture. "Birth control," she said, and watched him for his reaction.

"Well," he said, nodding. "That's a fine thing, Dr. Margot. A fine thing to do. Where is this clinic to be?"

"Right at the edge of the Valley," she said. She felt a little twinge of shame at having doubted Blake for even a moment. His views were always well reasoned, even when she didn't agree with them. "Where the women of the colored neighborhood and the Chinese neighborhood, and the Italian farm women, can go on foot, or on the streetcar."

"And what do you want Sarah to do?"

"Pretty much everything. I'll stop in at the clinic twice a week. We'll be looking for other physicians to help as well, but she would be the mainstay."

"She's a bit young."

Margot nodded. "I know she is. But she thinks for herself, and she's efficient."

"That she is," Blake said. He rubbed his chin with one finger, staring into the creamy depths of his coffee cup. "I would want to be certain she's safe," he said. "That can be a hard neighborhood."

"I have an idea about that, too."

He looked up, smiling. "You're thinking of William Lee Jackson."

"Yes, him, but even more, his grandmother." Margot chuckled. "That's a woman to be reckoned with."

"All you have to do is persuade her."

"Should I start with Mrs. Jackson, do you think?"

"No, you start with my Sarah. If she likes the idea, she'll have some thoughts about how to make it work, I'm sure."

"Do you know where she lives? How I might reach her?"

His smile widened to a grin. He looked, all at once, years younger. He looked more like himself than she had seen him all year as he struggled to recuperate. "Why, Dr. Margot, she'll be coming by here this very day. She wants to make certain you all are taking proper care of her patient!"

Margot laughed. "We'd better get ready, then," she said, and pushed her chair back. "I'll come back for lunch, Blake. Can you ask her to stay?"

"I'll do that."

They both rose, and Margot carried their two cups to the big sink to rinse. Blake was putting on his jacket when she remembered, and leaned against the counter to ask, "Blake, did you see anything last night? In the garden?"

He stopped with one arm in the sleeve of the coat. "See anything? Like what?"

"I don't know," she said and shrugged. "Really, I don't, I just—I thought there was someone outside, when I went out for a breath of air. Around ten."

"Ah. No, I'm afraid I was already in bed. I won't always retire so early," he said.

"Yes, you will," she responded tartly. "If you're the least bit tired, I want you to do just that. Doctor's orders."

He touched his silver curls with two fingers. "Yes, ma'am," he said.

She was laughing as she left the kitchen. Hattie was just coming in, tying on her apron, with the twins close behind her. Hattie said, "Now, Miss Margot, you go on and sit you down in the dining room. I'll have some breakfast for you in two shakes."

Grinning at Blake over her shoulder, Margot said obediently, "Yes, ma'am."

CHAPTER 11

Allison's cocktail was called the Bee's Knees, and Tommy swore it was all the rage in New York speakeasies. It tasted raw and burned her throat. She had wanted a champagne cocktail, like the ones she'd had on *Berengaria*, but Tommy told her that here they were just cheap gin mixed with ginger ale and sugar, and weren't really champagne at all, so she nodded, and drank her Bee's Knees without comment, hoping she looked very grown-up and worldly.

Tommy Fellowes, it turned out, knew all about how and where to drink, even in Seattle. Allison took another sip of the Bee's Knees, determined to drink it all. She swung her foot, admiring the strap pump and the shortened hem of her pink georgette dress. It was a little uneven, since she had taken it up herself with inexpert stitches, but she liked the way it draped just below her knees. She touched her side curls to make sure they were still in place. It was hot in this small, crowded room, and she was perspiring with a complete lack of delicacy.

Of course, she wasn't supposed to be here. Papa had forbidden her to go out in the evenings, or in fact to go anywhere without a chaperone. Mother would absolutely *loathe* Tommy for his lack of money or title or position, which was even better. Even thinking about that made the risk worthwhile.

Tommy grinned down at her. "Ready for another?"

She swallowed the last of the harsh gin-and-honey concoction, and nodded.

Tommy was on his way to Los Angeles, where he said he was going to work in the picture business. He claimed he had made the detour to Seattle just to see Allison. She wasn't sure she believed him, but that didn't matter. His appearance at Benedict Hall had been the first diverting thing that had happened since she got off the boat in New York.

She hadn't let him into the house, of course. News of his appearance would go straight to Papa if she did, and she could almost feel Ruby spying on her from the upstairs windows. Instead, she took Tommy's arm and pulled him around to the side garden, where they could talk in whispers behind a bank of rhododendrons.

"I'm not supposed to see you, Tommy," she said. "How did you find me?"

"Clip in the San Francisco papers," he said. "In the society column." He seemed to like the clandestine meeting, taking her hand in his gloved one, squeezing it in a way that made her stomach quiver. "It says you're spending Christmas at Benedict Hall with the Seattle Benedicts—too posh!"

"That's just like Mother," she said. "To put it in the papers!"

"But here you are," he said. "So it was true."

"Oh, it's true, but it's not like that. Papa's punishing me." She had begun to shiver, and Tommy put an arm around her, which made her cheeks flame.

"Punishing you for—you mean, that little party on *Berengaria*?"

"Yes. He says—" She looked down at her feet, embarrassed, feeling that she should be more sophisticated about it all, more blasé. She didn't know how to be blasé.

"Says what?" Tommy prompted. He was standing awfully close to her, and the heat from his body reminded her of that night, the sloshing water in the First Class swimming pool, the confusing cries of excitement coming from the cabanas—cries Allison hadn't really understood and yet felt, somehow, that she should.

"He says I'm compromised," she said.

Tommy barked with laughter, and she shushed him, glancing warily around to see if anyone had heard. "Compromised!" he said in a hoarse whisper. "What is this, the eighteenth century?"

"I think it is for my papa," she said forlornly. Her teeth were beginning to chatter.

"Well, First Class," Tommy said, squeezing her tighter. "Can't keep you freezing out here. Let's spring you from this cage! How's tomorrow night?"

Allison simmered with her secret plans as she sat through luncheon with the family the next day. She could see the difference it made in the household to have the butler back. Blake kept everything moving smoothly, the maids popping in and out under his watchful eye, the courses set and removed and replaced with efficiency. Everyone seemed more relaxed, as if they had just been waiting for everything to be set right. Blake spoke very little, but he had an air of authority as well as dignity. When luncheon was over, he changed his coat and put on a cap, and drove Uncle Dickson and Dick back to their offices, and Cousin Margot to the hospital.

As the women started up the staircase, Cousin Ramona said, "Isn't it marvelous to have Blake back, Mother Benedict?"

Aunt Edith responded, "I don't like that motorcar."

Ramona patted her shoulder. "I know. I know you don't."

Allison followed them up, with Ruby at her heels. At her bedroom door she said, "Ruby, I'm going to sleep for a while."

"Do you want to change? Shall I help you?"

"No. Just—go see if you can help the twins, or—"

Ruby sniffed. "I'm a lady's maid, Miss Allison. Not a housemaid."

"Well, then. Find something else to do."

"Yes, Miss Allison."

When the door was safely closed, Allison turned the lock, just to be certain. She found her pink georgette frock in the wardrobe, and a tiny painted sewing box she had received as a birthday gift. She had never opened it before, and the needles and thimbles were a little daunting, looking very sharp and shiny, but she meant to use them just the same. There were small spools of thread in different colors, and one of them was a good match. She held the dress up to her in front of the mirror, guessing at how much she dared shorten it.

As she labored over the stitches, she remembered *Berengaria* and the excitement of escape, of daring, and of bewilderment.

It had been great fun at first. Her new friends clattered up the stairs to the First Class pool deck, shrieking when the pitching of the ship made them stumble and crash together. The only light was that of the stars through the skylight. The water in the pool sloshed this way and that with the rocking of the storm, splashing green water up over the tiled deck. Everyone was made careless by the champagne cocktails they had drunk in the Second Class Lounge. A couple of the men didn't even bother to take off their tuxedoes before they threw themselves into the pool. The others, both men and girls, stripped off every stitch they had on. Brassieres, stockings, underwear, everything went in a colorful pile on one of the chaises longues. Allison, hanging back in the shadows, watched the naked bodies flash through the dark water like a school of great, shining fish.

They were so heedless, these girls. They climbed out of the water and dove back in, breasts and buttocks gleaming in the starlight, without the slightest reticence. Without any shame.

Until that night, Allison had never seen another human being nude. She had only glimpsed her own body by accident, always covering her nakedness with a towel or a dressing gown, averting her eyes if she caught sight of herself in her dressing table mirror. It was the way her mother was, and despite their differences, she had absorbed the habit, breathing it in as if it were part of the air of their home. She had never known anything different. Not even Ruby had ever seen Allison without at least some clothes on.

Despite that, naturally, she knew what a woman's body looked like. But when it came to men's bodies, she was completely, utterly ignorant.

Their silhouettes were familiar: wide shoulders, narrow hips, long arms and legs. Their naked bodies, though, were mysterious, dark, and distorted. They fascinated her, drew her—and terrified her. She wanted to look away, and at the same moment she wanted to see everything.

Tommy had come for her in her hiding place, seized her hand, and cried, "Come on, First Class! Don't be a baby!"

The one thing Allison wanted *not* to be was a baby. A child. Shyly, she slipped out of her dress and tossed it with her scarf onto an empty chaise. Everything was wet from the sloshing water, and would be ruined, but she couldn't help that. Tommy, in the same state of undress as everyone else, said, "Hurry up, old thing! Into the water!"

Allison had taken off her shoes, stripped off her stockings. Tommy flung himself into the pool with a great splash, and Allison seized her moment to step gingerly down into the pool, still wearing her chemise. She waded to a corner and sank up to her neck, hiding herself beneath the rolling water. The buzz of champagne evaporated, replaced by a fog of disquiet and embarrassment.

Tommy had just turned to find her, calling, "Hey, First Class! Where are you?" when the door to the staircase was thrown open. A shaft of light fell over the piles of clothes, the pale flesh of the men and girls poised at the edge of the pool, and Allison's face. The purser strode onto the pool deck, and a little gang of stewards followed. Amid shrieks of laughter and denial, only Allison froze where she was, trapped like a goldfish in a bowl. In moments, the Second Class usurpers had snatched up their clothes and disappeared down the staircase.

Allison, the only person who actually had a right to be in the pool, was caught.

* * *

The scheme to sneak out of Benedict Hall after dark took more courage than her escapade on *Berengaria*. Then, she had acted on impulse. Now she had to follow a plan, take deliberate steps. She let Ruby help her into her nightdress, then sent her off for the night. When the bedroom door was closed, Allison went to her dressing table to rouge her cheeks, to use her lipstick, to paste her cheek curls into place. She slipped into the pink georgette, taking care not to step on the hem, which would probably come loose under the slightest pressure. She wriggled this way and that, stretching her arms behind her until, with some difficulty, she managed to do up the fastenings.

She dared a peek out into the hallway. It seemed the family had gone to their beds and the servants to their rooms. With her heart in her mouth, Allison slipped on stocking feet down the back staircase, carrying her coat over one arm. The kitchen was dark, but a single small light glowed from the garage apartment. Allison stayed in the shadows while she put on her shoes, then dashed across the street to Tommy, waiting for her beside the brick water tower. They hurried down the hill in a wash of brilliant moonlight. At the bottom they caught the streetcar, sitting all the way in the back and giggling together like naughty children.

Tommy led her down several dark alleys, checking street signs, keeping her hand in his and helping her over curbs or around puddles. They found the building, but they had to pass through several doors, guided by the music that grew louder as they made their way down dim corridors with sticky floors and dingy walls. When they reached the final door, Tommy muttered something to a large, unsmiling man, and this person admitted them into a cramped space. There were perhaps a dozen tables crammed into it, in no particular order Allison could discern. A haze of smoke hung near the low ceiling. A trio of musicians was playing, crowded around an upright piano. There was no space for dancing, but three couples were attempting it anyway, sidling and kicking between the tables. Every table was occupied, but a raucous group at one of them waved to the new couple, inviting them to share.

Unlike the Benedicts of Benedict Hall, the Benedicts of San Francisco drank no alcohol. Adelaide claimed it was fattening. Papa gave up whisky when Prohibition came in, saying if the Congress of the United States thought people shouldn't drink, then that was good enough for him. Debutante parties mostly featured root beer and sweet tea. Adelaide had of course forbidden her daughter to sample the wines of Italy and France. Only on *Berengaria* had she tasted anything stronger than ginger ale. She accepted the Bee's Knees Tommy recommended, and told herself she would get used to the taste. The room was much too loud for talking, but she and Tommy grinned at the other revelers at their table, and Allison sipped her drink and watched people.

Drunk people, she decided, were fascinating. Their faces seemed to loosen, their mouths and eyelids slackening, their cheeks sagging as if the muscles beneath them had relaxed. Voices got louder, movements broader. Drinks spilled now and again, and once a chair fell over with a bang, kicked by someone trying to do the Black Bottom. At one point, two men started to shove and shout at each other, but the big man from the door appeared in an instant, and both men were gone before the altercation could really develop.

Allison and Tommy had both jumped up for a better look at the fight. Tommy took her arm to settle her in her chair again, but her head suddenly spun, and she stumbled against him.

"You all right, old thing?" he shouted in her ear.

Allison swallowed hard and clung to his hand. She didn't dare open her mouth to speak. Her second Bee's Knees was threatening to come right up her throat.

"Hang on, hang on," Tommy said. "You just need some air." He picked up her coat with one hand, and circled her waist with the other to turn her toward the door. She stumbled beside him, her head leaning on his shoulder. She felt horrible, sick and dizzy, so weak she could barely keep her feet.

She hardly knew how they made it out through the maze of

passages into the cold night air, but once there she did feel slightly better. Tommy bent over her as she leaned against the post of a streetlight, her eyes half closed with misery. "Food," he said. She shook her head, but he pulled her upright and propelled her a few steps down the street. "Come on, First Class, there's a café right over there. Some eggs and bacon, that'll fix you right up."

When he guided her into the warm, steamy atmosphere of the café, the smells of frying meat and toasting bread made her stomach turn again, and she shuddered with nausea. Tommy, ignoring this, ordered platters of fried eggs and sausages, potatoes fried with onions, and stacks of thick brown toast. With the food in front of her, the sensation in her stomach steadied and transformed into a ravenous hunger. She took a piece of toast, then a bit of egg. The spinning of her head slowed. She ate a sausage, crisp on the outside and running with juice on the inside. Her head felt much clearer now, better than it had all evening. Coffee came, and she drank some, then took another piece of toast, swirling it in yellow egg yolk, downing it in three great bites.

Tommy watched her with amusement. "Where are you putting that, First Class? You're as wispy as a grasshopper!"

Allison grinned at him and speared another sausage. She couldn't stop herself. Her belly, quivering with sickness only twenty minutes before, began to feel tight and full, and it was a wonderful sensation. She finished her eggs and all the sausage on her plate. She took a third piece of toast and smothered it with jelly. Tommy had finished his meal and pushed his plate aside, but Allison fed herself until there was nothing left. A waiter in a dirty white apron took their plates without comment, and left them a bill scrawled on a slip of paper.

Tommy paid the bill carefully, counting out his change. When they were on their way out, he said, "Feeling better, aren't you? I was right—you needed food!"

Allison tugged on her coat. "I guess so," she said.

"You must have! You ate enough for two hungry sailors!"

"I—I'm sorry about that," she said. Now that she had stopped gorging herself, the food in her stomach was growing heavy. Her belly felt distended, bulging against her chemise. She could still taste the richness of the sausages and the sweetness of strawberry jelly. Opposing sensations tumbled through her mind, pleasure and shame, relief and guilt. Her stomach, equally confused, began to rebel against its burden, rumbling and quivering, making her fear for what would happen next.

"Why be sorry?" Tommy cried, even as she swallowed a sudden, terrifying rush of saliva. "I love a girl who enjoys her grub!"

She looked up at him, suspecting he was making fun of her. His freckled face was wreathed in smiles, and his blue eyes danced with humor. His arm around her was warm and strong and friendly. He meant it, she thought. He really did. Nothing in her life had prepared her to expect such a thing.

She walked to the streetcar with one hand on her stomach and the other under Tommy's arm, and she pondered the mystery.

Allison's stomach had begun to churn in earnest by the time they climbed Aloha and reached Benedict Hall. She bade Tommy a hasty good night. He wanted to stay until she was safely in the back door, but she said in a shaking voice, "No, Tommy, you need to go. If I have to, I can knock, say I came down to the kitchen for something, then went out for a breath of air. If you're here . . ."

Gallantly, he said, "I can hide in the bushes!" but she gave him a little push, and he sauntered away, walking backward, waving and grinning and promising to write her from Hollywood. When he was finally out of sight, she hurried through the garden on trembling legs, stumbling around to the back lawn. Her stomach quaked, and she wanted only to reach the shrubberies before the inevitable happened.

Allison hated throwing up. When she tried it that once with the spoon, it was disgusting and messy. She never wanted to do it again. It was no more pleasant now, but she couldn't stop it. The muscles of her stomach clenched, saliva flooded her mouth, and everything she had consumed that night came rushing back. Her stomach seemed to turn itself inside out as she retched. Everything came up, and out, as she bent over the dry rosebushes and hoped no one was watching from the house.

When there was nothing left, she still gagged. She longed to go into the kitchen to rinse her mouth, to wash her face and scrub her hands, to get rid of all this embarrassment, but every time she started for the porch steps, her stomach clutched again. It seemed to go on forever, and she knew it was because her stomach was unused to so much food. She had done it all to herself, and the shame of that—the guilt over her unrestrained gluttony—made the whole thing worse. She hunched over the flower bed, her hands on her knees. Tears of weakness streamed over her cheeks.

"Allison? What's happening? Are you ill?" It was, of all people, Cousin Margot.

Allison couldn't prevent the whimper of surprise that escaped her. She was caught. There would be a fracas in the morning. She wiped her mouth with unsteady hands, straightened with some difficulty over the ache in her belly, and turned to face her cousin.

The moon had set, but the sky had begun to lighten over the mountains to the east. She could see Margot perfectly. She wore her wool overcoat with the fox collar, and a dark hat and gloves. She had her medical bag in one hand, and she reached toward Allison with the other.

"Why are you outside?" she asked, taking Allison's hand. "It's cold, and you—have you been out?" Her eyes took in Allison's clothes, her muddied shoes, her stockings, which must be revolting now, laddered and splashed with vomit.

Allison shuddered to have Cousin Margot touch her filthy hand. She tried to wipe the tears from her face, but she knew she was a complete mess, and she trembled with humiliation. "I did go out," she confessed in a rush. When Margot didn't look shocked, or disgusted, or anything except concerned, she blurted, "I went to a speakeasy!" and then held her breath, prepared for the onslaught of reproach that was sure to follow.

Instead, Margot drew her up onto the porch and in through the back door. She turned on the kitchen light, then pulled off her gloves and pressed her fingers to Allison's forehead. Evidently satisfied, she tipped up her chin to look into her eyes. "Did you drink anything?" she asked. "Were you sick?"

"I did," Allison said. She pulled her head away and dropped her gaze to her soiled shoes. "They're called Bee's Knees, but they taste like—I don't know, like turpentine. And I was sick in the rose bed." She wrapped her arms around her sore stomach, wishing she could just drop through the floor and disappear. Cousin Margot hadn't called Papa before, but she surely would now. She would tell him all about Allison's transgression, and when he heard—

But Margot was nodding. "It's just as well you were sick, Allison. You probably got it all out of you, and that's good. Bootleg alcohol can be dangerous." She went to the sink and ran a glass of water. "I'd like you to drink as much water as you can." She held out the glass.

Allison, hardly knowing how to react, accepted the glass and drained it. When it was empty, Margot filled it again and passed it back to her. Allison sipped it more slowly this time, cautious of her rebellious stomach. Margot was regarding her with that intent look, but Allison didn't mind it so much now, when she really did feel ghastly.

She finally said, "I'm awfully sorry, Cousin Margot."

Now Margot smiled, her narrow lips curving at the corners. There were smudges under her eyes, and she looked pale. She was tired, Allison thought. She must have been called to the hospital. She might not have been to bed at all. Margot said, "I suppose you went out with a boy tonight. I didn't know you knew anyone here in Seattle."

Allison answered cautiously. "It was someone I met on my crossing."

"Really? And he came here?"

"I think he likes me."

"Of course he does. You're a very pretty girl."

It was an offhand compliment, a statement made easily, as if it were obvious, and Allison didn't know how to respond. She would have to think about that later, when she didn't feel so sick. She lifted one shoulder, not quite a shrug.

Margot's smile faded, and she fixed Allison with that searching gaze again. "I have to ask you something," she said. "Despite your lack of menses, I need to make certain. There's no chance you're pregnant, is there?"

Allison had never expected such a question. It sent a shiver through her, one of surprise, but also of recognition. Somehow, she knew this was important. She wished she knew why. She stammered, "I—I can't be, can I, Cousin Margot? I'm not married."

Margot lifted one sleek eyebrow. "Surely you know, Allison, you don't have to be married to conceive."

Mute, lost, Allison shook her head.

Margot clicked her tongue and blew out a long, exasperated breath. Allison felt fresh tears start in her eyes, but Margot, seeing, put out a hand to touch her shoulder. "No, no, Allison, don't cry. The fault for this lies at someone else's door, I promise you. But you're nineteen years old, and you really should know about sex."

"My mother said—" Allison began, then stopped, tongue-tied with confusion. Adelaide hadn't said anything, in truth. She had said only that Allison would learn all about it from her husband, and she had implied that it would not be pleasant.

Margot dropped her hand from Allison's shoulder and gave her a tight, weary smile. "I'm so tired, Allison, I can hardly think. Perhaps we should talk about this some other time. But—" She held up one forefinger. "We should talk. It's not fair for you to go on in ignorance. Not fair to you, I mean."

Allison made herself ask, "Are you going to call Papa?"

At this Margot chuckled. "Oh, Lord, no, Allison. Nineteen! I can hardly blame you for wanting a little fun."

"I shouldn't have gone out, I know."

"You took a risk," Margot said. "Several of them, actually. But you don't know anyone your age here. You must be lonely."

Again, Allison didn't know how to answer. Her papa never worried if she was lonely. Adelaide only worried about how she looked. She just wasn't used to discussing—or even acknowledging—her feelings.

Margot gave a short nod and put her hand under Allison's arm. "Well, there's no harm done that I can see. Let's get you to bed, unless you're still feeling sick."

Allison shook her head. Her stomach felt tender, and her throat burned from having retched for so long, but she didn't think she was going to throw up again.

"Good," Margot said. She picked up her medical bag in her other hand, and steered Allison toward the stairs. The back stairs, Allison noticed. They went up together, and when they reached Allison's door, Margot pointed down the hall. She whispered, "If you feel ill again, knock on my door."

"Cousin Margot—"

Margot had released her arm, but she waited, eyebrows lifted.

Allison said softly, "You've been so nice."

"Not at all. I just want you to be safe," Margot said.

"Do you have to tell Uncle Dickson?"

"I don't think so." Margot smiled again, and Allison thought she had rather a nice smile. It seemed more special because she didn't use it very often. "Sleep, Allison. We both need to sleep. Let's talk about everything tomorrow."

CHAPTER 12

After her evening with Tommy, Allison slept fitfully. She had never had reason to believe that promises meant anything, and despite Margot's calm demeanor, she braced herself for trouble.

She came into the dining room to find her cousin already at the table, looking pale and a bit puffy-eyed. Margot glanced up, murmured a distracted good morning, then sat in tired silence, drinking her coffee. Ramona came in, talking quietly with Dick. Edith came in with Dickson and sat down without speaking. Uncle Dickson grunted a general greeting and retreated behind the shield of the *Times*, just as he always did. Cousin Dick nodded to everyone before tucking into a bowl of oatmeal and several rashers of bacon. Allison took her seat across from the empty place setting, feeling like a small, drab mouse waiting for a trap to be sprung.

It never happened. In a short time Margot and the men traipsed out the front door to meet Blake, waiting with the Essex. Ramona shepherded Aunt Edith upstairs. The twins peeked in to see if they could begin clearing the dining room.

It seemed the trap had never been set. Relief made Allison

tremble, and as she had suffered another bout of dizziness that morning, she ate an entire bowl of oatmeal with cream and brown sugar and raisins.

Margot had been as good as her word. It was something to think about, and as Allison and Ruby set about sorting through her wardrobe for her warmest woolen things to prepare for winter weather, she had to accept that she had misjudged her cousin. Ruby chattered away, tossing out tidbits of news she had picked up from the housemaids. Allison wasn't listening and missed most of it, until Ruby mentioned that Cousin Margot's new clinic was ready.

What interested Ruby, of course, was what had happened to the old one. "It burned up, Miss Allison," she said. "That's when your cousin Preston died. He got burned up, too."

"What?"

"Your cousin Preston. He died in the fire."

"I knew that, but—what are they saying about it?"

"Leona said—" She lowered her voice and looked around dramatically as if someone might be spying on them. "Leona said your cousin Preston started that fire. That he did it on purpose. Loena won't speak his name, so Leona told me when her sister wasn't in the room."

"Why won't Loena speak his name?"

Ruby shrugged. "Nobody said."

"Ruby, didn't you ask?"

"Oh, no, Miss Allison. My mother told me a lady's maid should keep herself to herself. I try to do that."

Allison considered Ruby's discretion to be a bit selective, but she didn't say anything. Ruby wouldn't understand if she pointed it out. Instead, she pulled a camel's hair sweater out of the back of the wardrobe, put it to her nose, and sniffed it. "This smells like mold," she said.

Ruby held out her hand for it and draped it over the bed. "I'll air it on the line. It's just been in the trunk too long." She turned to survey the now-empty wardrobe. "Is that everything?"

"It must be."

"But what about that?"

Ruby pointed, and Allison followed her gesture. A fold of pink georgette peeked out from beneath the bed, startlingly bright against the dull wool of the rug. Allison's heart thudded with fresh alarm. Even from here, she could see the dress was stained, soiled with dirt and rain and probably—revoltingly—sick. She started to push it out of sight with her foot, to kick it back into the darkness beneath the bed, but she was too late. Ruby was already bending, tugging it out, holding it up to the light. "What—what happened to your frock?" she exclaimed.

Allison reached for it and pulled it from Ruby's hands. "I must have dropped it," she said.

"Dropped it! Miss Allison, look at that hem! Who would have made such a mess?" Ruby, decisive for once, snatched the dress back and draped it over one arm. "It's all uneven and—" She turned the hem up with her free hand and stared from the ragged seam to Allison's face. "Did you try to do this yourself?"

Facing this new threat of betrayal, Allison sagged onto the stool before her dressing table. "I—I didn't want to bother you," she said in a faint voice. Her breakfast shivered in her belly.

"Bother me! More like, trying to do me out of my job," Ruby said sourly.

Allison caught her breath under a wave of guilty consternation. "Ruby, no! I wouldn't—"

Ruby interrupted her. "If you want to learn how to sew, you could just ask me, Miss Allison, though it ain't—I mean isn't—proper. You have me to do for you, don't you? Why would you want to—" She turned the frock over, and her little spate of words trickled to a stop.

The stains were even uglier in the wintry sunshine streaming through the bedroom window. They were multicolored, from rust and copper to an undigested, rank-looking brown. To Allison, they looked like exactly what they were. Spilled liquor, dirt from the speakeasy's filthy tables and sticky chairs, rain spots, a bit of mud from the rose bed, and . . . Her breakfast turned in her sore stomach.

Ruby asked, "Where did you wear this, Miss Allison?"

Allison stood up and snatched the dress from Ruby's hands. She rolled it into a tight pink ball. "It's ruined, Ruby," she said firmly. "I wanted to take the hem up, and I knew you wouldn't like it so short, so I tried to do it myself. I spilled a whole pot of tea on it."

"That won't never come out of silk georgette."

"As I said," Allison repeated, "it's ruined. If you're keeping track for Papa, you can add this to the list."

Ruby's eyes widened, and a flush crept over her plain cheeks. "Miss Allison, your papa—I mean, Mr. Henry—he—"

Allison, feeling she had regained the upper hand, patted the maid's arm. "I know all about it, Ruby," she said. "Papa set you to spy on me, didn't he? I hope he made it worth your while."

"Oh, Miss Allison," Ruby said miserably. "You weren't to know about it. Now I'll be in trouble with Mr. Henry."

"No, you won't," Allison said. "I'm not going to tell him, so you don't need to, either." She thrust the ruined frock forward. "Just get rid of this, will you? We don't need to talk about it anymore."

Ruby, her face stained an unbecoming red, took the rolled-up dress and carried it out of the bedroom. Allison wandered to the window to stare out at the winter landscape and wonder if there was any way to send Ruby back to San Francisco. It wasn't the maid's fault, she knew, and she didn't want to be the cause of Ruby losing her job.

At least it was all in the open now. Ruby had more or less admitted that her first loyalty was to Papa and Mother. She had taken her orders from Adelaide from the very first. It was too bad they couldn't be better friends. Allison had even less control over her life than Ruby did.

There had been a nanny once, when Allison was small, a sweet little woman called Rosy. She was a plump, warm-bodied person, ready with a grin or a kiss or a hug, whichever she deemed most useful in the moment. Skinned knees, pinched fingers, bad dreams, late-night thirsts, whatever small domestic crisis arose, the staunch and easygoing Rosy had a remedy. Rosy, in fact, was everything Adelaide was not, maternal and comfortable and uncritical. Allison had loved her with all the intensity a lonely child could muster.

One terrible day, six-year-old Allison refused to go to her mother when she was ordered to. She couldn't have known the consequences of her action, of course. She could only assess it now, recalling the scene as best she could. She had buried her face in the folds of Rosy's apron and clung to her sturdy legs until Adelaide tore her away. With Allison squalling all the way, Adelaide marched the little girl off to whatever task she had in mind. Allison couldn't remember Rosy saying anything, protesting or interfering in any way, but that didn't matter. Adelaide pronounced the nanny "too familiar." She was gone from the house the next day. No one told Allison anything about it, or offered the child any explanation. All she knew was that her protector, her friend, the only adult she could trust, vanished without a word of farewell.

Years later, coming upon a doll wearing clothes Rosy had sewn, Allison asked about her. Her mother sniffed and began a lecture on the proper behavior of servants and their mistresses.

Now, Allison knew that it was she who had been to blame for Rosy being sent away. She had revealed too much of her true feelings in front of her mother. It didn't matter that she had been six. It didn't matter that she was now nineteen. Adelaide was not to be trusted with feelings or confidences or anything else.

Eventually, Allison came to understand that her father had been complicit in the loss of Rosy. He could have intervened, spoken up for her, protested that Allison needed the nanny who had been with her since she was tiny, and who, by any measure that counted, truly loved her. By the time she discerned that truth, her father was firmly entrenched on her mother's side, a partisan in the war between mother and daughter. Ruby had been carefully selected and coached so as not to provide Allison with an ally, which meant that she had no one.

Until now. Was it possible that Cousin Margot . . . ?

* * *

Margot intended to reopen her clinic quietly, simply post hours in the window and let patients find her in the same way they had in the past. When she announced this to the family at breakfast, Dick protested that she should make more of a celebration of it. Her mother received the news in the absent way that had become her habit, as if she hadn't really registered what was being said.

Several days had passed since Margot came upon Allison being sick in the roses, but there had been no time for the promised talk. It weighed on Margot's mind, one of many things needing her attention.

Allison surprised her now by saying, "Let me help, Cousin Margot. You should make it an occasion." She had said so little since her arrival that every person at the table turned to her in surprise. Her cheeks colored under their regard.

"An occasion?" Margot asked blankly. "How does one do that?"

Allison gave her a shy smile. The first morning after the night of the speakeasy, Allison had looked like a frightened kitten, but when she came to understand that Margot truly wasn't going to report her misdeed, she appeared to relax. She had gone shopping twice with Ramona, and Hattie reported that Allison had eaten reasonably well before those trips. Margot took that as an assurance that Allison had understood her warning. No doubt the girl preferred not to faint in another tearoom.

"Well," Allison said now. "First, there should be a formal announcement."

Dickson said, "Good idea, young lady. I'll speak to C. B. Blethen. Get something in the *Times*."

Margot said weakly, "The *Times*?" It wasn't the newspaper that surprised her. It was the conversation, this discussion, treating the event of her clinic opening as if it mattered to any Benedict but herself.

Allison went on in a little rush, though Margot could see she was self-conscious about it. "You could have a—let's see—a reception. Or a tea. Invite everyone to see your office, tour the examination rooms. Emily Post says—" She broke off, her cheeks flaming now.

"No, do go on, Cousin Allison," Ramona said. "What does Emily Post say?"

Allison fidgeted with her flatware, but she pressed on. "She gives instructions for an afternoon tea. A tiered plate, if you have one—"

"Of course we do," Ramona said.

"She says to put the sandwiches at the top, and the sweets—cookies or cakes—on the lower tiers." She paused and added, haltingly, "I could pour, Cousin Margot. I know how to do that."

It was the longest speech any of them had heard the girl make. There was an odd moment around the table, everyone trying to adjust to this new Allison. The change in her demeanor was gratifying, but it was startling, too. Margot sensed the family members taking care not to look at one another as they judged how best to react.

It was Dick who broke the silence, saying heartily, "Excellent, excellent. You'll be a lovely hostess, Cousin Allison. Lucky you, Margot! And we'll all come, won't we, Ramona?"

"Of course we will."

Margot couldn't think whether this was a good idea or an insane one. Blake was in the dining room, his cane in one hand and coffeepot in the other, and he paused behind Allison's chair. He caught Margot's eye and gave her a subtle nod. Prompted by this, she said, "Allison, it's a very kind thought. Thank you. If you don't mind taking charge—I'd be happy to make an occasion of it." Margot couldn't help thinking, Perhaps Frank will come. But she didn't speak the thought aloud.

He had mentioned in his last letter that he expected to return to Seattle before Christmas, but that was nearly a month away. Sometimes Margot thought she couldn't bear to wait. She had taken care not to press him, not to ask him to promise, or to tell him how much she missed him. But she did. She missed him with a constant phantom ache somewhere in her body, no place she could name medically but which, emotionally, was as real as any physical location.

She pushed those thoughts down, to consider at a better time. She turned to Allison, thinking perhaps it would be good to have this distraction. "Tell me what we need to do," she said. "Do you think you can manage? Speak to Hattie, perhaps order flowers or whatever you do for such events?"

"I should come to see the clinic," Allison said. "To know what the space is like, see if we need to rent a table—"

Ramona gave a tinkling laugh. "I knew you had an eye for detail, Cousin Allison! What fun! Do let me be your assistant in this project, and tell me everything Emily Post says."

Allison's pretty smile broke out again, and Margot wondered that her parents didn't do more to encourage it. When she was happy—which she so rarely seemed to be—she was lovely, bright and youthful and pink-cheeked.

Margot looked around the table at her family and smiled. "Thank you all. I guess I'll—I'll just put myself in your hands!"

Only Edith said nothing. She sat pushing a bit of biscuit around on her plate with her fork, not seeming to hear the conversation around her. Margot noticed that no one, not even Allison, suggested that Edith should be included.

Still warmed by her family's unexpected enthusiasm, Margot excused herself and left the family to finish their breakfast while she went out to the hall to put on her coat and hat. Blake followed, leaning on his cane. "Where are you headed, Dr. Margot? I can drive you."

Margot bent to pick up her medical bag. She was about to refuse, but really, it was the perfect way to take Margaret Sanger to see the Women and Infants Clinic, and it would save a lot of time over the streetcar. "If you're free, Blake, it would be helpful. It's going to be a full morning. I need to go to the train station, then to the Women and Infants Clinic."

"Let me just change my coat."

Margot slipped out through the front door and stood in the

shelter of the porch while she waited. She felt the bite of winter on her cheeks and in her lungs. Pewter clouds shrouded the vista of the city, obscuring the Sound and the mountains beyond. Frank had left Seattle while the trees still blazed red and gold, and now they were sere, the deciduous ones bare of leaves, the layered greens of pine and fir providing the only spots of color.

She shivered a little against the cold and began to button up her coat. As she smoothed the collar with one gloved hand, she felt a new chill on the back of her neck, the vague prickle that meant someone was watching her. She spun sharply around to scan the porch behind her, and the gardens to either side. She couldn't find anything. She turned back again, but she frowned at the odd sensation.

As the Essex rolled down the driveway and pulled up at the curb in front of the house, Margot shook off the uneasy feeling and strode determinedly off the porch and down the walk to the gate. She was thrilled to be meeting Margaret Sanger at last. Today meant the culmination of months of letters and plans and petitions. She mustn't let it be shadowed by pointless anxiety.

Blake, now attired in his driving coat, his cap, and his black leather gloves, got out of the driver's seat to hold the passenger door for her. "Blake," she scolded. "You don't need to do that."

As she slid onto the seat, she saw the rebellious glint in his eye. "I'm managing perfectly well, Dr. Margot," he said.

She chuckled as he got into the driving seat. The cane waited in the seat beside him, but it was true, he had managed the doors with ease. "Patients like you keep doctors on their toes," she said.

"Do we indeed," he said, giving her a wry glance in the rearview mirror.

"Oh, yes," she said. "Yes, you do."

"Perhaps," he said, with a twitch of his lips, "that's a good thing."

As the Essex swept majestically down Broadway and turned down the hill to King Street Station, Margot said, "I had forgotten how nice this is, Blake. I took it for granted, and then when you weren't here—that is, the streetcar is fine, but this—this is marvelous. I've missed it."

"It's good to be driving again, Dr. Margot."

Margot was tempted to say that it was really Blake himself she had missed and not the automobile. She didn't speak the words, but she suspected he knew. She was still smiling when they reached the station.

Margaret Sanger was surprisingly small for a woman who had caused such a furor, not only in New York but in the whole country. She was slender and dark, with a slight overbite and a light, precise voice. She shook Margot's hand, refused to allow her to carry her bag, and insisted she wasn't tired in the least. "I won't be staying in Seattle, Doctor," she said. "So if we could go directly to the site, I'd prefer that."

"Of course. I've kept the whole day free."

"Very good. I'm due in three other cities this week."

If her tone was a bit peremptory, Margot let it pass. The woman had, after all, put her life on the line for their cause. She could be forgiven her lack of grace.

Blake emerged from the Essex and took Mrs. Sanger's valise to stow in the back. He touched his cap brim, said, "Good morning, ma'am," and held the door for each of the women, limping only a little without his cane.

As they drove, Mrs. Sanger asked where Margot had studied, how long she had been in practice, what her special interests were. She seemed collegial, pleasant enough, looking curiously out the window as the Essex rolled into the poorer section of Seattle. When Blake, following Margot's instructions, pulled the car up in front of a modest brick building, Mrs. Sanger said, "Is this it?"

"Yes," Margot said. "It needs a bit of work, inside and out, but the rent is reasonable, and the owners agreed to our purpose."

"A Negro section of town, I see."

Margot involuntarily glanced forward, to read Blake's reaction to this. He kept his gaze straight ahead as he reached for his cane and opened his door. She said, "Yes. Does that matter?"

Mrs. Sanger climbed out of the backseat without so much as a nod to Blake. "It's excellent," she said crisply. "It's a principal part of the community we want to reach." She added, in a casual way, "These people need birth control more than most."

Margot met Blake's gaze as she herself got out of the automobile. His features were perfectly blank, his eyelids hooded, his mouth straight. She left her medical bag on the seat, and she brushed the sleeve of Blake's jacket as she passed him. Her own voice, she thought, was equally crisp, even brusque, as she said, "Thank you very much, Blake. We'll try not to keep you waiting too long."

He answered, "I'll be right here, Dr. Margot." There was no inflection in his deep voice, but she heard the old echoes of the South in his accent, remnants that surfaced when he was angry. Margot's lips pressed together as she turned to follow her guest.

She used a key to open the door, but as she and Mrs. Sanger stepped inside, Sarah Church emerged from a back room. She wore a long paint-stained apron over a shirtwaist and ankle-length skirt, and her curly hair was bound up in a scarf. Her deep dimple flashed as she came eagerly forward, saying, "Dr. Benedict! Have you come to check on our progress?"

Margot nodded to her. "Hello, Sarah. Yes, in part. Also to show Mrs. Sanger our building. Mrs. Sanger, this is Sarah Church, the nurse who will staff the clinic and assist the physicians. Sarah, this is Margaret Sanger. You know her work, I believe."

Mrs. Sanger put out her hand to shake Sarah's, and then said, "A Negro nurse. Very good choice, Dr. Benedict."

Margot stiffened, and she saw Sarah falter in the act of extending her own hand. Mrs. Sanger seemed not to notice, briefly shaking Sarah's hand, then turning in a circle to assess the room. It smelled pleasantly of fresh paint. Sarah had cadged some simple furniture from one of the local businesses, a divan, a couple of mismatched straight chairs, and a low table.

Mrs. Sanger said, "You'll need a desk, of course. Will you be able to install a telephone?"

Margot moved to Sarah's side so the two of them faced Mrs. Sanger shoulder to shoulder. She heard the ice in her own voice as she spoke. "The matching funds should cover a telephone, yes. We're still working on the furniture."

"And the doctors? Are they Negroes also? We did that in New York, you know, and it was quite successful. Harlem, it was."

She walked toward one of the examining rooms, and Sarah and Margot stole the moment to glance at each other. Sarah's wide, delicate nostrils quivered. Margot gave an apologetic shake of her head, and beneath the cover of Sarah's apron, touched her hand before she followed Mrs. Sanger.

"I will be one of the physicians," Margot said. "I don't know yet who the other ones will be."

"Oh, I recommend using coloreds," Mrs. Sanger said offhandedly. She started into the first examining room, adding over her shoulder, "They understand each other, you know."

When Mrs. Sanger had moved out of sight, Margot turned to Sarah. "Blake is outside," she said quietly. "Why don't you go and say hello to him, and I'll—I'll—" She made an irritated gesture in Mrs. Sanger's direction.

"It's all right, Dr. Benedict," Sarah said. "Yes, I'd like to see Mr. Blake. Please don't worry about this. I'm used to it."

Margot's chin rose. "I don't want you to be *used to it*."

Sarah's eyes shone with wisdom far beyond her years, and her own small chin jutted in a matching movement. "This is our life, Dr. Benedict." She spoke without resentment, without even self-pity.

Margot nodded toward the outer door. "Go ahead," she said. "I'm going to have a word with our guest."

"Of course," Sarah said. "But you know, Dr. Benedict, you can't change the world singlehandedly." Something about the courage in her face, in the lift of her head and the decisiveness of her steps as she walked away, tightened Margot's throat. She had to clear it and draw a long, cooling breath before she followed the woman she had thought would be a mentor.

By the time she and Blake had returned Margaret Sanger to King Street Station and wound their way back up the hill to Benedict Hall, Margot felt so tightly strung she thought if anyone touched her she would reverberate. Blake left her in front of the gate, and she stalked up the steps and into the house, dropping her bag with a thud on the carpet in the front hall, tossing her hat at the mahogany coatrack and missing, cursing as she bent to pick it up. She heard the clink of glassware in the small parlor and knew the family had gathered for drinks before dinner. It was rare that a drink sounded like some sort of answer to Margot, but this was such a moment.

She shrugged off her coat and smoothed her skirt with her hands before joining the group around the piecrust table. Dick, with a single glance at her face, poured two fingers of whisky into a cut-glass tumbler and handed it to her without a word. She took a sip and settled onto the divan, cradling the glass in her hands and staring into the briskly burning fire. Everyone was there, Ramona and Edith, Dickson, even Allison. There was no sound except the crackle of burning wood until Margot blew out a long, exasperated sigh.

Her father asked in a wry tone, "Bad day, daughter?"

Margot threw him a look. "Not good, Father. I lost my temper."

He raised his bushy gray eyebrows and waited. Allison looked from one to the other of them, her eyes gleaming with curiosity. Ramona sat back, as if to move out of the way. It was Dick who said, "Who've you scolded now, Margot?"

She gave a sour chuckle. "Now, Dick? Do I scold so often?"

"All the time, I think," he said, but he was grinning. Ramona hid a smile with her perfectly manicured hand. Edith, in the chair opposite, gazed into space, her sherry glass tilting and forgotten in her hand.

"Well," Margot said. "You're right, Dick. At least, I tried to scold her. It didn't seem to take."

"Sanger," Dickson rumbled. "You were meeting Margaret Sanger today. I thought she was your heroine."

"My heroine has feet of clay, Father." Margot took another deep sip of whisky, and held the glass out for her brother to refill. "It doesn't mean she's not doing heroic things, but there's a flaw."

"Always is," Dickson said easily. He raised his own glass to watch the firelight flicker through the amber liquid. "That's the trouble with having heroes. They turn out to be human."

"Tell us about it," Dick said.

"You might not feel the same as I do," Margot said.

Allison surprised them all by saying, "I'd really like to know what happened, Cousin Margot. She made you angry?"

Margot turned to her, startled and pleased by this interest. "Yes, Cousin Allison, she did make me angry. I was looking forward to meeting her, and to showing her the progress we've made on the Women and Infants Clinic. It's a long story, but—"

Allison said, "There's a new law, isn't there?"

Dickson said, "There is indeed. Congress did something right for once. Hard to argue that the health of women and babies isn't worth a bit of national investment."

Margot nodded approval. "Thank you for saying that, Father. The infant mortality rate in America is appalling."

"Sheppard-Towner is a good law," Dickson said. "At least as far as it goes. I'm not sure we should let Margaret Sanger co-opt it, but there it is."

"I don't really think she's co-opting it, Father," Margot said. She let her head drop back against the divan and felt the tension in her body begin to release. It was good to be with her family, with her wise father and smart brother. And her interested cousin! She said, "Contraceptive education is an essential part of women's health concerns."

Ramona said, a bit plaintively, "Do we have to talk about that, Margot?"

Margot paused, trying to find a politic way to respond. She was aware of Allison's wide-eyed gaze, and of course, she hadn't yet addressed the issue with her. She didn't know how the girl would respond to blunt speech on the subject. "I know you're opposed to abortions, Ramona," she said finally. "The best way to prevent them, without doubt, is to prevent the pregnancy in the first place. It's my view—as it is Mrs. Sanger's—that treating women's health includes providing them with information about controlling the size of their families."

"It should be private," Ramona said primly. "Not a government matter."

Her sister-in-law's opinion was so similar to the one Frank had expressed that Margot had to look into the fire while she fought a fresh wave of irritation. It all seemed so obvious to her, so self-evident. How could it be, she asked herself, that she saw things so differently from her sister-in-law? The two of them had grown up in the same way, in comfortable and traditional families, never wanting for anything, never having to question the ways of the world.

To be fair, Ramona hadn't seen the things she had. She hadn't been present at the bedside of a woman dying of a botched and illegal abortion. She hadn't presided at the birth of a baby to a fourteen-year-old girl who thought she couldn't get pregnant her first time. She hadn't made house calls in poor neighborhoods where parents struggled to feed far too many mouths, or where women begged her for some way to prevent further babies from coming—and not, as a male physician in New York had jocularly suggested, by telling their husbands to sleep on the roof. These were women with few choices in life, all of them hard ones. They were women worn down by childbearing, by child care, by want and worry.

When no one else seemed inclined to speak, Allison asked in a hesitant voice, "Cousin Margot? I still don't understand what happened."

"Ah. Sorry, Allison. Of course you don't." Margot leaned forward to set her empty glass on the low table. "Margaret Sanger is a passionate advocate of what she calls 'family planning.' She was almost jailed for teaching women about it in New York, and she goes around the country speaking to people, trying to get the obscenity laws changed."

"But you agree with her," Allison said.

"Yes, I do. About that, I do." Margot drummed the arm of her chair with her fingers. "Ramona and I don't see eye to eye on this, but I don't think such information should be considered obscene. It's—I think the word for it is *humane*."

"The church doesn't agree," Dickson put in, but Margot saw the curl of his lips out of the corner of her eye. He was goading her, for the love of the argument.

"The opposition is impressive, Father. The church, the male legislators, the American Medical Association." Margot turned to face Allison directly. "But I keep getting distracted from your question, Cousin Allison. What I learned today, and what made me angry, is that Mrs. Sanger has a special interest in controlling the Negro birth rate. And that of the Chinese, as well, or any other group she thinks is inferior."

Dickson said, "Surely you read Sanger's book, daughter?"

Dick put in, "She believes in eugenics."

Margot nodded. "But she parts company with the movement in general, as I understand it. She wrote that heredity is not absolute. What I took from her book was that she wants to offer the same freedom to Negro women that she does to whites. But today, in the clinic, her manner toward Sarah was offensive. To say nothing of Blake! I was ashamed of bringing her here."

Ramona put in helpfully, and perhaps trying to be conciliatory, "Sarah was Blake's private nurse, Cousin Allison."

"Yes," Margot said. "She's a fine nurse, and Blake is fond of her. She told me she's used to being treated that way, and that infuriated me even further. Why should Sarah, an accomplished and educated woman, have to accept such treatment?"

"What are you going to do, daughter?"

"I'm going to move ahead with the Women and Infants Clinic," Margot said. "And I'm going to teach—" She glanced around at her listeners. "Family limitation," she said finally, choosing the euphemism with as much distaste as Ramona had expressed for the truer descriptor. "But," she added with determination, "I'm not going to invite that woman to Seattle again."

CHAPTER 13

Allison felt very grown-up and independent as Blake held the
door of the Essex for her, waited until she was seated, then
closed it after she had tucked in the skirt of her coat. When he
was in the driving seat, he said, "Straight to Dr. Margot's clinic,
Miss Allison? Or is there somewhere you need to go first?"

Allison tried to behave as if she were used to giving orders.
"I'll just go to the clinic." And then, hastily, "Thank you, Blake."

He touched his cap with his fingers and said gravely, "You're
most welcome, miss."

Allison settled back against the burgundy plush seat. She admired the automobile's pristine windows and the perfumes of
fresh polish and wax that filled it. It was ever so much nicer than
even the nicest taxicab. Blake drove at a decorous pace down
Aloha and onto Broadway, giving her time to gaze at the Christmas decorations that had begun to appear in picture windows
and storefronts. Just that morning, Hattie and the twins had
started hanging cedar garlands brought up to Benedict Hall on a
horse cart. Cousin Ramona had made Cousin Dick late for the office by cajoling him into climbing into the attic for the cartons of

decorations, because Blake was forbidden to use the ladder. Cousin Dick's loud, insincere complaints about being misused had set everyone laughing, even the maids and Hattie.

Allison's own home had never been like this, servants and family working together, everyone giggling and calling orders. Cousin Dick might pretend to be put upon, but he was obviously very much in the spirit. Allison's father would have simply snapped at Adelaide to get a handyman if the butler couldn't handle the task, and Adelaide would have pursed her lips and then snapped at someone else to vent her temper.

Allison thought about Cousin Margot as the motorcar turned off Madison onto Post Street. She had to admit there was something about her she liked, and it wasn't just that she hadn't betrayed her to Uncle Dickson and Aunt Edith or called her father to report her transgression. That was part of it, but not all. Cousin Margot had a way of speaking that made you think she meant every word she said. She had a trick of looking directly into your face as if she was really interested in you, not to find fault, but to understand you.

Allison knew her mother wasn't impressed by Margot. Adelaide had much preferred Cousin Ramona, and especially Cousin Preston, over the cousin who was a lady doctor. She derided Margot's plain skirts and shirtwaists, her simple hairstyle, her lack of rouge or lipstick.

Allison decided her mother was missing the point. Cousin Margot always looked—*right*, was the word that came to mind. She looked right, for her personality as well as for her profession. She looked right for herself.

"Here we are, miss," Blake said. Allison started and realized that the Essex had stopped and turned at the end of the short street. Blake was already getting out of the car, taking his cane in one hand, reaching for her door with the other. She gathered her coat around her and climbed out to gaze at the small, neat building that was her cousin's medical clinic.

You couldn't miss it, that was certain. A sign hung over the front door, reading in proud red letters, M. BENEDICT, M.D. A short brick walk curved up to two shallow steps and a small stoop. The walls were an inviting cream, and the entrance door was painted a cheerful blue.

"Aren't you coming in, Blake?"

He shook his head. "No, miss. It's better for me to wait here."

"But I might be a while."

He smiled, drawing deep creases in his dark face. "I have a book to read, miss. Don't you worry about me. Go on in."

She felt, suddenly, reluctant. Beyond that blue door were mysteries she couldn't fathom, illnesses and wounds and conditions she could never name. She thought of her mother saying, "Our *bodies*," in that voice of distaste. In this clinic Cousin Margot was M. Benedict, M.D. A doctor. A person who had secret knowledge of people's bodies, and who had power over them. Who looked at them, touched them.

What was she doing here, silly Allison Benedict, who didn't know anything? Perhaps she had made a terrible mistake.

Blake, behind her, said calmly, "I could certainly walk you to the door, Miss Allison."

She took a short, sharp breath to steady herself and glanced at him. "Oh, no, Blake. Thank you." She gathered her courage, such as it was, and turned back to the clinic. If she wanted to understand Cousin Margot better, this was a fine place to start. There probably weren't any sick people in there yet anyway. "I'm on my way," she said, and marched up the brick walk.

The minute she opened the blue door, Allison saw she had been mistaken about the sick people. The reception room, smelling of new paint and freshly ironed curtains, had been furnished with a handsome blue divan, several straight chairs, a low table, and a substantial oak desk at one side. A young woman in a nurse's apron and starched cap sat behind the desk, talking to a man in the coveralls and plaid cotton shirt of a workman. The man was bent forward as if he were in pain. He clutched his flat cap to his chest with one hand, and with the other he held a bloodstained handkerchief over one eye.

Allison froze just inside the door, her stomach quivering. The nurse, a stocky girl with black hair and thick black eyebrows, nodded to the man, rose, and disappeared through an inner door. She was back almost immediately with Cousin Margot. Margot, in a blindingly white coat and wearing a stethoscope around her neck, caught sight of Allison, and gave her a swift wave before she put her hand under the man's arm and guided him through the door.

The nurse closed the door behind them and turned back toward the desk. Seeing Allison, she said, "Goodness! We're not even open yet. Do you need to see the doctor, too?"

"No," Allison said, and then amended, "well, yes. But not as a patient." She straightened her shoulders and crossed the room to stand opposite the desk. "I'm Dr. Benedict's cousin. I've come to—to help plan the reception. The tea, I mean. For the clinic opening."

"Is the doctor expecting you?" the nurse asked, rather primly, Allison thought.

"Didn't she say anything?" Allison asked.

"No, but we've had a busy morning. The word got out, I believe, that Dr. Benedict is here. There were patients waiting on the stoop when I arrived."

Allison was surprised by the swell of pride this news gave her. Her cousin Margot was an important person. She wished her mother could see Margot here in her clinic, with her shining hair and direct gaze and confident manner. Indeed, Margot was so important she didn't need to worry about the opinions of people like Adelaide Benedict. Or care. That would be so marvelously emancipating!

She said to the nurse, holding out her gloved hand with her best debutante courtesy, "How do you do? I'm Allison Benedict. I'm going to plan the—the occasion," she added hastily, as the nurse's brows drew together. Truly, it wouldn't be mere vanity to pluck those. They looked like black caterpillars.

But then the nurse smiled and put out her own hand, and Allison saw that she was actually quite young. "I'm Angela Rossi," she said. "I hadn't heard anything about a tea, but I think it's a swell idea. Make it official!" The two girls shook hands, and Angela added, "I was lucky to get this position, you know, Miss Benedict. If Dr. Benedict does well, I will, too!" She grinned, and Allison found herself chuckling at her frankness.

The door to the reception room opened, and Margot put her head out. "Allison," she said, "can you wait a few minutes? Nurse Rossi, I need you here. We'll have to suture Mr. McDonald's laceration, and then you can bandage it for him."

They both disappeared, leaving Allison alone in the reception room. *Laceration. Suture.* Such interesting words, implying so much drama, but tossed off casually, as if Cousin Margot said them all the time. Allison was impressed. And, actually, she thought, as she turned to survey the room, the sight of the bloody handkerchief hadn't been that upsetting, not when Cousin Margot was about to set everything right.

Margot set Angela to cleaning the laceration over the patient's eye with hydrogen peroxide while she prepared an injection of cocaine solution. Mr. McDonald groaned once or twice while Angela worked on him, and Margot said, "It won't hurt for long, Mr. McDonald. I'm going to inject a topical anaesthetic, and then you shouldn't feel much at all beyond the tugging of the sutures. You were fortunate that the chain missed your eye."

"Foreman was afraid I'd gone blind," the patient muttered. He was a construction worker, Margot knew now, and had been helping to unload a stack of lumber. A chain under too much tension had apparently broken, and whipped back to catch Mr. McDonald across the forehead.

"You haven't gone blind, I'm glad to say. There's always a lot of blood with head wounds, because it's a highly vascular area. It looked frightening, but it's going to be fine. You're going to miss some work, though."

"I won't get paid if I don't work, Doc Benedict."

"You can't work if you get an infection, either, Mr. McDonald." It was a story Margot had heard many times, and it was the sort of thing she and her father argued about. She insisted there should be some sort of allowance made for workers injured on the job, and her father held the position that such allowances would create malingerers. They had never resolved the issue. She would do her best to insist, at least, that the shipping company pay her bill.

The procedure went smoothly, and Mr. McDonald, once the anaesthetic took effect, lay quietly on the examination table while she worked. She took time with her stitches. The wound was irregular, and she did her best to minimize the scar it was going to leave, removing one or two stitches, replacing them with better ones. When she was done, she stepped back, nodding to Angela as she pulled off her gloves. "Sprinkle with iodoform powder, Nurse, and then plenty of gauze. Mr. McDonald, no washing until I've seen you again, all right?"

Beneath Angela's hands, she saw him grin. "Will you tell the wife that, doc?"

Margot chuckled. "If I need to, absolutely." She laid her palm on his trousered knee. "Now, be sure the bandage stays clean. Nurse Rossi will finish here and give you an appointment to have the stitches removed. I'll see you then."

"Thanks, Doc Benedict. Thanks a lot."

"You're quite welcome, Mr. McDonald."

Margot was already out of the examination room when she realized what he had called her. Doc. Arnie at the diner called her doc, too, and some of the other working people on Post Street. Preston, when he was alive, had called her doc. She paused for a moment, her hand on the latch of the reception room door, and searched for some feeling about it, some reaction to the memory of Preston. Surely she should feel something. Nostalgia, sadness, even anger.

All she could find was relief. She gave her head a small, private shake and went out into the reception room.

"Cousin Allison," she said, glad to see the girl was still there. "Sorry to keep you waiting! It's been quite a day."

Allison smiled, and Margot noticed how much better her color was, how smooth her skin looked. "Nurse Rossi told me," Allison said. "You're already busy, and not officially open yet."

Margot smiled back. "Surprising, isn't it? In the past, sometimes we went entire days without seeing anyone. Now we'll just see whether any of these people can actually pay their bill."

"Sometimes they don't?" Allison said in wonder.

Margot laughed. "Often they don't!"

"But you—you see them anyway?"

"Oh, yes," Margot said. "They need help." She tipped her head to one side, looking into Allison's face in her direct way. "It's not that they don't want to pay, you know. Too many of the patients I see only come here out of desperation. We'll see if this spanking new clinic attracts a few patients who actually have something in their pocketbooks."

"Well," Allison said. She held out her hands to indicate the reception room. "It's very nice, Cousin Margot. I do think a table would be good, for the occasion, someplace to put the refreshments when people come to tour the clinic."

"It sounds fine, Allison. How about flowers?"

"Oh, people will send those," Allison said with confidence. "They always do, when they see the announcement. You just have to make sure it's printed in the *Times*. And the other papers, too."

"You have experience, I see," Margot said. "I leave it all in your hands, then. If you need anything, ask Ramona—she's a wizard with everything social."

"And Hattie," Allison said. "I thought I would ask Hattie to make cookies. At least, if Aunt Edith doesn't mind. Hattie loves to bake, I believe."

"That she does. She'll be delighted. Come now, I'll show you the rest of the place."

They passed Mr. McDonald and Nurse Rossi in the hallway, which was wide enough now for more than one person to walk at a time. With pride, Margot opened the door to the second examination room, then showed Allison the storage room. It was spacious and orderly, packed with cartons and boxes and carefully shelved supplies. Frank's hand was evident in every detail.

They paused in Margot's office, and Allison gazed up at her diplomas, replaced by the university since the fire, and displayed on the wall opposite the mahogany desk. Her gaze took in the shelf of medical books, the *Materia Medica* and her treasured Manual of Surgery. "You must have been in school a long time," Allison said.

"It certainly seemed like it! I had a lot to learn."

"I wish I could go to college," Allison said. Her cheeks reddened all at once, then paled again. "Papa says there's no point."

"Allison—sit down for a moment. We've had no chance to talk."

Allison turned obediently and settled into the armchair opposite Margot's desk. She looked suddenly tense. Margot said carefully, "I hope I'm not taking advantage of you, asking you to manage this party."

"No," Allison said. "Not at all. I've done it for Mother. We held one of the debutante teas in our house."

"That's wonderful," Margot said. "I wouldn't have the first idea how to begin. I'm grateful to you."

"It's fine," Allison said.

"Good. That's good."

Allison's eyes flicked away to the window that looked out over Elliott Bay, and her lips worked as if she were about to say something more, but changed her mind.

"As I said a few nights ago, Allison," Margot began, "I think at your age you should understand how pregnancies happen. It's the sort of thing I would expect your mother to teach you, though I'm aware mothers often don't."

"My mother doesn't talk about things like that." A pause. "Did yours?"

Margot sighed. "Well, yes. She didn't like doing it, though. She was embarrassed, and got through it as quickly as she could." She smiled a little, remembering. "For women of their generation—your mother's and mine—it's a difficult thing to talk about. But we're modern women, you and I."

Allison sat up a bit straighter. "You're talking about sex, aren't you, Cousin Margot?"

"Yes. I am."

"And that Mrs. Sanger—is that what she's teaching people about? Sex?"

Margot nodded. The girl wasn't completely ignorant, thank God. She had met pregnant girls who had no idea how they had gotten that way, and others who thought their babies were going to be born through their navels. "Did you understand much of our conversation last night? About Mrs. Sanger?"

"Not really. I'm sorry."

"There's no need for that," Margot said with warmth. "I just wish it would be a normal part of girls' education, so they know how to take care of themselves." She leaned down to open a drawer in her beautiful new desk and pulled out a pamphlet. "This," she told Allison, "I'm allowed to give you, because I'm a physician. No one else is, because it's considered obscene, but—"

"Obscene?" Allison said faintly.

"Afraid so. I hope you'll believe me when I say it's not."

"My mother says having a baby is messy. And hurts worse than anything you can imagine."

"Yet women go on having them," Margot said. "Just as they have for thousands of years." She pushed the pamphlet across her desk, and Allison picked it up gingerly, as if it might stain her fingers. "Bodies," Margot said with as much patience as she could muster, "tend to be messy, if you're sensitive to such things. Childbirth has some pain associated with it, but you can trust me, Allison, I've seen things that hurt far worse. And most of the mothers I've attended are so thrilled to see their little ones safely born that they would do it all again in a heartbeat."

"Not my mother." This was said flatly, without the slightest doubt.

"Are you sure about that?" Margot asked.

"Oh, yes." Allison picked up the pamphlet and folded it in half. "Yes, I'm quite sure."

"I think often parents and children don't understand each other. Uncle Henry was quite worried about you—"

Allison interrupted. "No, he wasn't, believe me. He was worried he wouldn't be able to sell me."

"Sell—?" Margot said helplessly.

Allison's features, usually soft and vulnerable looking, hardened, and her little pointed chin seemed to grow sharper as her lips pulled down. "Oh, yes," she said. "I'm on the market, you know. The marriage market." She spread her arms wide, and her small body seemed to suddenly thrum with resentment. She reminded Margot of a teapot starting to whistle. Suddenly, she was talking, words pouring out of her like steam.

"Oh, yes. The only thing Papa ever liked about me was my tennis game. I've always been Mother's problem, in his view. It's like a horse being groomed for auction, you know, the whole debutante thing. No young men are allowed at any of the events unless they have a pedigree, and all of us are paraded in front of them so they can make their choice. Everyone knows how much money you have, and what property is in your family, and—and they know your family history, too, which is why Mother and Papa were so worried I would make a mistake, because they're not proud of theirs."

Her cheeks were flaming red now, and her blue eyes sparkled with temper. "Your family is different, because Uncle Dickson has been successful for such a long time, and you have Benedict Hall and Cousin Dick in the business, but Papa—" Her energy evaporated, all at once, and the stream of her words sputtered and died. Her hands fluttered down into her lap like exhausted birds.

It took Margot a moment to think of how to go forward. The outburst both surprised her and, in some odd way, encouraged her. There was spirit in the girl, and that could only be a good thing. She said, choosing her words with care, "Allison, I don't think I understand the concern about your family's history. I believe your father is quite successful. Father has never intimated anything otherwise." She remembered that Dickson had worried about Henry's business not being diversified in the current economic climate, but this was not the time to mention it. "Are they really in a hurry for you to be married?"

"Oh, yes. Papa wants me off his hands. The expense, and everything, you know."

"Surely your family doesn't lack for money."

"It's never enough," Allison said. "That's what Mother says, in any case."

"Hmm. I suppose I don't know Aunt Adelaide very well."

Allison sat back in the armchair with a weary look on her young face. "You don't want to, Cousin Margot. My mother's a shark. She'll eat you up if you're not careful."

It had been, Margot thought, an odd visit. She walked Allison out to meet Blake, and stood watching, her hands in the pockets of her coat, as they drove off. The day was one of those cold, glittering ones, with icy sunshine glancing off the new bricks and paint of the clinic, and making a shining backdrop of the Sound and the snowy Olympic Mountains. Margot stood where she was for a short time to admire the view and savor the feeling of having created something fine.

Frank was partial to native plants, and he and the gardener had decided on a barrier of Pacific wax myrtle to ensure privacy at the back of the building. The hedge was small still, and looked a bit dilapidated in the cold. Margot walked around the side of the clinic, past her office window, to take a closer look so she could describe it to him in her next letter.

She touched the glossy, elongated leaves and pushed at the dirt of the bed with her foot. It seemed healthy to her, though she was no expert. They had planted six of them, and in years to come, the gardener and Frank assured her, the hedge would make a nice screen that would keep down some of the traffic noise. She crouched beside one of the plants and pulled one small, fragrant leaf from a low stem. It was a bit silly, perhaps, but she liked the idea of sending it to Frank. When he opened the envelope, it would slide out, a little bit of Seattle for him to hold in his palm.

She dropped the leaf into the pocket of her coat and walked around to the other side of the clinic, where the smaller windows of the two examination rooms faced north. That side lay in shadow now, the low angle of the sun falling below the roofline. Margot trailed her fingers along the wall, remembering the day when she and Frank had stood here, surveying the newly poured concrete footings. The day had been hot and clear, the sun burning their shoulders, pouring generously over the wet concrete. Today the air smelled of salt and smoke. That day it had been filled with the scents of raw earth and newly sawn wood, smells that would always remind her of the day she knew Frank Parrish loved her.

She had not, officially, accepted Frank's proposal that day. They had walked together down to the Public Market, and he had bought her an embarrassingly large bouquet of flowers from the Chinese flower seller. Somehow, though, the actual proposal got lost in the excitement, in the thrill of his new prosthetic, in their plans for the clinic. It was her fault, of course. She hadn't been all that sure she wanted to be a wife. Anyone's wife.

In fact, she still wasn't sure of that, but it didn't mean she didn't love Frank with all her heart. She had asked him once why they needed to be married, and his answer had been clear and succinct. He wouldn't ruin her reputation by not marrying her. He wouldn't ruin his own by living with someone not his wife. He wanted, he said, what his parents had. What *her* parents had.

A sudden shiver broke her revery. The shadows were too cold to linger in. She turned back toward the street and the front entrance, but at the corner she stopped.

Another memory, that of crouching down beside the fresh, uncured concrete to push the sapphire—Preston's sapphire—down into its gray, wet depths. She had watched the silver chain coil after it until it, too, sank and disappeared. Frank had said something about its value, but Margot had wanted only to get rid of it, to put it somewhere where no one would find it again.

The creeping Jenny starts the gardener had planted to cover the foundation were slow to spread. They grew in little clumps, their leaves stiff with cold and generously threaded with brown stems, and there were large spaces between them. In one of those spaces Margot saw a bubble in the concrete. It wasn't large, but it was definite, the only flaw in the otherwise smooth side of the foundation.

The chill that had made her shiver crept deeper. It settled in her chest, a familiar sense of dread she thought she had banished more than a year before.

She crouched down beside the flaw in the concrete, knelt in the exact spot she had on that sunny autumn day, before there had been walls or floors or windows in the building. She prodded the bubble with her fingers, but it was dry and hard and very cold. A sudden prickle on the back of her neck brought her to her feet. It had nothing to do with the cold and the shadows of the building. She had learned long ago, when she was still a small girl, to be aware of that prickling. She had learned the hard way that it was never wise to ignore it.

Now, though there should be no more danger, and nothing further to worry about, she spun to see who was watching.

There, was that a shadow, slipping between the shoemaker's and the Italian grocer's? The alley there was narrow, just a dirt lane where the businesses left their refuse and piled empty delivery cartons. Margot took a step, thinking if she hurried, she might reach the alley before whoever it was had disappeared.

"Dr. Benedict?" It was Angela Rossi, standing on the little stoop. She had taken off her apron and wore her cape over her long woolen skirt. Her handbag sat at her feet as she pulled on her gloves.

"Oh, Nurse Rossi. I kept you waiting. It turned out to be an interesting day, didn't it?"

Angela smiled cheerfully. "It was wonderful, Doctor! Real patients and all."

"I'm glad you didn't mind. I didn't expect to be working so much before we're officially open."

"I've left the ledger open on the desk so you can check it. The money is in the lockbox, in the big drawer."

Margot, anxiety forgotten in delight at this development, exclaimed, "Money! I can hardly believe it. Just a year ago, I could see this many patients in a day and not see a penny in actual income."

Angela bent to pick up her handbag. "Times are better, I suppose."

"Perhaps that's it." Margot went up the walk and put her hand on the latch. "I'll see you in the morning, then."

"I'll be here!"

Margot watched the young nurse tripping energetically along Post Street toward the streetcar stop, her cape fluttering around her sturdy black-stockinged legs. Rossi was proving, at least so far, to be everything Alice Cardwell had promised. She was hardworking, eager to learn, direct but kind with the patients, and deft with bandages. She would work out very well. Margot couldn't wait to tell Frank all about her.

She went back into the clinic for her own coat and hat, but as she passed the desk she took a swift peek into the cash box. She had put in some money, so the nurse could make change if need be. There had been five dollars in the box when she opened it that morning. Now, at a glance, she guessed there must be nine there, including two paper ones. She shook her head in wonderment at these riches as she shrugged into her coat and put on her hat.

It wasn't until she had gone around to put out the lights, and was locking the door, that she remembered that strange bubble on the side of the foundation. It was as if the sapphire, that object Preston had cared about so much, and which he had held as he died, was trying to emerge from its tomb.

She turned the key and dropped her key ring into the pocket of her coat. As she pulled the collar up against the cold, she told herself not to behave like a superstitious child. She stamped down the brick walk, impatient with the strange thoughts and impressions that had confused the final hours of what had otherwise been a most satisfying day.

She glanced up, and the smile returned to her face. Blake was there, just as he used to be. The Essex gleamed through the darkness, its headlamps lighting her way. Blake touched his cap as she walked toward him. "Good evening, Dr. Margot," he said, and there wasn't a trace of a Southern accent in his deep voice. "I trust you had a good day."

"Good evening, Blake," she said. "It was a wonderful day."

"Very good," he said calmly, as he held the door for her. "Very good."

CHAPTER 14

The alley was wet, and his shoes were heavy with cold mud by the time he slunk away from Post Street and down to Elliott Avenue. It seemed impossible that just two years before he had walked these streets proudly. Girls, like the pretty cousin who had driven off with Blake, used to turn their heads when he passed. They blushed with pleasure when he tipped his hat to them, and he often felt their eyes on him as he strode away, his head up, his back straight, a man without a care in the world. He had welcomed the sunshine on his neck, had removed his hat to feel the wind in his hair. He had gone into any establishment he wished, always welcome for his name, his status, and in no small part for his good looks. That life was gone now, lost forever.

She had won. She had destroyed him. If it hadn't been for Margot, he wouldn't be creeping through alleys, sheltering in shadows. She wasn't clever enough, despite what Father thought, to have effected this damage deliberately, but it was no less devastating for that. Now, if a woman caught a glimpse of him on the street, she averted her eyes. If he was careless enough to let his hat brim lift in the breeze or his muffler slide down his neck, children whimpered and buried their faces in their mothers' skirts. Men who caught sight of him winced with sympathy. They probably thought he bore the scars of the Great War, but their pity didn't lessen the revulsion they felt for his ruined face.

Indeed, he felt it himself.

The Compass Center, where he had been sleeping for months, had mirrors in the bathrooms. Rev. Karlstrom said they were so the men could shave and make themselves presentable before they went out looking for work. Mrs. Karlstrom—who at least didn't avert her eyes at the sight of him—advised him to accept his disability as part of God's grace. God! If there were a God, none of this would have happened. If there were a God watching over him, he could have grown up without having to fight *her* for every inch of ground. If there were a God who gave a tinker's damn about him, he would have held his rightful place as the adored son of a fine family. He could have gone on at the *Times*, writing his column, making his mother proud, acquiring a greater and greater readership that would eventually win even his father's respect.

He hated being at the Center, but he had no other place to sleep. He tolerated the sermons and the lectures, accepted the hand-me-down clothes, pretended humility and gratitude. The mirrors, however—reminding him every time he had to piss that his face had become monstrous—were too much. He had taken care of them. He had no choice, really.

There were plenty of discarded bricks lying around on the streets in Pioneer Square, and it was an easy matter to slip one under the coat they had given him, the coat that didn't fit and probably had belonged to some repulsive old man. He had carried the brick into the bathroom and made short work of the three mirrors hanging there. He didn't need to look at his scars every day. He could hardly forget how they looked. He had only to show his face on the street to be reminded, and in the most unpleasant way. It was only fair that, in the place he was forced to live, he didn't have to see them several times a day.

The Karlstroms, naturally, never knew who had smashed the

mirrors into gleaming splinters. He might look like a monster, but was still good at getting things done.

He would get this done, too, and do a proper job of it this time. He had made an uncharacteristic error the last time, confused by Parrish's presence, by the strangeness of Margot and Frank being at the clinic late at night, by a patient being there when the clinic should have been closed. And he had been betrayed by the sapphire, in which he had placed so much trust. More evidence there was no God. And no justice except that which a man achieved for himself.

This time he would be more subtle. This time he would use a scalpel instead of a pickax. He had remembered, at last, who the girl was living in Benedict Hall. Allison Benedict, little San Francisco cousin, the debutante. A pretty plum, ripe for plucking. She was just the tool he needed.

Of course his own life was over, and he'd be glad to be shut of it. There was nothing left for him but that achievement of justice, that balancing of accounts. Then he would be finished, and be damned to them all.

Allison waved farewell to Blake as he backed and turned the Essex to drive downtown to fetch Margot. He rewarded her with one of his generous smiles, a lovely flash of white in his dark face. She walked slowly up the steps to the front door, thinking about Blake, about Cousin Margot, about how different things were here from her expectations. Margot wasn't the enemy at all. She was—she was everything Allison wished she could be herself. Smart. Educated. Capable. No one, as nearly as Allison could tell, judged Margot by her appearance. They cared about who she was and what she could do.

The man with the bloody handkerchief had walked out neatly bandaged, all put together again, politely thanking the doctor and the nurse. How marvelous must it be to be able to fix things that way! Nurse Rossi was neither pretty nor particularly well spoken, as Adelaide would have hastened to point out, but like Cousin Margot, she was doing work that mattered.

The front door was unlocked. Allison let herself in to stand for a moment in the front hall, listening. It was still too early for the twins to be setting the table in the dining room. She could hear their light voices upstairs, above her head. The men had not yet returned from the office, and there was no sign of Cousin Ramona or Aunt Edith. The only sounds came from the kitchen, Hattie's rich voice humming as she clattered pans and walked this way and that in the kitchen, the floor creaking beneath her weight.

Allison hung up her coat and hat, then crossed the hall to knock on the kitchen door. The humming broke off, and a moment later, Hattie peeked out. She was drying her hands on her apron as she pushed the door open with her shoulder. "Why, Miss Allison! You were gone most of the afternoon, weren't you? Would you like a snack? A cup of tea?"

"Just a cup of tea would be nice."

"You go on in the small parlor, and I'll bring it."

"Hattie, really, I—I'd just as soon have it in the kitchen, if you don't mind. I need to talk to you."

Hattie paused, her apron caught up in her hands, a doubtful expression tugging at her plump features. "Talk to me? Is something wrong, miss?"

"Oh, no!" Allison smiled, and Hattie, after a second's pause, smiled tentatively back. "I just wanted to talk to you about Cousin Margot's tea. I know you're busy, but it seemed like a good time."

Hattie's smile widened. "Why, Miss Allison, of course." She smoothed down the folds of her apron and stepped back to pull the door open. "You're welcome in old Hattie's kitchen just any old time. I always liked the young ones coming in to have a cookie or cup of cocoa. It's been an awful long while, now they're all grown."

Allison was familiar with the kitchen in her own home. As a child, she had taken her meals there with Rosy, and later, before she came out, when her parents were entertaining. The San Francisco kitchen was dark, set beneath ground level and, like the rest of the house, narrow. This one seemed enormous in contrast, a long, bright room. A shining nickel-plated range sat on one side, and a tall white icebox on the other. The ceiling was high, and cloudy now with fragrant steam from a large bubbling stockpot. Something was baking in the oven, something that smelled of sugar and butter and vanilla. Allison's mouth watered suddenly.

Hattie walked to the sink to fill the teakettle, then walked back to put it on the range. "Set yourself down, Miss Allison." Allison slipped into one of the chrome-backed straight chairs arranged around a long table with a white enamel top. Hattie put a teacup and saucer in front of her, and then, as if she had forgotten—or ignored—Allison's refusal of the snack, she dipped her hand into a fat pottery cookie jar flanking a percolator. She set a plate of cookies beside the teacup. Now, as the kettle began to whistle, Allison picked up a cookie. It was every bit as sweet and rich as she had imagined, and her eyes closed with pleasure as the crumbs melted on her tongue. When she opened them, Hattie was grinning at her. "Lordy, I do like to see a child eat," she said with satisfaction. "Those snickerdoodles used to be the children's favorites. Now, here's your tea. Have another cookie, and tell me how I can help with Miss Margot's party."

Allison took a second cookie. She was afraid of bolting it, of gorging herself, as she had done at the diner with Tommy. The tea helped, though. She sipped it, and nibbled the cookie, and found she felt all right. Her stomach didn't feel desperate, and she felt at ease here under Hattie's approving eye.

A little swell of contentment rolled over her, a gentle, warm wave that made her smile. "I thought we'd put a table in the reception room," she told Hattie. "We can put the refreshments there, and you could do some cookies and finger sandwiches. If it's not too much trouble."

Hattie, who had crossed to the range to stir what was in the pot, said, "It's no trouble at all, Miss Allison, no trouble at all. So sweet of you to do all this! I'm sure Miss Margot is real happy to have you help."

"These cookies would be perfect, because they're small. People will be walking around with napkins, I think."

Hattie nodded agreement. She crossed to the table and lowered herself into a chair with a little grunt. "Hope you don't mind if I get off my feet a moment, miss."

Allison blinked. "Hattie! This is *your* kitchen. Why would I mind?"

"Well," Hattie said, fanning herself with the hem of her apron, "we do like to do things proper here at Benedict Hall."

Allison sipped tea and watched Hattie over the rim of her cup. The cook wasn't as old as she had first thought. Her forehead was smooth, and the skin of her round cheeks was glossy and plump. It was her eyes that had made her seem older, not wrinkles around them, but the set of the eyelids and the expression they held. Allison said impulsively, "I love the way you do things, Hattie. I mean, here in Benedict Hall."

Hattie made a little one-handed gesture. "Oh, well, Miss Allison, this is a good house. It always has been, until—well, until—" Her eyes suddenly reddened, and she looked away.

Allison said quietly, "I know. Until Cousin Preston died. I'm so sorry."

Hattie sniffed and dashed a hand across her eyes, as if the gesture could erase her ready tears. "You're a sweet girl, Miss Allison. You're being real sweet to old Hattie."

Allison knew her mother would have been appalled to see her sitting in the kitchen with a colored cook, having a conversation as if they were equals. But why should that be? In what possible way did a girl like herself—who didn't do anything but buy clothes and go to parties—bring more to the world than Hattie?

She said, with real melancholy, "I'm not a sweet girl, though. I'm a handful. That's what Papa says."

Hattie put one hand flat on the table and looked directly into Allison's eyes. "All I know is what I see," she said. She wasn't smiling now, and her eyes still glistened with the tears she hadn't shed. "I see a pretty girl being nice to an old servant and offering to help her cousin with a party. Nobody gonna tell me that girl is a handful."

"Oh, Hattie," Allison breathed. Tears started behind her own eyes, and for some reason that made her laugh. "Oh, Hattie," she said again, giggling and sobbing at the same time. "You just don't know what I've done!"

Hattie chuckled, too. "Well, you ain't killed anybody, I'm guessing, and you ain't got yourself in trouble. You're a good girl in my book, Miss Allison!"

Allison was laughing in earnest now at Hattie's frankness and at her kindness. "My mother," she sputtered, "would absolutely burst with fury if she heard you say that!"

Hattie's grin was wide and accepting. It felt marvelous to laugh with someone, and Allison didn't care that it was a servant. The fact that her mother wouldn't like it gave her all the more reason to enjoy it.

Hattie pushed herself to her feet and fetched the teapot to re-fill Allison's cup. "Well, I don't want to upset your mama. That's not my place. But everybody got to have someone to talk to." She picked up a long wooden spoon. " 'Course, you got that Ruby, don't you?"

Allison's laughter faded. "I can't talk to Ruby. She spies on me."

Hattie, shaking her head, stirred the pot with the big spoon. "Now, that's a shame," she said. "If I thought Loena or Leona was doing anything like that, I'd have a word to say about it!"

By the time she left the kitchen, Allison had Hattie's promise to make three different kinds of cookies, and to lend the electric percolator so they could make coffee for the reception. The twins came in just as she was leaving, and they glanced at her cu-riously, standing back to let her pass. She smiled at them. "Hello, Loena. Leona."

They bobbed curtsies, and Leona said, "Aren't you the clever one, miss, to be able to tell us apart!"

Allison was laughing again as she walked up the main staircase. It had been a day for laughing, and it felt good. It also felt good to walk upstairs without feeling as if she were climbing a mountain. She had felt tired and dizzy for so long she had forgotten what it was like to have energy.

Yes, it had been a day for laughing and a day for thinking. She felt better in every way than she had for months.

The night before the reception, the telephone in Margot's room rang at nine o'clock. She sighed as she reached for it. It would have been nice to have an uninterrupted night's sleep, to rise in the morning at a reasonable hour, take some care with her hair and her clothes for once. She put the earpiece to her ear and held the candlestick in her left hand. She said tiredly, "Dr. Benedict speaking."

"Don't sound like that," Frank said. "It's just me."

"Frank!" She wriggled back against her pillows, cradling the candlestick against her chest. "What a nice surprise! I was sure you were the hospital calling."

"Nope. Just me."

"I'm so glad."

"You sound tired. Are you all right?"

"I'm a little nervous, to be honest. I'm not very good with social things, as you know, and tomorrow—you did get the article I sent you? From the *Times*? Tomorrow's the reception at the clinic. Well, Cousin Allison is calling it a tea, so it's less formal. Very Emily Post!"

"It sounds nice," he said. "Big day for you."

"For us both, Frank, since you designed the building. The practice is already busy, though. It's as if they were waiting."

"Probably were."

"Yes. I suppose they were."

"So, your little cousin is handling the party."

Margot smiled, thinking of Allison's trips to the clinic, her solemn conferences with Hattie and with Leona, her order to Ruby—who wasn't a bit happy about it—to put on an apron and serve. "Allison looks happier than I've ever seen her. She even eats at meals—not a lot, but she does eat. She's quite a clever girl, I think. She just needed something to do."

"Good. I'm sure it will be a big success."

"I hope so. Some people from the hospital are going to come, which feels odd."

"Why? How many of them have their own private practice in their own private building?"

Margot laughed. "That's what Father said."

"Wise man, your pop."

"He is that." She paused, and then said wistfully, "I just wish you could be here."

"I want to be there."

"When is Bill Boeing going to let you come home?" She was afraid she sounded a little plaintive, but she couldn't help it. "You've been gone a long time, Frank, and we—" There she did stop herself. She had promised not to bring up their disagreements over the telephone. The calls were too precious for that.

"Too long," he agreed. "There's something I want you to do for me, Margot."

"Do you need something?"

"Sort of. What time does your shindig start tomorrow?"

"Eleven. I have rounds to make, and then I'm going to come home and change."

"Could you ask Blake to drive you out to Sand Point first? Do you know where that is?"

"I—what? No, I don't know where it is, but I'm sure Blake will. Why?"

"There's an airstrip there. It isn't much, but a Jenny can land. I'm sending you something, but you have to come fetch it yourself, Margot—you need to be there."

She caught sight of her face in the dressing table mirror, nestled among her white pillows. She looked younger and softer at this distance. She should try to smile more often, she thought. Try not to look so forbidding all the time. On a sleepy laugh, she said, "Frank Parrish, if this is a pony . . ."

He laughed with her. "Not a pony. I hope you like it, though."

The operator interrupted, saying formally, "I'm sorry, sir, but your time is up. Would you like to arrange another call?"

He said, "Better not. Thanks, operator. Margot, be there to-morrow! Ten o'clock!"

"I will. Good night, Frank."

The operator said, "Good night, sir," and added, "Ma'am. Thank you for using the Southern California Telephone Company."

The final click sounded before Frank could speak again. Re-luctantly, Margot replaced the earpiece in its cradle and set the phone on the bedside table. Sand Point Airfield! Now what could that mean?

She put out her lamp, took off her dressing gown, and slipped beneath the coverlet of her bed. Curiosity had vanquished her bout of nerves. She would, she thought, have a good night's sleep after all. It was lovely to drift off with the sound of Frank's voice still in her ear.

CHAPTER 15

The morning dawned under a heavy cloud layer that shrouded the tallest buildings of Seattle in folds of mist. Margot hurried her rounds at the hospital as best she could. She saw a little girl in the children's ward who had burned her arm on the family's charcoal stove. She prescribed picric acid and explained carefully to the mother how important it was to keep the burn clean. There was a surgical case, an operation at which she had assisted. She examined the incision and found the patient was healing well. She asked Nurse Cardwell to do a final check that afternoon before she released him to his family. Margot stopped to see a man in the charity ward whose stomach she had pumped the day before. She was concerned that the three-dollar gin he had consumed in such quantities could have neurological implications. She pointed this out to him, but she wasn't sure he was fit to comprehend her lecture. She left orders for him to stay another day, and for the duty nurse to administer a unit of Dakin fluid. Within the hour, she was hurrying home to change.

She was just unbuttoning her shirtwaist when Ruby knocked

on her door. Margot opened it and regarded her quizzically. She didn't think Ruby had ever been in her bedroom.

Ruby said, "Good morning, Miss Margot. Miss Allison sent me to help you dress."

"She—she what?"

"Sent me to help you dress," Ruby said. She sidled past Margot to go straight to the wardrobe, where the wool crepe ensemble hung in its layers of tissue paper. Ruby began unwrapping the tissue with an air of efficiency.

Margot said uncertainly, "Ruby, this is very nice of Miss Allison, but I don't need—"

Ruby turned to her with a look of utter disinterest. "Miss Allison told me to come."

Margot's lips twitched as she began again on her buttons. "Very well," she said. "Clearly, Miss Allison is in charge today. We'd better do as she says."

Ruby didn't seem to find this amusing. She folded away the last of the tissue and laid the skirt and jacket on the bed.

Ramona had persuaded Margot to go to Frederick & Nelson for a fitting. Margot protested that she didn't have time, but Allison was watching with such bright, hopeful eyes that she gave in. When she arrived, she found the suit already selected. It was a matter of twenty minutes for the saleswoman to take a few measurements, make tailoring marks, and send her on her way.

Even to Margot's uninformed eye, the ensemble was perfect for this iron-gray day. There was a pleated white silk blouse, and a jacket and skirt made in rose wool crepe, in a color so deep it couldn't possibly be called pink. It made Margot's skin glow, and though the hem of the straight skirt rose perilously close to her knees, the long jacket balanced it. She looked, she thought gratefully, appropriately professional, but she was fairly certain she didn't look the least bit stodgy. She wished Frank could see her in it.

Ruby helped her put on the blouse, then stood behind her to fasten the skirt. As she held the jacket for Margot, Margot said, "I understand you're going to help out today, Ruby. I appreciate it."

"Well, ma'am, I suppose a lady's maid has to do different stuff sometimes."

Margot raised her eyebrows. "Different stuff indeed," she said. "This will be a unique event, I believe."

"I s'pose so."

Margot slipped her feet into a pair of low-heeled pumps with ankle straps. She couldn't resist one slight, angled pose to admire herself in the mirror. Really, Ramona was good at this! She said, with satisfaction, "Thank you, Ruby. We're finished here."

Ruby said, "Yes, ma'am," and was gone without another word. Margot wrinkled her nose in the direction of her back and wondered how Allison put up with the girl. Or if she had a choice.

By the time Margot and Blake set out for Sand Point, the cloud cover had dissolved under chilly sunshine. Only scattered fluffs remained to float above the city, brilliantly white against the cold blue.

Her father had warned her that the road didn't go all the way to the airfield. He had been right, she saw, as Blake parked the Essex just at the edge of the Sand Point wilderness. There was going to be a navy airfield here one day, but the work was still in the planning stages. For now, there was nothing but dirt and trees and grass. Airplanes had landed there before. Eddie Hubbard had done it when there was no airfield at all, and three months before, a professor of military tactics at the University had been the first to land on the newly plowed five hundred feet of dirt that made up the landing strip. "Just to prove he could," Dickson had rumbled, describing it. "But it's a good location. Visibility, prevailing winds—all the stuff those fliers care about."

Margot knew nothing about fliers, or flying, but on this vivid day, it was an enchanting spot. Beyond the trees the waters of Lake Washington glittered a deeper blue than the sky. Gray-and-white gulls swooped and squawked overhead, and the traffic noises of the city faded into the distance. She pulled up her fox collar and struck out toward the frozen strip of dirt. Blake, leaning on his cane, followed her.

"You can wait in the Essex, Blake."

"Oh, no! I wouldn't miss this for the world, Dr. Margot."

"I hope we're not late."

"I don't see any airplanes. I don't think we can be late."

"Well, then, I hope the pilot isn't late! Allison has worked so hard. I don't want to ruin this for her."

"I'm sure you won't. And besides, this project has been good for her. Put some roses in those pale cheeks!"

"You're right. The difference is remarkable. Very good to see."

They picked their way through the stubble of mown grass and tree stumps, and though it was too cold and dry for mud, Margot was glad of her boots on the rough ground. They had just reached the edge of the airstrip, and Margot was casting about for someplace for Blake to sit down, when she heard the engine. She turned toward the sound, which was coming not from the south, as she had expected, but from the west, flying into the wind. She shaded her eyes with both hands, trying to pick out the airplane against the dazzle of sunshine and the scattered clouds.

"There it is," Blake said, pointing.

"Where? Oh, yes! Now I see it! Oh, my goodness, Blake, it's so tiny!"

Indeed, the airplane looked to her like a child's toy that had been tossed into the air. Its double wings glinted as it swooped above the boats and barges in Lake Union, heading north until it reached the shore, then banking to the east as easily as if it were one of the seagulls slicing the wind with its white wings. The airplane was white, too, and as it came closer she could see the fabric of the wings flex and ripple in the wind. The engine grew louder, drowning out the cries of the birds that flitted out of its path.

Now Margot could make out the figure of the pilot, the dark helmet, the gleam of sunshine on heavy goggles, the dull glow of a leather jacket. There were men in coveralls cutting trees and pulling stumps on the far side of the little airstrip, and they put down their saws and axes and gathered to watch the airplane's approach.

It buzzed above the plowed strip once. Blake said, "Getting a look at the landing surface, I would judge."

"Oh. Golly, Blake. I hope it's safe."

The airplane rose above the trees at the end of the strip. It turned in the sky at an angle so steep Margot put her hand to her throat, where her pulse raced in anticipation. A moment later the craft leveled off, aimed toward the spot where she and Blake stood, and began to descend.

It looked so light, a ridiculously insubstantial assortment of canvas and rubber and metal. Margot could hardly believe such a fragile construct actually carried a human being. She knew, of course, that airplanes had been widely used in the war, that they flew and fought and crashed. She knew the injuries pilots could suffer. As she watched this airplane touch down, bounce wildly on the uneven ground, and barrel forward, coming to a rough stop just short of the end of the airstrip, she was amazed that the pilots who flew such things ever survived their accidents.

The men watching erupted in excited cheers. Margot found, to her amazement, that she was clutching Blake's arm. When she released it, they both laughed.

The airplane was no more than a hundred feet from her, the closest she had ever been to a flying machine. This, she reminded herself, was what Frank cared about. What he was studying at the army base in California. What Bill Boeing and the engineers who worked for him believed was going to transform the future. She tried to see the beauty in its ungainly lines, in its wires and wheels and battered propeller, but it wasn't clear to her at all.

The pilot unbelted his harness and stood up to put first one long leg and then the other over the side of the cockpit. He jumped down, and reached up with his right hand to thrust his goggles onto the top of his helmet. With his left hand—a little stiffly—he waved to the cheering men and then, turning, to Margot and Blake. He strode toward them over the uneven dirt, and Margot breathed, hardly believing her eyes, "Frank! It's Frank! He—Blake, he *flew the airplane!*"

Blake made some response, but Margot didn't hear it. Casting all dignity aside, she dashed forward, nearly tripping on the uneven ground, to meet Frank halfway. She stopped an arm's length away to take in the sight of him. He stopped, too.

His face was grimy, except for where the goggles had protected his eyes. The helmet completely hid his hair. He wore a heavy leather jacket that made his shoulders look bulky as mountaintops, and a pair of military coveralls and heavy boots. He grinned, his teeth showing white in his tanned face.

He said, "Surprise!"

"Oh, my God. Oh, Frank, my darling! A surprise in every way!" She stepped forward and into his arms. He held her tight for a few seconds before he bent his head to kiss her firmly, hungrily. He tasted deliciously of salt and fresh air and dirt, and she thought she might never let him go.

The men on the other side of the airstrip hooted their appreciation of the embrace, but Margot didn't care.

Allison stood behind the desk in Cousin Margot's reception room, watching people come in and out. A gray-haired, stern-looking woman introduced herself as Alice Cardwell, and marched herself straight back to the examining rooms. Margot smiled, and followed, murmuring to Allison that this was the matron of Seattle General. Other people from the hospital had come and gone, most just to shake Margot's hand, glance around with their eyebrows raised, and depart. Allison didn't know if the raised eyebrows were surprise or disapproval, or perhaps—the more likely, she thought—envy.

Surely no one in Seattle possessed a clinic that was more up-to-date, more modern, than this one. Everything was the best that could be found. Uncle Dickson had seen to that. He and Dick, with Ramona and Aunt Edith in tow, had been some of the first to appear. In a rare demonstration, Uncle Dickson had actually kissed Cousin Margot's cheek before he left, and murmured something to her that made her smile. Aunt Edith had said nothing, but Ramona had cooed over all the fine details, the curtains, the furniture, Cousin Margot's tidy office and elegant desk. Cousin Dick said, "Good work, Margot," in a gruff voice that made him sound a lot like his father, and they had smiled at each other.

The hospital matron emerged from the back with a restrained smile on her rather craggy face. She nodded to Allison and shook hands with Cousin Margot. She stopped long enough to sip a cup of tea, which seemed to please Margot, before she, too, departed.

Allison had gone in person to each of the businesses on Post Street to deliver special invitations to the tea. She was gratified that every one of them came: the Italian grocer, the cobbler, the owner of the diner two doors down. They stepped gingerly into the reception room as if afraid their boots would dirty the floor. They held their caps in their hands as they greeted her politely, nodded to Nurse Rossi, and shyly congratulated "Doc Benedict" on her handsome new building. They ate Hattie's cookies and drank cups of coffee. They declined seeing the examination rooms, but they inspected the windows and floors with critical eyes before taking their leave.

The guest who really mattered, of course, Cousin Margot's great surprise of the day, was Major Parrish. He looked very much as Allison remembered from her debutante party, tall and lean and dashing, except now he had an artificial arm and hand that really worked. He held a coffee cup with it, which seemed a marvel. He didn't say much, but his vivid blue eyes sparkled with what Allison assumed was pride. Pride in the new building, she thought, but also pride in Cousin Margot. Allison couldn't think why they weren't already married. The connection between them was nearly tangible. They were so bound together she was surprised they could walk in different directions!

Allison knew she must also glow with pride. The party was a quiet success, not flashy, like the debutante parties had been, but welcoming to all sorts of people. If it had been too fancy, the cobbler wouldn't have been comfortable. If it had been too simple, the doctors and nurses and the man from the *Times* might have thought it dull. It was just right. The reception room bloomed with the flowers people had sent, including an enormous bouquet from Uncle Dickson and Cousin Dick's office. The trays of refreshments had to be refilled several times. People were quiet at first, but then they relaxed, talking and laughing. Ruby was the only person who didn't seem to enjoy herself. She poured coffee and tea, but she hadn't smiled once, and she spoke to no one.

When three o'clock arrived, the hour when the tea was to end, there were still three people in the reception room, a trio of Chinese women in bright cotton jackets and straight wide pants. One of them, the oldest, tottered on improbably tiny feet, and Allison winced as she realized they were bound to half their normal size, fitted into embroidered silk shoes. The youngest woman translated for the others as they stood in the very center of the reception room, delicately sipping tea.

Allison said, "Take the cookie tray to these ladies, Ruby." Ruby gave her a resentful look, but she did as she was told. Each of the Chinese women accepted a single cookie, and the youngest, a girl hardly older than Allison herself, smiled and bobbed her head to Ruby and then to Allison.

Cousin Margot came back from showing Major Parrish something in the storage room and greeted the Chinese ladies warmly. "Mrs. Li, you look very well," she said to the youngest. "How are your children?" She shook hands with all three.

Major Parrish stood just behind her. Allison thought he had looked divine in his flying jacket and made both him and Margot laugh by saying so, but he had been eager to get out of his flying clothes and to wash the grime of his flight from his face and neck. There had been no time for him to go to his boardinghouse to change, so he had left everything in the storage room. His belted tweed jacket was a bit long for fashion, and he had no vest, but his dark trousers fit him well. He apologized for having no hat, having carried no valise with him—something about the weight of it. Margot had waved her hand and said it didn't matter at all. Allison thought he still cut a fine figure, and there was something appealing and masculine about the simplicity of his clothes.

The old Chinese lady, when she saw Major Parrish, hobbled

forward, smiling widely, nodding to him, and chattering in swift Chinese. Mrs. Li translated. "My grandmother wants you to know, Dr. Benedict, that she is looking forward to doing the flowers for your wedding."

At this, Cousin Margot flushed bright pink. Her mouth opened, but it seemed she couldn't think of any response. Behind her, Major Parrish also seemed struck dumb. There was a long, tense moment of silence, the couple staring at the old Chinese woman, the three Chinese ladies gazing back in sudden consternation. Ruby, rather stupidly, held the serving tray out from her body as if it offered some defense.

Allison stepped forward, bobbing her head carefully to the three guests, since that seemed to be the thing to do. "How kind of your grandmother," she said swiftly to Mrs. Li. "Please tell her how much the Benedict family appreciates that."

Mrs. Li smiled at Allison and thanked her. She spoke to her grandmother, and to the middle-aged woman, who must be her mother. A few moments later, they were gone, Mrs. Li and her mother supporting the old lady between them. Allison escorted them to the door, then closed it behind them.

When she turned back, Cousin Margot and Major Parrish had disappeared again. Only Ruby was left, unplugging the percolator, stacking the used cups and saucers into their carton. Allison said, "Gosh, that was awkward, wasn't it?"

Ruby glanced up. "Awkward? What was?"

Allison gave the maid a sour look. "Oh, Ruby! You're hopeless."

Margot said, "Sorry about the embarrassing moment, Frank."

She did look sorry, a furrow marring her smooth forehead, her narrow lips curving downward. He caught her hand and brushed her hair away from her jaw. "It doesn't matter, sweetheart," he said. "Don't let it spoil this day."

"It's not just the flower seller, Frank, though she's a dear old thing."

"She's grateful to you."

"I know. Her daughter does look well now, doesn't she? Though she hasn't returned to be examined in a long time."

"No money, I suppose."

Margot nodded, and the strand of hair fell forward over her jaw again. He put out his hand and brushed it back, not because it needed it, but because he loved the silky feel of her hair, loved the touch of her skin. "They've always paid me in embroidery. Or flowers," she added, and colored again.

"Well," he said, as lightly as he could. "The old lady has an excellent memory. She at least is hoping for a wedding."

"Not all our guests today feel the same."

"Don't they? Who objects?"

"*Object* is probably too strong a word." Margot turned away from him in the small space of her office. She grazed the surface of the desk with her fingertips, then the tops of the row of medical texts standing to one side. "Alice Cardwell—she's the matron at Seattle General—she asked if you were my young man, and when I said you were, she asked me if I was going to throw away my career by getting married."

She kept her back to Frank as she said these words. He said quietly, doing his best to keep the emotion out of his voice, "What did you tell her, Margot?"

"I said—" She turned abruptly to face him, jutting her chin in that way that made her look so much like her father. "I said it didn't have to be one or the other. That I could marry and still practice as a physician." Her eyebrows were up, her dark, direct gaze challenging. "Do you agree with that, Frank?"

"I've said that I do, sweetheart."

"Yes, but—we've hit a bit of a snag, haven't we? We have some things we have to talk about. To settle."

"Yes. But not today." He stepped closer to her, gazing down into her face. "Today was a big success, wasn't it?"

She smiled suddenly, and her dark eyes shone. "Oh, Frank!" she exclaimed. She found his right hand, his good hand, with her left. "What a wonderful surprise you gave me! I have a hundred questions, about your flying, about your being here—and there's been no chance to ask them! Are you staying? Does Mr. Boeing know you're here, and does he know—"

Frank, laughing, put his left arm around her waist, pulled her close, and kissed her lips. He felt them curve beneath his, and in a moment they were both chuckling. "Come on, Doctor," he said. "Let's get everyone back. I believe Blake is waiting."

She leaned forward, pressing her cheek to his chest for a long moment. She murmured, "It's so good to have you home."

Huskily, he said, "It's damned good to be here," and dropped a kiss on her fragrant hair.

CHAPTER 16

Blake drove Frank to his boardinghouse on Cherry, with a promise to be back to pick him up for dinner. Frank tried to protest that it wasn't necessary, that he could take the streetcar, but Margot laughed. "You'll never persuade Blake into that, Frank," she said. "He's so pleased to be driving again. Let's indulge him."

"All right." Frank nodded to Blake, who had insisted on getting out of the Essex to unload Frank's flying clothes and helmet. "I appreciate it, Blake," he said. "I'll be ready." Blake touched his fingers to his cap and held the door for Margot to get back in.

Ruby and Allison were in the car, and the back was loaded with the percolator and cups and trays. Over her shoulder, Margot watched Frank as the Essex pulled away. He saluted her, and she waved. She sighed with satisfaction as the car turned onto Broadway. Blake caught her eye in the mirror. "Very nice to see Major Parrish again."

"Yes, it is," she said and saw his lips curve with amusement at her understatement. She leaned forward. "Frank, a pilot! I couldn't believe my eyes."

"It's an impressive accomplishment," Blake said.

"Did you know?"

He coughed slightly. "Well, Dr. Margot. I suppose I can admit it now. Major Parrish wrote to me, a personal note, to explain what he was planning. He was afraid you might not think the 'delivery' at Sand Point was important enough for you to be present."

"Such drama! It's not like Frank, really, but it was marvelous to see." She felt Allison's eyes on her, and she leaned back again and smiled at her young cousin. "I had no idea he was flying airplanes himself. He was supposed to be studying them—but flying!"

"It's so exciting," Allison said. "I've never heard anything so romantic!"

Margot laughed. "In the usual run of things, I'm not much of a romantic, but in this case, Allison—I have to agree with you. It was a very romantic thing to do!"

In a cheerful mood, she and Allison went into Benedict Hall together. Ruby went with Blake to unpack the automobile by the back door. Margot started toward the stairs to change for dinner, while Allison said she was going to the kitchen to thank Hattie for her help. "That's a very good idea," Margot said. "Please tell her for me how much I appreciated it."

"I will," Allison said. She moved across the hall to the kitchen with a light step. Margot paused on the staircase, watching her. Allison had gained a little bit of weight, and it looked good on her, rounding her thin cheeks, swelling her bosom just a bit. Her color and her skin tone were vastly improved, but it was more than that. The tension that had gripped the girl when she first arrived, that quenched her appetite and depressed her mood, seemed to have lessened, perhaps even released completely.

Surely, whatever had happened on board *Berengaria* could not have been so serious as to cause it. Margot had no doubt Uncle Henry and Aunt Adelaide had greatly exaggerated its importance. Indeed, Margot thought, as she reached the landing, it was more likely to be a symptom. But a symptom of what?

"Oh, Margot, good!" Ramona emerged from the end of the

corridor where she and Dick had their bedroom and bath. "Dick's just telephoned from the office." She hurried forward in a flutter of blue wool crepe. Margot thought it might be a new dress, though she didn't always notice such things. It was loose, falling just to Ramona's ankles, not her usual style.

Ramona reached her, cheeks pink with hurrying. "It's your Uncle Henry and Aunt Adelaide," she said. "I know this isn't the best day, because you were so busy at the tea, but—they're coming here. Tomorrow! Mother Benedict doesn't—that is, I'm not sure what I should—"

Margot put up her hand to stem the flow of words. "Ramona. You've been wonderful while Mother hasn't been herself. Whatever you think is best will be perfect, I'm sure."

"Well, thank you, Margot. We do what's necessary, don't we? Now, do you think perhaps the bedroom over the big parlor? It hasn't been opened for years, Dick says, and it's probably a bit musty."

"Tell Blake. But he's to have the twins take care of it! He's not to go cleaning the room himself, but he'll know what needs to be done. On second thought, let me speak to him, and he can confer with you."

"So odd, that they would decide, all at once—"

"It *is* odd, and you're right, the timing is not the best. But perhaps they wanted to be with Allison for Christmas?"

"No doubt." Ramona paused, first putting her hand to her throat, then passing her fingers over her forehead. She drew a little breath and blinked. "Goodness, I suppose I shouldn't rush like that."

"Ramona—are you feeling well?" Margot moved her hand to encircle Ramona's slender wrist with her fingers. Her pulse was quick, but steady and strong.

"Oh, I feel marvelous!" Her sister-in-law blushed an even deeper pink, and though she drew her wrist away, she smiled up at Margot. "I just needed to catch my breath."

"Are you sure you—"

Ramona laughed. "Oh, Margot!" She leaned closer and said

softly, "We haven't told anyone yet, and we thought we should wait until we were sure. I wanted to tell you first, really, but we . . . Well. Dick and I are expecting!"

"Oh! Oh, Ramona—how nice for you both! For all of us! I don't need to ask if you're happy—it's painted all over you!"

Ramona giggled and breathed a contented sigh. Margot overcame her usual reserve to embrace her sister-in-law and send her on her way, a bit more slowly this time. Thoughtful, she went on to her bedroom to change.

She hoped the presence of the San Francisco Benedicts wouldn't be one burden too much for Blake. He had been back such a short time, and the leg still dragged, though he tried to disguise it. She would admonish him, of course, but she wasn't sure that would help. Perhaps she could persuade Father to take on more staff, at the very least another housemaid, and perhaps someone to assist in the kitchen. The twins and Hattie were busy all the time. She would speak to Father tonight, before Frank arrived.

And, she decided, as she ran a comb through her hair and smoothed the skirt of her black wool dinner dress, she would speak to Blake now. She took a critical glance in the mirror and decided she would do. Her cheeks, from the excitement of the day, were almost as rosy as Ramona's. She could never be bothered with cosmetics, although when she was younger her mother had tried to persuade her. She could see, though, that a little natural color was rather nice. Perhaps, before Frank arrived, she would smooth on the smallest touch of lipstick. There was a push-up tube somewhere in her dressing table. Her mother had presented it to her years ago, and she had never, before now, had the urge to use it. She didn't know if it was still good, but she could try.

She found Blake in the dining room, supervising the twins as they laid the table. She beckoned him out into the hallway. "Dick telephoned from the office just now," she said. "It seems Uncle Henry and Aunt Adelaide are arriving tomorrow from San Francisco."

"Are they? I don't think anyone expected them."

"No, it's quite a surprise. Ramona thought we should open the bedroom over the big parlor, but it will need airing."

"Yes, that's the best choice. I'll go up to open the windows, but keep the door into the hallway closed. No need to chill the whole house."

"Blake, please. Send the twins up to do it. And I'm going to ask Father to add some staff. This is going to mean a lot of extra work, I'm afraid."

"How long are they staying?"

Margot shook her head. "I don't know. Maybe Father does—Henry might have telephoned him."

"So odd that they're arriving with no notice."

Margot knew what Blake really meant. It was rude. To say nothing of presumptuous, though he wouldn't think of saying that himself. He would say it wasn't his place to criticize any Benedict, even ones whose manners didn't meet his standards. She said, beginning to be amused by the whole thing, "It's really odd, Blake, you're absolutely right. To be charitable, I suppose it's possible they simply wanted to see Cousin Allison at Christmas."

"Who wants to see me at Christmas?" Blake and Margot turned together on hearing Allison's voice. She had emerged from the kitchen and stood now at the foot of the staircase. Her cheeks had gone pale, and her eyes stretched too wide in her small face. "Who is it, Cousin Margot?"

It seemed such a straightforward thing, to tell the girl that her parents would arrive the next day, but Margot could see in Allison's expression that there was nothing simple about it. She had guessed, of course, though she couldn't have heard their whole conversation. Her face had closed down, and her body stiffened. Even her voice showed strain. "Who's coming?"

Margot wished she could put her arms around Allison and ease her tight shoulders, but the girl's very tension created a sort of chasm she didn't know how to bridge. She said, aware that her own voice sounded artificial, "Why, Cousin Allison, it seems your parents are coming to Benedict Hall. Tomorrow, in fact." Allison didn't move, but she seemed to shrink, to draw into herself, like a balloon with a puncture. Margot did her best to pretend reassurance. "Won't that be nice?"

Allison's voice carried no conviction at all. "Oh, yes, Cousin Margot. Certainly." She moved up the staircase on feet that dragged, all the lightness of her earlier step drained away in a heartbeat.

Margot watched her go. When Allison had disappeared she said, "Blake, whatever could be the matter with her?"

He was on his way back to the dining room, but he paused, leaning on the marble lion head of his cane. "I don't know," he said slowly. "But this news didn't make her happy."

Margot blew out a slow breath. "There's something going on in that family," she said. "And for that girl's sake, I'd better find out what it is."

Frank felt a wave of sadness at how much the elder Mrs. Benedict had faded over the past months. Gray had crept into her fair hair, dulling it to a metallic color. Her face bore shallow, dry lines that weren't there before. She didn't smile at Frank, though she greeted him with her usual stylized courtesy, calling him Major and asking briefly after his work.

Margot said, "Mother, Frank is a pilot now. I saw him fly an airplane into Seattle today."

Edith Benedict said in a pale voice, "A pilot. My, my. Isn't that interesting." She turned away from them and went to sit on the small divan, facing her husband in his armchair.

Margot showed no reaction, and Frank guessed she was used to her mother's inattention by now. Margot looked vibrant, her dark eyes shining, her smooth skin set off nicely by her black dress. She wore a long strand of pearls he had never seen before, and she had a pair of matching earrings clipped to her ears. He flattered himself that she had made a special effort because he was here. It both gratified and stirred him.

They were in the small parlor. Dick was doing the honors with a whisky bottle and a tray of cut-glass tumblers. The young cousin, Allison, sat at one end of the sofa, staring into the fire. Frank wondered if something was bothering her. She had been animated all afternoon, moving here and there to welcome guests, inviting them to take refreshment, managing coats and hats. Now she was so still that if her eyes hadn't been open, he might have thought she was asleep.

Dick handed him a glass of whisky. Frank saluted his host, and Dickson raised his glass in return. "Major, it's a treat to have you here again."

"Thank you, sir. It's certainly a pleasure for me."

"Blake tells me you're one of our flying men now. Well done."

"I was lucky to have the opportunity," Frank said. He had taken a straight chair and set one next to him for Margot. He felt her shift beside him, her arm brushing his. "No feeling like it, sir." He sipped Dickson's excellent whisky, thinking how good it was to enjoy it without really needing it.

"I envy you. If I were a younger man, I'd want to try it myself." Dickson drank, then glanced across at his wife, who gazed into space, as silent as Allison.

The younger Mrs. Benedict, Frank thought, was prettier than ever, her color high, her cheeks plump and smooth. Her radiance made her mother-in-law seem even paler by comparison. Ramona said, "It's so exciting, Major Parrish! But aren't you frightened sometimes?"

He inclined his head to her. "Any pilot who isn't sometimes frightened is a fool, Mrs. Benedict," he said. "But being in the air is the greatest excitement I've ever had." He glanced at Margot. "Worth the risk," he added.

"Blake and I watched Frank land this morning," Margot said. "It was beautiful to see."

Ramona asked, "What do you wear? Those leather helmets and long white scarves?"

"Ramona!" Dick said, but he cast his wife an indulgent look.

"Helmet, yes," Frank said, amused. "The scarves are just in films, I think."

"I saw *The Skywayman* down at the Guild Theater," Ramona enthused. "What those pilots could do! It was terrifying."

Frank judged it best not to mention that two pilots had crashed and died making that film. He said, "Well, those are stunt pilots. I just fly Jennys. Nothing fancy."

"Could you take me up?" Margot asked, surprising him into a laugh.

"Is it safe?" Dickson demanded.

"Yes, sir, I believe it's safe, but the Jennys belong to the army. I don't have one of my own."

"One day," Margot said.

"Maybe. One day."

Blake, attired now in his serving coat and a pair of pristine white gloves, came to the door to announce dinner. Everyone rose, and Frank stood back to allow the senior Benedicts to precede him, then the younger ladies. Allison didn't look up as she passed him, and she didn't speak.

In the dining room, Frank felt a quiver of unease when he saw that Preston's empty place was still being set. No one else remarked upon it, and the maids, when they began to serve, simply ignored it. Frank caught Margot's eyes and raised his eyebrows. Beneath the cover of the tablecloth, she touched his hand with her long cool fingers, a promise to explain later.

The Benedicts' cook had not, it seemed, improved her skills. The sweets she had made for the reception had been well received, but the cuisine at dinner was much as Frank remembered. The soup was a fish chowder, heavy with flour. The roast chicken was overdone, and the potatoes with it were the opposite. No one commented. Margot and her father, as well as the younger Benedicts, did their best with the indifferent food. Edith, Frank noticed, ate very little.

Allison Benedict ate nothing at all.

Margot was watching Allison, too, her heart constricting with pity. Allison had been at her best today, surely the bright, happy girl she was meant to be. That girl had disappeared again, taken refuge behind some private barricade, like a soldier under fire. Margot had no doubt it was not a happy place to be.

When dinner was over, Margot borrowed one of Dick's overcoats for Frank and wrapped herself in an old rabbit fur coat of her mother's. She told Blake they were going for a walk, and he nodded approval, holding the front door for them to pass through.

It was lovely to be alone together. Margot tucked her gloved hand under Frank's arm, and he pressed it tight against his side as they walked. The night was bitterly cold, every breath a little cloud of mist dissolving into the darkness. The December sky was clear and black and spangled with stars.

They crossed the road, skirting the foot of the water tower to walk on into the park. Idly, Margot told Frank about the flaw in the foundation of the clinic. He suggested remedies and promised to look at it next time he was home. They passed the Conservatory, its glass-paned walls gleaming with starlight, and they paused to admire the lunette window above the entrance. They stopped at the crest of the hill beyond it and gazed down at the city laid out beneath their feet. Here and there Margot saw houses with electric lights strung around their Christmas trees. Their little blooms of color were just visible through the shrubbery. "I like those," she said, pointing. "I suppose it's frivolous, but we should be frivolous at Christmas, don't you think?"

He put his arm around her shoulders and drew her close to his warmth. "My mother has a collection of German ornaments," he said. She let her head touch his shoulder, enjoying the smile in his voice. "Her family has had them for years. Brought them over on the boat, I suspect."

"You haven't seen your mother in a long time, Frank."

"Yes. Almost a year."

"Do they have a telephone?"

"No. At least none of the ranches around there did when I was there last."

She let the subject drop, though there were questions she

wanted to ask. There had been a girl. Elizabeth. Frank wouldn't talk about her in any detail, but there had been some ugly scene when he was first released from the hospital in Virginia, when his amputation was still agonizingly painful, and—at least in his mind—hideous to look at. Elizabeth, evidently, had fled in horror when she saw it.

Margot slipped her arm around Frank's waist and wondered if Elizabeth was sorry now. She wondered if Frank had seen her when he went home to visit, but she didn't want to ask. She didn't want to give the impression she was insecure, or worried, or—whatever the impression might be. It was, naturally, none of her business.

He turned his head and shifted the brim of his hat so he could press his lips to her forehead. "Margot," he said. His voice had gone husky in that way that made something come alive deep in her belly. "Sweetheart. We should talk things through."

"I know." She closed her eyes, breathing in the scent of him, soap, aftershave, the thick wool of the borrowed coat. "This is just so nice, this one moment. I wish we didn't have to worry about what comes next."

He put his hand under her chin and lifted her face so he could kiss her mouth. He did this firmly, demandingly, and her body seemed to melt against him of its own volition. "Tired of waiting," he whispered against her lips and kissed her again.

Breathless, she pulled back, but just a little. "Why should we wait, Frank? We can find a house, move into it together—"

His hand came up, his good hand, and stopped her lips with two fingers. "Don't. Don't even suggest it. It's not right."

Gently, she pushed his hand away, saying with asperity, "I'm not a conventional woman, Frank. You know that already."

"You're also not some silly film actress whose reputation doesn't matter."

"I don't care what people think."

He grinned down at her, looking so handsome in the starlight she could have wept with wanting him. "You do care," he said. "You have to, Margot. And so does your family."

She wriggled her shoulders, wanting to deny it, but knowing he was right. She said, after a moment, "All right, then. What do we do? I can't compromise my principles just because I want—" A small laugh bubbled in her throat, and she finished in a throaty whisper, "Just because I really, really want to go to bed with you!"

For long moments after that, neither of them could speak. They were embracing and laughing at the same time, and neither had much breath for speaking. At last Margot pulled back. "It's getting colder," she said. "My toes are freezing."

He kept one arm around her as they turned to walk back. She adjusted her hat, which had been knocked askew, and smoothed the ruffled wings of her hair with her fingers.

Frank said, "You haven't told me how the Women and Infants Clinic is coming along." She heard the caution in his voice, felt it in the slight tension of his arm around her waist. He was trying to make a start to the conversation they needed to have.

"It will open in February," she said. "Sarah Church is working there, arranging things. She's doing excellent work." She kept her eyes down, watching the icy pavement as they passed the tower and started across the street to Benedict Hall.

"Did Mrs. Sanger come to Seattle?"

It was a question freighted with implication. It was what lay between them, their essential disagreement as to how women's freedoms should be addressed.

Margot paused on the wide porch, just inside the circle of light cast by the windows, and looked up to meet Frank's eyes. She said simply, "She did come, Frank. She was awful."

He was startled into laughter. "Margot! I thought you admired her!"

She sighed and took a last look out into the starry darkness. "Oh, Frank. I should have known, I suppose, from her newsletter, but I thought people were misinterpreting her. That she meant something much more subtle. The way she spoke to Sarah, the way she talked about which populations most needed to curb their birth rate—it was ghastly. I had to apologize to Sarah for bringing Mrs. Sanger there, for putting her through that."

Frank bent, and kissed her cheek. "I'm sure Sarah knows you don't agree with that sort of nonsense."

"I made sure of that." Margot turned to the door, and Frank reached for the latch. "But, Frank," she said, "I'm still going to offer birth control services at the clinic. Education is the only hope those women have."

He stopped, his hand already on the door. His eyes were steady, very blue, full of affection. "I'm not good at putting things into words, Margot."

"You're not worried about your own reputation, Frank?"

"No." He took his hand from the latch and turned to lean his back against the door. "No, it's not that."

"Surely you don't think this information should be denied to women."

His mouth worked a little, twisting, quirking at one corner. "It's not that exactly. It's—" He made a frustrated gesture with his left hand, a movement that looked so natural it was hard to remember the hand was artificial. "Things are changing so fast. A man can't keep up." He bent to kiss her forehead. "I'm still just a cowboy, I guess."

"I may not be the right woman for you," she said, her heart swelling with a potent mix of longing and misery and love.

"Have to be," he said. He pulled the door open before she could ask him what that meant.

CHAPTER 17

At breakfast, when everyone was served, Blake came into the dining room and stood at the end of the table. "Miss Allison, would you care to accompany me to the train to meet your parents?"

She felt every eye upon her and didn't dare refuse. She said, "Yes, thank you, Blake," in a voice so small she was surprised he could hear her.

He nodded. "Very good, miss." He refilled several empty coffee cups and carried the pot out of the dining room.

Ramona said, "We were going to go Christmas shopping, weren't we, Allison?" in a bright tone. "Perhaps we'll postpone, so your mother can go as well. What do you think, Mother Benedict?"

Aunt Edith was staring at the empty chair on her right hand. Uncle Dickson prompted, "Edith?"

She started and said, "What? I'm sorry, did someone speak to me?"

Ramona repeated her suggestion. Aunt Edith turned her pale blue eyes to Allison. "Adelaide," she said.

Allison felt a rush of shame for her, that she should be so confused. She was about to correct her, but Aunt Edith went on. "Adelaide is such a strange woman. She came from a bad family, didn't she, dear?" Her gaze shifted to her husband at the far end of the table. "Do you remember? Her father was horrid, all those mistresses, and—"

"Now, Edith," Dickson said hastily.

Ramona said, "We shouldn't speak so about Allison's grandfather."

Allison, who had been staring miserably at the stack of griddle cakes on her plate—one of the things Hattie did well—glanced up at Ramona. "It's all right, Cousin Ramona. My mother told me about it."

Before anyone could alter the course of the conversation, Edith said, "Oh, yes, and he used to take these women out in public, to the theater and to restaurants. It made his wife furious, and her parents threatened to sue. It was a dreadful scandal. Everyone talked about it."

An embarrassed silence followed this elaboration of the tale, filled only by the scraping of knives and forks, the rustle of napkins, and the sounds of coffee being drunk. Allison took up her own knife and fork and began the process of slicing her griddle cakes into slivers. The slivers fell from the stack, one by one, to dissolve into nothingness in a pool of warm maple syrup.

She had used the spoon the night before, though there wasn't much in her stomach to eject. She had done her best just the same, then spent a quarter of an hour examining herself in the mirror. She saw, with a stab of panic, that her hips had swelled to twice their usual size. Her bosom stretched the lace border of her chemise, and her thighs had taken on enormous and humiliating proportions. She took the plaid frock out of the wardrobe and tried to put it on. It was so tight she couldn't fasten it.

She wished she could get rid of it. She even took scissors from the dressing table drawer, thinking she would cut the dress into ribbons, slip it out of the house and into the burn barrel. The trouble was that Ruby would know if the dress disappeared.

Ruby knew more about her wardrobe, about the stacks of sweaters and lingerie and stockings that had come with her from San Francisco, than she did herself.

And so, before accompanying Blake to the station, she tried on four dresses to find the largest. The one she settled on had a dropped waistline and a gathered skirt, with a narrow belt that fit just at the top of her hips. She cinched this firmly, and fastened her brassiere in its tightest hooks. Over everything she wore a long black sweater. She hardly ever wore the thing, a baggy creation with painted wooden buttons, but it covered her from shoulders to thighs.

She didn't feel grand and grown-up, riding in the back of the Essex, as she had done the day before. She felt like a dog about to be whipped. When Blake spoke to her, she gave monosyllabic responses, and he was soon as silent as she was. The Christmas decorations seemed to have proliferated from the day before, every front door festooned with greenery, every window boasting red and green and blue lights, but the pleasure they had given her turned to dread. There were just two weeks left until Christmas, and she feared her parents meant to stay the whole time.

Or perhaps they meant to drag her back to San Francisco. As much as she hadn't wanted to come to Seattle, now she wanted, with all her heart, to stay in Benedict Hall. But when her mother saw how fat she had gotten, how much she had let herself go, she supposed she would want her home in a trice, where she could once again bend her critical eye over every detail of her daughter's appearance and behavior.

She followed Blake into the station, shrinking into the baggy black sweater. The train was a bit late, and Blake said, "Can I fetch you something while we wait, Miss Allison? I believe they sell Coca-Cola at that kiosk in the corner."

She shook her head. "No, thank you."

"Are you feeling all right, miss?"

She looked up, seeing the concern in his dark eyes and in the drawing together of his thick white eyebrows. A servant, she reminded herself. Not a friend. Indeed, she had no friends. "I'm fine," she said. She feared she had sounded curt, or imperious, but Blake's face showed only sympathy and kindness. She felt a betraying tremble in her lips and a stinging in her eyes. She folded her arms tightly around herself and glared out into the cold, bright day.

It gave her an odd feeling to watch her parents come into the station. They could have been strangers, a couple she had never seen before. Her father was stocky and rather worn-looking, his hair more gray than she remembered, the pouches under his eyes more pronounced. Her mother looked small and faded, lost in the thick folds of her mink coat. Her neck was corded and hollow beneath her sharp chin. Her face powder accentuated the wrinkles bracketing her eyes and mouth. The hand she extended so languidly felt like bird bones inside its kid leather glove.

They touched their cheeks to hers. Her father said, "How are you, Allison?"

Her mother, pulling back from the brief embrace, eyed her narrowly. "That awful sweater, Allison. Surely you have something better to wear."

Allison said in resigned fashion, "Hello, Papa. Mother." And then, awkwardly, "This is Blake. Uncle Dickson's butler."

"You're the driver?" her father asked.

"Yes, sir," Blake answered and tipped his cap to them. "If you will give me your luggage tags, sir, I'll fetch the bags."

Adelaide dug in her handbag for the tags. As Blake took them from her gloved fingers, she said, sharply, "Be careful with the bandbox. The lid is loose."

"Yes, ma'am." Blake touched his cap again before he crossed the marble floor toward the luggage carts, where the Pullman porters were unloading bags and trunks.

Adelaide clicked her tongue. "I don't know why Dickson has to employ coloreds," she said. "There are so many people looking for work these days."

Allison said, "They're very good, Mother," though she dreaded her mother's thoughts on Hattie's cooking.

"That's not the point, is it, Allison? It's the way it looks. And this one walks with a cane."

Allison was about to reply, to defend him, but Blake was already limping back toward them, somehow managing his cane and two valises, the bandbox tucked securely under his arm.

Papa stepped forward and took one of the valises, and Blake nodded his thanks. "This way, please, Mr. Benedict," he said and led them all out of the station to the car.

The car, at least, met with Adelaide's approval. She settled onto the plush seat, her mink spilling around her, and said, "We should have one of these, Henry. A closed sedan. So much warmer, and no wind."

Her husband made a noncommittal sound and gazed out the windows at the streets of Seattle. "I expected rain," he said.

No one had a response to this. Blake drove at his usual deliberate pace, turning left on Broadway, rolling slowly up Aloha. Adelaide tapped her foot with impatience. "Can't we go any faster? Surely everyone's waiting for us," she said.

Allison took pleasure in saying, "Oh, no, Mother. Everyone is busy. Cousin Margot is at the hospital, and Uncle Dickson and Dick are at the office. Cousin Ramona is working on menus with the cook, and Aunt Edith is resting." The sideways twist of her mother's lips, her short, exasperated snort, gave Allison a little rush of satisfaction.

In the mirror she caught a glimpse of Blake's face. Though his features were impassive, his eyes, ever so briefly, met hers before they flicked away. Feeling exposed, she turned her head to gaze out at the mansions of Fourteenth Avenue.

Dinner at Benedict Hall, that night in December, felt to Allison like one of the minefields she had read about, where the doughboys hardly knew where they dared put their feet, and if they made a mistake they got blown to bits. Her mother, stiff and wary in one of the dark embroidered gowns she had bought in Paris, and with her hair pinned up in elaborate loops, tried to engage Aunt Edith over their glasses of sherry. Cousin Ramona did her best to smooth the conversational path, but there were long silences between the women, in which Adelaide looked offended, Aunt Edith looked vague, and poor Ramona looked desperate.

Papa had accepted a single glass of whisky, to be sociable, he said. Speaking slightly too loudly, he talked business with Uncle Dickson and Cousin Dick, and asked blunt questions about what Dickson saw in the future. Allison could see Uncle Dickson choosing his words carefully, trying to avoid criticizing while still offering insights into what he expected from the decade. "Prices are rising too fast, Henry," he said. "I don't trust it."

Her father objected. "Hell, no, Dickson. We're coming out of a depression, the aftermath of the war. Now is the time to take our profits, put them in the stock market so they can grow without our having to work so hard."

"Hmm. You could be right, but I have some concerns about the viability of the market."

"Nonsense, nonsense," Henry exclaimed, waving his glass.

Throughout, Allison perched on one of the straight chairs, a glass of lemonade held carefully in both hands. Her mother had frowned when she saw it and snapped, "What's that, Allison? What are you drinking?"

Blake, who had served it to Allison on a small tray, said with dignity, "If you'll permit me, Mrs. Benedict. Our cook makes lemonade especially for Miss Allison."

Allison said, "Thank you, Blake." Blake inclined his head and limped out of the room with the empty tray.

Adelaide said in an undertone, "I hope you haven't gotten used to special treatment, Allison." Allison felt Ramona's eyes on her and didn't answer. She did, however, drink the entire glass of lemonade before they all went in to dinner.

Cousin Margot reached home barely in time to change. Major Parrish was already there, looking handsome in a black dinner jacket. Margot hurried down the staircase and into the dining room just as they were all taking their seats. Uncle Dickson held Adelaide's chair for her, and Papa, taking the cue, held Aunt

Edith's, though he looked awkward doing it. Blake stood inside the door, watching as the newly hired maid, a plump middle-aged woman in a black dress and a professional-looking white apron, filled water tumblers. Cousin Margot slipped into her chair, saying, "Hello, Aunt Adelaide, Uncle Henry. I'm sure Ramona has made you feel welcome. I'm sorry I couldn't be here when you arrived."

Everyone murmured vague courtesies, and Leona came in with the soup tureen. She, too, wore a frilly white apron, though she had no black dress. Allison kept her head down, but she watched her mother from beneath her brows. Adelaide was assessing everything, she could see. She would take note of Leona's lack of uniform. She would probably count the silver place settings and make guesses at how much the candelabra cost. Allison saw her eyes sweep over the arrangement of Christmas greenery on the side table, and prayed she wouldn't say anything. Cousin Ramona had lamented the lack of flowers at this cold season, but had nevertheless done a pretty job with sprays of cedar and tiny scarlet berries cut from the shrubs in the garden.

The new maid, called Thelma, ladled soup from the tureen as Leona held it for her. She filled every bowl except the one at Aunt Edith's right. She paused behind the empty chair, the ladle in her hand. Leona had already placed the tureen on the sideboard. Blake cleared his throat, beckoned to Thelma, then led both maids back out into the corridor. Allison saw her mother look at the vacant place, the soup bowl resting, empty, on the charger. Adelaide said, "Are we waiting for someone?"

Allison had to avert her face to hide the laugh threatening to burst from her lips. She saw that Margot was watching her, and her cheeks flamed with sudden shame, but it was too late to save the moment. Ramona, trying as always to put a brave face on every situation, said, "Mother Benedict likes to keep Preston's place there, Aunt Adelaide. It comforts her."

Allison kept her eyes down, but she was sure her mother was embarrassed. She should have warned her about the empty place, of course. It didn't seem to matter much. It was only another skirmish in their prolonged conflict.

It wasn't even the first one of the day. She had gone into the bedroom prepared for her parents and found her mother gazing disconsolately into the mirror and stroking her abdomen. Allison had said, in imitation of Adelaide's frequent plaint, "You've gained weight, Mother." She added, in her sweetest tone, "It looks good on you."

Adelaide had shot her a look of the purest fury and resentment, but Allison pretended not to notice. "I came to let you know the family is gathering for drinks. You can come down anytime, and Blake will show you where." She escaped from the bedroom without waiting for a response.

In truth, she thought, as she dipped her spoon into the soup and sipped, Adelaide deserved it. Though she hadn't accused Allison of letting herself go, she had eyed every part of her with the steely glint that meant Allison was going to hear every detail later. It had felt good to fire the first shot in this particular sortie.

By the end of the evening, Adelaide had regained the advantage.

The dinner had gone smoothly enough, because Major Parrish and Uncle Dickson found a great deal to talk about. Uncle Dickson had all sorts of questions about flying and Jennys and the Boeing Airplane Company. Allison thought it was interesting, though none of the other women seemed to agree. Except Margot, naturally, but then Major Parrish was—or was supposed to be—her fiancé. Margot had questions, too, questions that sounded smart, about the effect of altitude on pilots' breathing and the limitations of their body weight. Allison listened to all this with admiration. She liked watching the way Cousin Margot and Major Parrish looked together. They leaned toward each other when they were speaking, and their eyes met directly. They laughed at the same things, and Margot's eyes were bright with happiness.

It all made Allison wonder if such affection could survive the disappointments of actual marriage. Of course, Uncle Dickson was unfailingly kind to his wife, no matter how strangely she behaved, but her own parents lived in a state of constant tension. They spent their lives waiting to catch each other in any infraction of the rigid contract that was their marital relationship. Was it possible they had once been in love with each other, the way Cousin Margot and Frank Parrish so clearly were? Or had her mother simply seen Henry Benedict as a chance to achieve the role in society she craved?

They all trooped back into the big parlor after dinner for coffee. It was a room Allison had barely glimpsed before this evening, but there were so many of them—nine in all—that Blake had decided the big parlor would be more comfortable. Allison saw the room through her mother's eyes, estimating the price of the long velvet divan, the massive cherry sideboard, the brocaded chairs, the cost of maintaining the large chandelier. The fireplace in this room was twice the size of the one in the small parlor, and when Blake and Thelma came in with coffee, they set their trays on an oval table inlaid with polished pink marble.

The room would have taken up an entire floor of their tall, skinny house in San Francisco, and Allison could guess that her mother would have a great deal to say about it when she was alone with her husband.

It was while they were drinking their coffee, Ramona trying to draw out her mother-in-law, Margot and Frank standing by the crackling fire, speaking quietly to each other, that Adelaide lifted her spear to mount a fresh assault.

"I do thank you, Dickson," she said in her brittle voice, "for taking Allison in this winter. I hope she hasn't been any trouble."

"Not at all," Uncle Dickson said. He was snipping the end of his cigar with little silver scissors, dropping the discarded end into the biggest cut-glass ashtray Allison had ever seen. He smiled at Allison. "It's been nice having a young person in the house."

Allison was surprised. It seemed to her that her uncle had barely noticed her presence.

"Well," Adelaide said. "Perhaps you're accustomed, having raised three children, but I think it can be a terrible strain."

"Hardly know she's there," Dickson rumbled, and struck a thick match to light his cigar.

"Really? She can be so noisy. Even as a little girl, her voice was so loud, sometimes I wanted to put a pillow over my head."

"Mother, don't talk about me like that," Allison said in a low voice.

Adelaide's laugh sounded just as if someone had thrown a glass into the fireplace. "Oh, Allison, do have a sense of humor, for pity's sake! You were always a handful, you know that."

"Now, Adelaide," Henry said, and Allison cringed. Whenever her father stood up for her, it was like throwing a gauntlet at his wife's feet. She saw the stiffening of her mother's neck and heard the resentment in her voice. She was aware of Cousin Margot's sudden attention, and she wondered if she could hear it, too.

"Oh, Henry, how would you know? You were always at the office, or off at one of your business dinners!" Adelaide smiled at everyone in an effort to make her complaints seem playful. "You know how it is, don't you, Edith? The men are off making money, and we women are left to manage the children."

Aunt Edith looked up, startled at hearing her name. She didn't respond, and Allison was fairly certain she hadn't been following. Her mother, though, seemed not to understand this.

"And for you, so many children! You must have been exhausted. But perhaps, with three of them, they entertained each other. That must have been nice."

Allison felt the sudden tension that gripped the room. Margot's face had a fixed look on it, as though someone had said something offensive. Even Uncle Dickson, meeting his daughter's gaze across the room, looked oddly sad. Or was it angry? It was hard to tell, the way his bushy eyebrows drew together, making a straight line across his forehead.

Adelaide, oblivious, pressed on. "I thought it would be easier during Allison's debutante year, but there were so many invitations, and fittings, and all the dances and parties. I never had a moment to myself, and then there was her Grand Tour—"

Allison interrupted her, muttering, "Mother. I never wanted any of that."

Her mother's brittle laugh rang out again. "Oh, Allison, don't be ridiculous! What girl doesn't want that?" When Allison didn't answer, Adelaide went on, "You were a success, too, if I do say so myself. Your picture was always in the papers, even though there were prettier girls."

Major Parrish spoke up. "Hard to believe there were girls prettier than Miss Benedict." Margot gave him such a sweet smile that Allison's heart contracted.

But her mother was in full attack mode. "So gallant of you, Major, but we women have to be objective about these things."

Uncle Dickson murmured, "Eye of the beholder," but Adelaide paid no attention.

"Of course, I had to work to keep her slim," she said. Allison dropped her gaze to her coffee cup, turning it and turning it in her hands, but she could *feel* Cousin Margot stiffen at this volley. "I can see you've been feeding my daughter well, Dickson!" This was uttered gaily, as if in thanks. "I suspect your cook of tempting her with all sorts of treats!"

Even Aunt Edith lifted her head at this remark. She said, "Oh, Hattie," as if in answer to some unasked question. "Poor Hattie. A dear woman, but a terrible cook."

It was such an odd, even inappropriate, thing to say that even Adelaide Benedict was silenced. Major Parrish, in his courteous, quiet way, set down his cup and said, "I hope you will all excuse me. I have to be on my way in the morning. Deliver the airplane back to the army. Thank you for dinner, Mrs. Benedict."

Aunt Edith made a vague, trembly gesture with one pale hand. Major Parrish said, "Sir," with a nod to Uncle Dickson. Dickson hefted himself out of his chair to shake the major's hand. "Good to see you again, son. Won't you let me call Blake to drive you?"

"No, sir, thanks. Enough work for Blake to do here. I can catch the streetcar."

"I'll walk you out," Cousin Margot said.

Ramona and Dick both said their farewells, and Papa stood up to shake the major's hand before he and Margot left the room. When the door of the big parlor had closed behind them, Adelaide said, "Such a handsome man. Is he going to be your son-in-law, Dickson?"

Uncle Dickson settled himself back into his chair with a sigh and picked up his cigar from the ashtray. "I hope so, Adelaide," he said, reaching for a match to relight the cigar. "I expect that will be up to Margot. That girl has a mind of her own."

It was said with unmistakable pride. Allison heard it in Uncle Dickson's voice, and recognized it in his small, satisfied smile.

Her mother missed the point entirely. "We certainly understand that, don't we, Henry? Allison always has to have everything her own way."

Allison shrank back into the corner of the divan and wished she could disappear.

CHAPTER 18

The weather had changed dramatically since the night before. Margot stepped out onto the porch with Frank, pulling her collar high under her chin. The stars were invisible, and even the light of a half moon was obscured by the blanket of cloud that rolled in to embrace the city, softening its rooftops and chimneys, wrapping its steeples and the top of the water tower in gray, damp folds. "Will you be able to fly tomorrow?" Margot asked.

Frank was shrugging into his camel's hair overcoat, throwing a plaid wool scarf around his neck. He carried his Stetson in his hand. "It depends on how low the cloud cover is."

"It's so cold, though, Frank." She moved close to him, loath to let him go. His body felt warm and strong, and she could hardly restrain herself from pressing against him.

"Best for flying," he said. "Cold air is denser. More lift."

"You'll be back soon?"

"Christmas Eve," he said. "Already have my ticket." He put his arm around her shoulders and kissed her. "We'll both do some thinking, Margot."

"Yes." She kissed him back, and then, on an impulse, slipped her hands under his coat and hugged him with both her arms. "Although I've already—"

He interrupted her by kissing her again, then whispering against her mouth, "I know, sweetheart. Give me a little time."

"I wish you could just stay in Seattle."

"Someone has to fly the airplane," he said and chuckled. "It's a hell of a lot of fun, Margot."

She pulled one arm from behind his back and tweaked the lapel of his dinner jacket. "So I gather! You're like a boy with a brand-new toy."

He grinned down at her, looking very boyish indeed. "Yup."

Reluctantly, she released him. As she slid her arm from beneath his coat something papery crackled against her elbow. "I'm sorry we couldn't have gone out tonight, Frank, had a bit of time for just the two of us, but I didn't like to leave Ramona to deal with Uncle Henry and Aunt Adelaide on her own. She's been marvelous since—well, you know, since Mother fell apart. I don't like to take advantage."

"I know. It's all right."

"My aunt is awful, isn't she?" she murmured, smoothing his scarf with her fingers. It didn't need smoothing, but she couldn't resist touching him, even if it was just with her fingertips. "She looks starved, but you saw her at dinner—she ate everything in sight, even Hattie's lumpy creamed spinach."

"Maybe thinness runs in the family," he said. "Your little cousin isn't much more than bones herself."

"You should have seen her when she first arrived! I know I wrote you. She frightened me, frankly, but she looks much better now. The food at Benedict Hall isn't always the best, but she recently started eating much better."

"Not tonight," he said, arching one dark eyebrow.

"No. I saw that, too. I worry that all her progress will be destroyed. As you saw, her mother's hard on her."

"It's rotten," he said. "Poor kid has no one to stand up for her."

Margot moved back a little and hugged herself against the cold. "She has me."

"Good," Frank said. His eyes twinkled gently in the faint light of the moon. "Lucky girl."

"There's a diagnosis, something called anorexia nervosa, though I'd never heard of it until I went looking. The clinical research is awfully sketchy, but it seems some people—especially young girls—stop eating. At worst, they die. At the least, they harm their health, sometimes permanently."

"Why do they do that?"

Margot shook her head. "I've been asking myself that question. There are three different ideas, from three different doctors."

"You'll figure it out," he said with confidence.

She gave a small, tired chuckle. "That's what Blake said. You both may have placed too much confidence in my skills."

He kissed her one more time, a lingering, longing kiss. "I'll see you Christmas Eve," he said softly. He put his arms around her to draw her close. She pressed her cheek to his shoulder and felt again the crackle of paper.

"You have something in your pocket, Frank," she said, drawing back.

He frowned, and reached into the pocket to draw it out. It was a long envelope, creased and stained. He turned it over in his hand to read the address. "Oh! Forgot about that."

"Something important?"

He shrugged. "Don't know. Haven't opened it."

"Why?"

He hesitated, looking past her into the dim silhouettes of the shrubberies. "Not sure I want to," he said.

"Have I—am I intruding, Frank?" They stood a little apart now, Frank with his hat in his hand, Margot with both hands under the fur collar of her coat. She wished she had never mentioned it, let the envelope stay unnoticed—perhaps forgotten—in his pocket.

He thrust his hand back into his coat pocket, and she heard

the rustle of the unopened envelope against the silk lining. His jaw muscle flexed, but a moment later he turned his gaze back to hers and laughed a little. "It's silly," he said. "Mrs. Volger was holding this for me. It's from Elizabeth."

"Oh. Oh, I see." It was her turn to look away, to gaze at the mist-shrouded water tower, its brick surface nothing but shadow now, all detail lost in the darkness. She would have felt better if he had opened the letter, read it, and thrown it away. The act of keeping an unopened letter seemed to carry some sort of weight, have meaningful implications. Elizabeth's horror over his ruined arm had been part of the reason he had never wanted Margot to examine it.

She was not so delicate as Elizabeth. She had seen nearly everything, and when she looked at his arm that night in the operating theater, all she could think of was how to repair the wound that was causing him such pain. Did that make her unfeminine? Possibly.

"Margot—I may never open it."

She turned back to him, and she heard the slight edge that crept into her voice too late to soften it. "Of course you will, Frank. When you're ready. She was—or is—someone important to you."

His face, as she watched, seemed to harden. Of course, the memory must still hurt. Elizabeth's reaction to his wound, while he was still in the hospital in Virginia, had been a nasty moment for him, a cruel punctuation to the suffering he had already experienced. But it worried her, that letter, and the uncharacteristic impulse that made him carry it in his pocket. He must mean to read it eventually. And what would it say? That Elizabeth was sorry, that she wanted to make it up to him? That she still cared?

It hadn't been so long, after all. Not quite two years since Frank left the hospital and came to Seattle, hurt, bereft, in constant pain and persistent worry. It was all different now. He had a fine job, and his arm was repaired. The prosthesis worked well. He had prospects again.

He said only, "Yes. You remember."

"Of course."

He bent to kiss her one more time, a cooler kiss this time, as if he were distracted. Perhaps it was merely that his mind had turned to the flight tomorrow.

Or perhaps, she thought dismally, his mind had turned to the letter, to what it might say, to how he might respond. Perhaps he was thinking about Elizabeth.

She feared the shameful jealousy that burned in her heart. She didn't want it to show in her face or in her voice. She made herself say, with as much dignity as she could command, "Safe journey, Frank."

"Thanks." They gazed at each other for a long, uncomfortable moment, and then he was gone, striding down the walk, out through the gate, off toward Aloha. Margot watched him until he turned the corner and disappeared from her sight into the thickening fog. It would not do, of course, to run after him. Her dignity would truly be in shreds if she did that. She felt the urge just the same, and had to force herself to turn back toward the house and go inside.

The family and their guests were still gathered in the large parlor. Blake was just coming out with the coffeepot, the good silver one. He stopped at the foot of the staircase as Margot closed the front door. "Do you want coffee, Dr. Margot?"

She shook her head. "Thanks, Blake. I think I'll leave them to it and just go to bed."

"I could have driven the major home."

"Father offered that, but Frank didn't want to trouble you." She sighed, thinking of Frank on the streetcar and, even more, in the air tomorrow, borne aloft by those preposterously fragile bits of wood and wire and metal.

Blake said gently, "Try not to worry, now. Major Parrish will be back before you know it."

"Oh, I know," she said. "I know that, Blake, but—" She felt an urge, as irrational as the one she had just resisted, to tell him about the damned letter, to see if he had some idea what it might mean. How strange that she, surrounded by people as she was in Benedict Hall, had no one to talk to about her romantic troubles! What normal woman had no friend to confer with, to turn to for advice? She rubbed her forehead with her fingers. "Never mind," she said. "I just need to sleep. Could you tell them for me?"

"Of course. I'm sure they'll understand. Rest well, Dr. Margot."

"Thank you. Good night."

As she climbed the stairs, the murmur of conversation reached her from the big parlor. Aunt Adelaide's voice sliced through the others with the piercing quality of a cat's screech. It rose up the stairwell to pursue Margot into her bedroom. It was a relief to shut her door and close the sound away.

When she had shed her dinner dress and wrapped herself in her dressing gown, she went to the window. She settled into the window seat, pulling back the curtains so she could gaze out, past the winter-dry skeleton of the camellia, into the shifting mist that hid the park and the water tower from her view. Frank should be back at Mrs. Volger's by now. She wondered if it was possible for him to feel as lonely as she did.

More likely, she thought, he was eager to return to Sand Point and his airplane, to rise above the trees and the lakes and the houses, to fly off over the mountaintops to the warm California valley full of other men just like him—aviators, engineers, soldiers. He couldn't know how she hungered for him. Should she have told him? Was that what women did? Or did they instinctively, as she was doing, hold something back to protect that small, tender spot in the heart where love resided?

And why, oh why, was Frank carrying Elizabeth's letter in his pocket?

She let the curtain fall, rose from the window seat, and crossed the room to her bed. As she extinguished the lamp and pulled the comforter up over her shoulders, she reflected that she was like two different women living in one body. She couldn't imagine not being a physician. She couldn't abandon the passion and dedication that had always ruled her life. But she was also a woman in love, in the manner of romantic stories, the most old-fashioned stories of all. That woman couldn't bear the idea of life without Frank. She longed to find a way to merge both those women into one.

For some reason that line of thought brought her back to Allison. She released her worry over what would happen between her and Frank and fell asleep worrying about what was wrong between Allison and her mother.

She had been asleep for perhaps an hour when she woke to shouting in one of the rooms down the hall. In that first, heavy sleep of the night, she wasn't sure what she was hearing. Accustomed to responding instantly to the telephone or to her alarm clock, she was out of bed and into her dressing gown almost before she realized she was on her feet. She threw open her door just in time to see Allison, her hair mussed and her cheeks flaming, charge out of her bedroom and down the stairs. The front door banged open, and an icy draft swept into the house and up the staircase.

Margot the physician knew better than to run in an emergency, but she strode so swiftly down the corridor it was almost a run. The door to Allison's room stood open, and inside, huddled on the floor, wailing like a cornered cat, was Aunt Adelaide. She bent forward from the waist, her legs crumpled beneath her. Her dun hair tumbled every which way, with hairpins spilling onto her shoulders.

Margot reached her. "Aunt Adelaide, what's the matter? Are you hurt?"

The face Adelaide turned up to her was a mask of bitterness. Her carefully painted eyebrows were smudged, and tears made rivulets through the powder on her cheeks. She sobbed, open-mouthed, and Margot thought she was very near a fit of hysterics. "My arm!" she cried. "That little bitch broke my arm!"

Margot would have said she was long past being shocked by anything she saw or heard, but somehow, hearing her aunt apply such a vicious phrase to her own daughter made her pull back in disgust. Adelaide, still weeping, pleaded with her. "Aren't you going to help me? You're a doctor! Help me!"

She was braced, shaking, on her right hand. Margot could see, even from where she stood, that her left arm was indeed broken. She didn't need to palpate the forearm to know that it was fractured, both the radius and the ulna clearly deformed, and the left hand flopping, useless, over her thigh.

A voice from the doorway said, "What's happened? Where's Miss Allison?"

Margot glanced over her shoulder and saw Ruby, wide-eyed with alarm. She wore a thick chenille robe that fell to her toes, and her hair was braided for the night. "Ruby, there's been an accident. Allison ran out the front door. Could you get your shoes and see if you can find her? I'm going to get Mrs. Benedict up on the bed."

At this Adelaide wailed louder, and Margot repressed an impulse to slap her. She inched around her to lift her up, one hand under her good arm and the other, gingerly, under the opposite armpit. This caused Adelaide to screech that she was killing her, that her arm was shattered, and other complaints Margot didn't bother to try to understand. Ruby had run for her shoes. Uncle Henry appeared in the doorway, at least five minutes after he should have, in Margot's opinion.

"Uncle Henry," she said in a flat voice. "We'll need the motorcar. Could you go to the garage and tell Blake?"

She was settling Adelaide, whose sobs were subsiding into a steady, irritating whimper, onto the edge of Allison's bed. Adelaide was still in her dinner dress, and she had torn the hem of it. She looked down at her legs and moaned something about having laddered her stockings, but Margot ignored this. Loena appeared, and Margot said, "Loena, good girl. Stay with Mrs. Benedict while I change, will you? We're going to the hospital."

Loena's eyes were as wide as Ruby's, but she looked more excited than alarmed. "Yes, Miss Margot," she said. She crossed the room and stood beside the bed, but Margot noticed she didn't stand close enough to touch Adelaide. "Oh, gosh," she exclaimed, gazing down at Aunt Adelaide's arm. "That must hurt like blazes!"

Adelaide groaned. Margot was on her way out of the room, saying, "I'm sure it does, Loena. Just keep Mrs. Benedict from falling off the bed, will you?"

"Yes, miss. Gosh!"

Margot was used to dressing quickly. In moments she had on a skirt, sweater, stockings, and shoes. She ran a comb through her hair without bothering to look in the mirror, and went back down the corridor. She encountered Dick in the doorway of Allison's room. He was frowning, obviously reluctant to go in. He turned with an expression of relief when he heard her step on the hard carpet. "Margot, what's happened?"

"I'm not sure yet, Dick, but I'm going to have to take Aunt Adelaide to the hospital. Her arm needs setting, and I can't do it here. Uncle Henry's gone to call Blake."

"Ramona's awake, of course—I'm sure everyone is!—but I told her she shouldn't get up."

"That's right. There's nothing she could do. Blake and I will manage. I expect Father and Mother are up now, too, and everyone else."

He nodded and was gone in an instant. Glad, she thought, to get away from Adelaide's whining. She wished she could. She said, "Loena, I'll take over now. Could you go to Mrs. Adelaide's room and find her coat?"

She had been right about everyone being awake. The only person missing, as she maneuvered Adelaide down the corridor and onto the staircase, was her mother. Even Ramona had given up trying to sleep. She stood at the bottom of the staircase, wrapped in powder-pink flannel and wearing knitted slippers. As Margot shepherded Adelaide down the stairs, Ramona said, "The Essex is waiting in front, Margot. I saw it from my window."

"Good. Thanks, Ramona."

"Here's Hattie. I'll ask her to make some cocoa, calm everyone down."

Margot cast her sister-in-law a look of admiration. Ramona behaved as if handling a frantic household were just what she had been born for.

Loena, Leona, and a surprised-looking Thelma were gathered in the hall, hugging themselves against the chill. Hattie stepped forward to meet Ruby just coming in. "Did you find Miss Allison? Oh, that poor child!"

Ruby shook her head. "I don't know what to do now."

Margot and Adelaide had just reached the foot of the stairs. Margot said, "Get dressed, Ruby, and keep looking. Ask Mr. Dick to help you." Adelaide cried out as Margot draped her mink coat over her shoulders, but Margot said only, "You need your coat. It's cold outside."

Henry was searching the dining room and the two parlors for Allison, but with no success. They all stood in the hall, a shocked audience in dressing gowns and overcoats, as Margot and Adelaide, who was moaning steadily, moved out the front door, across the porch, and down the steps to the gate.

Dickson followed them. He said, "Shall I go with you, daughter?"

"Thanks, Father. Blake and I can manage. I'll take Aunt Adelaide to the accident room. We should be back in an hour or two."

Blake held the car door and assisted Margot to seat Adelaide, then went around to the driving seat. Margot, as she climbed in herself, said, "Father, Allison is outside somewhere, all alone."

"I'll call the police," her father said.

Uncle Henry said, from the porch, "No! No police." Dick, standing beside him, gave him an odd glance.

Dickson scowled but didn't comment. He closed the automobile door and was back through the gate and up the walk before Blake pulled away from the curb. Margot sat on Adelaide's right side, and did her best to ignore her aunt's groans and gasps. She spent the fifteen-minute drive calculating how much codeine

phosphate she dared inject into a woman who probably weighed
no more than ninety pounds.

His patience had paid off. His instincts must be as sharp as
they ever were, which was pretty damned sharp. In the face of a
dearth of other things to take pride in, that bolstered his resolve
and strengthened his self-respect.

After a revolting dinner at the Compass Center—greasy soup
and a roll so stale it could cost a man a couple of teeth—he had
felt the tug of his obsession, that intuitive call to come here
again, to stand in the cold fog. He had lost count of how many
nights he had spent this way, wrapped in his hand-me-down coat,
charity scarf obscuring his face, gaze fixed on the windows and
doors of Benedict Hall. Waiting. Waiting for his chance.

At first he thought he might have made a mistake. It seemed
like any other night, except for having to endure watching Margot and her one-armed cowboy on the front porch. They could at
least have had the decency to go to the back if they were going to
carry on that way, but Margot had never had the slightest sense of
propriety, or even a modicum of consideration for the family
name. It had been tempting to follow Parrish down the street,
but that wouldn't serve his purpose at all.

Instead, he lounged against the cold bricks of the tower and
waited. He didn't know what he was waiting for, exactly, but he
had a feeling, and despite the chill of the December night, it energized him, kept him rooted there, watching.

His reward came an hour after Parrish left and Margot went in-
doors. Someone, someone whose voice he didn't recognize, set
up a god-awful caterwauling. It caused lights to flick on in nearby
houses and doors to slam at Benedict Hall. He knew what a cry of
pain sounded like, of course. He had plenty of experience with
pain. These shrieks were caused by pain, but intensified, he was
certain, by outrage and resentment. Something dramatic had
happened in Benedict Hall, something that had set the house by
its ears.

Whatever it was, it was precisely what he had been waiting for. It propelled the young cousin straight out of the house. Pretty little Allison, hatless, coatless, running as if pursued by the devil, flew out the front door, leaving it open to the cold. She dashed down the walk and out the gate, leaving that standing open as well. Hair askew, flimsy dress rippling around her, she barreled across the road.

Straight into his waiting arms.

CHAPTER 19

The radiographs confirmed for Margot what she had already observed, but there was more. Aunt Adelaide's arm was fractured, the two bones of the forearm snapped cleanly in two. Margot also saw, studying the image, that Adelaide Benedict's bones were shockingly fragile, a condition that could only show on the radiograph if it were already far advanced. It would have taken very little strength to break them.

Adelaide, even after being given a hypodermic, wept and complained throughout the setting of her arm and the application of plaster of Paris. She rolled her head to and fro on her pillow, and the nurses in the accident room raised their eyebrows at one another.

"Dr. Benedict, do you have other orders?" The night nurse stood close beside the bed, keeping watch that Adelaide's antics didn't cause her to slide right off the edge.

"Yes," Margot said wearily. "She'd better have a sedative. Four ccs of valerian tincture, Nurse. I'll stay with the patient while you prepare it."

"Yes, Doctor."

Margot bent over the bed. She was tempted to just strap the woman down and leave her, but she forced herself to speak kindly. "Aunt Adelaide. Your arm is set now, and you've had a good dose of codeine phosphate. You shouldn't be in pain."

"She broke my arm," Adelaide whimpered. "She threw the spoon at me, and then she broke my arm!"

"Spoon?"

"Yes, the spoon! I gave her one just for herself, but she won't use it, and she—she—"

Margot said, "Never mind, Aunt Adelaide. Never mind that now. Here's the nurse, and she's going to give you something to help you relax. I'm going to telephone to Benedict Hall to see if Allison is all right."

"She has this filthy pamphlet on her dressing table, this obscene thing, and she said—"

"All right, Adelaide," Margot said, feeling her temper fray to the breaking point. "I'm the one who gave Allison the pamphlet. There's no need to be angry at her about that."

Adelaide glared around the accident room as if looking for someone who would listen to her complaint. "She *broke my arm*," she cried in her piercing voice. "My own daughter! *My arm!*"

Margot took a slow breath through her nostrils and stepped back from the bed. The nurse gave her a questioning look, and Margot nodded, not trusting her voice. When Adelaide had swallowed the valerian tincture, grimacing at the bitter taste, she lay back on her pillow, seeming a bit calmer already. Margot didn't trust this sudden change, and she motioned to the nurse to resume her position on the other side of the bed.

"Aunt Adelaide," she said. Adelaide stared at the ceiling, her thin lips pressed so tightly together they almost disappeared. "Aunt Adelaide, the X-ray of your arm shows your bones are very weak. The condition is called osteoporosis, and it may have come about because you're so thin. If Allison even bumped your arm, the bones could have broken."

"She didn't *bump* me," Adelaide grated. "She threw the spoon at me. I picked it up, and told her to use it, and she pushed me! She broke my arm!"

"What was she supposed to do with the spoon?"

The valerian began its work, and Adelaide's eyelids trembled and drooped. "She's getting fat," she said. "I let her come to Seattle—"

Margot's resolve evaporated. "You forced her to come to Seattle, Aunt Adelaide. She didn't want to."

Adelaide spoke with her eyes closed. "She had to. Everyone's talking about her. She's ruined."

"Why?" When there was no answer, Margot spoke more sharply. "Adelaide, why is Allison ruined?"

"Naked," Adelaide mumbled. "She was naked. God only knows what else . . . Everyone's talking."

The nurse put a hand to her mouth to hide her smile. When it was clear Adelaide had fallen asleep, Margot said, "I didn't understand a word of that, did you?"

The nurse dropped her hand and bent to smooth the pillow beneath Adelaide's head. "It may not mean anything, Doctor. She won't remember saying it, either."

Adelaide's sleeping face looked pitiful, the layers of cosmetics like a film of dust settled across her gaunt features. Automatically, Margot took a clean washcloth from a nearby basin and began to wipe away the rouge and powder. The nurse held out her hand to relieve her of the cloth. "Let me do that, Doctor."

"Thank you. I think I'd better admit her. It would be hard to get her home in this condition, and I'd like to bring in our family physician, ask him to do a thorough examination."

The nurse nodded, dropped the cosmetic-stained washcloth into the basin, and set off across the accident room to call for a gurney. Margot stood where she was, gazing down at Adelaide. Her aunt's slight body barely made a silhouette beneath the brown hospital blanket, and her face, in repose and free of paint, more resembled that of a starving child than an ill-tempered middle-aged woman. "What's going on with you?" Margot whispered. "Why are you all so unhappy?"

Adelaide exhaled a long, relaxed sigh, and slept on.

Allison gasped a lungful of foggy air. She wanted only to escape, to flee from her mother's accusing shrieks, to evade Ruby's restraining hands. She didn't stop to close the door or to latch the gate. The mist enveloped her and softened the raised voices from the house. She dashed headlong into the street and across it without so much as a glance left or right.

The cold air shocked her out of her incipient hysterics, but one of the Louis heels of her evening shoes caught on the far curb. She lost her balance, stumbled, and began to fall, throwing out her hands to catch herself on the concrete of the sidewalk.

What her hands encountered was the bulk and heat of a man's body, swathed in some stiff, slippery fabric. Her hands gripped the material without meaning to. Her face, propelled by the momentum of her fall, collided with his chest.

Strong arms encircled her before she could push herself back. Hard hands gripped her close, as if in an embrace, but it wasn't one of safety or of desire. The moment she felt the encircling pressure of his arms, she knew there was danger. He squeezed her against him and blew sour breath down the back of her neck.

He hissed, "At last!" in a hoarse voice that made her blood— so recently running high and hot—turn instantly to ice.

Her tears of fury cooled swiftly in the night air. She choked, "Let me go! Sir, please!" She beat at his shoulder with her hands and tried to scrabble away with her feet. The heel she had tripped on broke off and dangled precariously from her shoe.

His laugh was more a growl than a sound of amusement. He loosened his grip, but kept hold of her wrist with one hard hand.

Allison drew back as far as she could and stared at him. This new threat jumbled in her fevered brain with what had just happened in Benedict Hall.

She had struck her mother. She hadn't done it on purpose, but it had happened just the same. Adelaide had been brandishing the spoon, threatening to stick it down Allison's throat with her own hand. Allison batted it away, with no more intent than if she were swatting at a buzzing hornet, but something had snapped. She heard it break, and so did her mother. They both froze for one horrible instant, gazing at Adelaide's forearm, and then Adelaide began to scream.

Allison might have tried to help her mother, might have gone in search of Cousin Margot to set everything right, but she didn't trust herself to do it. What really drove Allison out of Benedict Hall was the impulse that swept over her, the nearly irresistible urge she felt to put her two hands around her mother's bony neck and squeeze until the shrieking stopped.

She had fled from that awful impulse, and now—

The man's breathing rattled as if he had something stuck in his throat. As her eyes adjusted to the dim light, she made out a limp wide-brimmed hat, a drab overcoat of canvas or something like it, and a dark wool muffler. His eyes glinted pale blue, but the rest of his face was hidden, the scarf pulled up over his nose and wound around his neck.

She twisted her arm, trying to loosen his hold.

"Don't bother," he said. There was something wrong with his voice, though his accent was cultured. "We're just going to take a little walk, you and I together."

"No," she cried and tried again to jerk free.

He grabbed the back of her neck with his other hand. She felt the pinch of his long nails and shuddered. "You might as well relax," he said in that awful voice. "I'm going to need you for a little while. When I'm through, I'll probably let you go."

"Need me for what?"

"Why don't you wait and see?" The tone might have seemed conversational if his voice weren't so ghastly. It was more than just hoarse. It sounded—broken. Shredded.

"No!" she said again. "I don't want to!"

He gave her a shake, as if she were a recalcitrant puppy. "Used to getting what you want, aren't you? Spoiled little rich girl?"

"That's not true!"

"I think it is." His grip on her neck tightened. "But it doesn't matter. Let's go."

"I'm not going!" She pulled back on both heels, one intact and one broken, and pushed at him with her free hand. He wasn't tall, but his body was as hard as stone, and she might as well have pushed a brick wall. He shook her again, harder this time, and she gasped at the pain in her neck. "What do you want? Why are you—"

"The more you fight me," he grated, "the worse it will be." He loosened his grip just a little, but she still felt the bite of his fingernails at the base of her skull. "I mean that, by the way," he added offhandedly. "If I have to hurt you, I will enjoy every moment. Seems only fair to tell you that, little cousin."

"Cou—cousin?"

Another hideous laugh. "Yes indeed!" He pushed her ahead of him, forcing her deeper into the park, down the curving sidewalk lined with dark shrubbery. She fought him at every step, kicking, struggling to loosen his grip on her neck, to turn her head to bite his hand. None of it did any good. She stumbled onward, limping on her broken shoe, her fear rising as they approached the water tower. The top of it was lost in fog. Below the park, only a few streetlights glimmered through the mist. The bay was invisible, but a freighter's horn blasted its bone-piercing call from somewhere out on the water.

None of it seemed real. The hideous scene in the bedroom, the reckless flight from the house, her mother's shrill screams, and now—in the rolling fog, with the brick tower looming above her—this man! Was he—whoever he was, whatever he wanted—was he truly going to hurt her?

His breathing was terrifying, each breath rattling in his chest as if it were his last, but his fingers were as implacable as iron claws against her tender flesh. They were as cold as iron, too. Everything was cold, her bare arms, her feet in the thin shoes, her hands, the tip of her nose. She began to shiver and stammered through chattering teeth, "I'm not your c-cousin!"

"Oh, but you are! Allison, isn't it? Miss Allison Benedict, I believe, debutante of San Francisco."

"But—who are *you?*" She twisted again, trying to see his face.

He pushed her forward, and she almost tripped. He said, "Preston Benedict, at your service. Cousin Preston to you!"

She could barely speak for the sheer outrageousness of the idea. She breathed, "No! That's not possible."

"And yet"—another push—"here I am!"

"No, no! You're *dead!* There was a funeral. There's a grave, and a tombstone—everything!"

"Sentimental, isn't it?" He laughed, then coughed. His coughing made a fearsome tearing sound, as if his lungs were ripping apart. Their progress slowed as he fought for breath, and they paused at the foot of the granite stairs leading to the tower entrance.

When he could speak again, he rasped, "They buried an empty coffin, you know."

"Wh—what?"

"Wh-what?" he mimicked, a bizarre echo in his ruin of a voice. "Didn't tell you that, did they? There are no bones in that grave. There can't be, because those bones are right here." He slapped his chest. "Nothing under that headstone but an empty box."

"I don't believe you."

"Why should I care? Now, go."

Allison, her head spinning, limped up the steps. Ahead, past the curving wall of the tower, the glass walls of the Conservatory shimmered through the fog like the walls of a fairy-tale palace. She could no longer see the lights of Benedict Hall. When she faltered at the last step, he gave her a vicious shove, and she fell to her knees on the landing. Her silk stockings tore, and she heard the beads from the hem of her frock scatter across the granite.

All at once she was angry, and it felt much better than being afraid. She was furious at this person, whoever he was. He was no better than Papa and Mother and Dr. Kinney, all of them doing their best to control her, not one of them caring how she felt or what she wanted, all of them using her to get what *they* wanted. This man was exactly the same.

Rage cleared her spinning head. "You're a liar!" she cried, still on her knees. "I'm not your cousin! My cousin Preston is dead!" She jumped to her feet, and with a swift motion, yanked the muffler away from his face.

For one sickening moment they stared at each other.

Allison's fury died away under a swell of profound pity. This man, whoever he was, had been rendered monstrous. The skin below his eyes was puckered and blurred as if it had dissolved. His mouth was a slash, what was left of his lips distorted, pulled to one side and down. His chin and neck ran together as if the skin had melted and then frozen again into thick, reddened ridges of flesh. His eyebrows were gone, and his eyelashes, too.

No wonder his voice was so awful. He had been in a fire. He must have breathed flame and smoke, destroyed his voice, scarred his lungs.

She realized her mouth was open in horror, and she closed it. He said, "Pretty, aren't I?" and lifted the muffler again to hide his disfigurement.

She didn't answer. She tensed her muscles, then spun on her uneven shoes to dash away. His hand shot out, seized her arm, and wrenched her back against him. "I told you, don't bother," he snarled.

She struggled now with everything she had. She shouted, but there was no one to hear. She kicked, and fought his hands, but he was as cold as he was hideous. Though she waged her battle until her strength gave out, until her throat hurt from screaming, it was useless.

When she was limp with fatigue, her breath coming in little sobs, he said, "That's better." He gripped her elbows and rattled her until she felt her bones crack. "I meant it, you know," he said, very close to her face. "I like this. Love it, actually." He gave a little shrug. "It's the way I am. The more you resist, the better it is."

Allison, looking into those lashless blue eyes, believed him.

* * *

Margot refused to let Blake drop her in front of the house, though he tried to insist. "I'm not having you maneuver your cane in and out of the damned automobile any more than you have to!" she snapped, and then said, "Oh, I'm sorry, Blake. I'm so tired, and I'm worried."

"It's all right, Dr. Margot," he said mildly. "This has been a hard evening."

"Awful. Just awful. I want to blame it all on Aunt Adelaide, but I suppose Allison bears some responsibility."

They left the Essex in the garage and walked together across the lawn to the back porch. Blake said, "I know it's not for me to have an opinion, but Miss Allison seems far younger than nineteen. A child, in many ways."

Margot glanced up at him. "I agree, Blake," she said. "I suppose it's not unusual, in a family like hers." He held the back door for her to pass through. She walked ahead of him, through the darkened kitchen, on into the hall. It was dark there, too, but the door to the small parlor stood open, and light spilled out. Margot hurried toward it, with Blake limping behind her.

Empty cups rested on the piecrust table, and a pot with a ladle on a sideboard. Ramona, still in her dressing gown, but now with her hair combed and a thick shawl around her shoulders, jumped up from the divan. There was no one else in the room. The fire had died down, and the air felt chilly. "Margot! How is Aunt Adelaide?"

"She'll be all right, I think," Margot said.

Blake said, "Mrs. Ramona, why are you alone, and the fire dying out? Three maids in the house—four, if you count Ruby—"

She shook her head. "It's all right, Blake. I sent the twins and Thelma to their beds. And Hattie. There wasn't anything else they could do tonight."

He said, "But Ruby, at least—"

"Ruby is out with Uncle Henry and Father. Searching."

Margot said, "Searching? Ramona, you can't mean—Allison hasn't come back?" She glanced at the onyx corner clock and exclaimed, "It's two in the morning!"

"I know," Ramona said. "She's been gone for hours, with no coat, no gloves—and it's freezing outside."

Margot began stripping off her own gloves. "I don't know what to do," she said. "I was so taken up with Aunt Adelaide!"

"Where is she? Still at the hospital?"

"I admitted her. Her arm is set, but I don't think she's well in general, and I want Dr. Creedy to give her a full examination in the morning. And, Ramona, you need your rest. You should be in bed."

"I couldn't possibly sleep," Ramona said. She pulled the shawl tight around her shoulders and worried at the fringe with her fingers. "I'm afraid for Allison, poor little thing. If she knows her mother's hurt, or thinks she was responsible—"

"She should have been back hours ago," Margot said. "I would have thought the cold would drive her back, if nothing else." She had begun taking off her coat, but she stopped with one sleeve on and one off. "I wonder if I should join Father and Uncle Henry."

"No," Blake said firmly. "I'll get the Essex out again, and see if I can help. You two ladies should both rest, but I suppose you won't be able to. I'll just put some wood on this fire."

Margot pulled her arm out of her other sleeve and took her hat off. "You're right, Blake. Ramona, lie down on the divan, at least. Put your feet up." Ramona did this, and Margot arranged the shawl to cover her. Blake disappeared briefly, and limped back with both his arms full of small logs. "Blake, your cane!" Margot said.

"I'll get it in a moment."

"I think I'll make coffee," she said. "We're going to want it."

When she reached the kitchen, though, she found Hattie already there, with an overcoat over her nightdress and thick knitted slippers on her feet. "Hattie, I thought you were sleeping."

"Oh, I couldn't, Miss Margot. I just couldn't, not with poor Miss Allison out there somewhere in the dark!" She was filling the percolator at the big sink.

"I can understand that," Margot said heavily. "I can't sleep, either. I admitted Aunt Adelaide to the hospital, and do you know,

Hattie—" She hesitated, knowing her mother wouldn't approve, then rushed ahead just the same. Hattie and Allison had established a relationship of their own, and Hattie would understand. "Do you know that Aunt Adelaide never once asked about Allison? Just went on whining about her broken arm, and then, when she had an injection for the pain, rambling on about whatever it was Allison was supposed to have done. 'Ruined,' she said. What on earth could the child have done that was so awful? I don't even know if a girl can be 'ruined' anymore."

Hattie was scooping coffee grounds into the top of the pot. "She didn't tell me about it, Miss Margot, but that girl was awful unhappy. Bored, of course. Lonely, too. She took to arranging your little party like a duckling takes to water. Sat here at my table afterward and actually ate something!"

"She was looking so much better," Margot mused. She pulled out one of the aluminum chairs and sat down, kicking off her shoes and stretching her legs out with a sense of relief. The percolator began to bubble, and she thought what a comforting sound that always was in the morning, the promise of a full day to come. It was strange to hear it in the wee hours.

Hattie said, "I just don't know why a young girl like that would go off her eats like she did. She was better, eating a bit every meal. Then, the minute she knows her parents are coming, she goes off again. That ain't right."

"No. I agree, Hattie."

Hattie took the bottle of cream from the icebox and laid cookies on a plate. She had started her Christmas baking, and the cookies were shaped like Christmas trees and angels. They made Margot feel sad, such gay little sweets in the midst of a night of crisis.

When the coffee stopped bubbling, Hattie said, "There now. You go on in the small parlor, Miss Margot. I'll bring this in."

"I could wake one of the twins," Margot suggested.

"Better they get their sleep, if you ask me. We don't know what tomorrow will be like."

The truth of this chilled Margot to her bones. She shoved her feet back into her shoes and started into the hall. The front door opened just as she passed it, and the searchers trooped in, red-nosed and tousle-haired. She saw that Blake had returned with the Essex, but had left it parked in the street. She said, "Father? No luck, I gather?"

"None. It's strange. I don't see how she could have gotten very far."

"The streetcar," she suggested.

"But would she know where to go?" Uncle Henry demanded. "Has she gone off before?"

"No," Dick said in a tight voice. Margot saw that he, too, was angry. She hadn't realized how much Allison had become part of the household—part of the family—until that moment. "No, Uncle Henry. She hasn't gone off before."

Dickson said, "I think it's time to call the police, Henry."

"No! That will mean publicity. Surely the silly girl will come home in the morning."

The other Benedicts—Margot, her brother and sister-in-law, her father, and Blake and Hattie—stared at him. He turned his back to stamp away up the stairs, leaving the rest of them standing in the hall.

CHAPTER 20

Allison wished she had long sleeves so she didn't have to feel the ridges of Preston's burn scars. They seemed to have no circulation. They felt like the cold claws of an animal, without feeling or flexibility, and her skin prickled with revulsion at their touch.

As he forced her toward the door of the tower's south entrance she said, "That's locked at night. You can't go in."

He barked his ugly laugh. "Always hated people telling me what I can't do," he said. He held her arm with one hand while he dug an enormous iron key from the pocket of his disreputable coat. She tried to seize the moment, to wrench her arm free, but only succeeded in making him grip her more tightly. Her arm would be covered in bruises, she knew, when there was light enough to see it.

He had the door open a moment later, and he pushed her through it, closing it behind them with his foot. She heard the heavy lock click into place.

She said, for the tenth time, "What is it you *want?* If it's something from the family, why not just ask?" but he didn't answer.

He drove her ahead of him to the stairs. They were steel, faintly shining in the darkness, and slippery. Preston's breath whistled in his lungs as they climbed. The exertion briefly warmed Allison. "Where are we going?" she panted.

"Climb," he gasped. "One hundred six steps, and we're going all the way."

"Why?"

"Because I say so."

She didn't ask again. She saved her breath for the ascent, and watched him warily for any sign he meant to make her fall. It would be easy in the dark stairwell, and there was real danger in these hard, icy steps. She couldn't think what it would gain him to throw her down the curving staircase, but he wasn't in his right mind, which she feared meant it didn't have to make sense. It was obvious he had no qualms about hurting her. He might even do it just for pleasure. For kicks, as Tommy Fellowes might have said. She placed her feet carefully in the dimness, as he propelled her higher and higher. When they reached the top, he released her, but he stayed close, and she had no doubt he would seize her again if she tried to bolt.

They were in an observation deck, a great circular space surrounded by arched windows. Ironwork grates barred the windows, but there was no glass, and they were open to the icy night air. Allison hugged herself against the cold, the warmth of the climb draining swiftly away. "I'm going to freeze to death," she said.

The laugh again. "So much more pleasant," he said, "than death by burning. I know all about that!"

"You really are my cousin, then," she said sadly.

"Yes, I really am."

"Isn't there something the doctors can do for you? For your face, I mean?"

"No. Soon enough it won't matter, anyway." He turned away from her, leaning his elbows on one of the windowsills. She cast a glance at the stairwell, wondering if she dared to dash down those slick steel steps. He said, without looking at her, "Don't try it. You'll just slip and fall, and the door's locked at the bottom anyway."

"What are we doing up here, Cousin Preston?"

He said, gazing out into the mist, "We're waiting."

"For what?"

"For them to really get the wind up."

"I d-don't know what that m-means." Her teeth began to chatter again, and her words came out in staccato bits that felt like crushed ice between her teeth.

He turned his head to speak over his shoulder, readjusting the scarf when it slipped. "It means I want them all to get good and worried about you. To be frightened."

"Wh-why?" She was rubbing her arms now and stamping her feet.

He said, "Christ," and slipped off his overcoat. He held it out to her. "Put this on, but don't mistake it for kindness. I just don't want to listen to you stutter for hours."

The coat was noisome and greasy, but she put it over her shoulders anyway. The pockets were heavy with things she had no wish to explore, and she kept her hands away from them. An automatic thanks for the coat rose to her lips, but it died unspoken. He didn't deserve gratitude. It was his fault she was freezing, after all. "Tell me why you want the family frightened, and I'll tell you they probably don't care what happens to me."

He spun to face her. "What do you mean, they don't care? Precious little cuz, I'm sure they've all got their knickers in a twist, thinking you've run off or been abducted for ransom!"

"*Have* I been abducted for ransom?" she snapped. Part of her knew she should be afraid, but another part of her—a larger part—found the whole situation absurd. And after what she had done this evening, after hearing her mother squalling about her broken arm, none of this seemed to matter much. Nothing mattered much.

"No. Money can't help me now."

"Then what? If you wanted to hurt me, you would have done it by now."

The ghastly chuckle. "Not necessarily. Although, the more you seem like *her*—thinking you know everything—the more I feel like hurting you." He took her earlobe in one of his cold, disfigured hands and tweaked it, hard. It hurt, but she bit back her cry. She wouldn't give him the satisfaction. Goose bumps ran down her neck and across her shoulder, but she thrust out her chin and glared at him.

"Why aren't you afraid of me?" he demanded.

She shrugged inside his big, disreputable coat. She wandered away from him, walking to one of the windows to peer out through the grate. There was nothing to see but a cloud of fog, but she supposed, when the sun rose, the view was very nice. "You don't know me," she said.

"Oh, but I do," he said sourly. "Pretty little deb, downy chick getting all plumped up for the market! Parents sparing no expense or effort!"

"You don't know anything about it." Her tone was every bit as sour as his. "The market part is right. Not the rest."

"Poor little cuz. The heart breaks." He coughed and spat. "See those lights down there? They're looking for you. Searchlights, the Essex rolling around the streets, no one getting any sleep."

She peered through the fog and saw that he was right. Lights bobbed here and there around the park and along the street. She could just see, through the mist, that lights still burned in Benedict Hall, though it must be nearly three in the morning.

"What happened there tonight?" Preston asked. "What did you do?"

She turned to face him, putting her back to the brick wall. "I broke my mother's arm."

He made a sound that might have been a gasp of surprise or a chuckle of amusement. "You amaze me, little cuz. I suspect you're trying to shock me."

"No. It's true. We had an argument, and I—I didn't mean to hurt her, but I—" She raised both hands in a gesture of surrender. "You might just as well toss me down these stairs, Cousin Preston. They've been threatening to put me away in a sanitorium. Now they'll do it for sure."

Margot watched in astonishment as Henry started up the staircase, undoing his tie as he went. She said, "Uncle Henry! Allison went out with no coat, no gloves—it's freezing out there."

He didn't pause. "She'll remember them next time, then," he said, and stripped his tie from his shirt. As he reached the landing, he was already at work on the buttons. "Ruby, you go to bed, too," he ordered. "I'm not paying you to walk the streets in the middle of the night."

Margot turned back to face her family and found Hattie with tears in her eyes. "Miss Margot—Mr. Dickson—you won't just leave her out there? That poor little mite—"

Margot said briskly, "Of course not, Hattie. If Uncle Henry won't telephone to the police, I will."

Her father moved toward the telephone resting on its pedestal in the hall. "Let me do it, daughter. I'll call Searing directly, and he'll know how to keep it out of the newspapers." He rummaged in the little drawer below the telephone and came up with a city directory. He started thumbing the pages.

Ramona said, "I don't know what to do to help."

"Ramona," Margot said, "I really think you should go to bed. Dick, she shouldn't get overtired."

At this both Hattie and Blake turned to look at Ramona, and Ramona colored and gave a small, embarrassed wave of her hand. "I'm sorry, Hattie. I was going to make the announcement soon—that is, we were, Mr. Dick and I."

Hattie exclaimed, "Mrs. Ramona! It's a baby, isn't it?" She gave a small sob and pressed her hands to her plump cheeks. "Just as I thought, just what I was suspecting! Oh, my lands, that's just the best news I've heard in such a long time! Go on now, you and Mr. Dick, you go off to bed. You hungry, Mrs. Ramona? Some warm milk, maybe?"

Ramona denied wanting anything but sleep, and Dick shepherded her up the staircase. In the hall, Dickson leaned against the wall, the earpiece of the telephone in his right hand, the base in his left, speaking in a low voice. Blake said, "Shall I go out again, Dr. Margot? Have another look?"

"I'm gonna go with you!" Hattie said, which at another moment might have made Margot laugh. Hattie was notorious for avoiding the Essex whenever she could. Funerals, weddings, and sick calls, she had always declared, were the only reasons for climbing into that motorcar.

"Hattie, that's not necessary," Margot said. "You should go to bed, too." As Hattie began to protest, Margot put up her forefinger, but she took care to speak gently. "We'll need you in the morning, Hattie. Blake and I will go out and search again, I promise."

"Oh, Dr. Margot—but you have the hospital, and the clinic—"

"First things first," Margot said firmly. "We need to find Allison." It was true, she had rounds to make in the morning, but fortunately no surgeries. She glanced outside at the heavy fog roiling over the shrubs and curling around the bare trunk of the camellia, and thought of Frank. He wouldn't try to fly in this, surely!

Her father strode back to the foot of the stairs, jamming his hat on his head and beginning to search his pockets for his gloves. "Searing's sending two officers," he said. "I'll meet them outside. If Henry comes down, tell him—oh, tell him to go to the devil!"

Margot said, "With pleasure, Father, but I suspect he's already enjoying the sleep of the just."

"What kind of father is that?" Dickson muttered, stamping toward the front door. "Little girl like that, out in the dark with no one to protect her. . . ." He was already on his way down the walk, still grumbling.

"We'll leave the door unlocked, in case she comes back while we're out." Margot was putting her coat on again. "Hattie, please. Try to sleep."

Reluctantly, Hattie made her way toward the kitchen and her own room. Like Dickson, she muttered to herself as she shuffled past the staircase, untying her apron as she went. "Poor little mite," Margot heard her say. "What is this world coming to? With parents like that!"

Moments later, Margot and Blake were in the Essex, prowling through the foggy streets with the headlamps turned low. Margot sat in the front, beside Blake, and for once he didn't demur. They crept through the mist, the lights from the automobile stabbing at the gray fog, reflecting uselessly back at them. Margot wondered if it wouldn't be better to just extinguish the lamps altogether.

"By now she could have walked quite some distance," Blake said gravely as he turned out of Fourteenth Avenue and started down Aloha.

"I know," Margot said. "I thought of the streetcar, but I doubt she has any money."

"She could make her way down to Broadway."

Margot said, "I should tell you, Blake. She did slip out once, though I promised I wouldn't tell anyone. She went out with a young man she met on her crossing. They went to a speakeasy—" She felt, rather than saw, his sidelong glance. "She was sick under the roses," she said drily, watching the sides of the road for any sign of a shivering girl in a short-sleeved dinner frock. "But she never mentioned the name of the place."

"I wouldn't know it even if you told me," Blake said. "I've never had occasion to drive to a speakeasy."

"Nor have I, Blake. Nor any inclination."

"No indeed."

She searched the foggy street. On Broadway, nothing moved at this hour except the occasional stray cat and, once, a dog rising from a shadowed doorstep, its hackles lifting. They drove slowly to the very end of Broadway and back again. Misty streetlight halos illuminated the fog here and there. Alleyways melted into gray dimness. Margot peered into the mist until her eyes ached, and tried to imagine Allison somewhere safe and warm.

She looked fragile, he thought, though she acted tough. Her neck was as slender as a child's, and her ankles, hidden now by the drooping panels of his overcoat, looked as if they could barely hold her upright. Her eyes were huge above her little pointed chin. It occurred to him that those eyes were the same blue as the sapphire, and he liked the synchrony of that. It seemed a good omen. A promise that he would, at last, complete his purpose.

When he held out his hand and said, "I'll need the coat for a few minutes," she didn't protest or question him. She slid out of the coat, but she dodged his hand, letting the coat fall in a puddle to the floor of the observation deck. The pockets, heavy with his special treasures, clanked on the hard floor. Allison, stepping out of the folds, looked like a chick emerging from its broken eggshell. She hobbled on her uneven shoes to one of the arched windows, where she stood hugging herself against the chill.

"I'll give it back soon," he found himself saying, which was ridiculous. What the hell did he care if she froze to death? Surely he had learned by now that being softhearted was a waste of his time.

He shrugged into the coat, avoiding her eyes as he felt in his pockets. Just touching the stone, even disguised as it was, encouraged him. From his other pocket he drew the straight razor. Turning so she could see him, he opened it. Even in the dimness, its polished blade glimmered. Her eyes grew even wider, the whites gleaming in the darkness. He supposed her face went pale, though the light was too poor to show it. She fell back a step, her bravado gone. It was utterly gratifying, and his loins stirred in answer to her fear.

The razor was nearly new, from Sheffield, with a pearl Bakelite handle and a blade that had been freshly honed when he lifted it from the barbershop down on Post Street. He held it up so she could see it clearly, and advanced toward her with an unhurried step. She emitted one small whimper and shrank back against the brick wall. The starlit fog outlined her fair hair and her slender silhouette, and he was tempted—oh, so tempted!—to do exactly what she feared, to slash through that tender throat and see the hot blood pour over her georgette dinner frock.

He had done it before. He relished the feeling of power, of reckless daring. It was how he had acquired the stone in the first place. He could imagine it with no difficulty, a single swift stroke, her body crumpling to the floor, himself leaping back to avoid being stained by the spray of her heart's blood. He could take what he needed, wrap it in something—what? A scrap from her dress, perhaps? His message would carry the greatest impact that way, but . . .

The image faded. Margot would never come to him if Allison were already dead. He needed her alive, his pretty little cousin, cowering now in terror against the brick wall.

He reached her, stretched out his hand, and lifted a lock of her pale hair. A good, thick strand, one that would be easily identifiable, too much to have been given up willingly. He lifted the razor with his right hand.

She cried out and tried to duck away from him. He held tight, forcing her to dangle from his handful of her hair. Some of it came away on its own, tearing free of her scalp, but the rest held so her head was twisted upward, her eyes turning to him in the most pitiful way.

He grinned behind his mask of dark wool. "Shhh," he said. "I'm not going to cut you, little cuz. I just need a hank of this." He poised the blade close to her head and wielded it. The blade was sharp, even sharper than the saber he had wielded in Jerusalem. It cut through the strand easily, instantly. Her support gone, she fell to her knees.

He held up the fistful of hair in triumph. At his feet, Allison sobbed, which made his groin tingle again, but he ignored that. He needed to be moving, to get this done.

"I," he told her, turning toward the stairs, "will be back before you know it."

He clattered down the long curving staircase, unlocked the door with the key he had lifted so neatly from the maintenance shed, and locked it again when he had gone through. He laid his palm on it, briefly, a gesture to reassure himself he had her safely stowed. It was all going just the way he had planned.

He had known, once he had the sapphire in his possession again, that it would. Margot had shown him herself, though she would never know it. She had poked at the building's footings where the stone was buried, drawing him to where the bubble had emerged from the cement, practically begging for him to retrieve it. The hammer and chisel had been laughably easy to lay his hands on, lifted from a toolbelt hanging by the back entrance to the Compass Center. He had only to wait until it was too dark for anyone to see what he was doing, and then it was a simple task to chisel out the stone. It practically met him halfway, in any case, bulging out of the concrete that way. He had to repress an urge to apologize for taking so long, as if it were an abandoned child or a pet left behind! That was laughable, too, but he couldn't help thinking that if he had only had it with him, all those months while he tried to heal in an obscure country hospital, he might not look like a monster now.

The good thing, he saw, once he got the chunk of concrete into the light and could see the stone, was that its true color had returned. It was alive again, its depths glistening, reflective, gleaming almost as vivid a blue as it had that day in Jerusalem, when he had *liberated* it from that arrogant Turk. He had made mistakes, he knew. He had pondered each one of them while he lay in the hospital swathed in such layers of bandages he could barely see. He had examined them, considered them, assessed where he had gone wrong, what he should have done.

He understood clearly, now, what he had to do. He wouldn't try for subtlety. He wouldn't take the indirect approach, as he had in his attempt to burn down Margot's building. He had his bait, and he had a plan. It wasn't in his nature—as it hadn't been in *hers*, the incomparable Roxelana—to flinch from what was necessary. Roxelana had imbued the sapphire with all her power, and despite the price he had paid for his mistakes, he would wield that power effectively this time, and then his work would be finished. He could leave this earth without regret, and be united with Roxelana wherever it was people like the two of them ended up.

He listened hard to be certain no automobiles were approaching on Fourteenth Avenue before he dashed across. He took care not to let the gate creak as he came through it. He crept up the porch to the front door in perfect silence. He left his shoes there, gingerly lifted the latch, then tiptoed across the hall and up the staircase.

It was strange, being in Benedict Hall after all this time. The smell of it was achingly, even perilously, familiar. The air was redolent of the past, of easier times. His half-destroyed nostrils flared at the reminiscent scents of cooked food, of floor wax and furniture polish. He detected random ghosts of perfume in the air, like imprints of the ladies who had passed through the house. Lights burned in the small parlor and in the hall, lighting the staircase from below. The second floor, where the family's bedrooms were, was dark, every door closed, every light off. He breathed slowly, wary of the sounds his lungs made, and which he couldn't control. He stepped gently on the strip of carpet as he moved to the front of the house, where Margot's bedroom faced north, to the park.

Despite the need to hurry, as he passed his old bedroom, opposite hers, he was tempted. Just one peek, one quick glance inside. It would be his final glimpse at his boyhood sanctuary. It was sentimental, no doubt, but in the face of what he was about to do, surely he was entitled.

He listened at the door first, to be sure there was no one occupying it. He wondered if it was Allison's room now. That would have been logical, placing her close to the front of the house, next door to Margot. If it was hers, of course, it was now conveniently empty. That made his scarred lips curl beneath the cover of his muffler, and he gently, slowly, eased the door open.

He caught a breath before he could stop himself, and the whistle of it in his scarred throat sounded like an explosion in his ears. He tensed, listening for any sign that someone else had heard, but there was nothing, only the natural sighs and creaks of a big sleeping house. He sidled into the room, pushed the door closed behind him, and looked around the bedroom he had slept in since he was a child.

It was, in this room, as if the past year had never happened. It was as if he could turn back the hands of a clock and make it once again the summer of 1920, when he was still Preston Benedict, popular columnist for the *Seattle Daily Times*. When he was the handsome war veteran, scion of one of the city's best families, the sought-after creator of "Seattle Razz." In this bedroom, nothing had changed. Nothing had been moved. Nothing had been added.

There was no smell of dust or mold or mildew, so clearly someone was cleaning it. His silver-backed brushes lay where he had left them, and the little case for his cuff links and tie tacks still rested on the dressing table. The silver-inlaid tray, where he used to drop his keys and the change from his pockets, waited, empty, on the chest of drawers. His red onyx fountain pen lay across it at a neat angle. No doubt, if he opened the wardrobe, he would find all his clothes hanging there, waiting.

Waiting for whom? For him to come back from the dead?

His scarred flesh was too stiff for a proper grin, but he tried. He felt his cheeks twist with the effort, an appropriately bitter and pointless one. This mausoleum of a room was the perfect memorial, and he had no doubt who was responsible for it.

It was Mother, of course, his bereft, grieving mother, and it was his fault. If he had done it right, he would have come home to her as if nothing had ever happened. He would have driven Margot off to make her life somewhere else, out of his way, out of his life. Mother could have accepted that. She would have recovered from that loss, and swiftly.

Damn, Preston. You'd better get it right this time.

He took one last look around the room, feeling an undeniable stab of regret, then padded out of the room and closed the door behind him. He turned to Margot's room, where the door stood open. He stepped inside, hurrying now, not bothering to take in the details of her private life. On her narrow bed, with its white quilt and lacy pillows, he laid the chunk of concrete he had chiseled out of the clinic foundation. He arranged it so the sapphire buried in it faced upward, into the dim glow from the window. Next to it, he laid the hank of Allison's hair, nicely fanned, bright gold against the white.

When Margot returned, exhausted from the fruitless night's search, she would know. Margot was hateful and selfish and revoltingly mannish, but she wasn't stupid. She would know he had been there, and that she was the only one who could save Allison.

CHAPTER 21

Before turning for home, Margot asked Blake to drive her to the hospital. He parked the Essex near the entrance, and she went in to ask if anyone had been admitted overnight, or if anyone had tried to visit her patient with the broken arm. The receptionist shook her head, and assured her she had been at her desk since nine the previous evening. Margot thought of trying the other hospitals, but Blake argued against it.

"You can telephone to them," he said reasonably. "Or, if Miss Allison went to a hospital, they will undoubtedly telephone to Benedict Hall."

Margot collapsed against the seat. "You're right, of course. It's probably better to go home, but I'm really worried."

"Maybe when we get back, she'll be there."

"From your lips to God's ear," Margot murmured.

"Ah. Quoting Hattie," he said.

"Sometimes she's the only one who knows the right thing to say."

It took longer than usual to make their way up the hill to Benedict Hall. The fog had persisted through the hours of darkness, and though the sluggish light was beginning to rise, Blake was wary of early-morning vehicles emerging without warning from the mist. As he pulled the Essex into the driveway and around to the garage, Margot looked over her shoulder. Benedict Hall looked much as it had when they left, lights on in the hall and the small parlor, everything else dark.

She felt dry-mouthed and edgy as they left the garage and walked across the lawn to the dark kitchen. Hattie, it seemed, had taken her advice and gone to bed. Blake turned on the light, and Margot saw by the Sessions wall clock that it had just gone six. She went out into the hall and into the small parlor, where she found her father, still fully clothed, sound asleep on the divan. She left him there, turning off the lamp on its side table, closing the door as softly as she could.

The rest of the house was quiet. The maids weren't due out of their beds for another half hour. Margot slipped off her shoes before she climbed the stairs to go to her room, glancing toward the back of the house. Allison's door stood open. The door to the bedroom Henry and Adelaide were sharing was closed.

In the vain hope she might find her, she walked down the hall to look in Allison's room. As before, the bed was made, though it was rumpled. A plaid frock had been tossed on a chair. Allison's nightdress and dressing gown waited at the foot of her bed, and her brushes and face creams were arranged before the mirror, but there was no sign of Allison.

Margot sighed and turned toward her own bedroom. There would be no sleep tonight, but she could at least wash her face, change her clothes, and—

She was only two steps through her own bedroom door when she saw it. An icy wave of shock swept over her, making her skin crawl and her face go cold. A cry of protest, wordless, involuntary, rose in her throat and died there. Her bare feet carried her forward almost without her realizing it, and she fell to her knees beside her bed in the gray half-light, staring at the—the *thing*—awaiting her.

It looked gross and offensive on her clean white quilt. The jagged bits of concrete clinging to it couldn't disguise it, and she could see at a glance it had been arranged with care, so she would recognize it in an instant.

The sapphire. Preston's sapphire, the one he had placed such faith in. It had been an uncharacteristic bit of mysticism for her brother, his belief that this stone gave him strength and influence, and he had died—supposedly—with this jewel in his hand. Only Frank knew where she had buried it, how she had pressed it down into the wet concrete of the foundation. They had smoothed the spot with a trowel, the two of them together, and agreed the stone would remain there, out of anyone's reach.

Margot knelt there for a full minute, staring at the sapphire in its jagged coating. It stared back at her, glinting faintly as sunrise began to filter through the mist. When she reached out her hand for it, the shattered cement scratched her palm, but the sapphire glowed an invitation.

It meant nothing to her, of course. It was a stone. A rock, as she had declared before she interred it. It possessed no inherent powers except the ones her brother, a man out of his mind with rage and hatred, conferred upon it. She remembered the bulging spot in the footings of her clinic, and the tingle on her neck that day, that old familiar sense of danger. He had been watching. He had seen her examining the flaw, and he had dug the stone out of the concrete, and he had left it here for her to find. She knew precisely what this meant.

Preston was alive.

He had escaped the fire after all. Slid from the stretcher, and left the sapphire behind in the folds of the ambulance blanket. He had run, fled from the consequences of his actions, hid himself somehow, somewhere. Left his mother to grieve until she very nearly lost her sanity. Let the family bury an empty coffin beneath a meaningless headstone.

She was just about to push to her feet, to carry the thing downstairs to show Blake, when she saw the lock of hair.

She couldn't mistake it for anything else. It was Allison's, silky and fair, the way Edith's used to be. She wished she could think it meant something else, that it had come from some other source, but she couldn't. Somehow, in some twisted plot only he could concoct, Preston had taken Allison, and he intended Margot to come after her. There was no mistaking the message.

Margot rose to her feet. She would have to go, and go alone. Allison was in more danger than any of them had suspected.

Jars and bottles in mysterious shapes and colors crowded the shelves in the back room of Margot's clinic. The air held that undefinable tang of medicine, a smell that called up memories of icy stethoscopes, nasty-tasting thermometers, gleaming steel needles poised to puncture tender flesh. Without Margot there, so brisk and efficient and calm, the clinic seemed to Allison a place of horrors, of tortures half-imagined. The inner door to the examining rooms was locked, and though Preston had made short work of the lock on the back door, he didn't bother with the second one.

It had been a long, frigid walk through the foggy darkness. Preston knew every street, every alley. He knew just how to dodge the policemen who walked the streets, flashing their Daylo searchlights into the shadows, looking for the missing girl. Half a dozen times he had covered her mouth with his loathsome hand, dragged her away from the dancing beams of light, forcing her to crouch behind garbage bins, huddle beneath stacks of firewood, hide behind piled shipping cartons. He had given her the coat again when he returned to the water tower, but she suspected that was more to disguise her than for her comfort. He made her walk fast, despite her broken heel, and by the time they reached the clinic, her back ached from walking on uneven shoes. Her arm stung from his ruthless grip on it. The straight razor had disappeared, but she was sure he had it in his pocket, within easy reach. She felt light-headed with hunger, having not eaten more than a few bites of anything in two days, and that didn't help. She couldn't think clearly enough to devise a means of escape.

"What are you going to do?" she asked, when he had finally released her. "The nurse will be here in the morning."

"Don't fret yourself," he said shortly. "It will all be over by then."

"What will be over?"

He didn't answer.

The long hike had taxed him, too, she could tell. He was sweating, though she had the overcoat and he was dressed only in a shapeless sweater and some sort of high-collared shirt. He found the storeroom light and switched it on, making her blink against the sudden brilliance. When her eyes adjusted she saw that he kept the muffler raised around his scarred face. Above it, his eyes glittered as if with fever.

Or madness. He was insane. What person in his right mind would sneak into Benedict Hall and out again, then bring her all the way downtown to Margot's clinic?

He said, "Give me my coat. It's warm enough in here."

She took it off and handed it to him. He put it on, though beads of perspiration dripped down his forehead.

Allison kicked off her uneven shoes and leaned against the wall, rubbing her bare arms against the chill of the room. "What am I doing here, Cousin Preston?"

"It's not about you," he grated.

"You didn't need to haul me down here, then!" She glared at him. "I *hate* people trying to control me!"

"Trying? I didn't try, cuz. I *did* control you."

"Give me one chance, and I'll be gone," she said, and pointed to the door. "You broke the lock."

In answer, he pulled the razor from his pocket and brandished it. He had folded the blade away, but she had seen how easily it opened. She understood very well how wickedly sharp it was. Looking at it, she put a hand to her head, where a thick patch of hair was now missing. He said, "Don't fret, cuz. It will grow back. It was necessary."

She could tell he meant to speak lightly, but his shredded voice spoiled the effect. She remembered the way he had seemed at her deb party, sophisticated, wry, clever. Good-looking and confident. She dropped her hand and folded her arms around herself. "I don't see the point of any of this."

"There's a point," he rasped. "And when she gets here, you'll see."

"When she gets here? Who?"

"Don't be stupid," he snapped. "Who do you think?"

"Cousin Margot? If you wanted to see her, you could have just waited at Benedict Hall! This is crazy—"

He was standing near the door, but now he spun to face her. "I'm not crazy!" he shouted.

"I didn't say *you* were—"

In three swift steps he had crossed the room. He gripped her throat with one hand, choking off her words. He hissed, "Goddammit, I'm warning you, little cuz. You're not the one I want, but I wouldn't hesitate. You don't know me, and you don't know what I've done, or what I can do, but believe me, you wouldn't like it. You wouldn't like it at all."

Tears of pain sprang to her eyes. She could breathe—just—but she couldn't speak. It was all so bizarre, the whole evening, her mother screaming, Preston dragging her all over Seattle, now nearly strangling her. This couldn't be happening. She was imagining it. It was a nightmare. If she could only breathe, surely she would wake up and find herself tucked up in her bed.

"Stop tempting me." He opened his fingers, releasing her. He took a step back as she clutched at her throat and sucked in noisy breaths.

He spoke faster and faster, his voice so raw it must hurt. He waved the razor in front of her face. "Little idiot. I've seen you, dangling after the great Dr. Benedict." His burned throat whistled when he drew breath. "You have no idea what she's like. You think she's the great healer, kind and clever and all that nonsense? She's fooled you. You're as blind as the rest of them!"

He began to play with the razor, opening it, closing it, opening it again, testing the blade with his thumb, turning this way and that as if he were looking for something. The sour odor of him increased, filling the small space. Allison's skin prickled with goose bumps, and the room seemed to contract around the two of them. She backed toward the inner door to the clinic, wondering if there was some way to get it open, to lock herself in some other room or escape through a window.

"Don't even think it!" he shouted. He opened the razor and slashed the air with it, once, twice. Allison's heart fluttered, and she felt as if there weren't enough air in the storeroom to sustain them both. She wished with all her heart she had eaten Hattie's overbaked salmon tonight. This battle was real, not the artificial one she and her mother had been fighting for so long. She needed strength. It had been a long, cold, taxing night, and she was nearly at the end of what she had.

She braced herself against the inner door, her hands behind her. Her voice sounded thin to her, but she had to ask. "What do you want me to do?"

"Shut up!" he shrieked, in a voice that made her bones shiver. "I want you to shut up!"

That, at least, she could do. She pressed her lips together. She let her spinning head drop back against the wood, telling herself she didn't dare faint. If he came for her, if he lost the last shreds of control he had, she had to try to protect herself.

From beneath her lowered eyelids, she watched the erratic sweep of the straight razor as Preston, muttering to himself, tugging at the muffler over his face, paced the room. Every time he came near her, her stomach tightened and her heart thudded, but she kept herself upright. It was tempting to slide down, to sit on the floor, to rest, but the glitter in his bloodshot eyes convinced her she didn't dare.

When Margot, in stocking feet, crept down the main staircase, she saw by the light under the kitchen door that Blake was still there. She debated furiously with herself.

It would be much faster to go in the Essex. Blake would be deeply upset if she didn't tell him what she had found, and what she had to do. But could she keep him safe? His heart still wasn't as strong as she would like it to be, and the dragging of his right leg worried her.

On the other hand, when he realized she hadn't returned, he would come looking. He would guess where she had gone, and follow, unless she lugged the chunk of concrete with her, and took the lock of Allison's hair as well.

Trust, she thought. There was no one in the world she trusted more than Blake. Except perhaps Frank, but he wasn't here.

She glanced to her right, where the small parlor was still dark, and from which she could hear her father's heavy breathing as he slept on. The rest of the house, from the servants' attic bedroom down to Hattie's, behind the kitchen, was silent, sleeping. Waiting.

She descended the staircase, and turned left, toward the kitchen.

When she opened the swinging door, she found Blake leaning against the counter, a mug of coffee in his hand. He straightened when he saw her face. "What is it?" he asked in a low voice.

She said, "Get your coat, will you, Blake? I'll explain on the way."

"You can stay with the car," Margot said. She peered down Post Street, but it was too early—not quite seven—for any of the businesses to be open. The shifting fog hid doorways and windows. Only one light showed on the street, shimmering through the mist.

"I don't want you going in there alone," he answered. *Theah.* His accent had turned more Southern than she had heard in months.

"I know you don't, but until we see what's going on . . ." She opened the passenger door and climbed out of the Essex.

"I'm not going to argue, sweetheart. This is the way it's going to be."

Despite everything, despite the sleepless night and the blood-chilling anxiety that gripped her, hearing the old endearment from Blake's lips gave her strength. She managed a wry smile across the top of the automobile, and she made no objection as he got out of the driver's seat and walked around the front, leaning on his marble-headed cane. "You see the light?" she said.

"I do." *Ah do.* He reached her, and side by side, they started around the building.

It made Margot's blood rise to know that her clinic had been invaded, that someone—that *he,* who was supposed to be gone from her life—still held power over her. She was grateful for Blake's bulk at her shoulder. Despite her brave words, this was not a confrontation to take on by herself. Blake understood that better than anyone.

He hadn't argued with her interpretation of the artifacts lying in wait for her. He knew how devious her younger brother had always been. And evidently, though the idea was almost too bizarre to take in, still was. She had described the bit of concrete, the stone half buried in it, and the stomach-churning sight of a strand of Allison's hair, deliberately laid out to show how long and thick it was. It was not possible that either had come to rest on her bed by accident.

Blake had said only, "Good Lord. He survived."

"He screamed, that night in the fire," she said in a shaking voice. "Both Thea and I heard it, a shriek I was sure meant he was dying. Burning to death."

Blake was turning down Madison, driving as fast as he dared through the fog. He said, speaking a sentiment that hadn't yet occurred to Margot, "Poor Mrs. Edith."

"Oh, my God, Blake. I can't imagine what this would do to her. How could he? How *could* he?"

Now, they approached the back door of her clinic. The lock was broken, the brand-new brass Schlage Frank had installed himself, to keep out the occasional tramp in search of alcohol. It had a glass doorknob on each side, a pretty carved thing Margot had taken pleasure in. The doorknob hung loose now, shiny with mist. The lock had been gouged out of the wood, splintering the door above and below it. The door was closed, but loosely, light showing through the broken lock and around the edges of the doorjamb. Margot paused on the step to gather herself before she put her hand on the slick glass knob. When she felt she was as prepared as she was going to be, she pulled on it. The door swung open, and she walked over the sill and into the nightmare.

Now that the moment was here, now that he had maneuvered her into position, exhilaration at having succeeded made his heart pound. He whirled when the door opened, alerted by the rush of cold air, and saw her in the doorway.

Margot. His lifelong enemy. In his grasp at last.

He sidestepped swiftly to seize Allison with a hard hand on her neck. She yelped in surprise and pain as he jerked her forward. He thrust her in front of him, but he hooked his arm around her throat, pressing her fair head against his shoulder. In his other hand he held up the straight razor so its blade glittered in the light. He found he was breathing too fast, the air rasping through his scarred throat. He forced himself to breathe deliberately. He didn't want anything to spoil this moment or betray his excitement. It was almost over, all his pain and suffering and misery. It was almost over for both of them.

"Doc," he said. He saw the jerk of her body as she heard his altered voice for the first time. He felt her alarm over the razor's blade as clearly as if she had screamed, and that gave him pleasure. There had been no pleasure in his life for a very long time. "I see you got my little invitation."

"Preston," she said, spreading her hands in entreaty. "Why? Why did you let us all believe you were dead?"

"What do *you* care?" he demanded. Allison wriggled in his grasp, and he pressed the flat of the blade against her cheek to stop her. She emitted a tiny gasp, and froze. He rewarded her by lifting the blade away from her skin, but only slightly. He kept it high enough to be in her line of sight, and he felt by the tension in her body, pulled tight against him, that she knew it was there.

Margot said, "You're hiding your face. Are you burned?"

"Trust you, doc," he snarled, "to want the disgusting medical details before you even ask if our little cousin is all right!"

"I can see she's all right," Margot said. "I want her to stay that way."

"Oh, good. Motivation!" He lifted the blade again and slid the flat of it down Allison's cheek. It was probably cold. She shuddered, and he laughed. "I would hate to scar this pretty face," he said, his eyes on Margot. "Wouldn't you just hate to see that?"

"Of course," she said. She took a step forward, into the room, and now he saw that Blake was behind her, on the outer step.

"Blake!" he cried. "I might have known the doc wouldn't make a move without you!"

"What do you want, Preston?" Margot said. Her voice, that deep, mannish voice he had always hated, was as even as if he weren't standing here with a razor blade held to her protégé's cheek. "Tell me what you want, so we can get this over with. Let Allison go home to her parents."

"God, Margot, I hate it when you tell me what to do." He tried to purr the words, as he could have done once, but they came out as a growl.

Margot made a small, uncertain motion. "I'm not," she said, and her voice trembled just a little. He wanted to hear it tremble more, wanted to see her shake with fear. He wanted her to beg him for mercy.

Then he could end it.

"I'm just asking," Margot said. "I'm not telling. You wanted me here, and I came. You can let Allison go home with Blake, and you and I will—"

He felt rivulets of sweat running down his ribs inside the hand-me-down shirt. A wave of fury made him tighten his hold on Allison's throat, her chin tucked tight into the crook of his elbow. She stumbled, losing her balance, but she didn't make a sound.

She really was a tough little thing. And so pretty. He could have done things with a girl like that, seen her rise to the top of the social circle. She could have been a sister he could boast about, someone to be proud of.

Instead, he had been cursed with Margot, more man than

woman, Margot with her hands always into the most disgusting things, the filthiest stuff, then coming home to Benedict Hall and sitting down at the dinner table, touching the flatware and the crystal and the napkins with those hands. . . .

"Preston," she said now. "Let me see your face. Surely we can help you—"

With one swift motion, he tore the muffler off and threw it aside. Margot's voice trailed off in what must be horror at the destruction of his face and neck. Behind her he heard Blake's sudden, swiftly indrawn breath, but he ignored that. Blake wasn't important.

He sneered at Margot with his stiff, scarred lips. "You think you can help me, doc? I think you've done enough already."

"Oh, Preston," she whispered. He saw pity in her face. He had grown to hate that look of pity, no matter whose face wore it. It was useless. It was offensive. She said, "You've suffered terribly."

Allison, held tight in the crook of his arm, quivered against him. She was crying, he thought, but silently. Oddly, this gave him no joy. He rather liked her, and he admired her spirit. He loosened his hold on her neck, but he kept the razor blade close to her face to forestall any shenanigans.

He looked past Margot to the outside step, where Blake stood in a tense posture, leaning on his cane, ready—it seemed—to dash into the room if necessary. "Hello there, Blake," he said. "Haven't turned up your toes yet?"

"Mr. Preston," Blake said heavily. "Won't you let Miss Allison go? We can talk about what you—what you need."

"Need? I need what I've always needed!"

Margot took another step forward. "Plastic surgery, Preston," she said. "They're doing amazing things these days, and I can help you find—"

"Stay where you are, doc! We're doing this my way!" He pressed the blade against Allison's cheek once again and felt another sob shake her small body.

"Doing what?" Margot asked. "What is it we're doing, Preston?"

"Don't take that doctor tone with me, Margot," he grated. "It's all over for you and me. It's your fault I look like this, and it's your fault our poor little cuz is in this fix."

"That makes no sense," Margot said and took another step.

He pressed the blade tighter, and a thin line of blood oozed from Allison's tender cheek and dripped under his hand. "You want her to look like me?" he cried.

Margot froze. "Don't!" Allison twisted backward, away from the razor.

"Stop it," he hissed in her ear. "You'll make it worse."

Allison said, shakily but clearly, "It's already worse, Cousin Preston."

He wanted to laugh, but he couldn't do it. The tension in the storeroom was as thick as the fog outside, a miasma of sweat and fear and rage. Somewhere a clock ticked and ticked, maddeningly, scraping his nerves.

He had thought he would like this. Thought he would enjoy this moment when he had the power, and could force Margot to do what he wanted. He hadn't expected to feel sympathy for Allison, hadn't expected to see pity on Margot's face. He needed the sapphire back, he thought. He needed Roxclana's strength to do what had to be done. He wished he had it here, with him, but then Margot would never have understood, would never have come . . .

Damn it. It had to be done, with or without the stone. The time had come. The end for both of them.

He said, "I can't take this life anymore, doc. Not this way."

"I can understand that. It must be awful. But, Preston, if you'll just let me—"

"Shut up!" His voice was too rough to have any power, but the razor had plenty. He pressed it against Allison's little white neck, and she trembled against him like a leaf in the wind. "Just shut up, Margot! You've fooled everyone, all these years, but you can't talk your way out of this one. I'm going, but I'm by God not going alone!"

Blake drew a swift, alarmed breath. "Preston, you don't mean that."

"Be quiet! I'm only letting you stay so you can take our little cousin home," he snarled.

"Let her go then," Blake said.

"In a moment. When I have what I want."

Margot said, warily, "What *do* you want, Preston?"

He braced the razor under Allison's chin and whispered, "What I've always wanted, Margot. You. Come here."

CHAPTER 22

Frank knew the moment he opened his eyes that there would be no flying today. The fog, unusually thick for Seattle, blanketed the streets and clung to the shrubberies and rooftops. Even the few lights on in the houses along Cherry Street were nearly suffocated by the mist.

He sat up swiftly and looked at the alarm clock beside his bed. It was only six thirty, but he didn't think he could go back to sleep. He got out of bed, strapped on his prosthesis, and went into the bathroom to wash and brush his teeth. When he returned, he found himself at a loose end. He couldn't fly, that was clear. He should probably go down to the Red Barn, call March Field from there to warn them of the delay. He could get some work done, check in with Mr. Boeing.

He dressed quickly in a freshly pressed shirt and trousers from his wardrobe. He put on one of his belted jackets, and then, anticipating the chill of the foggy morning, he shrugged into his overcoat.

The rustle of paper in his pocket reminded him. Slowly, he

drew out the envelope, still sealed, bearing his name in Elizabeth's careful handwriting. He gazed down at it, wondering what she would have to say. He couldn't remember her face anymore, at least not all of it at once. He could dredge up the way her eyes looked, or her hair, or sometimes her mouth, but he could no longer put the pieces together.

The only face he could call to his mind was Margot's. Margot in her white doctor's coat. Margot smiling at him across the candlelit table at Benedict Hall. Margot in the darkness, her eyes gleaming up at him, full of affection.

Margot's face when she realized he was carrying around a letter from Elizabeth.

"Damn, Cowboy," he muttered. "Not fair to her."

He would make it up to her. He would go down to the clinic, repair the flaw in the footings she had told him about. If it needed fresh concrete, or to be sanded down, he would figure it out. He could be waiting for her when she arrived.

Hurrying now, he trotted down the stairs and let himself out of the rooming house. He strode swiftly to the streetcar stop. He had time to get coffee at the diner, chat with Arnie for a few moments, then walk up Post Street to the clinic as soon as it was light enough to see the problem. He would surprise her, since she thought he was on his way back to March. He pictured himself smoothing the furrow from her forehead, bringing the smile back to her face. He would give her the damned letter, tell her to burn it. He would remind her—dredge up the words somehow to express the truth of his heart—that she was the only woman he cared about.

He hopped off the streetcar, saluting the operator as he did so, and strode up to Post Street through the fog. The shoe repairman and the barber hadn't opened their doors yet, but the Italian grocer had lifted his awning and was setting out trays with braids of garlic, piles of onions, fat red potatoes. The door of the diner was open, its rooster doorstop wedged against the sidewalk. Frank was on his way there, thinking of coffee and eggs and bacon, when he spotted the Essex at the end of the street.

He glanced at his watch. It was just past seven. Surely Margot wouldn't be at her clinic already.

No light shone from the reception room, or from the window of her office, which he had planned so carefully for the view of the bay. He paced faster, hurrying past the diner and on toward the clinic. A rectangle of light fell on the raw ground behind the storeroom, where eventually there would be a barrier of shrubs to separate the clinic from the alley behind. What was she doing there so early? Had there been a delivery? He could step in and help, he thought. Blake shouldn't be doing that sort of work.

Frank moved up the sidewalk, then around to the back of the clinic. With a little jolt of alarm, he saw there was something wrong with the door. The glass knob, special ordered from Tweedy and Popp, hung loose, and the lock was broken, gouged out with some tool, a screwdriver or perhaps a chisel.

He called, in a low voice, "Margot? Blake?" There was no answer. Alarmed now, he leaped up the steps.

Margot knew what Preston was capable of. She had experienced the depth of his cruelty throughout her childhood, and she still bore the scars.

Only Blake had believed her then. Preston had been Edith's golden-haired, blue-eyed darling. If he sometimes hurt his sister, it was always an accident. It was never intentional. All of those incidents were just a little boy's antics. Only Blake knew how close Preston had come to doing real and permanent harm to Margot.

Margot's belly trembled with dread, but she couldn't see any choice. None of this was Allison's fault, and the situation was beyond Blake's ability to defuse.

She did as Preston told her. With her hands open by her sides, she walked toward him. "I'm coming," she said.

"Closer." He grinned, horribly. The scars were glazed, shiny with keloid tissue, and they filled her with sorrow. They were the perfect symbol for Preston's twisted nature, the tortured thinking that had driven him all his life.

She came within an arm's length of him, and stopped. "No farther," she said in a low tone. "Not until you let her go."

Behind her she felt Blake tense, as if ready to leap, but what could he do? That blade, that straight razor—even if it hadn't been stropped, it could be deadly. It could slice through Allison's flesh with even a halfhearted stroke. If Preston turned it on himself, it could sever an artery in a flash, requiring no strength at all. And if he turned it on her—as he so clearly meant to—

But she couldn't think about that. She said, turning her head slightly to Blake, "Stay where you are. Nothing you can do."

Preston laughed, a sound of pure horror. "Right-ho, doc! Nothing he can do. Or you, either."

It seemed that his madness gave him energy. They were all exhausted, from tension, from sleeplessness, from fear, but Preston, with the sort of swift, brazen movement that had always made him dangerous, shoved Allison away from him and seized Margot's wrist.

Allison stumbled forward and fell into Blake's arms. At the same moment, Margot tried to wrench her wrist away from Preston's hard hand, but he was ready. Without hesitating, as if this was the moment he'd been waiting for, he held her tight with one hand while with the other he lunged at her with the razor. He held nothing back. He poured all his strength into that vicious slashing motion, grunting with effort.

Margot threw up her free arm, palm out, more by instinct than by plan. She meant to deflect the blade before it reached her throat. In this, at least, she succeeded, but the blade sliced easily through the sleeve of her coat. In the grip of adrenaline, she didn't feel the laceration, but she knew it was there, a deep cut on the inside of her forearm, where the precious, essential tendons ran down to her fingers. Blood sprang forth to stain her sleeve and drip like hot syrup over her skin.

She couldn't help crying out. He had cut her before, when they were children. He had burned her, pinched her, pushed her when he had the chance, but in comparison with this, those events were minor. The straight razor blade was lethal. She knew what a blade like that could do to a person, and despite every-thing, it stunned her to think her brother would use it on her.

In the space of a heartbeat, Preston raised the blade again. This time, she knew with dread certainty, it was going to reach her throat. It was as if he knew precisely where to strike to achieve the swiftest, the surest destruction. It was as if he had studied—as she had—just where the carotid artery carried heart's blood clos-est to the surface. If he reached that artery, she would be uncon-scious in thirty seconds. She would bleed out in under five minutes. Stress meant her blood pressure was high, and her blood could spray as far as six feet away, spattering everything in the room. Her tidy storeroom would be awash in it, the floor and the walls and the shelves—and Preston himself—splashed with it.

Time slowed to a crawl. Every instant became an eternity. There was noise behind her, Allison screaming, Blake shouting, the door banging. Margot didn't try to sort out the sounds. She was fully occupied in trying to twist away from the descending blade. In the slow march of seconds, she assessed every action, and she understood she would be too slow. Grief filled her at the waste, the pointless tragedy of it. It was a moment of violence that would change lives forever.

Still, she tried. She threw her weight back and struggled to lift her bleeding arm. The razor fell with deadly speed, its silver blade already red with her blood. She observed it with crystal clarity, and acceptance shuddered through her. There was even a distant sense of relief at this inevitable outcome, this end to the specter that had haunted her all her life.

When something—a jar, perhaps a bottle—spun past her head to strike Preston full in his face, it knocked him off balance. The blade flashed past Margot's eyes, missing her by centimeters. Preston roared a protest, wordless, harsh, as he scrambled to his feet again. He lifted the razor, but a hand—not her own, and not even human—snatched it from him as if it were no sharper, no more dangerous, than a silver butter knife from the dining table in Benedict Hall.

Preston howled with impotent fury. Frank—Frank!—threw

the straight razor into a corner, where it clattered to the floor, well out of reach. Frank's arm, his wonderful, nearly invincible Carnes arm, seized Preston in an irresistible grip of metal and leather. Time, for Margot, resumed its normal flow with a snap that took her breath away.

Blake joined Frank, and together they held Preston's arms, even as he shrieked curses and fought to free himself. Allison appeared at Margot's side, guiding her back with her small hands, exclaiming over the blood running over her hand to drip on the floor. She made Margot pull off her coat. She found a roll of gauze on a shelf, rolled up Margot's sleeve, and began binding the cut with sure, swift movements.

The men who worked on Post Street—the Italian grocer, Arnie from the diner—crowded into the storeroom, drawn by Allison's screams and Preston's shouts, which went on unabated, and which made Margot wonder if his mind had broken at last. Soon there were policemen, and even an ambulance, which Margot knew she didn't need, but which bore her away just the same, with Frank at her side.

She was the only person, in all the crowd that gathered to deal with the crisis, who hadn't spoken a word. She would always know, after this day, what shock felt like to her patients. She knew the symptoms, of course—dry mouth, damp skin, tight chest. What she had never guessed was the emotional effect, the sense of disconnection, the impression of having stepped through a curtain into some other, alien world and knowing there might not be a way back. She had thought she knew all about dying, but this—this was something she had never imagined.

Nothing seemed real to her, not Frank's warm hand on her shoulder, nor the gong of the ambulance, nor even the pain beginning to burn in her arm. The only thing that seemed real to her, at this moment, was the propinquity of death. She had been ready for it, albeit reluctantly. She had seen it coming. She had felt the curtain of shadow ready to fall, the profound mystery about to be revealed. It had been thwarted, for now. But it hovered nearby, for all of them, for everyone she knew and cared about.

She had not died today. No one in that room had died. But it could have happened. It could so easily have happened. How did people live with that knowledge?

Allison shivered with a violence she wouldn't have believed possible. The warmth of the Essex's heater hadn't helped, and the blankets Ruby wrapped around her, as she huddled by the fire in the small parlor, didn't help. Nothing eased her shaking until Uncle Dickson brought her a small glass of golden liquid and said, gruffly, "Drink up, Allison. Best medicine there is."

She did, and he was right. The heat of the brandy ran like fire through her throat. She could trace its warmth down her chest and into her stomach. At last, hours after the awful scene in Margot's clinic, she began to relax.

"Is she all right?" she had begged, over and over, of anyone who seemed to know what had happened to Cousin Margot. "Is it bad?"

It was, again, Uncle Dickson who soothed her fears, once she was calm enough to listen. He said, "My own physician is seeing to her. Don't worry. Dr. Creedy says it's a superficial laceration."

"It's my fault, Uncle Dickson." Allison's throat was so tight she could barely speak. "If I hadn't run out like that—"

He patted her hand. "No, my dear," he said. He looked so sad she felt sympathetic tears sting her eyes. "No, all of this is my fault, going back a very long way."

Blake came in, carrying a tray with cups and a teapot. Uncle Dickson said, "Blake, I want you to go to bed. That's an order."

"Yes, sir." Blake nodded, but the order didn't stop him from setting the cups on the piecrust table and pouring out the tea. Ramona was there, in her pink flannel dressing gown, and Dick in a thick sweater and plus fours. Cousin Ramona had been crying. Cousin Dick had tried to comfort her, but he was white around the lips, and Allison saw that his hands, rubbing his wife's shaking shoulders, trembled so that when he tried to pick up a teacup, it rattled violently against the saucer. She could only guess at their feelings. They had mourned Cousin Preston all this past year. Learning he was alive must be staggering. Incomprehensible.

Her father was fully dressed in his usual suit and vest. He paced beside the tall windows, sometimes glaring at Allison, other times peering in confusion out of the window. He had taken to scrubbing his head with nervous hands until his hair stood up like a rooster's comb.

Blake said, "Mr. Dickson, Hattie would like to know what to do about luncheon."

"Tell her we'll have cold sandwiches, or soup if she has it. Whatever's convenient."

"She sent Leona up to see to Mrs. Edith."

"Good. That's good. Thank you, Blake."

Uncle Dickson put two more small logs on the fire and stoked it a bit, then sat down in his chair near the divan where Allison was curled in her nest of blankets. He watched to see that Blake had left the room before he said over his shoulder, "Henry, sit down. Have some tea. Or would you prefer brandy? There's nothing we can do now but wait for Margot and the major to telephone."

"What about Adelaide?" Papa said fretfully. "Margot was going to arrange something for Adelaide today."

"It's a good hospital," Uncle Dickson said. "They'll take care of her." He put his head back, staring at the flames in the fireplace beneath heavy eyelids.

"I just don't understand," Papa said, pacing again. "First Adelaide in the hospital, and Allison running around in the dark—how did all that add up to Margot and Preston—" He broke off and ran his hand through his hair again.

Allison, encouraged by the warmth of the brandy, said, "I wasn't running around, Papa." She was about to explain that Preston had seized her, forced her into the water tower, but the grief on Uncle

Dickson's face stopped her. She pressed her lips together and was silent.

Uncle Dickson's eyes flicked over to her, then away. "Allison couldn't have known."

"She knew better than to strike her mother!" Papa exclaimed.

Allison hung her head. There was no answer to that. She shouldn't have struck her mother, spoon or no spoon. In truth, it had been more of a collision than a blow, but Papa wouldn't care for that excuse, she was sure.

"I'm sure Dr. Kinney will have a word to say about all this," he pronounced. Allison clenched her teeth and stared at the folds of her blanket.

Uncle Dickson said, "Henry, we don't know for sure what happened yet."

"My wife's in the hospital!" Papa exclaimed. "Her own daughter put her there!"

"No. My daughter, the physician, put her there, and not for her broken arm. She thinks she's ill." Uncle Dickson closed his eyes and spoke with infinite weariness. "But, Henry, my son's in jail, and I have to find some way to tell his mother that he's been alive all this past year, while she mourned him and took flowers to an empty grave. Keep some perspective."

Allison said softly, "I'm so sorry, Uncle Dickson. About everything."

He murmured, "Thank you, my dear."

Her father shot her a furious glance, but she pretended not to see it.

She drank the cup of tea Blake had poured, then, feeling stronger, she unwrapped the blankets and stood up. Ramona and Dick were huddled in a corner, Dick with an arm around Ramona, Ramona with her head on his shoulder. Papa came to stand by the fire, his arms folded over his paunch. He stared down at her, unblinking.

"I'm going to take the tray into the kitchen," Allison said quietly.

Papa said, "Call one of the maids."

"All the servants were up half the night, Papa. Cousin Ramona said so."

"So were you."

"And you're angry at me for that."

"It doesn't mean I want you doing servants' work."

"I don't like being useless," she answered pointedly, and was rewarded by seeing his cheeks redden. She picked up the tray with the teapot and unused cups without looking at him again. She carried the tray out of the small parlor and across the hall, backing through the swinging door into the kitchen. She found Hattie stirring something in the big stockpot. Ruby was seated at the enamel-topped table with a cup of tea and a plate of toast and jam.

"Oh, Miss Allison! Let me take that from you." Hattie hurried across the kitchen to reach for the tray. "You shouldn't oughtta do that sort of thing."

Allison cast Ruby a reproachful glance, but Ruby only stared back at her as she put the last piece of toast in her mouth. She made no move to get up, but watched as Allison relinquished the tray into Hattie's hands.

Hattie said, "You poor chile. You must be exhausted!"

"You must be, too, Hattie," Allison said. "I think everyone is." And then, with a touch of bitterness, "Except perhaps Papa."

"Well, now," Hattie said, not meeting her eyes. "I wouldn't know about that. Did you have some tea? Maybe you should go up to your bed and get some rest."

"I don't think I could sleep, Hattie. I keep seeing Cousin Margot, and Cousin—" She broke off, remembering. Hattie had grieved for Cousin Preston, too, had wept over his empty place in the dining room. She didn't know if Hattie had heard yet, if Blake would have explained—

When she looked up into Hattie's face, she saw that the cook already knew. Her eyes were red, the lids swollen. Tear tracks marked her cheeks, and her lips trembled as if she had only just managed to stop crying.

Hattie swiped at her eyes with the hem of her apron, and said,

"I know, I know, Miss Allison. This is a terrible time. I thought, when Mr. Preston got burned up in the fire, that was the worst thing that could ever happen to Benedict Hall, but this—" Her voice broke on a fresh sob, and she turned back to the stove.

"Oh, Hattie," Allison said. She stood awkwardly by the enamel-topped table, staring at Hattie's rounded shoulders, her bent head. Hattie was right. It was terrible. It wasn't just that Cousin Margot had gotten slashed with a straight razor. It was her *brother* who did it, and who had hidden himself all this past year while people who loved him grieved his death. It was stranger than any novel or film, and she had no idea what was going to happen next.

While she struggled to think of something she could say, some comfort she could offer, she became aware of Ruby's gaze, bright with avid curiosity. "Ruby," she said sharply. "Go see if Aunt Edith needs anything."

"Leona's up there, Miss Allison," Ruby said.

Allison very nearly stamped her foot. "Leona is not a lady's maid. Aunt Edith may need her hair dressed or something. This is going to be a hard day for her."

"Why?"

"Ruby. Do as you're told." Allison lifted her chin and did her best to mimic the decisive tone Cousin Margot used when people were behaving badly. She turned her back as if she had no doubts about Ruby's obedience. She heard the chair scrape, the teacup clatter in its saucer, and then the swish of the swinging door. She would remonstrate with Ruby later, she promised herself, about leaving her things on the table for Hattie to clean up.

When she was sure Ruby was gone, she walked across to the stove so she could look up into Hattie's face. Big, shining tears rolled down Hattie's cheeks, even as she stirred and stirred the pot. Allison, no longer caring whether it was appropriate or not, put out her hand and took the long wooden spoon from Hattie's hand. She laid it on the spoon rest, put the lid back on the pot, and then, putting her arm around Hattie's plump waist, she guided her to the table and pressed her into a chair.

The cook was shaking her head, pressing her fingers to her eyes. "No, no, Miss Allison, you shouldn't—old Hattie will be all right, if I just take a minute—"

"Sit right there," Allison said. She went to the counter, where the teapot rested on its tray, and poured a cup. She carried it back to the table and set it in front of Hattie, then pulled a chair up beside her. "Drink some tea, Hattie. It will make you feel better."

Hattie sniffled, and reached for the cup. When she saw it was one of the good china ones, she hesitated, but Allison touched her shoulder, and said, "It's not a day to worry about rules." Hattie sniffled again, and drank, while Allison sat back and waited for her to calm herself.

When Hattie had drained the cup, she set it down, pulled a large handkerchief from her apron pocket, and blew her nose. "So kind to old Hattie, Miss Allison. I'm sorry I'm so weepy, but it's a real sad day."

"I know it is."

"We all thought," Hattie said in a trembling voice, "that Mr. Preston was gone. Mrs. Edith didn't never get over it, you know, and now—I don't know but what this is a whole lot worse."

"Uncle Dickson is trying to think of how to tell her."

"It was just—it was so *cruel* of Mr. Preston. He knew—he knows—" Her words died away, and she sat twisting the handkerchief in her hands. She drew a painful, uneven breath, and brought her eyes up to Allison's face. In a voice tight with apprehension, she said, "Blake says Mr. Preston got burned. Does he look—is he very—" She gave a shake of her head and looked away, to the view of the garden stretching behind the house.

"He's terribly scarred," Allison said. "I'm so sorry, Hattie."

"Oh," Hattie said, keeping her gaze on the window. The fog had burned away at last, and the weak December sunlight picked out the bare stalks of the rosebushes. "That's a sad thing. He was a handsome boy."

"I remember."

"He cut Miss Margot, Blake said." Hattie's voice was steady

now, but weighed down with grief. It was the voice, Allison thought, of one who doesn't see a way forward.

Allison knew she was too young, and too inexperienced, to offer anything that could ease Hattie's sorrow. She could say only, "Yes. He's so angry."

"But he didn't hurt you," Hattie said.

"Not really," Allison said. "He wouldn't let me go, and he cut a hank of my hair, but he didn't hurt me. Well, just a scratch on my cheek." She touched it with her fingers. It hadn't been deep enough even to bandage, and it was already nearly healed.

Hattie turned to look at her. Her voice shook as she said, "You musta been scared, you poor chile, but you know, I don't think he ever meant it. It's the fire. The scars. They've changed him, hurt his mind, maybe."

"That makes sense," Allison said gently. "Anyone would be changed."

Hattie gave her a tremulous smile. "You're the sweetest chile," she said. "Sitting here and listening to me go on."

"I like being here. I like being in your kitchen. And it's one place I know Mother and Papa will never come."

Hattie sighed, and wiped her eyes one final time. "I'm sure your mama and papa love you, Miss Allison."

Allison shook her head. "No," she said. She spoke with regret, but it was nothing like the grief Hattie was feeling, and she knew it. "No, I don't think they do, Hattie. I guess mothers and fathers don't always love their children."

Hattie dropped her apron and smoothed it over her lap. "That's a hard truth, and I can't deny it. It was that way for me."

Allison leaned forward, surprised by this confidence. "Was it, Hattie? Your mama, your papa—"

Hattie gave her head a shake. "I didn't have no papa, Miss Allison. And my mama—well, I s'pose she did the best she could. We had some mighty hard times, but I s'pose my mama did the best she could."

Allison put an impulsive hand over Hattie's, finding her skin warm and slightly rough. "Do you think that's it, Hattie? They do the best they can?"

"It's the Christian thing to think, Miss Allison. I never had no babies, but I sure do know being a mama is hard." Hattie removed her hand from beneath Allison's, but gently. She put her hands on the table edge to push herself up.

"My mother didn't want babies," Allison said. "She never wanted to be a mother."

"Oh, now. I expect she changed her mind once you came along."

"No, she didn't. She told me. She didn't want *me*."

Hattie sank back down in her chair. "Oh, poor chile. That must hurt your heart something fierce. I always thought, if you grow up with enough food and a safe place to live, that meant you were lucky."

"You didn't have enough food, Hattie?"

"No, Miss Allison. Not till I came here to work for the Benedicts. I surely didn't."

Allison stared at her empty hand lying on the table. "I did. There was plenty of food. I just wasn't supposed to enjoy it."

Hattie drew a sharp breath. "How's that?"

Allison watched her fingers curl into a fist, then open again. "There was food. I was supposed to eat it, but then I was supposed to throw it up."

"I don't—that doesn't make sense."

"It's what my mother's done, for years. It's how she stays so thin."

"But you don't do that, do you, Miss Allison? That can't be good for a person."

Allison's laugh made a sad, hollow little sound. "No, I don't do that, Hattie. I hate that. I just—I sort of stopped eating."

"I thought you just didn't like my cooking. I know I'm not too good at fancy cooking, but that's what Mrs. Edith wants, so I—" She gave a shrug. "I'm glad to hear it wasn't that, why you didn't want to eat."

"Mother says I'm too fat. She hates me to get fat."

"She can't mean it!" Hattie protested. "A pretty girl like you!"

Allison looked up into Hattie's sympathetic face. "You can't imagine, Hattie. You can't imagine how twisted up it all is, with my mother and me."

Hattie shook her head, and her dark eyes shone with fresh tears. "This is awful sad to hear," she said. "I'm awful sorry."

"I am, too."

Hattie drew another, slower breath, and gave Allison another trembling smile. "Oh, now. We're a pair, aren't we?"

Allison smiled back, comforted. "I guess we are, Hattie. I guess we're a pair, you and I."

Hattie pushed herself up and crossed to the stove. "One thing I know, Miss Allison," she said. "Everybody gotta eat. I'm gonna finish this soup. Everybody feels better after they have some soup."

CHAPTER 23

"I was lucky," Margot told Frank, as the nurse finished bandaging her arm. "My sleeve caught the blade, prevented it from severing the tendons. That would have meant the end of my surgical practice—maybe all of my practice." She looked up into his face, and saw that he was still angry, his jaw pulsing with tension, the blue of his eyes darkened to indigo. "Mostly, I was lucky you were there," she added softly. "I don't know what might have happened."

The nurse, a woman she had never seen before, glanced up from beneath her cap, then quickly away again. They hadn't spoken Preston's name, but everyone in the accident room knew something terrible had happened in the Benedict family. Dr. Creedy had treated Margot's arm and then told them he was going to the jail to treat—he had paused, and spoken in an undertone—her brother. There had been two nurses in the room at the time, and Margot's cheeks burned under their curious glances. She knew hospitals. The nurses would have their heads together the moment she and Frank were gone. She couldn't see how even her father could quash the rumors that would fly.

The other nurse came back into the room and crossed to her. "Dr. Benedict, your driver is here. He's waiting with the car."

"Thank you. We're coming." The bandaging process was finished, and Margot nodded to the nurse, then swung her legs off the bed. "We can go, Frank. Do you have my coat?"

"Wear mine," he said, shrugging out of his jacket, draping it around her shoulders. "Yours is gone."

The nurse said, "We threw it away, Dr. Benedict. I hope that was all right. It looked—" She broke off, spreading her hands.

Margot nodded again. "Of course. I should have realized. I'm sure it's ruined."

The nurse supported her as she stood up, and Frank took her other arm as the three of them walked toward the door. "If there's any sign of infection," the nurse began, but Margot forestalled her instructions.

"I know," she said. "Thank you, Nurse. I'll come back if there is."

As they crossed reception to the front doors of the hospital, Margot felt curious eyes on her, and kept her head down to avoid them. Frank kept his arm around her shoulder, which helped. Blake was waiting in the Essex, and he climbed out to open the rear door.

"Thank you, Blake," Margot said. "When we get home, I want you to go straight to bed."

"I'm fine, Dr. Margot," he said. "I had a bit of a rest already."

As Blake pressed the starter, Frank said, "You're the one who needs to go to bed, Margot. I'll go clean up the clinic."

"Is it bad?" she asked. "The storeroom?"

"Not too bad. I'll repair the lock on the door. Mop up the floor."

"You'll need hydrogen peroxide for that. And we'll need to disinfect it."

"Fortunately, there's no carpet there."

"I don't know what to tell Angela."

"Truth is best," he said shortly.

She sighed, and let her head drop back against the plush seat.

It was warm in the automobile, and she had allowed Dr. Creedy to give her an injection of scopolamine, which was now making her drowsy. Textbook reactions, she thought. First, shock. Second, a burst of nervous energy that had made it hard to sit still while Dr. Creedy made his sutures. Now, exhaustion.

"What's going to happen to him?" she murmured to Frank.

He didn't need to ask whom she meant. "It's either jail or an insane asylum."

"I don't know which is worse."

Frank shifted his shoulder to move closer to her. He didn't answer, but she sensed his thought in the hardness of his muscles and the pressure of his hand on hers. Her brother had nearly succeeded in killing her. Frank didn't care what happened to Preston.

They found Dick and Ramona alone in the dining room, seated at the table. The soup tureen waited on the sideboard, and Blake insisted on serving both Margot and Frank from it before he disappeared into the kitchen to have his own luncheon.

"Where's Father?" Margot asked.

"Gone to the hospital with Uncle Henry," Dick told her. He looked pale, but calm.

"You've heard everything, Dick?"

"I think so. It's hard to believe that he—that Preston—" Involuntarily, he looked over his shoulder, as if Edith might be there.

"If I hadn't seen it, I'm not sure I would have believed it myself," Margot said. "He's hidden himself, all this time. It's astounding."

"He was burned, Blake says. Badly scarred."

"It's awful, Dick. As bad as anything I've seen."

Ramona said, with a shudder, "I can't take it in, Margot. I just can't take it in. And I don't know what we're going to do about Mother Benedict."

"I don't, either," Margot said bleakly. "I have real concerns about what a shock like that could do to her. She's in such a fragile state already."

"How could he let her suffer that way? Couldn't he have—at least he could have—I don't know! Anything to let her know he was alive!" Ramona covered her face with her hands, and Dick put his arm around her shoulders.

"I can't give you an answer," Margot said sadly.

Frank said, "Margot, you need to eat something. There will be time to deal with this later."

She cast him a grateful glance. It was true, despite everything, she was hungry, and the chicken soup, thick with homemade noodles, was rich and comforting. She was halfway through a bowlful when the dining room door swept open.

Allison, showered and dressed in a fresh frock but looking haggard, stood in the doorway gazing at Margot with desperate eyes. There was a chunk of her hair missing, just beside her right temple, which she had tried to disguise with pomade. "Cousin Margot! Are you all right? I've been so worried!"

Margot held out a hand in invitation, and Frank rose to pull out the chair closest to her. Allison hurried around the table, grasping Margot's hand even as she settled into the chair. Margot squeezed the girl's fingers. "I'm fine," she said. "There was no permanent damage. Nothing at all for you to worry about."

Allison's cheeks were pink with emotion, though her eyes were hollow and shadowed. "It would have been my fault!" she whispered. "If I hadn't gone out—that is, if Mother and I—"

"Hush," Margot said. "We can talk about all of that later. Have a bit of soup, and you'll feel better."

Frank, without waiting to be asked, had gone to the sideboard, and returned now with a bowlful. He set it in front of Allison, and resumed his own seat.

Margot held up her arm so Allison could see the bandage. "See? A few stitches, probably not even necessary. You did very well with the gauze, and I'm as good as new. Now, please, Allison—eat Hattie's good soup. It has magic powers."

Allison's eyes were fever-bright with unshed tears. She blinked, and pressed a forefinger to her trembling lips.

"I mean it," Margot said, gently.

Ramona added, "Cousin Allison, Margot is right. Everything's going to be fine."

Allison picked up her spoon. Margot watched until she saw that she really was going to eat her soup, then winked at Ramona, and returned to her own serving with good appetite. Frank, on her other side, did the same. When Loena came in a few minutes later, the tureen was nearly empty.

It wasn't until Loena had gone out with the tureen and the tray of soup bowls that Allison gasped, and put her hand to her mouth again. "Mother!" she said in a horrified whisper. "I forgot to ask about Mother!"

Dick made a small noise in his throat, one that sounded like disgust. Margot wondered what that was about. "Uncle Henry has gone down to the hospital," Dick said. "With Father."

Allison turned wide eyes to Margot. "She's in the hospital?"

"Not because of her arm," Margot said. "Her arm breaking may be because of some other illness. I thought she should be examined by our family physician."

"Some other illness?"

"That's right, Allison. Some other illness. Her arm shouldn't have broken so easily."

"You mean it wasn't my fault?"

It was Ramona who answered this sad little question. She said, in the firmest tone Margot had ever heard her use, "Cousin Allison, you're barely an adult, and your mother has been one for a long time. She's the parent, and you're the child. You're not to blame for any of this. Not the smallest part."

It was a strange day, and a long one, all the normal rhythms of life disrupted. After luncheon, Margot went to bed and slept for four hours without moving. When she woke, she pressed the bell for one of the maids, something she almost never did. It was the new one, Thelma, who appeared at her door, and Margot sent her to run a bath and to find out whether Major Parrish was still in the house. Word came that he had gone to his boardinghouse, but would return for dinner.

Margot glanced out the window as she made her way toward the bathroom, and saw that the last of the fog had burned away. No doubt Frank would be on his way back to March Field in the morning.

But for tonight, she meant to make herself as presentable as possible. She might even ask Ramona to help. She had things to say to Frank, and she wanted to look her best when she said them.

She had just finished dressing when someone knocked on her bedroom door. When she opened it, she found her father, looking so tired he could barely stand. She took his hand, and pressed him down to sit on the edge of her bed. "Have you rested at all?"

"Not yet. I went from the hospital to the jail. I had to see Preston, of course."

"Oh, Father. That must have been hard."

"Ghastly." He passed a shaking hand over his eyes. "He's in this hideous place. Bars everywhere. An open toilet in the corner."

"Awful."

"He just sat on the bunk—no mattress, just these rusty wires—and stared at the wall. He wouldn't talk. Wouldn't look at me. I could see, though, his scalp—his neck—he's so badly burned, Margot."

"Father, we could get him help for his scars. Plastic surgery is a fairly new field, but I've read of some good work being done in California."

Her father dropped his hand. His eyes were bloodshot, and his cheeks sagged. "Did he really do those things, Margot? What they said he did?"

"I'm afraid so."

"He tried to—to hurt you."

This made her choke back a bitter laugh. "To hurt me. Yes, he did indeed try to hurt me."

"Blake thinks he meant to hurt himself, too."

"I believe that was his intent, Father. He said it was the end for both of us."

Dickson's sigh shook his whole body, and he covered his eyes again. From beneath his hand, he said brokenly, "This was behind us. Done with. Now, again . . . I don't know how to face it."

"I'll talk to Mother, if you like."

"I was thinking of not telling her, Margot." He lowered his hand again and pushed himself up from the bed. "I was thinking of committing him to Western State Hospital. And keeping it quiet. Out of the papers."

Margot frowned. "Can you do that? Will it work?"

"It will work. Nothing really happened, in the end. I'm not excusing him, you understand." He gave her a worried glance, his eyes full of guilt and grief.

"I understand that, Father."

"I know enough judges, and Creedy can make the recommendation. These weren't the actions of a sane man."

"No. That's true."

"Let's go down to tell the family. We'll have to get everyone to agree not to mention it to Edith."

"Father, it's a very big secret to keep. If the maids find out, or Hattie . . ."

"Hattie knows already."

"Oh, Lord. Poor Hattie. Well, you know she'll want to protect Mother, either way."

"Without a doubt."

"I'm not sure if this is a good idea or a spectacularly bad one."

He gave a shaky laugh, and put his arm around her waist to escort her out into the hall. "I'm not either, daughter. But it's the only one I have."

Frank returned to Benedict Hall, dressed in his black dinner jacket and a dark silk tie, at eight o'clock. The house was resplendent with Christmas decorations, boughs of pine and cedar draped along the banisters of the porch, colored lights festooning the picture window. Blake greeted him at the door with his usual composure, as if the two of them had not just that morning been present at a scene of such melodrama it already seemed impossible.

"Major Parrish," Blake said. "How good to see you again. If you don't mind my saying so, sir, that's a very handsome jacket."

Frank grinned at Blake as he handed him his overcoat and his Stetson. "Don't mind at all," he said. "I hope Dr. Benedict feels the same."

Blake's eyes twinkled briefly. "I have no doubts about that, Major." He hung the overcoat and hat on the mahogany coatrack before he led the way down the hall to the small parlor. He held the door, spoke Frank's name to the family assembled there, then turned away toward the kitchen. The newest maid was just coming out, and she curtsied to Frank before following Blake.

The only person missing from the gathering was Allison's mother. Frank shook hands with Dickson Benedict, thinking that he looked as if he had aged a decade since the night before. He greeted Dick and Ramona, who sat very close together, their hands entwined, as if they couldn't bear to be apart. Allison came to take his hand in both of hers, and to murmur in an undertone, "Major Parrish! Thank you so much for what you did!"

She was the only person to acknowledge what had happened. Margot, looking slim and elegant in a narrow frock of some deep blue fabric, drew him to the little divan without saying anything. Her mother looked up in the vague way that had become her habit, and said, "Major Parrish. How nice to see you again." She seemed unchanged from the night before, and when Frank raised his eyebrows to Margot, she gave a slight shake of her head.

After dinner, Margot drew Frank aside to stand near the window in the small parlor. Someone had arranged sprigs of pine in a wide glass bowl and sprinkled bright red cranberries among the greenery. The bowl rested on the sideboard, where Blake had set out glasses and two or three bottles from Dickson's cellar. Dickson and the rest had settled themselves near the fire, Dickson with his cigar and cut-glass ashtray close at hand, Dick and Henry Benedict with tumblers of whisky. Allison had tucked her feet up under her, and rested her chin on her hand as she stared into the flames. She hadn't spoken to her father at all throughout dinner. She had, however, eaten a good meal. Frank saw Margot give her an encouraging smile.

They stood now beside the half-open drapes, gazing out into the dark garden. The moon was rising above the mountains to the east. The mists of the night before had evaporated, and the moonlight cast shadows across the grass. The cloudless sky meant there would be frost by morning. He was in for a chilly flight until he reached California.

He glanced across at the quiet group by the fire. Ramona was speaking to Dick, and including Allison in the conversation. Allison was nodding, adding short remarks to whatever the discussion was. Frank said, "Your cousin seems to have recovered."

Margot looked over her shoulder at her family, then turned her face back to the moonlit night. "She's young," she said. "It was exciting, but nothing terrible happened, in the end."

"Depends on your perspective."

"Oh, yes, Frank. That it does."

She gazed out into the garden, and he watched her clear profile, the smooth curve of her bobbed hair against her cheek. He said, "And you? Have you recovered?"

She didn't turn her head. "I don't know. It was a very close thing, and that's hard to accept. If you hadn't come . . ."

"But I did come."

"Yes. You saved me. In a way, you were the only one who could save me, because of your hand."

He held up his left hand, the prosthesis now bearing a deep score where he had grasped the straight razor blade. "Don't forget, Margot, I have this hand because of you. So it balances out."

She breathed a long, trembling sigh. "Still, it feels odd to think that if you hadn't come, if something hadn't brought you there, I might have—" She stopped and swallowed. A moment later she lifted her face to look into his eyes. "Frank. Why *did* you come? You couldn't fly in the fog, of course, I knew that. But you couldn't know what was happening, or even that I was at the clinic at that hour. Why were you there?"

He shifted his shoulders to block the view of the people around the fireplace before he dug the envelope out of his pocket. "I came to bring you the damn letter," he said. "Because it upset you. I never meant that to happen." He held it out to her. "Burn it, Margot. I don't want to read it."

She made no move to take it. "Why would you not read it, Frank?" Her eyes searched his face. "What is it about the letter—a letter from Elizabeth—that gives it so much power?"

He folded the envelope in half. He shoved it back in his pocket and turned away from Margot's piercing gaze. "Don't know," he said dismally. "Don't know why I didn't just open it in the first place, and now that I've put it off so long . . ."

She moved closer to him, so the lean length of her pressed, ever so slightly, against his hip. Despite everything, despite her parents in the room, the strangeness of the day, the tension of what lay between them, he felt a rush of desire. She said, "You can't hand this off to me, Frank. You have to deal with it yourself, whatever it is."

He slipped his arm around her. The urge to kiss her, right here in front of everyone, almost overwhelmed him.

She gazed out at the winter darkness, her face set and still. "If you still care for Elizabeth, Frank . . ."

"Can't even remember what she looks like, Margot."

"Maybe she's sent you a photograph."

"God, I hope not." He blew an exasperated breath, and released her. "I wish she hadn't sent the thing. I don't want to think about the ranch, or about Montana."

"But it's part of who you are." She tensed beside him and withdrew, just a little. He felt the absence of her body next to his, and it gave him a chill. "You could go back," she said. "If that's what you wanted."

"It's what my father wants. My mother."

"Of course they do."

He said, clumsily, "You wouldn't want to go, Margot."

She lifted her chin to meet his gaze. "I wouldn't want to leave my clinic. Or the position at the hospital I worked so hard for."

He felt a wave of shame, and had to look away from those eyes that seemed to see right into his soul. The truth was, he supposed, he might have asked her, even knowing how selfish that would be. It would mean moving out to Missoula with him, being a country doctor, making calls on remote ranches, seeing children and old people and ranch hands at all hours of the day or night. In ranch country, the doctors even worked on animals when the veterinarian wasn't available. Their family doctor had come out more than once to help a cow calve, sew up a horse cut by barbed wire, try to help a sow with a blocked intestine.

He said, "No, Margot, I would never ask that," but he wasn't sure she believed him. Wasn't sure he believed it himself.

By the time he said good night to her, he already knew what he should have said. He should have said that he didn't want to go back to Missoula, despite his parents' wishes. He liked his work with Boeing. He loved flying airplanes. He wanted to be part of the future of airplane travel, and that future was here, in Seattle.

The damned letter had confused him, and he couldn't blame Elizabeth for that. His confusion was all about his mother missing him, his father mourning the lost dream of a bigger ranch, of his son taking over as he grew old. It was all mixed up with the war, and the hard times that followed, and the immense changes they found in their country and in themselves. Why, he berated himself, couldn't he have found the words to explain all that to Margot?

As he rode in the streetcar back toward Cherry Street, Frank pulled the letter from his pocket and used the stiff metal of his left thumb to slit the envelope open. There was a photograph, as it turned out, one of those careful ones people posed for in photographers' studios. He didn't look closely at it, but tucked it back into the envelope and turned to the letter. Elizabeth's handwriting was familiar to him from the letters he had received

when he was out in the East, fighting with the British Army. She
had seemed to like that part, sending letters to a soldier, being
the girl back home. It was the reality she hadn't been able to tolerate.

> Dear Frank:
> I'm sorry I didn't come to see you when you
> came to visit your folks. I should have, and I
> meant to, but I was embarrassed about what
> happened at the hospital in Virginia. You were
> in pain, I could see that, and your injury was
> so terrible. You needed me, and I failed you.
> That nurse gave me an awful scolding. I thought
> she was being mean to me, when I was so upset,
> but I can see now that she meant to help.

Frank knew the nurse she meant. He laid the letter on his
knee for a moment, remembering Rosa Gregorio's plain features,
her New York accent, the grim look in her eyes as she warned
him to show Elizabeth his arm before they were married and not
after. Elizabeth had proved her right, of course, but Nurse Gregorio hadn't been happy about it. He could imagine her scolding
Elizabeth, telling her exactly what she thought of her reaction.
Rosa Gregorio was a plain-speaking woman, and she had fought
hard for each and every one of her patients.

That had been an awful moment, watching Elizabeth's face as
he exposed the debacle of his arm to her. It hurt even to remember it. He sighed, and picked up the letter again.

> I went to see your folks after Thanksgiving.
> Last year I heard you were maybe going to get
> married, to a lady doctor out in Seattle, but

*they tell me you didn't do it. I thought maybe I
could come out to Seattle on the train and visit
you. Your folks and mine would sure like it if
you and I could take up where we left off. Your
mother says your arm is all fixed up now.*

Frank lowered the letter again. He had told his parents about
Margot when he went to visit last March. His mother had been
nervous about meeting her, a physician, a girl from a wealthy
family. His father had scowled and said it was a shame about
Elizabeth. Frank hadn't told them about the painful scene in Virginia. It hadn't seemed fair to Elizabeth, and now . . .

He shook the photograph out of the envelope and held it up to
the light as the streetcar clicked down Broadway. It was a pretty
picture. Elizabeth was a pretty girl, with fair, curling hair done up
on top of her head, and soft, full lips smiling out of the photograph. She wore a lacy dress, belted tightly beneath her full
bosom. Frank smiled down at the picture, remembering how
nice it had been to have a sweetheart when he was young, someone to write to when he was off at college, someone who sent regular letters from home when he was at war halfway around the
world.

It was interesting that the girl he had lost evidently wanted
him back. That was nice, in a way. Flattering.

He put the photograph back in the envelope, tucked it into his
pocket, and swung down from the streetcar, feeling sure of himself again. He knew what he had to do. All that remained was to
make a good job of it, and it had nothing at all to do with Elizabeth, or Missoula, or even his parents.

He had no doubt there were dozens of men eager to claim a
pretty young woman like Elizabeth. He just wasn't one of them.

CHAPTER 24

Dickson and Margot sat side by side in the passenger seat of the Essex while Blake steered carefully down Broadway toward Madison. Dickson, wrapped in an overcoat with a thick wool muffler, kept the brim of his homburg pulled low over his forehead, but Margot had seen the exhaustion in his eyes and the tension in the set of his mouth. She wished she had some comfort to offer, but what was there to say to a father who had learned such terrible things about his son?

They rode in silence for a few minutes. Dickson coughed, adjusted his hat with his gloved hands, and said, "I'm sorry you had to do this, Margot. Not very pleasant for you. And the major's gone? Headed back to March Field?"

"He flew out this morning. Blake and I picked him up and drove him to Sand Point. Bill Boeing was there, too, Father."

"Was he," her father said. "That's something."

"He wanted to see the airplane."

"Major Parrish has made a wonderful impression."

"Yes. Frank was pleased."

Except Boeing's presence had meant they couldn't speak privately. She was trying not to worry about any of it, the letter, Frank's preoccupation, the question that lay between them. He had, at least, kissed her cheek, right there in the presence of his boss. She would cling to that memory until he returned.

"Is someone covering for you at the hospital?"

"Yes. Matron Cardwell is handling it. I thought I'd go to the clinic this afternoon."

"Good. Yes, you should do that." He fell silent again, watching as Blake maneuvered the motorcar onto Yesler and turned cautiously down the steep hill.

The beige brick wedge of the Public Safety Building stood four stories high. During her training, Margot had spent several weeks in the City Emergency Hospital on the third floor. She had never been to the fourth floor, nor had she ever wanted to go there. It was kept separate, with its own elevator, and even from the street, she could see the steel bars on its windows. Now, with her father beside her, she walked into the lobby and turned in the opposite direction from the hospital elevator. They passed several men in suits and bowler hats, and a policeman and policewoman in uniform with a manacled prisoner walking between them. Dickson's step faltered.

Margot glanced at him, but his head was up, his chin jutting in the familiar way. He would deal with it, she knew. In many ways this was a much harder thing to face than the supposed death of his youngest son, but he was a strong man. He knew how to manage difficult circumstances. And, in this case, he understood the truth of the matter.

Except for the uniformed operator, they had the elevator to themselves. As it carried them to the top of the building, Margot said, "Has Mother asked any questions?"

"No."

"I thought, after the disturbances the other night—"

"You would have thought so," her father said. "She doesn't notice very much these days."

The elevator stopped, and the operator touched his cap and said, "Fourth floor, sir. Ma'am."

"Thank you." Margot took her father's arm as they stepped out. She felt the tension trembling in his muscles, but his voice was steady as he explained to the supervisor of the jail, a small, dark man with hard eyes, who they were and why they had come. The supervisor gave them sidelong, curious glances as he led them down the central corridor to a heavy locked door. He selected a key from the ring at his belt, and unlocked the door, which opened with a forbidding clang.

They found themselves in a corridor between a row of barren-looking cells. A few prisoners watched listlessly as Dickson and Margot passed by, but no one spoke, and Margot preferred not to look at them, to see the damaged humanity imprisoned here. The whole echoing space smelled of a rather unnerving mix of bleach and boiled vegetables. Beyond the barred windows the open sky was a perfect, cold blue, and it seemed to intensify the sense of despair within.

The cell was just as her father had described it. It was clean, but offered little comfort. Someone had provided Preston a blanket and a pillow and added a thin ticking mattress to the cot. There was no chair or any other furniture. The toilet in the corner had no lid, but the fixture seemed to be in working order. There was a rudimentary sink, rust-stained and slightly askew from the wall, with two taps. A window was set in the outer wall, too high for anyone to look out. The inner wall of the cell was made up only of bars, which meant there was no privacy at all for its inmate. Preston was sitting on the end of the cot, facing the blank wall at the back.

The supervisor said, "You don't need to go in, right?"

Dickson said, "This will be fine."

"Just the same. I'll be right here, sir." The small man retreated to a spot near the door, but stood with his arms folded, his gaze focused on Preston.

Dickson removed his hat and held it with one hand in front of his chest. His other hand gripped one of the bars, the knuckles white with tension. Margot stood in the center of the aisle, feel-

ing both awkward, because she had no role here, and angry, because she could see how the situation pained her father. Even
Preston's slumped shoulders, the vicious scars she could see on
his scalp and neck, engendered only impersonal pity, a feeling
she might have had for a stranger. Her brother was her enemy,
and though he was pitiful to behold, damaged and powerless, she
couldn't pretend affection for him.

Dickson said, "Preston."

Preston didn't move. Didn't react at all.

"Preston, we need to talk about what to do. We have to make
a decision."

There was no response.

Dickson cast a pleading look over his shoulder at Margot. She
hesitated, certain Preston would not welcome her intervention,
but her father looked so stricken she couldn't refuse him. She
moved forward just enough to stand at Dickson's shoulder, and
spoke to her brother. "Preston. Father wants to help you."

At the sound of her voice, Preston stirred. He moved his feet,
side to side, forward and back, then settled them on the bare
floor and pushed himself up from the cot. Still facing the back
wall, he straightened the colorless shirt he wore and tucked the
tail firmly into his baggy, unbelted trousers. Margot didn't know
if these were his own clothes, or those of the jail, but she knew
how deeply Preston must loathe them. He turned slowly to face
them.

Dickson shuddered from head to foot, and Margot realized it
was the first time he had seen the full extent of Preston's burns.
She should have prepared him, should have warned him that
Preston's face was disfigured, was unrecognizable.

If Preston felt anything, he didn't reveal it, or perhaps his
scarred features no longer showed emotion. He stepped around
the end of the cot and walked toward the wall of bars. Margot had
to force herself to hold her ground, despite the protection of
thick steel.

Her father put a hand through the bars, though the movement
caused the supervisor to take a step forward with a small sound of

warning. Dickson ignored him. He touched Preston's shoulder with his fingers, and said, in a voice of pure heartbreak, "Son."

"Pater," Preston said. It should have been a light response, offered with Preston's old insouciance, but his voice could no longer respond to his intention. "Doc." He nodded to Margot. "New coat. It's about time."

She just stopped herself from touching the shawl collar of the blue wraparound coat Ramona had ordered for her, and had delivered to Benedict Hall. The coat fastened with a single, enormous Bakelite button that had made her laugh at first, but which Ramona assured her was perfect. Preston said, "I could feel bad about spoiling the old one, but really, it was past time for that thing to go."

Dickson said, "Preston. What does any of that matter?"

Preston leaned one shoulder against the bars of his cell, almost pulling off the man-about-town attitude, despite his ugly clothes and his disfigured face. "What does matter these days, Pater? It's all over for me, that's obvious."

"It's not all over. It doesn't have to be. In the end, nothing really happened."

"That you know about," Preston said.

"Don't add to your problems," Margot said. He shrugged.

"We're going to send you to Western State Hospital," Dickson said.

"Western State Hospital for *the insane*," Preston responded, with emphasis.

"It's not called that anymore," Dickson said. "And conditions have improved, I'm told."

"Oh, I'm sure, Pater. I'm sure now it's a real treat. A resort. A spa!"

"It's the only way to keep you out of prison."

Preston waved a scarred hand to indicate his surroundings. "You hadn't noticed? I'm already in prison."

"It doesn't have to be for long. Dr. Creedy will—"

"Creedy! That clacking old woman. He'll do whatever you want, won't he?" Preston's mouth contorted in his effort to pull off a smile, and Dickson made an involuntary sound in his throat. "Going to have me committed, Pater?"

Margot began, "Preston, listen to reason. If you go to the hospital, we can get you some surgery, improve those—"

She never finished her sentence. Without the slightest warning, he lunged at her. He thrust both arms through the bars, his fingers curved into claws. Margot was standing behind her father, and the clutching fingers fell on him instead, gripping his coat, knocking the homburg from his hand. Dickson cried out, but Preston, showing his teeth like an angry dog, tried to reach past his father to get to Margot. His eyes were awful to see, the pupils swelling, the lashless lids stretched wide.

Margot fell back away from him. She tried to pull her father with her, but he stood where he was, tolerating the scratching of Preston's hands, the futile grappling. Preston tried to shout, but his voice defeated him. "You *bitch!*" he croaked. "You arrogant *bitch!*" His whole body banged against the bars as he tried to reach Margot. His face distorted, pressed against the bars.

The jailer reached them, wielding his nightstick. He whacked the bars with it, and ordered the prisoner to back away. Preston paid no attention until the next blow of the nightstick fell on his outstretched arm, right at the elbow. Margot was sure it must hurt like the devil.

Preston fell silent. He withdrew his hands, and stood with his arms hanging uselessly by his sides, glaring at Margot.

"Why?" Dickson asked in a low tone. He waved the jailer off, and the man retreated a short distance. "Why did you do it, Preston? Your mother has suffered agonies this entire year. I don't think she'll ever be the same."

Preston's eyelids dropped, for just a moment, and when they lifted again Margot thought there might be something there, sadness perhaps, some remnant of human feeling. She couldn't be sure. It might be wishful thinking, a longing to see something that meant her brother was not a complete monster.

Preston said, "Is she coming to see me?"

"I haven't told her you're here," Dickson said. "In fact, Preston, I haven't told her you're alive."

"Good. Don't."

"If you'll go to the hospital," Margot said swiftly. "If you'll go willingly, commit yourself, admit your illness, Mother doesn't need to know what you did. I don't see the point in telling her."

Preston's pupils began to contract again, and in the pale blue of his eyes, Margot saw a shred of the pretty boy he had once been, the handsome young man he had become, who was now lost forever. He said, "How much does she know?"

"She thinks you were trying to put out the fire in my clinic. To save it."

She was stunned to see tears rise in Preston's eyes. They swam there, little tragic pools of misery. Despite everything she knew, everything she had been through with him, her heart ached for the grief that lay ahead. He swallowed so hard she could see the reflexive spasm of his throat.

He said tonelessly, "All right, doc. I'll go to the booby hatch. As long as you don't tell her about me." He tossed his head in a grotesque imitation of his old charm. "Let's allow the mater to believe her boy is a hero, shall we?"

Allison lay down on her bed after lunch and was sleeping so soundly that Ruby had to shake her shoulder to wake her. "Miss Allison," she said. "Miss Allison, Mr. Dickson wants you. Wants everyone."

Allison could hardly lift her eyelids. She yawned, and tried to pull away from Ruby's hand, but the maid persisted until Allison blinked, pushed a hand through her hair, and sat up. The little enamel clock on her dressing table told her it was past five. "Oh!" she said. "I slept so long."

"Mr. Dickson wants you to come to his study."

"Really?" Allison had never been to her uncle's study. She understood it to be his private lair, where even the maids were forbidden to go unless he gave express permission.

Ruby didn't seem to appreciate the novelty of the invitation.

She went to the wardrobe and got out the plaid dress. "You might as well dress for dinner now, Miss Allison."

"Not that dress, Ruby."

Ruby turned, the plaid frock in her hands. "I thought this would be good. You haven't worn it for some time."

"I'm never wearing it again." Allison pointed to the wardrobe. "The cream chiffon, Ruby. You can take the plaid away."

"What do you want me to do with it, Miss Allison?"

Allison pushed herself up from the bed and went to her dressing table. "Burn it. Cut it up. Make curtains out of it." She sat down on the stool and picked up her hairbrush. Ruby, the plaid dress still in her hands, stared at her, open-mouthed. "If you won't do it, Ruby, I will."

"But, Miss Allison—Mrs. Adelaide especially likes this one."

"Let her wear it, then."

Allison hurried her toilette and, dressed in the cream chiffon, descended the main staircase to the hall. She found Blake waiting for her at the foot of the stairs, and he guided her to the study, which turned out to be much smaller than Allison had expected. There were books everywhere, on shelves, on a low table, piled on a writing desk next to one of Uncle Dickson's ubiquitous ashtrays. This one was brass, and Uncle Dickson was seated nearby, tapping ash into it in an abstracted way.

"I'm sorry if I kept you waiting," Allison said. Every face turned to her. Her father was there, scowling in a corner. Cousin Ramona sat on a straight chair, with Cousin Dick standing behind her. Allison took a low stool, the cream chiffon pooling around her on the carpet.

Uncle Dickson said, "That's all right, Allison. I know you were tired."

She looked up in surprise when Blake ushered Hattie into the already crowded room, and closed the door behind the two of them. The servants stood, looking stiff and self-conscious, just inside the door. Hattie had taken off her apron and put on a fresh housedress. Her hair looked as if she had just combed it with water. Small drops glistened in the light of the desk lamp. Blake stood with his hands on the lapels of his jacket, his face drawn in somber lines.

"Margot will be a bit late tonight," Uncle Dickson began. "She telephoned from the clinic."

"And Adelaide?" Henry asked.

"I'll get to that, Henry," Uncle Dickson said. "There are things I need to say. Hattie and Blake, thank you for joining us."

Blake said, "Of course, Mr. Dickson." Hattie touched her hair as if to be certain it was still in place, and gazed at her feet.

"I would have preferred, Hattie," Dickson said heavily, "not to burden you with this, but we have a problem. I know how much you care about Mrs. Edith. This is a good time to tell you that you've been invaluable to all of us in this past difficult year." He paused to crush out his cigar, and Allison was sure he was giving himself time to choose his words with care. It all seemed terribly exciting and mysterious, and it was all she could do to sit still.

"Fortunately for our purposes just now," he went on, "Edith has not seemed to notice the—shall we say, drama—that has unfolded around us in the past two days. She has kept to her room, except for dinner last night, and so I think we can manage what I have in mind." He paused again, and Allison hardly dared breathe. "Hattie, this will be hardest on you. If you find it impossible, I hope you will tell me now." He looked up, and Hattie, fidgeting with the buttons of her dress, brought her eyes up to meet his gaze. "You learned about Preston," Uncle Dickson said. "From Blake."

Hattie's lips parted, but she seemed not to know what to answer. Blake, seeing, said, "I'm sorry, Mr. Dickson. I wasn't thinking clearly."

"There's no blame to attach, Blake," Uncle Dickson said. He drew a long, sibilant breath. "No need for an apology. This is a profound shock to us all, and you naturally thought of confiding in Hattie."

Allison had to clutch at the stool beneath her to keep from

bouncing on it. She could hardly wait to see what would happen next.

"The reason I mention this, Hattie, is that Miss Margot and I feel it would be best not to tell Mrs. Edith that Mr. Preston survived the fire."

Ramona pressed a hand to her lips. Dick patted her shoulder.

"This means," Uncle Dickson went on, "that we will be keeping a big secret, for Edith's sake. Ramona and Dick have already heard my thoughts about this, but Henry, and you, Allison, need to understand our reasons. My wife has had a terrible year, and her mental state is not the best. You have no doubt noticed this already."

Allison took a surreptitious glance at her father. He stood with his hands in his pockets, listening with his head on one side. When he didn't say anything, Allison said, "We don't need to tell Mother, do we, Uncle Dickson? I'm not sure she can keep this secret."

Her father said, "I don't like keeping secrets from my wife."

Allison lifted her head. "You do it all the time, Papa," she said, winning a glare from him and a sympathetic glance from Cousin Ramona.

Uncle Dickson said, "I would like your promise, Henry. Please don't speak of this. It will serve no purpose to tell Adelaide."

There was an uncomfortable pause, and he finally said, "Yes. Of course, Dickson. Allison and I will both respect your wishes in this matter."

"I've already said so," Allison said. "You don't need to speak for me." She turned her head to escape his angry expression. There was going to be trouble later, and plenty of it. Just now she didn't care.

Cousin Ramona asked quietly, "What's going to happen to him, Father Benedict? To Preston?"

Uncle Dickson sighed. "Of course you're concerned, my dear. Thank you. Preston is going to be committed to Western State Hospital."

"The insane asylum," Dick said.

"I don't care for that description, but yes, Dick. He needs psychiatric care. He agreed to it as long as we—that is to say, on the condition that—his mother is kept in ignorance. Of all of it. When he's been there long enough to satisfy the courts—to speak frankly, that is, to avoid criminal prosecution—Margot and I will find an appropriate place where he can be cared for." He cleared his throat and added sadly, "Indefinitely."

Blake said, with dignity, "Hattie and I have discussed this, Mr. Dickson. She will tell you herself, but you can count on us." He nodded to Hattie and moved a little aside, as if to leave her in center stage.

Hattie, staring at her shoes, spoke so softly Allison wondered if Uncle Dickson could hear her. "I think this is a good thing, Mr. Dickson. Mrs. Edith has suffered enough. She don't need more grief in her life."

"Thank you, Hattie," Dickson said gravely. "Your loyalty humbles me. I hardly know what we would do without you."

Cousin Ramona said, "Father Benedict, I usually go up to Mother Benedict at this time to help her get ready for dinner."

"Please do, Ramona. We'll gather in the small parlor, and carry on as usual."

"Adelaide," Henry said sharply. "I'm still waiting to hear something about *my* wife." Allison turned to stare in disbelief at her father's tone.

"Oh, yes," Uncle Dickson said. He stood up and pushed his chair under the writing desk. "Dr. Creedy will meet with you in the morning, at the hospital. Your appointment's at ten. Margot will be there, and the three of you can discuss Adelaide's condition."

"What condition?"

Uncle Dickson shook his head. "I'm not a medical man, Henry, but apparently there is one, or Margot wouldn't be concerned." When Henry began to bridle, Uncle Dickson held up one hand. "You can trust her," he said, firmly. "My daughter is an excellent physician, and if she thinks Adelaide needs treatment, then you should seek it."

Blake said, "Drinks, then, Mr. Dickson?"

"Please, Blake."

Blake held the door for Hattie and ushered her out into the corridor. Uncle Dickson rose, grunting a little, and waited for Ramona and Dick to go out ahead of him. Allison followed close behind, but her father caught her arm to hold her back. She tried to pull free, but he held tight, and she gave in so as not to make a scene.

He waited until the others had gone out into the hall. He gave her arm a small, angry shake before he released it. "Just because you've fooled Dickson and the rest of them, Allison," he said, "don't think you've fooled me."

"Fooled you how, Papa?" Allison was proud of the steadiness of her voice. She thought of the way Margot stood up to Cousin Preston, her bravery in the face of that terrifying blade, and she met her father's eyes without blinking.

"Acting like butter wouldn't melt in your mouth, my girl. I know better. I know how you really are."

Allison tried to hold on to her dignity, to be as much like Margot as she could, but this was too much. She stamped her foot, and angry tears sprang to her eyes. "You don't know *anything*, Papa," she whispered. "You don't know anything about me, and you know even less about Mother." She stepped around him and turned toward the door.

Before she reached it, he said, "I'm warning you, Allison! Dr. Kinney—"

Her tears dried instantly. She spun, in a twirl of cream chiffon, to face her father. "I have Cousin Margot now. She's a *good* doctor. She knows perfectly well I'm not a hysteric. I am not going to a sanitorium no matter what you or Dr. Kinney or any other stupid old man says!" She spun again, full of defiant energy, and marched through the door and down the corridor to the small parlor. She didn't bother to look back to see if her father was following.

CHAPTER 25

Margot met Dr. Creedy at the door to Aunt Adelaide's ward and greeted him. "Father asked me to tell you how much we appreciate your help with this situation."

Creedy nodded. "Of course, Margot. You don't mind if I call you Margot?" He smiled at her with the familiarity of long acquaintance. "After all," he said, thrusting his hands into the pockets of his white coat, "I've known you since you were a toddler."

"Of course I don't mind," she said. "I'm grateful you're here to explain things to my aunt and uncle. I doubt they see me as fully qualified."

"Families are like that," Creedy said. "My mother never let me prescribe anything for her, much less examine her! But I'm happy to help. The Benedicts are keeping me busy these days."

"I know. Here's my uncle now. I'll introduce you, and we can go in."

Uncle Henry looked wary as he shook Creedy's hand, and the look he directed at Margot could only be called truculent. They went into the ward, and Margot asked the nurse to bring them a privacy screen. Adelaide was sitting up in bed, her arm in its cast supported by a sling, with a thick pillow under her elbow. Without the cosmetics she always wore, and with her hair lying loose on her shoulders, she looked younger. Softer, somehow. Margot could see, also, that she was frightened.

She touched her hand. "Aunt Adelaide, how do you feel this morning?"

"Why are you all here?" Adelaide asked in her reedy voice. Her eyes flicked from one to another of them, and Margot thought it must look like an inquisition to her. "What's the matter?"

"There's nothing to worry about," Margot said. She turned to Henry. "Uncle Henry, why don't you bring that chair over so you can sit beside Aunt Adelaide? Dr. Creedy wants to talk to both of you."

When Henry was settled, she moved to the end of the bed to let Creedy manage the consultation. As he talked, she watched her aunt's fear dissolve into resistance, and then denial. Her face set in stubborn lines. Henry's eyes darted from side to side, as if he were trying to escape, as if he didn't want to hear any of it.

Creedy was good, speaking in clear, simple language. He mentioned the osteoporosis, and the poor condition of Adelaide's teeth. He described the heart murmur he had detected, and discussed the possibility of anaemia.

"These could all have different causes, Mrs. Benedict," Dr. Creedy said. "But in my view, the simplest explanation is usually the right one. Because of your extremely low body weight, I think my diagnosis is correct. You're exhibiting symptoms of malnutrition."

"What's that?"

"Malnutrition, Aunt Adelaide," Margot said quietly. "Starvation."

"Ridiculous!" Henry erupted. He seemed to select Margot as the troublemaker. "That's a preposterous thing to say. No one is starving in my house."

Margot gave him an exasperated look. "Uncle Henry, two people are starving in your house. Why don't you see that?"

"What? What are you talking about?"

Adelaide said, "I'm not starving! I eat perfectly well."

"If that's the case, Mrs. Benedict, then we should conduct other tests to assess why you're not absorbing nutrition from your meals."

Henry said, "Margot, why did you say *two* people?"

A burst of impatience made Margot snappish. "Have you looked at your daughter recently?"

Dr. Creedy raised his eyebrows at this, but did Margot the courtesy of letting the conversation continue. Henry said, with the air of someone much put upon, "I don't have any idea what you mean."

Adelaide said, "Allison is slender, as a young girl should be. I've made sure of that."

"How?" Margot demanded. She realized she had put her hands on her hips, like an angry parent, but she didn't bother to correct the posture. "Tell me, Aunt Adelaide. How have you made sure?"

Adelaide sniffed. "That's between a mother and a daughter. I think I know what's best for my—"

"Stop it," Margot said firmly. "You've made yourself ill—how, I don't know, but I expect between us, Dr. Creedy and I will figure it out. I won't have you making Cousin Allison ill as well."

Creedy rose at that and beckoned to Margot. She followed him past the screen and on to the far side of the ward, where a nurse was preparing medication trays. Creedy leaned against the wall and pushed his spectacles higher on his nose. "What's this about a daughter? Does she have the same symptoms?"

"Extreme thinness. Probably amenorrhea, although she hasn't confessed that. Oh, and quite low blood pressure. She fainted a few weeks ago."

"What do you think it is, Doctor?"

Margot didn't realize at first that he had called her by her title. She was too absorbed by the problem before them, the puzzle to be solved. She said, "Allison has been living at Benedict Hall for two months. I noticed how thin she was, of course, and then realized she wasn't eating her meals. Our cook was upset, and I was worried. Have you read the studies on a condition called anorexia nervosa? The studies are French and German—they're hardly exhaustive, but Pierre Janet seems to have done the best work. His opinion is that it's a psychological condition. He distinguishes two types—obsessive and hysterical. I didn't know which might apply to Allison, but listening to her mother just now—"

Creedy was nodding, rubbing his upper lip with a forefinger. "We could ask one of the psychology men, but obsessive seems to fit. So the girl—how old?"

"Nineteen."

"Young Allison starves herself, and Mrs. Benedict has some other way to make herself thin."

"I should mention the Simmonds opinion about pituitary insufficiency as a cause for extreme weight loss, but I found a paucity of clinical evidence. His paper didn't convince me."

"I haven't read it, but I'll take your word for that, Doctor." Creedy pushed away from the wall. "I'll test your aunt for anaemia, and recommend she see her own physician for the heart murmur. If both Mr. and Mrs. Benedict deny there's a problem, I don't know if there's anything further we can do."

"I'd like to keep Allison at Benedict Hall, though. She was getting much better—that is, she was until her parents arrived."

He considered this, alternately pulling on his lip and pushing at his spectacles. Finally, he said, "I could recommend a rest cure for Mrs. Benedict. I believe there are a number of reliable places in California. Expensive, though."

"I don't think the money's a concern."

"Good. Well, if Mrs. Benedict takes a cure, no doubt the two of them would be willing to leave their daughter with your branch of the family. You can call me if the girl doesn't continue to improve."

As they walked back to the patient's bedside, Margot felt the knot of worry that had been tightening in her belly begin to release. Perhaps, somehow, they would find a way through this.

* * *

The whole family was at lunch when Henry and Margot returned. Allison tensed at the sound of her father's voice in the
hall, but when he came into the dining room, he looked subdued,
and said little beyond greeting Aunt Edith and Cousin Ramona.
Uncle Dickson said, "How did things go at the hospital?"

Henry said only, "Fine. Creedy's a good man."

At this, Uncle Dickson raised his eyebrows at Cousin Margot,
but she—looking more rested than she had in days—only gave a
small shrug. She felt Allison's gaze on her and winked across the
table. Allison's cheeks warmed with pleasure. They were friends
now, she thought. They had been through a great adventure—
well, a tragedy, of course, poor Cousin Preston!—but they had
come through it together, with Major Parrish to help, and everything was going to be fine.

Aunt Edith was just as she always was, composed, well groomed,
inattentive. Cousin Ramona had roses in her cheeks and a sparkle
in her eye, and Allison was sure she was so happy about the coming
baby that even her sorrow for Preston couldn't spoil her mood.
Cousin Dick and Uncle Dickson had gone to their office this morning, but come home for lunch, and Hattie had made a special effort.
There was a shepherd's pie, hot and filling on this icy December
day, and silver baskets filled with hot bread. The Christmas tree
had been delivered, and rested now in all its piney fragrance on the
back porch, ready to be brought in on Christmas Eve. Fat new can-
dles, red as rubies, waited to be lighted at dinner, and someone—
Leona, Allison suspected, who had the most initiative of all the
maids—had made twists of greenery down the center of the table.
They filled the dining room with spicy scent.

Allison collected her thoughts enough to ask politely, "How is
Mother, Papa?"

This might have been an opening for him to chastise her again
for causing the injury, but he looked distracted and uncertain. He
said, "Your mother is going to need a long rest, Allison. Dr.
Creedy recommended a place he knows in Monterey."

"Oh! California," she said.

"We'll speak about it after lunch."

Uncle Dickson leaned forward. "Henry. If Adelaide is going to take a cure, why not leave Allison with us? We've enjoyed having her so much."

Allison held her breath. It was said so easily, as if it didn't mean everything in the world.

Her father said, with his customary scowl, "I don't want my daughter to be a burden, Dickson."

Cousin Dick, with a grin at Allison, said, "That could never happen, Uncle Henry. We'll put her to work."

Margot said, "You know, Uncle Henry, Allison could take some classes at the University. I did my undergraduate work there. They have excellent courses for young women."

Allison squirmed in her chair and twisted her fingers together to keep from begging.

On any normal day, under ordinary circumstances, this would have been Henry Benedict's cue to expound on the pointlessness of higher education for girls. In Benedict Hall, with his accomplished niece sitting just across the table, this avenue of argument was closed to him. Allison could have predicted that.

What surprised her, what she would never have predicted, was the hesitance in his answer. It was unlike her father to doubt himself, but whatever it was that had happened this morning, he clearly doubted himself now.

He said, "Very kind of you. All of you. It might be . . . that is, with Adelaide away, and only Ruby . . ."

Cousin Ramona said sweetly, and pointedly, "Oh, won't that be marvelous, Cousin Allison? When the baby comes, you'll be here to help!"

Angela Rossi came to Margot's office and knocked on the open door to get her attention. Margot glanced up. "Are they here?" She pushed the surgical manual she had been studying back into its place on the shelf beside her beautiful new desk and gave it a satisfied tap with her fingers. Her father had insisted on providing the very newest editions of all the books she had lost, and the up-to-date research was both fascinating and useful.

Angela said, "Yes, Doctor. That is, Miss Benedict is. I believe your driver is waiting in the motorcar. Shall I show Miss Benedict back?"

"Please do," Margot said. "And if we have no more appointments today, you can go home. I'm sure you have things to do for the holiday."

"I do," Angela said. "I have all that baking still to get done, and a few gifts to wrap."

"Gifts!" Margot breathed. She spread her hands. "I haven't done a thing about gifts."

"A bit late now, I think," the practical Angela said. "But I'm sure your family will understand."

Margot had to chuckle at that. The Benedicts were used to her never getting around to Christmas shopping, and they were well accustomed to her yearly apologies.

Angela disappeared down the short hallway and returned in a moment with Allison, red-cheeked from the cold. She wore a scarlet wool coat with fur trim on the cuffs, black stockings, and a pair of strapped pumps. Her fair hair had gotten damp somehow, destroying her careful spit curls. It curled charmingly around her head, making her look like one of the cherubs on a Christmas card.

Allison waited until Angela closed the office door, then burst out, "They're gone, Cousin Margot! I kept worrying Papa would change his mind at the last minute, but he didn't, and they're gone! Ruby, too!"

"That was a good choice. You don't really need a lady's maid, and your mother can use the help, since she only has the use of one arm."

"And all her dresses will need altering, to fit over the cast," Allison said. "I pointed that out to Mother, and that convinced her." She took the chair opposite the desk, perching on the edge as if she might fly away at any moment. "She is going to be all right, isn't she? Mother, I mean?"

Margot considered her answer with care. "Her arm will heal, Allison. It will be slow, because she's not very well, but it should heal well. It was a clean break."

"And the other—thing?"

"The other 'thing' is why I wanted to see you, and see you here, in my office. As a physician."

The nervous energy seemed to drain out of Allison all at once, and she sank back in the chair and began rather listlessly to fiddle with the buttons of her coat. "Oh. I thought perhaps we were just going to talk about the University."

"We *will* talk about that, Allison," Margot said firmly. "I'm going to help you with your admissions, and if you like, help you choose a course of study. Nothing has changed."

Allison brightened noticeably. "Oh! Thank you! I can hardly wait."

"Excellent. Now." Margot rested her linked hands on the desk blotter. "You know Dr. Creedy suggested your mother spend some time in a sanitorium, Allison. She's much too thin, and he feels—and I agree—that we need to understand why that is. It's not only her bones that are affected. She shows signs of anaemia—fatigue, weakness, thin fingernails—some of which you exhibited yourself. I believe there is also some cognitive impairment, which—well, you don't need to worry about that. Dr. Creedy discussed all this with your father. In the sanitorium, your mother should be able to put on some weight, and—"

"Oh, she won't," Allison said with confidence.

"Pardon?"

"She won't put on weight. She'll see to it she doesn't."

Margot frowned. "What do you mean? How can she 'see to it'? She'll have a lot of rest, and nourishing meals—"

"She throws them up, Cousin Margot." Allison emitted a gusty sigh.

"What—do you mean, she vomits?"

"Yes."

"Does food make her ill?"

"No, I don't think so. She does it on purpose. All the time."

Allison spoke with resignation. "Mother stays thin because after she eats she puts a spoon down her throat and—" She gave a slight shudder. "I know it's disgusting. It's because she doesn't want to get stout like her mother did."

Margot pressed a fingertip to her lips, thinking. In truth, despite all her experience, it *was* disgusting. She thought back over the papers she had read. Neither Simmonds nor Janet had mentioned behavior like this. After a moment she dropped her hand and said, carefully, "Allison—do *you* do this?"

"No!" Allison shook her damp curls. "She gave me a spoon of my own, but I—"

"She did *what?*" Margot stared at her young cousin in horror. "She wanted you to do the same thing?"

Allison fell silent, gazing at Margot with wide eyes and parted lips.

"Oh, my dear," Margot said helplessly. "I can't—I hardly know what to say about that."

Allison looked away, and spoke in a small voice. "I didn't like it, Cousin Margot, but Mother said I was getting fat. I just—I couldn't make myself do what she wanted. It was easier not to eat in the first place."

"Fat," Margot echoed. "She said you were fat." She eyed the slight girl opposite her, nearly swallowed by her scarlet coat. Her cheeks were hollow, her neck slender and fragile-looking. "Allison, you're not fat. You're the opposite of fat."

Allison lifted her eyes to the window, and Margot followed her gaze to the view of the bay. The early winter darkness had already fallen, but white ship lights glimmered here and there like stars dropped into the water. Margot waited, giving the girl time. It was a moment to be silent. To let understanding grow in the empty space that must exist in Allison's young heart.

Allison let her coat fall from her shoulders and sat hugging herself as she gazed out into the night. "Sometimes," she said mournfully, "I know I'm not fat. Sometimes I can see it in the mirror, that my stomach and my—my bust—that they look normal. Even sort of thin." She turned pleading eyes to Margot. "But other times, when Mother's been telling me, I see this awful shape. My thighs, and my waist, they look like they belong to someone else. Someone I don't recognize. Sometimes I think I'm hideous." Shining tears rose in her eyes, and she wiped them away with her fingers. "Sometimes," she finished in a whisper, "I get so confused I think I must be crazy. Because I don't know what's real."

Margot took a clean handkerchief from a desk drawer and handed it across the desk. She wanted to get up, to put her arms around the girl, but she made herself wait. It was too soon. Just now Allison needed a doctor, not a friend. She spoke as gently as she knew how. "Allison, I think your mother is even more confused than you are. I don't know if we can help her, but I want to help you."

"Hattie says my mother loves me," Allison said, her voice catching in a sob. "Do you think so?"

"I'm not much of a judge of love," Margot said. "I wish I were better at it."

Allison blew her nose and dabbed at her wet eyelashes, then crumpled the handkerchief in her lap. "I'm sorry," she said.

"You have nothing to be sorry for," Margot said. "You're having a natural reaction to an unhappy situation." She tapped her fingers on her blotter and tried to think how best to proceed.

"Is my mother crazy? Is that why she does these things?"

"I don't think *crazy* is the right word," Margot said cautiously. "But I do think Aunt Adelaide has gone too far. For both of you," she added. "She's created a situation, for whatever reason, which has made her ill. My concern is that it threatens to make you ill, too."

Allison surprised her with a tremulous, tearstained smile. "I'll be all right, Cousin Margot," she said. "I'm working on it."

"May I help you with that?" Margot asked. "One reason I wanted you to come here was to weigh you, check your blood pressure, examine you—because these are the things I know how to do, and because I hope I can help that way."

"Yes. Yes, we can do those things, and I think it's really nice of you. Also—" Allison hesitated, her gaze shifting away, and then back. "I hope you won't think it's strange, but Hattie helps me, too. I know she's just your servant, your cook—"

Margot chuckled. "I think you've guessed by now that none of us thinks of Hattie or Blake as just servants."

Allison's smile steadied. "Hattie's kitchen is my favorite place in Benedict Hall."

Margot thought of her early-morning chats with Blake at the white enamel table, while the whole house slept around them. It was nice that even in an enormous place like Benedict Hall the kitchen felt like home, at least to one or two of the family. "Well, then. As long as you're amenable, let's get you on the scale, and I'll record your blood pressure. Can you promise, do you think, that if you feel you're having trouble, you could come and talk to me?"

"Yes. And I can talk to Hattie. I always feel better when I talk to Hattie."

Margot knew what her mother would think of such an answer, and even more, what Aunt Adelaide would think of it. But since she herself had relied on Blake countless times, over the entire length of her life, she could only say, "Yes, Allison, you could certainly talk to Hattie. Sometimes we find comfort in the most surprising places."

In the circle of someone's prosthetic arm, for example. But she couldn't think about that now.

CHAPTER 26

When Margot emerged from the hospital, she stepped into a swirl of fat snowflakes that spangled the sleeves of her new blue coat and caught on her eyelashes as she hurried across the sidewalk to the waiting Essex. The automobile looked as if it had been sprinkled with confectioner's sugar, and Blake's driving cap, when he stepped out to open her door, was soon glistening with snow.

"We'd best get up the hill before this gets any worse," Margot said from the backseat. Even a small amount of Seattle snow, wet and slippery, could make Aloha impassable.

"We will, Dr. Margot. Don't worry."

"It's pretty, though, isn't it, Blake?"

"We'll enjoy it more from the windows of Benedict Hall." She laughed and sat back to leave the problem of negotiating the hill to Blake. Christmas Eve of 1921 fell on a Saturday, and Margot had decided that was a good reason not to hold clinic hours. She gave Angela Rossi the day off, and except for three patients at the hospital, she meant to do the same.

The snow thickened on the streets and sidewalks by the time

Blake dropped her at the front gate. All the windows of Benedict Hall glowed with light, and someone had looped a string of red and green Christmas lights in the picture window. They twinkled gaily through the flutter of snowflakes, and Margot took her time moving up the walk, savoring the holiday mood. The tree had been set up at the foot of the staircase, towering all the way to the molded ceiling. Boxes of ornaments, dusty from the attic, waited nearby. The hall smelled marvelously of evergreen boughs and Christmas baking.

Margot hung up her coat and was unpinning her hat, smiling a little at the familiar voices sounding from the small parlor. Her father. Dick. Allison and Ramona, laughing.

And—she could hardly believe it—it was Frank she heard with them, just a word or two, but unmistakably Frank!

She hastily straightened her skirt with her hands and tried to sort out her disordered hair. Frank must have heard the front door, because he came out into the hall and strode toward her. He looked wonderful, his hair freshly cut, his jacket some new tweed thing she hadn't seen before, his eyes bright with pleasure. He didn't say a word, but folded her into his arms and pressed her against him for such a long time that she began to laugh and wriggle to get free. He kissed her then, firmly and at length. He released her only when Blake, coming out from the kitchen, ostentatiously cleared his throat.

Margot and Frank moved apart, smiling. Blake said, with exaggerated gravity, "How good to see you in Benedict Hall again, Major Parrish."

Frank's lean cheeks flushed, but there was laughter in his voice. "Thank you very much, Blake. Merry Christmas."

"And to you, sir." Blake, carrying a tray, walked past them and down the hall to the dining room. At the door he turned back and said, "Luncheon is in twenty minutes, Dr. Margot. You and the major have time to join the family for a cup of cider, if you like."

"We will. Thank you." When Blake had disappeared, Margot said, "Frank, why didn't you tell me you were coming? You keep surprising me!"

"Yes, I know," he said. "But today—well—I had something to talk to your father about."

"To Father? About what?"

He hesitated, and his cheeks colored even more deeply.

"Frank Parrish, you're blushing like a boy! What are you up to?"

"Well, Margot." He coughed a little and let his gaze drift above her head, to the very top of the fir tree. "What do you think a man speaks to his girl's father about?"

"Oh, Frank, don't be silly. I'm hardly a girl. I'm nearly thirty. . . ." The impact of his words came a heartbeat too late, and she broke off. "What—you didn't!"

"I did." He looked terribly young with his cheeks so flushed, despite the streaks of silver in his hair. She wanted to put up her hand and touch his face, but at that moment Thelma appeared with a soup tureen, passing them with a bob of a curtsy.

Frank seized Margot's left hand in his natural right one. "Can't talk in here, Margot. Too many people around. Let's go out on the porch."

"It's freezing! Did you know it's snowing?"

"Put your coat back on."

He was smiling, but she saw that his hand trembled slightly as he helped her into her coat and shrugged into his own. They stepped out onto the porch, where the falling snow sparkled under the lights of the windows. "It's beautiful," Margot said. "We don't get a lot of snow in Seattle."

"Different snow from Montana."

"Much wetter, yes." She turned to him. "Now, tell me, Frank."

He took her hand again, this time holding it in both of his. "I've spoken to your father," he began.

Margot felt a giggle rise in her throat, from embarrassment, from wonder, from hope. "So old-fashioned, Frank!"

"Old-fashioned cowboy," he said. "And you can stop laughing. This is serious."

She put her free hand to her mouth and tried very hard to look solemn.

"Not very convincing," he said.

"You're taking too long about it!"

"You're making it hard."

"I'm sorry," she said and reached up to kiss his cheek. "There now, I'm serious."

He stepped back a little, so he could see her face. "Margot, I—the thing is, when Elizabeth wrote to me, I realized—" He made a little exasperated sound and said, "I'm no good at explaining things."

"It's all right," she said. "You finally read her letter, I suppose."

"Yes. She said her folks and mine still hoped to put the ranches together."

Margot drew a breath, but couldn't think of any response. He tightened his grip on her hand to reassure her. "I miss the ranch," he said. He inclined his head toward the snowy landscape beyond the porch. "If you think this is beautiful, you should see the Bitterroot Valley in the snow."

"Frank—the letter."

"The letter. Yes." He cleared his throat again, but he smiled down at her. "Elizabeth is a nice girl, but—after knowing you, Margot—there's no other woman in the world for me. There never could be."

She closed her eyes, savoring the import of those words, letting the comfort of them—the joy in them—wrap around her like cotton wool, warming her heart, easing her fears. When she opened them again she breathed a sigh. "Frank—all the things between us? Not just your family's ranch, but the Women and Infants Clinic, my practice?"

"I wrote my mother to explain why I couldn't come back to Elizabeth or to the ranch. I told her about the clinic, and she said—I should have seen this myself, I suppose, but—"

Margot made herself wait. She was usually good at waiting, at allowing her patients to find the words they needed, to share their secrets, but this was hard. She bit down on her lower lip to restrain her impatience, and she watched Frank search for how to say what he wanted to say.

He finally said, "Mother said some things are too important to be kept secret. I should have known that already."

"Does that mean you don't mind anymore?"

"I still have complicated feelings about it—but then, I'm a man. I don't know what it feels like to be a woman, to have to deal with such things. But you do, and I know you have good reasons for wanting to help."

"I will thank your mother for her wisdom when I have the chance."

"She'll like that, Margot. She'll like you."

"Is she terribly disappointed about you and Elizabeth?"

"She didn't say so. Said she wasn't surprised."

"And how are you going to feel if I'm still Dr. Benedict? If I want to keep my name?"

"That's hard, too, for an old-fashioned man. But you're the woman I love, and you're not old-fashioned." He shrugged. "I guess film actresses do it all the time."

"Film actresses. Oh, dear."

The snow began to fall faster, cutting off the outside world, encasing the two of them in a shifting curtain of white. Snowflakes glistened beneath the Christmas lights, ruby and emerald sparks floating through the cold air. Margot gazed at them for a moment and said, almost to herself, "Is everything spoiled, I wonder?"

"Spoiled? Why, Margot?"

"Oh, Frank. Because you carried a letter from your old sweetheart around in your pocket. Because your parents would prefer you to marry a girl from home—and because I'm so different from Elizabeth. From most women, I guess."

"Sweetheart," he said. He drew her close to him to kiss her forehead and cradle her against his chest. "No, this isn't a fairy tale to be spoiled by such things. We're real people. With real problems."

Her voice was muffled against his camel's hair overcoat. "I love you, Frank."

"I love you, Margot." He put her away from him, just a little, so he could put his right hand into the pocket of the overcoat. "Now, don't interrupt me. I practiced this." He took out a small brown velvet box and held it up on his palm.

Margot opened her mouth to speak, but he shook his head, grinning now. "Nope. Wait."

He opened the box, and she caught the glisten of jewelry inside as he knelt on the damp surface of the porch. He held the box up to her and said, his eyes twinkling at least as much as the diamond ring in its nest of satin, "Will you marry me, Margot Benedict? I promise to always let you be yourself. And I'll do anything that lies in my power to make you happy."

"That was good, Frank," she said, smiling. She knelt down herself, heedless of the hem of her brand-new coat, and looked up into his face. "Oh, yes," she said. "Yes, I will most definitely marry you, Frank Parrish. And I'll do my very best to make you happy, too."

He held the box in his prosthetic hand while he took the ring in his natural one. It was beautifully understated, a small square diamond in a frame of even smaller ones. It was the sort of ring she could wear all the time, even in surgical gloves, and the thoughtfulness of the choice made her heart flutter. He slipped it on her finger, kissed her hand, then took her in his arms.

When Blake came to call them to luncheon, he put his head out the door, then immediately stepped back inside. He closed the door as quietly as he could, managing to avoid even the softest click. He went to the dining room, smiling to himself, and informed the family that Major Parrish and Dr. Margot would be delayed for a few more minutes. "They would prefer you to begin your luncheon without them," he said.

Dickson said, with satisfaction, "Excellent, Blake. Just excellent."

CHAPTER 27

Western State Hospital was a forbidding place. It was huge, made of brick, with sprawling wings that looked almost unintentional, as if they were added as an afterthought. Margot and her father approached the entrance with dogged steps, passing a set of soaring sandstone pillars, making their way through heavy double doors, not pausing until they were inside the cavernous, echoing lobby.

Even Margot, veteran of hospital lobbies, found this one oppressive. After the gaiety and color of the Christmas celebration at Benedict Hall, the grimness of this place was particularly hard to bear. A pervasive smell of cleaning products hung in the air. Straight vertical bars topped every window, and though the lower parts of the windows bore a curlicue pattern, they were still iron bars, merely bent into shapes meant to be easier on the eye. There were locks on every door, and in the distance, half-heard cries and screams sounded from the wings, making goose bumps rise on her neck.

Dickson tensed, the muscles of his arm shivering beneath her fingers. He muttered, "Better than the city jail, at least."

"We're not abandoning him, Father. We'll do our best to see he's well treated." She hoped that was possible. There had been horrific stories, when she was a medical student, of abuses of mental patients. It had been a running joke among the interns that if they turned out to be really bad doctors, they could always get work at Western State Hospital.

Her father's cheeks were drawn into deep, unhappy furrows that made him look older than his years. Margot stayed close beside him, her gloved hand under his arm. She had left her medical bag with Blake, in the Essex, and she felt exposed without it. In her free hand she carried a small valise, lovingly packed by Hattie with fresh underwear, sweaters, a wrapped box of Christmas cookies and gingerbread. No few of Hattie's tears had fallen on these things, though Margot doubted Preston would ever know.

The police had moved Preston the day after Christmas. Technically, commitment to Western State Hospital was involuntary. Preston, true to his side of the bargain, did nothing to resist it. Dickson's friends in the courts had done their work with efficiency and without attracting notice from the newspapers. Only one official had pressed Dickson for details on the son everyone believed deceased, and that one, an associate of decades, expressed more sympathy than surprise. The whole thing had been handled with her father's usual deftness, and Margot suspected she was the only person in the city who knew what it had cost him in heartbreak and shame.

They found the administrator's office without difficulty, but they had to press a bell before someone came to the door and admitted them. They had to wait even longer while the managing physician, Dr. Keller, read them a long list of rules and restrictions. He said, "As you're a medical professional, Dr. Benedict, we'll allow you and Mr. Benedict to go up to the ward. As a general rule, we restrict visiting, but we'll make an exception in this case. This once, you understand."

"We understand," Dickson said. His voice was harsh with tension.

Margot said nothing. She was sure Preston would not want to see her, but she had come in support of her father. Neither Blake nor Frank had been in favor of it, though she had assured them there was nothing to worry about. Most of the inmates were deemed criminally insane and treated accordingly. Preston would be no exception.

Dr. Keller called for an orderly and gave instructions. The orderly, a thickset giant of a man with the unlikely name of Small, led Margot and her father to an elevator that carried them up two floors. Mr. Small pushed the elevator doors open, and ushered them out into a long ward with a gray linoleum floor and dull green walls. A tiny nurse's office, with another locking door, faced a common room where books lined one wall and a cabinet radio dominated the other. Beyond the office the corridor stretched the entire length of the wing. Rooms—no, cells, Margot thought, there was really no other word—lined the corridor, each with a tiny window and a handwritten nameplate beside the locked door. Voices came from behind the doors, calling, muttering, weeping. The whole thing felt Gothic to Margot, and she could only imagine how appalling it must seem to her father.

The orderly spoke to the nurse on duty, a woman wearing a long brown sweater over a white uniform. She set off briskly down the corridor, a huge ring of keys clanking at her waist, and Mr. Small followed her.

The nurse unlocked a door, and she and Mr. Small stepped inside. Margot said, "Let's sit down, Father. Preston may need to get dressed or something."

Her father, looking numb, settled onto a straight chair. Margot almost sat on the sofa, but its array of stains discouraged her. She took another straight chair, resting the valise on the floor beside her. She was scanning the bookshelf, wondering who had chosen these nineteenth-century titles, when the nurse and Mr. Small reappeared. They had Preston between them, supported by their hands as he made a slow, shuffling progress down the long corridor.

Dickson said, "My God, Margot, what's wrong with him?"

Margot murmured, "I don't know, Father. Let's wait and see."

They both rose and watched Preston's approach. His head drooped, and his eyelids were heavy, as if he had been sleeping. The nurse and Mr. Small bore a good deal of his weight, Margot could see, as if his muscles were too slack to bear it himself.

When the trio reached the common room, the nurse and Mr. Small helped Preston into a chair. Mr. Small stayed behind Preston, his eyes never leaving him. The nurse went into her office, but returned a moment later with a blanket. She spread this over Preston's lap. "If you need anything," the nurse said, "I'll be right over there." She pointed to her office. "But Mr. Small will see that everything is all right."

Mr. Small folded his arms and dropped his chin to his chest. His presence was a security measure, obviously, but Margot could see it wasn't necessary. Preston was incapable of threatening anyone at the moment. She leaned over him, causing Mr. Small to stiffen. Margot shook her head. "It's all right," she said. "We're fine." Mr. Small didn't move.

Margot touched Preston's wrist with her fingers and lifted his eyelids. Delicately, she touched the conjunctiva of his left eye. He didn't flinch or blink. She said, "Preston? Can you hear me? It's Margot. And Father."

Preston struggled to lift his head, and his scarred lips twisted as he tried to speak. It took a few seconds for him to slur, "Doc. H-hiya, doc. Come to f-finish me off?" His eyelids drooped, and he gave a short, strangled laugh. "N-not much left of me."

Margot straightened, and glared at Mr. Small. "Who's been medicating him? And what is it? Potassium bromide, I would guess. The dose is far too high."

The orderly said, "I don't know, miss. I don't do medicines."

"Doctor. I'm Dr. Benedict. Get the nurse, please."

"Yes, miss." He backed toward the office door, not taking his eyes from Preston.

Dickson, stiffly, crouched in front of his son to take one scarred hand in his. "Preston," he said. "We've brought some things from—some things for you. Clothes. Some of Hattie's gingerbread. She knows you love that."

Preston's eyelids lifted, but awkwardly, first one and then the other. A silvery thread of saliva slid from his lips and down his scarred chin. Margot stripped off her gloves and reached into her pocket for a handkerchief. As she wiped his chin clean, he said, "Wh-what's this, doc? D-diamonds?"

"Yes," she said. "Frank Parrish and I are going to be married."

"G-God. P-poor Cowboy."

The nurse, with Mr. Small close behind her, came hurrying across to the common room. She stood beside Preston's chair, frowning at Margot. "You're a doctor?" she demanded. "Someone should have told me."

"It didn't seem important," Margot said. "But now I want to see my brother's records. Who prescribed for him? And why is he sedated so heavily?"

"The admitting physician prescribes potassium bromide for all incoming patients. It eases the transition. Helps them settle in."

"How? At this level of medication, I doubt the patient remembers a single thing about the transition."

"Doctor, I'm not the one to ask. It's hospital procedure. I'm sorry."

Margot drew a noisy breath and released it. It wasn't the nurse's fault, and it wouldn't help to alienate her. Her father was still kneeling by Preston, holding his hand. His lips were clamped tight, and his thick eyebrows drawn fiercely together.

She bent over the two of them, aware that this motion brought Mr. Small to attention again. She said, "Preston, they've given you too much medicine. I'll speak to the doctor in charge, I promise."

Her father pushed himself to his feet. The nurse pushed a chair forward, and he accepted it with a nod. "Now, son," he said gruffly. "Let's go through these things we brought, shall we? Just a few little—" His voice caught, and he coughed. "Just a few things to—to make you feel better."

Margot's own throat ached, watching her father's attempt to converse with Preston. She couldn't avoid the bleak thought that it would have been better—better for everyone—if Preston had died in the fire. Her brother was accustomed to a life of style and comfort and sophistication. Being in this place, for Preston, must feel like a living death.

They spent a few more minutes with him. Dickson took each item out of the valise, described it to Preston, and laid it back inside. Preston said, "P-p-pater. Tell Hattie I l-love her gingerbread."

"I will, son. I'll tell her."

"N-not Mother."

"No. As we promised."

There was more saliva whenever Preston spoke. The nurse moved to help, but Margot was already there, wiping the spittle from his scarred chin with her handkerchief. She said, "These scars should be treated, Nurse. First, sweet almond oil as a demulcent, then an emollient. Petroleum jelly will be fine. Do you have those things here? If not, I'll send them from my office."

"I can get them."

"Please do. I'll leave you my telephone number in case there's a problem."

"Yes, Doctor."

Preston said, "Even h-here, d-doc?"

Margot answered quietly, "Yes, Preston. Even here. For your own good."

His eyes opened, and he looked into her face. He said, very clearly, "Hell."

Dickson said, "What?"

Margot said, "I know, Preston. I understand." His eyelids drooped again.

The nurse signaled to Mr. Small, and the two of them helped Preston to his feet. The nurse said, "Say good-bye to your family, Mr. Benedict."

Abruptly, Preston threw up his head to fix the nurse with a glance of such hatred that Mr. Small uttered a warning sound. The three of them turned toward the corridor and managed a few slow steps before Preston shuffled to a halt. He mumbled,

"W-wait. Th-there's something . . ." This time the look he bent on the nurse was reminiscent of the old Preston, limpid eyes, persuasive angle of his head. Even as disfigured as he was, there was something there, some remnant of his personality.

Dickson hurried to Preston, and Margot followed.

The nurse said, "Sir, be careful—" but Dickson was already there, stepping past the orderly to stand in front of his son.

"What is it, Preston? What can we do?"

Margot watched her brother narrow his eyes, struggling against the drug-induced fog that slowed his mind and dragged at his speech. He looked at his father, then past him to Margot. There was life in his eyes at that moment, a flash of clarity, and with it the familiar look of malice.

Preston leaned toward Dickson, as close as the orderly's firm grip would allow him to. "It's a child," he said, enunciating with effort.

Dickson said, "What? What child?"

"My child," Preston said. The life began to fade again from his eyes, and his head sagged to one side. He drew a noisy breath through his scarred throat. "I th-thought you should know."

Margot said, "Preston, this is cruel to Father. On top of everything else—"

" 'S true," Preston said. "S-Seattle. S-somewhere."

The nurse said, "Dr. Benedict, our patients often make odd statements. They usually don't mean anything."

"B-bitch," Preston mumbled. "D-don't s-speak for me, b-bitch, you—"

Mr. Small gave Preston's arm a jerk, forcing him forward. Preston gagged, as if the action caught him by surprise. Dickson and Margot had to move out of the way and watch as Preston was guided ungently back into his room and locked inside.

They left the valise with the nurse, and Mr. Small escorted them back to the elevator and pushed the call button. The doors had just opened when they heard Preston's hoarse voice from his cell. "It's a bastard!" he cried. He must have been standing right beside the door, shouting through the screened window. "A

Benedict bastard!" He fell into a spate of croaking laughter that ended in a fit of coughing.

As the elevator doors closed, Dickson said, "My God. What does that mean, Margot?" He was white to the lips, and he trembled like a sapling in the wind. "Does it mean anything?"

She held his arm in her two hands, steadying him as best she could. "I don't know, Father," she said, choking with misery and horror and sadness. "I just don't know."

CHAPTER 28

On her wedding day, Margot crept down the stairs before sunrise. She was still in her dressing gown, with thick socks on her feet against the February chill. She had been awake for hours, and when the clock at her bedside ticked over to six o'clock, she gave up on sleep, and went in search of coffee.

The kitchen was dim, illuminated only by the faint gleam of Hattie's polished appliances. Margot found the small cupboard light, and used that to spoon coffee grounds into the percolator, to fetch the bottle of cream from the icebox, and to get a mug from the cupboard. She leaned her hip against the counter as the percolator bubbled, and pondered the new direction of her life from this day forward. The diamonds of her engagement ring twinkled with promise in the low light. They should have reassured her, she thought. Bolstered her confidence. Instead, her mind whirled with questions.

She was pouring out her first cup of coffee when the back door opened with a tiny click. Margot smiled, and as she reached into the cupboard for another mug, she heard Blake chuckle, and one of the aluminum chairs creaked as he sat down.

She set his coffee in front of him and put her own on the table, with spoons from the drawer of silverware. As she settled into a chair, she said, "It's like old times, Blake. Just you and me in the wee hours."

He lifted his mug to her. "Old times and new times, sweetheart. I'm very happy about today."

"Are you?" She cradled the warm mug between her palms. "That's good. I am, too."

"No second thoughts?"

She laughed. "Oh, yes. Many second thoughts. But I always come back to the main one."

"I hope your main thought is for Major Parrish."

"It is." She gazed into the swirl of cream in her mug. "It's going to be an interesting life for him, I'm afraid."

"He loves you," Blake said.

"I hope he loves me enough!" she said with another laugh.

"On matters of marriage, I am of no use to you, Dr. Margot."

She looked up at him, and her heart stirred with affection. "You have already been of use to me, Blake. To us both."

He gave a little shrug, but his lips curved and his eyes shone with contentment. "I'm so happy to see you settled."

"Settled? It sounds good, doesn't it? But I'm not sure I'll ever be *settled*."

Blake picked up his cup and leaned back in his chair. In the dim light he looked almost as young as he had the day she first took her courage in her two hands and went off to medical school. He looked as young as when she had sat here, quaking with nerves on the morning she was to begin her internship. Of course, when he rose from the table he would be leaning on his cane, and when the light was better she would see how white his hair had grown, how lined his face. But just at this moment, he sat across from her as he always had, wise, dependable, strong. Her touchstone. Tears sprang up at the thought, and she touched the heels of her hands to her eyes to press them away.

"Are you all right?" he asked.

She sniffled and laughed at the same time. "Oh, yes, fine. I was just thinking of how many times you and I have sat together in this kitchen. How many times you gave me courage when I was afraid. Now you're doing it again. You're giving me courage."

"I don't give you courage," Blake said. "You have plenty of that on your own."

"Confidence, then."

"Yes, I suppose you could say that. I've always had confidence in you."

"Even now, Blake? Do you have confidence in this, too?" Her voice was a little unsteady, and more tears threatened.

He put out his hand to briefly touch hers. "I do, sweetheart. I have all the confidence in the world."

Ramona was in her element. Now six months pregnant, dressed in flowing lavender satin, she gave orders like a queen— or perhaps like a general. Florists, caterers, the string quartet she had hired, two waiters in formal wear who would assist Thelma and Leona and Loena, all marched here and there at her commands. Benedict Hall was transformed. Branches of viburnum with delicate pink flowers bloomed in tall vases on the stairs, bowls of winter roses filled the dining room, and evergreen garlands festooned the hall. A spectacular arrangement of forsythia and winter jasmine, lovingly created by the Chinese florist from the Public Market, waited in the large parlor to be the backdrop for the ceremony.

Allison, pink-cheeked with excitement, dashed up and down the main staircase with updates for the bride while Margot hid in her bedroom, away from the fuss. While she and Frank were on their honeymoon journey, taking the train south to California so he could show her March Field, Leona and Loena would move all her things, and his, waiting in modest cartons beside her wardrobe, to the far end of the hall, the large bedroom at the back of the house. It had its own bath and a small balcony facing south over the garden. They would use the back staircase most of the time, for convenience, but Blake had assured Margot the servants wouldn't find that a problem.

Father had moved Margot's telephone to their new bedroom, but he apologized to Frank for it. "Rings at all hours," he warned his son-in-law to be. "You'll see being married to a doctor has its drawbacks."

Frank had said, "Yes, sir," and Margot flashed him a look that made him smile.

Her gown—her wedding gown, the very idea of which still amazed her—hung now in front of her wardrobe, the tissue stripped away, the folds carefully draped to avoid wrinkling. It seemed to her a wonder of stitches and beads and buttons. There was no veil, because the idea of it made Margot shudder. "It's so medieval," she had complained. "Pretending the bridegroom has never seen the bride."

Ramona sniffed. "Mine was beautiful," she said. "With a coronet of pearls to hold it."

"Ramona, *you* were beautiful," Margot said with sincerity. "The veil suited you perfectly. But can you see me in a coronet of pearls?"

They had been in the fitting room of the bridal department of Frederick & Nelson. The saleswoman looked disapproving, but both Ramona and Allison had dissolved in giggles. Allison said, "You have to admit it, Cousin Ramona. Let's just keep her from wearing a stethoscope." At that they all laughed, while the saleswoman, a tape measure in her hands and lengths of white satin hanging everywhere, waited for the Benedict women to return to the serious matter at hand.

They had, of course, eventually, but there had been much more laughter and a great deal of arguing, mostly between Ramona and Allison. Margot had cleared the whole day for the exercise, so she stood as patiently as she could while the saleswoman measured her, Ramona fingered fabrics and frowned over beads and laces, and Allison brought an assortment of *prêt-à-porter* gowns for Margot to consider.

As it was winter, and an afternoon wedding, they settled on a gown with long net sleeves, a dropped waist, and an exquisitely hand-beaded bodice. Margot pleaded with Ramona and Allison to spare her the train, and they had agreed on an ankle-length hem, with white silk stockings and white *peau de soie* shoes with a modest heel. There was no coronet, but there were tiny pearls on the headband that Margot would wear over her freshly shingled hair.

It was Allison's task, on the day, to help Margot into her dress and make sure everything was in place. When it was time, she came dashing up the stairs for the dozenth time. "He's here!" she gushed. "Major Parrish is here, and he looks *divine!*"

"Did you think he wouldn't come?" Margot asked, laughing.

Allison laughed, too. It was a day for laughing. For happiness.

Margot could hardly recognize Allison as the same wan, gaunt creature who had arrived at Benedict Hall in the autumn. She had gained some weight, though no one could call her plump. Her skin had regained the dewiness appropriate to her youth, and her hair looked full and healthy. She dutifully presented herself every week at the clinic so Margot could check her blood pressure and her temperature and listen to her heart, but her real healing, Margot was convinced, had been effected by Hattie. It wasn't just food. It was Hattie's affection, freely offered without criticism or demands, that had made the difference for a lonely, unloved girl.

The only blemish on this day had been the argument about the guest list. Edith Benedict had roused herself just enough to oversee this element of a Benedict wedding, and she had objected with surprising energy to the inclusion of Sarah Church.

"She's my colleague, Mother," Margot had said. "We've been working together since Blake's accident."

"You can't put a Negro on your invitation list, Margot. You just can't. It would make everyone uncomfortable."

"Then *everyone* can just stay away," Margot had said irritably. Of all the things to catch her mother's attention! It was enough to make her want to elope.

It was Blake who solved the problem. He came to Margot at breakfast the next day, bowed, and asked to speak with her.

When she followed him out into the hall, he said, "I hope you'll forgive me, Dr. Margot, but I heard your argument with Mrs. Edith yesterday. I took the liberty of telephoning Nurse Church."

"You did? Why?"

"Because I felt certain she would be just as uncomfortable at receiving your wedding invitation as Mrs. Edith believes the other guests would be. I was correct, as it happens."

"She won't come?"

"She would prefer not to have to refuse."

"But, Blake—she's my friend! I don't have many women friends."

"She is both your friend and your admirer. I know that." He gave her a gentle smile, and nodded his head toward the dining room, where the family was gathered. "She will be happier—and Mrs. Edith will—if you can manage to let this one go, Dr. Margot. If you could see your way to letting this issue pass, I think it would be the wise thing to do."

Margot had pressed her lips together in exasperation, but she knew Blake had everyone's best interests at heart. In the end, though it galled her, she did as he suggested. Sarah Church didn't receive an invitation to the wedding. In fact, as Margot perused the list later, she saw that most of the people who would attend were ones she barely knew, friends of her parents, business associates of her father's. There were a few people from the hospital. Angela Rossi would come, and Matron Cardwell.

And of course, there were Frank's parents. Margot had met them briefly the day before, work-worn, cheerful people. Frank's father shook her hand, and called her Doctor. Frank's mother embraced her, though shyly, as if uncertain whether such a demonstration would be welcome. They were a bit awed by the magnificence of Benedict Hall and the number of servants who kept popping in and out of the dining room and the small parlor, but Ramona, as hostess, was gracious and unpretentious. They seemed to relax after a time.

When she and Frank had said good night, and Blake had driven the Parrishes off to the Alexis Hotel, she said, "I'm going to love them, Frank. I'm sure of it."

"And they will love you." He kissed her greedily, and said in a husky voice, "Tomorrow, Margot. Finally."

She kissed him back. "Tomorrow!"

And now, at last, the day had arrived. Allison helped her into her gown, and combed her hair before slipping on the pearl-encrusted headband. Margot submitted to her young cousin's deft fingers as she applied a bit of powder, a touch of lipstick, a dab of perfume. She put on the *peau de soie* shoes, smoothed the skirt of her dress, and turned to the mirror to face her reflection.

She said, "Good God, Allison, who *is* that woman?"

"Why, I believe that's Mrs. Frank Parrish," Allison said with a giggle, and Margot giggled with her.

CHAPTER 29

Blake met them at the train station with a formal, "Welcome home, Dr. Margot. Major Parrish."

Margot and Frank, grinning like children, could only just restrain themselves from hugging him right there in the center of King Street Station. Blake said, "You both look very well."

"Blake, it was marvelous!" Margot said. "So relaxing. I think every honeymoon should begin with a train journey."

"I gather you enjoyed yourselves, then."

"More than I could have imagined!" she said. "I can't remember the last vacation I took."

"That might be because you haven't taken one in years."

Frank insisted on helping Blake with their bags, and Margot thought Blake was indulging him, under the circumstances. When they were on their way up the hill to Broadway, she leaned forward from the backseat. "Blake, Frank took me up in an airplane! One of the Jennys, at March Field. It was absolutely the most exciting thing I've ever done."

"That sounds wonderful. I envy you," Blake said in his dignified way.

"Would you like to fly, Blake?" Frank asked. "I could arrange that."

Blake drew a breath to answer, but Margot burst out, "Now, don't say no automatically. Think about this, Blake. It's the most amazing experience—the wind in your face, and the wings vibrating around you—it's like being a bird! You just leave everything behind, all the silly things people think are so important. Everything's tiny and far away, and none of it seems to matter very much at all."

She could see the curve of Blake's cheek, and she knew he was smiling. "Very well, Dr. Margot. I won't say no. If Major Parrish finds it convenient sometime . . ."

"It would be my pleasure, Blake," Frank said. He found Margot's hand and held it. "I think I've become the Boeing Airplane Company's expert on the Flying Jennys."

The staff was waiting when they reached Benedict Hall. The day was typically Seattle, weak shafts of March sunshine illuminating a misting rain. All three maids stood under the shelter of the porch roof, and Hattie, in a freshly ironed apron and wearing an enormous smile, stood with them. Ramona was there, her pregnancy evident even from the street, and Allison, bouncing on her toes with excitement. Only Edith was missing, but Margot hardly noticed. She had become used to her mother's absences.

Blake stopped in front of the house and got out, leaning on his cane, to open the back doors of the Essex. When Frank said, "Let me get the bags, Blake," he shook his head.

"No, sir. I'll bring them in from the garage, Major Parrish, and see they're carried up to your rooms. You go and say hello to the family."

They were soon all seated in the small parlor, and Hattie sent Loena in with a tea tray. Margot and Frank handed out the gifts they'd brought, including a silk scarf for each of the maids, which they sent back to the kitchen with Loena.

"Your wedding gifts are stowed in the large parlor, Margot," Ramona said. "You and Frank can open them when you have time. I had thank-you cards printed for you, but not too many, in case you don't like the paper I chose."

"Thank you, Ramona. I'm sure I'll love it. I don't have any idea how to do that sort of thing."

"Actually, I wasn't sure . . . they're printed in the names of Major and Mrs. Frank Parrish. Was that all right?"

Margot smiled at Frank, and reached across to touch Ramona's hand. "Perfect," she said. "It's just perfect. I'll be Dr. Benedict when I'm working, but Mrs. Parrish everywhere else."

"Well," Ramona said, relieved, smiling. "That sounds like a sensible arrangement. Good for you, Margot!"

Margot picked up her teacup and eyed her sister-in-law over the rim. "You look really good, Ramona. You're feeling well?"

"Perfect! Two and a half months to go. We're doing up the room next to ours as a nursery. It's big enough so the nurse will be able to sleep in there, too."

"Goodness! Benedict Hall is going to have a huge staff."

"Yes, but Blake says it's fine. We've kept Thelma on, as you saw, to help Hattie."

"Good." Margot glanced at Frank. "Leona went up to unpack for us. I hope that was all right with you."

"Takes some getting used to," he said. "But I'm sure she'll make a better job of it than I usually do."

Margot set her cup down. "Is Mother all right?" she asked Ramona.

Ramona's smile faded, and she linked her hands over her swelling abdomen. "Something happened," she said. "Just this morning, actually. I don't know what it was."

"Really? She seemed to enjoy the wedding. It brought her out of herself a bit, and I thought perhaps she was getting better."

"I did, too, or at least I hoped so. But this morning—she was in your old room, after breakfast, helping the twins to clear out the last of your things, and—I don't know what it was. Leona said she had something in her hands, and she went into Preston's room and locked the door. She hasn't come out."

Margot's mouth went dry, and her heart began to pound. She

rose, and tried to smooth the creases from the skirt of her traveling dress. "I think I'd better go up." Frank started to get up, too,
but she waved him back. "No, you stay. Tell Allison about the
seals we saw from the train."

Anxiety churned in her stomach as she climbed the staircase.
Where had she left it? She had just jammed it into a bottom
drawer after that terrible night, when she was too tired to think,
too emotionally drained to plan anything, and then she had forgotten all about it. There had been the rather lovely Christmas,
with the excitement of her engagement. She had been busy all of
January with the Women and Infants Clinic, her own clinic on
Post Street, and the wedding preparations. She had spent every
spare moment with Frank, going to her bedroom only to sleep or
to change. Frank had repaired the gouged-out hole in the footings of her clinic, and the shrubs were budding now, stretching
their branches up toward the wintry sun. They would soon hide
the foundation.

Preston had been on her mind, of course. She planned a visit
to Western State Hospital after she had seen to things at her
clinic, picked up rounds again at Seattle General. She had written to Dr. Keller explaining her concerns about Preston's medication, requesting that someone have a look at his scars, but she
thought it would be best to follow up in person.

But the sapphire—she had put the stone out of her mind. She
had forgotten all about it.

She drew a deep breath and squared her shoulders before
knocking on Preston's door. "Mother? It's Margot. We're home,
Frank and I." She raised her hand to knock again.

The door flew open before her knuckles struck the wood.
Edith stood before her, wild-eyed, graying hair disheveled,
cheeks flaming. She stood taller than she had in months, and her
voice rang out in a way it hadn't in more than a year. "What have
you done to Preston?" she demanded.

Margot said, "What? What do you mean, Mother?"

Edith held out the chunk of concrete, lifting it up in her two
hands so the half-buried sapphire gleamed blue in the light from

the hall. Edith's eyes blazed a matching blue fire. "Where is he, Margot? Why are you hiding my son from me?"

Margot slumped against the doorjamb. She couldn't think how to answer.

Within the hour they were on their way to the hospital. A terse telephone call to Dickson's office had brought him swiftly home, and he was closeted with Edith for no more than ten minutes before emerging with a thunderous expression to tell Blake they would be taking the Essex out again. Margot made another telephone call, but she had to put her father on before obtaining permission to see Preston immediately.

Dickson said, "You don't have to come, daughter."

"I do," she said. "If Mother—that is, you might need me." She had her medical bag, and after Frank helped her with her coat and she had put on her hat and gloves, she carried it with her to the waiting automobile. Dread made her stomach roil.

Frank repeated, "Margot, I can come with you."

"No, darling," she said. "Father and I can manage. You go on to the Red Barn."

"Be careful, Margot."

She nodded. "I will. It's Mother I'm worried about."

Edith was so frantic to depart, once she heard where Preston was, that it took both Margot and Dickson to persuade her to take the time to put on her coat and gloves. In the backseat of the Essex, she sat twisting her hands together and asking, over and over, "Why? Why didn't you tell me?"

Dickson said, glancing at Margot above Edith's head, "He's terribly scarred, Edith. You will hardly know him. We thought— in your fragile state—"

"My state," she said in a brittle voice, "has been fragile because everyone said my son was dead, but I knew, I *knew*. You've all been lying to me, deceiving me!"

"No, Mother," Margot said, a little more loudly than she intended. "That's not true. We didn't know Preston was alive until just before Christmas."

"Why didn't you tell me then?"

"Edith, calm yourself. Try to listen," Dickson said

She shook her head, and twisted and twisted her hands. "I don't understand. He was burned; he's been suffering. He needs me, and you didn't *tell* me!"

It did no good to explain that Preston hadn't wanted her to know. It seemed pointless to relate the story of that long night when he had seized Allison and nearly killed his sister and himself. Edith talked on and on, asking, pleading, accusing, and by the time they reached the hospital, Margot was debating with herself over whether she should give her mother a sedative before she saw Preston. This time she kept her medical bag with her as they crossed the grounds of the hospital and went up the steps between the sandstone pillars.

Edith finally fell silent when they stepped inside the echoing entrance hall. Margot wanted to hold her arm, to steady her, but Edith wriggled free and watched with fierce attention as Dickson walked to the office and spoke to the secretary there. A moment later Dr. Keller himself, with Mr. Small in attendance, came out to escort them. They went up in the elevator and emerged onto the ward, where a nurse—a different one this time, younger, less mild in her speech and movements—came to meet them.

"We'll bring the patient to you," the nurse said, with a gesture to Mr. Small.

Edith said, "No! No, I want to go to his room."

"Mother," Margot warned. "I want to prepare you for—"

Edith turned on her with a sound so much like a cat's hiss that Margot fell back a step before she could catch herself. "Haven't you done *enough?*" her mother cried. "Haven't you caused *enough* trouble, Margot?"

Margot was aware of Dr. Keller's attention on them, and the nurse was poised, one hand in the air, as if she might need to seize someone or something. Mr. Small, stolid and silent, folded his arms, watching and listening.

Dickson, with a weary sigh, put his arm around his wife. "All right, Edith," he said. "That's enough, now. It's not Margot's fault. You mustn't speak to her that way."

Edith pulled away from him. "You always take her side, Dickson. Now leave me alone. I want to see my son."

There seemed to be nothing for it but to allow her, with the nurse at her side and Dr. Keller and Mr. Small just behind, to walk down the long corridor. The ward was oddly silent today, and Margot suspected the sedatives had been increased when Keller learned they were coming. She heard mumbled voices here and there, an occasional querulous call, but that was all. She and her father came last, and Margot wished she didn't have to go at all. Keller had no medical bag with him, but she kept hers close, thinking of what she might be able to do if her mother fainted, or had hysterics, or, God forbid, suffered a breakdown when she saw Preston's scarred face.

The nurse lifted the heavy ring of keys at her waist and sifted through them for the correct one. Edith fidgeted impatiently beside her, calling, "Preston? Preston, are you there?"

Margot heard, from inside the cell, her brother give a prolonged groan of recognition. The lock clicked, and the nurse began to pull the door open. Edith started to push past her, and Margot, alarmed, took two long strides, to go into the cell with her mother whether she wanted her there or not. It was going to be a ghastly shock. Edith had never been good at shocks.

The door was open. Edith stepped through and stopped abruptly, one hand pressed over her mouth, gazing at Preston. He was standing by the barred window, the weak sunlight falling full on his disfigured face, the ridges and whorls of his burn scars, the distortion of his mouth, the absence of his eyebrows and most of his hair.

He said, "Mother. Oh, God."

Edith said, in a tone of pure grief, "Oh, Preston. Preston, son. My poor, poor darling." She put out both her arms, crossed the cell, and took Preston in her arms. She cradled his head and caressed his scarred skull, murmuring over and over, "Oh, my poor darling. How awful for you. My poor, poor darling."

CHAPTER 30

Allison didn't know for certain how long she'd been asleep. It was still dark when she heard footsteps in the hall and on the stairs, doors opening and closing. Light showed beneath her bedroom door, punctuated by moving shadows as people walked to and fro. She sat up, wondering what was happening. A moment later she heard Margot's deep, calm voice, and Cousin Dick answering her. Someone groaned, a sound that seemed louder because of the strange hour.

Ramona! The baby!

She scrambled out of bed and seized her dressing gown from its hook. She found her slippers with difficulty, one buried deep under the bed and the other tossed under her dressing table, and she opened her door to listen.

Downstairs, Cousin Dick was speaking on the hall telephone. From Ramona's bedroom, she heard Margot and Ramona talking in normal voices, as if the groan of a few minutes before hadn't happened. From the other big bedroom, where Uncle Dickson and Aunt Edith slept, there was no sound, but below stairs, she

heard the muted bang of the kitchen door, and knew that someone had roused Blake.

Allison moved tentatively to the door of Ramona's bedroom.
She had never actually been in it, but she could see the end of
a big bed with a dark comforter on it, and catch a glimpse of
Margot's back as she bent forward. Allison rapped gently on the
open door. "Cousin Ramona? Cousin Margot? Is there anything
I can do?"

Margot straightened and beckoned to her. "Oh, yes, come in,
Allison. You can sit with Ramona while I go and get dressed. Her
labor's started, but it's going to be some time yet before baby
comes." She did something with her hands, and Allison realized
she had been wearing surgical gloves, which she was now stripping off. "I'll be right back."

Ramona, in a nest of pillows, smiled a bit palely at Allison, and
patted the bed beside her. "Do come sit with me, Allison. I've
just had a few pains, and Margot says I'm in for a bit of a wait."

"Did it—do they hurt a lot?" Allison said, sinking down beside
Ramona.

"Yes!" Ramona said, on a ghost of a laugh. "Yes, they hurt, but
I keep thinking how much I want the baby, and . . ." She winced
and pressed her lips together. Color rose in her face and receded
almost as quickly, and the same groan Allison had heard earlier
came from her, a deep sound she wouldn't have thought Ramona, so delicate and feminine, could produce. A moment later
the pain seemed to pass. Ramona breathed a sigh and lay back on
her pillows.

Allison tried to imagine her mother going through this, riding a
pain like that without crying out or screaming or weeping, but
she couldn't do it. She took Ramona's hand in hers, not knowing
what else to do. "You're so brave," she whispered.

"Oh, no," Ramona said. "Not brave at all. I'm really frightened, Allison. But this is what women do, isn't it? Everyone else
has done it, and I can, too." She closed her eyes and breathed
carefully in, then out. "Whew. This is going to be hard work."

"Is Dr. Creedy coming?"

"He's busy with an emergency at the hospital. And in the meantime, I have Margot. Thank goodness."

"Oh, yes. I think Margot must be the best doctor in the whole city!"

She knew Ramona had chosen to have her baby at home, in Benedict Hall, instead of going to the hospital. Margot thought it was a good idea, as long as there were no complications—whatever those might be—and apparently Dr. Creedy didn't mind, either. Ramona had confided to Allison that she didn't want to have her baby at the hospital because she had heard so many stories of babies getting mixed up. Allison didn't think that sounded right, but she didn't say anything. She wanted Ramona—all of them—to trust her. Instead, wondering about the issue, she had gone to Hattie.

She had fallen into the habit of taking all her embarrassing questions to Hattie. When her monthlies reappeared, she asked Hattie where to get supplies, and Hattie accompanied her to Bartell's on the streetcar so she could buy Lister's Towels. When she wanted to get rid of the plaid frock and two others that had always been too tight, she asked Hattie if she knew of someone who could use them. Hattie took them from her, and said she would take them to the jumble sale at the church. When she was trying to understand the Women and Infants Clinic, it was Hattie who explained that Cousin Margot and that pretty Sarah Church were teaching poor women how not to have babies, and when Allison frowned and asked how you could do that, Hattie explained it to her in succinct and specific terms. Allison had blushed hotly, over and over, but she didn't mind that too much in front of Hattie. She tried not to think about Cousin Margot and Major Parrish on their honeymoon, and what that must be like, but sometimes it bothered her. Hattie only patted her shoulder and said not to worry, that when it was her time and she met a man she really loved, it would all sort itself out.

To the question of babies getting mixed up in the hospital, Hattie only chuckled and shook her head. "There are lots of good reasons to have babies at home, though," she said. "It helps that we're here to take care of Mrs. Ramona when her time comes."

And now, here it was. Here was Cousin Ramona, about to give birth. It was exciting, and it was scary. And it must be messy, because Margot brought in a basin and a stack of clean towels and an enormous sheet she spread over the bed, tucking it under Ramona and covering the pillows. She also had her medical bag, but when she saw Ramona looking at it, she said, "Just a precaution, Ramona. You're doing beautifully, and baby's head is down, just as we want it. Everything looks perfect."

Much better than being in a hospital, Allison was sure. Hospitals were so cold and noisy and impersonal. Here, in Ramona's pretty bedroom with its thick velvet curtains and family pictures arranged on the bureau, surely here she could concentrate on what she needed to do.

When the next pain came, Ramona scowled, closed her eyes, and emitted that deep groan again. She gripped Allison's hand, and Allison gripped back, breathing and scowling just as Ramona did. When the pain passed, Ramona sighed and asked for water. Allison looked a question at Margot, who nodded. "Just a sip," she said. "We don't want anything extra in there with baby just now."

Allison went down to breakfast at Margot's urging. She found everyone at the table. Uncle Dickson was reading his paper, as usual, though he looked up anxiously when Allison came in. Aunt Edith was nibbling at her breakfast and looking as if she wasn't quite sure what was happening. Frank was just finishing his coffee, but Dick was pushing with his fork at the stack of griddle cakes on his plate, and it didn't look as if he had eaten anything. He jumped when Allison appeared, as if he was ready to fly up the stairs at a moment's notice.

Allison sat down next to him, in Ramona's usual chair, and Thelma set a plate in front of her while Loena poured her coffee.

When the servants had left the room, Allison said, "Don't worry, Cousin Dick. Margot says Ramona's doing fine."

Uncle Dickson said, "Good, good. I'm glad you're lending a hand, Allison. Good girl."

"It's just taking so long!" Dick groaned. He gave up pretending to eat his breakfast, laying down his fork and slumping in his chair. "Should it take so long?"

Aunt Edith said, "What, dear? Do you need more coffee?"

"Mother!" Dick exclaimed.

Allison said, "Aunt Edith, Cousin Ramona is having her baby. It started last night."

"Oh, that's nice," Edith said and put a bite of griddle cake in her mouth.

Frank wrinkled his nose at Allison and gave a slight shrug, but Dick blew out an anxious breath and rubbed his forehead with his palm.

Uncle Dickson folded his paper and laid it beside his plate. "You were a long time coming, too, Dick," he said. He smiled at his eldest son, and Allison felt a twinge of envy at the affection between them. Uncle Dickson went on, "I walked the floor for hours, waiting to hear something from upstairs." He pointed at the ceiling. "Right up there, they were, in our bedroom, your mother, her maid, and the doctor. I thought I'd go mad with worry, and in the middle of everything the doctor came down and ate a leisurely luncheon as if nothing at all were happening. I still remember," he added with a laugh, "that ham sandwich he was having. For months afterward I couldn't look at a ham sandwich!"

"Margot says she'll stay with Cousin Ramona until Dr. Creedy comes," Allison offered.

"Why isn't he here now?" Dick demanded. Allison had never heard him sound so querulous. It made her feel very grown-up and important that she was sitting with Cousin Ramona when her own husband wasn't allowed to go anywhere near her. She had thought the whole thing would be upsetting, but it seemed marvelous instead, an important task, a life-changing event, and it was all being handled by women.

She said, "Cousin Margot spoke to Dr. Creedy on the telephone. He has to do a surgery, evidently, but Margot said she would stay." She unfolded her napkin and said with pride, "Margot and I have been with Cousin Ramona all night."

Frank nodded appreciation of this.

Uncle Dickson said, "Very good, my dear. I'm sure you're a great help." He pushed back his chair and stood up. "I'll be off, Dick. Telephone me when you have some news."

Allison was just coming out of the dining room when she heard Margot, from the head of the stairs, calling her name. She drew a swift breath and dashed up the staircase. "Is everything all right?" she whispered when she reached the second floor. "Is Ramona—?"

Margot was just pulling on a pair of fresh surgical gloves, and Allison saw that her dress was spattered with water, as if she had been washing her hands. "We're going to have a baby soon," she said, without alarm. "I don't think Ramona is waiting for Dr. Creedy."

"Oh! Oh!" Allison cried. She started toward the bedroom, then stopped. "What—what do I do?"

"You don't have to help," Margot said, snapping the gloves down over her forearms. "But if you think you'll be all right, it would be nice for Ramona to have you there."

"I'll be all right," Allison said, and though her nerves quivered at the mystery of what was to come, she was certain it was true. If Ramona could do this, and Margot could help her, how could she do any less?

"Go and let Hattie know first, will you, please? Hattie will know what we need."

Allison did as she asked, hurrying down the staircase once more to knock on the kitchen door. "Hattie," she said breathlessly, "Cousin Margot says the baby is coming!"

"Oh, my Lord," Hattie exclaimed. She tossed the dish towel she was holding over the edge of the sink. "Leona, Loena, you'll do these dishes and clear the dining room. I'm going to collect a few things and go on up to Mrs. Ramona."

Allison flew back up the stairs and met Margot in the hall. "We're here," she said breathlessly. "That is, Hattie's on her way. *I'm* here."

"Excellent," Margot said, with a calm that amazed Allison. Her own heart was beating like a drum in her chest, and her hands trembled with nerves. Margot said, "Now, Allison, we still have some time. Just remember, if you feel faint, move away from the bed. Get to a chair, or—" She smiled to soften her words. "Or just faint on the floor! We'll pick you up, but we don't want you toppling over onto Ramona."

Allison said, with confidence, "Oh, I won't feel faint. I promise." She hurried to the head of the bed, where Ramona lay panting and perspiring. "Cousin Ramona, I'm right here! Give me your hand, and squeeze all you like. We're going to have a baby!"

Just as Margot had said, there was some time to go. Ramona alternated between drowsing and mumbling words that didn't always make sense, but which Allison and Hattie answered just the same. When the pains came, Ramona came fully alert, her eyes narrowed, her face contorting and her breathing fast and shallow. She often made the deep groan Allison had first noticed, but when the pain passed, she relaxed, exhaling, closing her eyes while Allison bathed her forehead with a water and vinegar solution Hattie had prepared.

Near lunchtime, Margot went down to the dining room, leaving Allison and Hattie to keep Ramona company. When Margot returned, she sent Hattie down. "Leona's doing very well with ham-and-cheese sandwiches, Hattie, so you go and have some. Allison, you, too. I'll be with Ramona."

"I don't want to leave," Allison said. "In case the baby comes while I'm not here!"

"I don't think that's going to happen," Margot said.

Ramona whispered, "I'm ready now!"

Margot chuckled and patted her thigh. She examined her again and said, "Soon, now, Ramona. I know you're getting tired, but you're doing very well. It won't be much longer." She waved Allison out, indicating ten minutes with her raised fingers. Allison gave Ramona's hand a last pat and hurried down the staircase.

She found Dick there. He jumped to his feet when he saw her, and she gave him her best reassuring smile. "Cousin Margot says everything's going well, Cousin Dick. It will happen soon, she says."

"Thank God," he muttered. He looked haggard, his cheeks flushed but his lips pinched at the corners.

Allison considered him, her head tipped to one side. "I think Cousin Ramona looks better than you do just now," she said.

He rewarded her with a laugh. "It's so hard just waiting," he said. He was at the table, a half-eaten sandwich on a plate in front of him. "If only there was something I could *do*."

"Why not go out and buy some flowers?" Allison suggested. "Cousin Ramona would love that, once the baby is here."

Dick said, "Allison, that's a damned good idea," and was gone from the dining room almost before she realized she had given an adult her advice, and he had actually taken it.

She was just finishing her own sandwich when Hattie came in. "Miss Allison, Miss Margot wants you." In a good imitation of Dick's speedy retreat, Allison was up from the table and dashing up the stairs almost before Hattie finished speaking.

She came into the bedroom to find Margot with her head bent and both hands on Ramona's belly. She glanced up when Allison came in. Her expression was intent, but calm. "Oh, Allison. Good. Come sit at Ramona's head, will you? Her pains are coming quite close together now, and she's fully effaced. Just give her something to hold on to, your hands, your arms, whatever works best."

Another pain came, and Ramona groaned, much louder now. Allison, as she reached for her, was glad Dick had gone out. She could see that it was part of labor, but if he was pacing the hall below, listening, he might find the sound upsetting. Ramona gripped her forearms as the pain shook her, then lay back with a little gasp.

Margot said, her voice slightly lower this time, "The baby crowned with that contraction and with the last one, too. If we don't make progress with the next, I may ask for your help, Allison. Can you do that?"

Allison swallowed. "Of course," she said, and though her heart skipped a beat, she thought her voice sounded assured. Calm, like Margot's.

"Good," Margot said. She put up one forefinger and watched as another of the deep, hard pains shook Ramona's body. Ramona grunted now, pushing, her eyes squeezing tight and her lips pulling back over her teeth in a sort of animal grimace, one Allison could see was completely involuntary.

When the pain passed, Margot nodded. "Yes," she said. "We'll need a bit of help, Allison. Here, let me show you."

Ramona said in a breathless whisper, "Is everything all right? Is my baby all right?"

"Everything's going to be fine, Ramona. Allison and I are just going to help the baby on its way. Take a deep breath now. Get ready for the next one."

Ramona breathed, while Margot took Allison's two hands and arranged them, one over the other, low on Ramona's swollen belly. "When I tell you, Allison, you push with the heels of your hands, right here." Allison's hands trembled, but she kept them where they were. Ramona's body was hot to the touch, and the whole room seemed overheated, charged with energy and effort. Margot said, very quietly, "Baby's shoulder is catching on the pubic bone, here. We're going to help it bend, so it can slide past. When the next contraction comes—yes, here it is. Now, Allison, gently, but firmly."

Allison thought if her eyes stretched any wider they'd come right out of her head, but she did precisely what Margot said. She braced her hands, one on top of the other, and at the peak of the contraction, in the midst of Ramona's long, agonized groan, she pressed down.

Nothing happened, at least nothing that she could see. Margot, who now had long silvery-looking forceps in her hand, said, "There's the crown. Allison. Can you press a little harder? Don't be too shy. Straight down, both hands. Ramona, keep pushing."

To Allison, the moment seemed to go on forever. Ramona stopped grunting, but Allison was pretty sure it was because she was out of breath. Her muscles still flexed and strained beneath her hands. It was odd, to be pushing on Ramona's body when she was already working so hard, but Margot encouraged her.

"Keep it up, Allison. Straight down, with both of your hands. You're going to free up that little shoulder, just flex it enough so it can get past the bone."

"Like this? I'm not hurting Ramona?"

"No, you're not hurting her. You're helping—oh, good. Excellent. We just need a moment more. . . . Oh, good work!"

It was the most awe-inspiring sensation Allison had ever experienced in her life. Beneath her palms, even through skin and bone, she could feel the shape of the tiny body. She felt the soft shoulder bend, and then there was a sudden, smooth slippage as the baby moved. There was a quiet rushing sound, as of a distant waterfall. Ramona cried out, not in pain, but in relief. Margot made no sound, but Allison, looking up at her, saw the curve of her lips, the satisfied expression in her eyes. A moment later, while Ramona sobbed and Allison caught her hands in hers, Margot held up the baby, red and wet and glistening. Safe and sound.

The infant took a breath and began to wail.

Margot stripped off her gloves and bundled them into the basket Hattie had brought up, along with the stained sheets and towels. Hattie was remaking the bed around Ramona, who sat up in a nest of fresh pillows, her brand-new infant, wrapped in a new, puffy receiving blanket, snuggled in her arms. Allison was brushing back Ramona's hair, freshening her face with a cool cloth, and arranging a satin bed jacket around her shoulders.

Allison straightened just as Hattie made her way out of the bedroom with the basket of laundry, and assessed her efforts. "There, Cousin Ramona. You look very nice."

"Let's just open the window for some fresh air, Allison," Margot said. "Then you can call Dick."

Allison pushed up the sash and pulled back the curtains to let in the midmorning sun. She glanced around the room, as if it were her responsibility to make sure everything was in order for this first meeting of father and child, and then, with a proprietary nod, went out into the hall and down the stairs.

Margot smoothed the bedspread a little, though it didn't need it. "You can rest soon, Ramona."

Ramona murmured, over the head of her sleeping baby, "Thank you so much, Margot."

"My pleasure," Margot said.

"Allison was wonderful, wasn't she?"

"Amazing," Margot agreed. "Who would have thought, when that sad girl showed up here six months ago, that we might have a budding nurse in the family?"

A crisp knock sounded on the bedroom door, and Allison peeked in. She said, "There's a new papa out here eager to meet his baby daughter."

Ramona touched her hair with her fingers, and gave Allison a brilliant smile. "Please show him in. We're ready."

Dick came in, beaming and relieved, with an enormous bunch of flowers in his hands. Behind him, Margot saw Dr. Creedy. She picked up her medical bag and carried it with her out into the hall.

Creedy put out his hand. "Dr. Benedict," he said. "You've left me nothing to do here, I gather."

Margot shook his hand. "I think everything's fine now."

"Any complications?"

"Yes, actually. There was a shoulder dystocia, but it resolved well, and the shoulder didn't dislocate. I had forceps ready, but I didn't need them. I would be happy if you would examine my sister-in-law before you go, and the baby, of course. The infant looks perfect to me, but I'm not sure I can be objective in this case." She rubbed her eyes, feeling the weight of the sleepless night, but buoyed with excitement at the appearance of her brand-new niece.

Creedy said, "You know, I delivered one of my own children, Doctor. When it's your own flesh and blood, it's not the same."

Margot nodded. "Thank you for saying that. I was wondering."

"When father and daughter have said hello, I'll check on everyone," Dr. Creedy said. "But I have no doubt Mrs. Benedict was in the best possible hands."

"Kind of you to say so. I'll send a maid up to see if you need anything. I'm going down to telephone to my father and my husband, and give my mother the news."

She found the entire staff collected at the foot of the staircase. Hattie had already told them, of course, and they all stood smiling up at Margot as she descended. "Everyone is fine," she said. "Mother and baby—and worried papa—all doing well."

There were murmurs of delight and congratulations. Hattie said, with a twinkle, "And Auntie Margot? How is she doing?"

"Hattie, I'm so happy, you would think that baby is my own!" Margot said.

Margot went to do her hospital rounds and then her clinic hours. The day seemed endless, not just because she hadn't slept, but because she could hardly wait to get back to Benedict Hall. When she said good night to Angela and went out the front door of the clinic, she found Blake waiting faithfully in his usual place. They drove to the Red Barn to pick up Frank, then straight home, as Dickson was already there.

"Everything went well?" Frank asked.

"Yes, it did in the end. There was a shoulder dystocia, which surprised me, because the baby's not very big, but then Ramona's not big, either. In any case, with Allison's help, we managed just fine."

"And the baby?"

"Oh, Frank! She's just precious!" He smiled, and held her hand until they reached Benedict Hall.

Ramona had slept most of the day. The nurse, a middle-aged woman with a beaky nose and long chin, had arrived in the afternoon and was installed in the nursery next to Dick and Ramona's bedroom. By dinnertime, she had prepared for everyone to meet the baby girl. One by one, the staff was allowed to climb the front staircase and stand in the open doorway of the bedroom. Nurse peeled back the receiving blanket to show the red-faced, wrinkly infant with her stiff thatch of dark hair. Every one of the staff made the appropriate compliments.

Margot met Blake just as he was coming back from his visitation. He leaned on his cane, making a cautious way down the stairs, and he inclined his head to her when he reached the hall. "A great day for the family," he said.

"Yes, it is, Blake. You must be feeling—I don't know—grandfatherly?"

He put his finger to his lips. "Don't let Mrs. Edith hear you say that! But yes, in a way, I suppose I do."

"Where is the grandfather, by the way?"

"Mr. Dickson is fortifying himself with a whisky," Blake said. "Mrs. Edith is in the small parlor, too. I'll fetch them now."

"Blake—Mother hasn't seen the baby yet?"

"No. She didn't ask, and I wasn't sure what I should do. Hattie said to leave her be."

"Hattie would know best," Margot said. "But that makes me sad."

"Yes. It does seem a pity." Blake moved down the hall toward the small parlor.

He was back a moment later with Dickson and Edith. Margot followed them up the stairs, noting the protective arm her father kept around Edith's waist. They walked to the open door of Ramona's bedroom, where Dick met them. Edith stopped in the doorway, but Dick urged her to come in. "Don't you want to hold her, Mother?"

Edith, limply acquiescent, followed him to the bedside, where Nurse set a chair for her, then lifted the infant from her cradle. She laid the baby in Edith's arms, but Margot saw with approval that she stayed close, ready to step in. She could see by the expression on the nurse's plain features that she had assessed Edith and judged her not to be trusted with her infant charge.

Dickson stood at the end of the bed, smiling down at his daughter-in-law. "Well done, Ramona, my dear," he said. "Your little girl is a real beauty."

She wasn't, of course. In part of her mind, Margot knew that, and she suspected this was what Dr. Creedy had been hinting at. The baby looked beautiful to all of them who would love her, who already loved her because of who she was. She was red and wizened and scruffy-looking by any objective measure, but by the subjective judgment of every self-respecting Benedict—and, Margot suspected, all the servants as well—she was infant perfection.

Nurse said brightly, "Mrs. Benedict, this is your first grandchild, isn't it? How do you like becoming a grandmother?"

Edith, gazing down at the baby girl in her arms, said, "Oh, no. Not my first."

Frank had come up behind Margot, and she felt him stiffen. Her father turned to face them with a stricken look.

Margot shook her head. Preston had laid one more burden on his mother's shoulders. Poor Edith, who could barely remember what day it was, remembered everything Preston had said to her, even in the grim cell of an insane asylum.

Ramona, fortunately, was spared any knowledge of the Benedict bastard, if such a child even existed. She said, "No, you're right, Nurse. This is the first Benedict grandchild. My mother-in-law might be a bit confused. It's been a long day."

Edith didn't seem to hear any of this. She bent her head and pressed her pale lips to the baby's forehead. She murmured, "You're my first granddaughter, though, little one. I'm quite glad to see you."

"Louisa," Ramona said mistily. "Her name is Louisa, Mother Benedict. Do you like it?"

Dickson cleared his throat. "It's perfect, my dear. Louisa Benedict. Just lovely."

Edith sighed and said, "Louisa. Louisa. It's like music, isn't it?"

Dickson patted her shoulder. "It is, dear. It really is."

Then it was Frank's turn. He held out his arms, cradled the warm little bundle, and gave Margot a smile of such delight that it drove every other concern from her mind. After everyone else had gone downstairs to dinner, after Ramona turned on her side and drifted off to sleep, Frank and Margot stayed beside the cradle in the nursery. They sat side by side, watching little Louisa Benedict sleep, admiring her dark eyelashes, the exquisite scrolling of her tiny ears, the pink, wrinkled delicacy of her fingers and toes.

When she squirmed awake and began to cry, Frank picked her up and held her against his shoulder as if he had held dozens of weeping babies. She snuffled once or twice, then subsided again into sleep.

Frank gazed above the child's head at Margot. His vivid blue eyes were brilliant in the low light. He said, huskily, "Let's not wait too long for our own, Mrs. Parrish."

Despite her resolve, she had found that she liked being called Mrs. Parrish very much indeed. She liked the way he looked with the baby in his arms, and at this moment, in this cozy dim room, nothing seemed to matter but the many forms of love that filled Benedict Hall.

She said, "Very well, Major Parrish," and reached above the baby to kiss him. "We won't wait too long."

ACKNOWLEDGMENTS

The writing of a historical novel is not a straight road, but one that winds and curves and doubles back on itself as new facts and details of the period are uncovered. I'm deeply grateful to the people who guided me down this particular road, and for a few who popped up on unexpected corners.

Nancy and Dean Crosgrove are invaluable as medical sources. My sister, Sarah Phillips, is intimately acquainted with social services in the Pacific Northwest, and advises me on psychological issues. My mother, June Campbell, was a child in the 1920s, but helps me understand the flavor of the times. Catherine Whitehead was my first reader on this book, and I'm lucky to have her eye and her instincts. All the Tahuya Writers—Catherine, Brian Bek, Jeralee Chapman, Dave Newton, and Niven Marquis— have been my steadfast companions on this long writing journey.

At www.catecampbell.net, readers can find a bibliography that includes reference books, historical websites, and other sources, such as the Museum of History and Industry in Seattle.

One special person who appeared unexpectedly along this road will remain unnamed, by personal choice, but was generous and courageous in sharing with me a personal story of bulimia and anorexia. I could not have created Allison's story line without that input, which I suspect was painful to revisit. Thank you, my friend.

HALL OF SECRETS

Cate Campbell

About This Guide

The suggested questions are included
to enhance your group's reading of
Cate Campbell's *Hall of Secrets*.

Discussion Questions

1. Fashions for women changed more rapidly in the 1920s than at any earlier time. Do you think the narrower silhouette of women's clothes was responsible for the increase of eating disorders in the twentieth century, or do you think such disorders already existed? Were you surprised that Margot had difficulty finding research to aid in her diagnosis of Allison's condition?

2. Allison Benedict is a young woman coming of age in a time of great social change. What role models did she have as she struggled to be her own person? How was her experience different from that of the English girls she met on *Berengaria*?

3. Women's fashions in the 1920s—free of corsets or hobbling long skirts—symbolized new freedoms for women, but they also dictated a certain body style, which was the genesis of the first diet fads. Did the new style create a new form of restriction for women?

4. Does Edith Benedict's reaction to her son's terrible injuries seem the healthy response of a mother's unconditional love, or is it more evidence of her emotional disturbance?

5. Hattie, in accepting Allison's confidences, hints at her personal secrets without revealing them. What do you think holds her back?

6. Secrets are at the heart of *Hall of Secrets*. Preston uses them as weapons. How do the other characters use them? How does Edith surprise her son and the rest of her family when she learns his secrets?

7. Margaret Sanger is a controversial figure in history, a woman who championed the rights of women to have con-

trol over their lives and their bodies, but who also had strong opinions about whose families should be limited. She met strong opposition not only from the Church but from the American Medical Association. Do you think, on the whole, Mrs. Sanger had a beneficial influence on society?

8. Is Allison Benedict as much a victim of the rigid social distinctions of the time as Hattie? Do you think, without Margot's example and encouragement, she would be able to break out of her preordained role?

9. The period of the 1920s fascinates later generations. We seem to be compelled by the fashions, the music, Prohibition, even the impending Great Depression. Why do you think this period of our history holds such lasting interest?

10. Are there aspects of society in the 1920s you find appealing? Are there others that offend you?